# THE BALANCE OF POWER

※※※※※※※※※※※※※※※※

Antryg dragged at the massive door, but it stood firm, bolted from the other side. Pressing his ear to the oaken slabs, he caught the faint scratching of broomstraw and a whisper speaking words of dissolution.

*"No!"* Antryg's fists slammed the door with a force that nearly broke the bones. Then rough hands dragged him backward; someone twisted his shoulder to drop him to his knees.

"Hold him!" the Witchfinder snapped, striding into view.

"Get that door open!" Antryg shouted, struggling to his feet. Someone twisted his arm; the pain turned Antryg's knees to water. "Please! The spells in that room are the only thing holding the Citadel in balance with the Void."

"So this is the heart of the Council's secret plot?" The Witchfinder's pale eyes flickered over the room.

"There's no plot. But if anyone disrupts those circles, the entire Citadel may be destroyed!"

"Is it so?" the Witchfinder whispered. "A small price to pay . . ."

By Barbara Hambly
*Published by Ballantine Books:*

DRAGONSBANE

THE LADIES OF MANDRIGYN
THE WITCHES OF WENSHAR
THE DARK HAND OF MAGIC

*The Windrose Chronicles*
THE SILENT TOWER
THE SILICON MAGE
DOG WIZARD

*The Darwath Trilogy*
THE TIME OF THE DARK
THE WALLS OF AIR
THE ARMIES OF DAYLIGHT

RAINBOW ABYSS
THE MAGICIANS OF NIGHT

THOSE WHO HUNT THE NIGHT

SEARCH THE SEVEN HILLS

# DOG
# WIZARD

## Barbara Hambly

A Del Rey Book
BALLANTINE BOOKS • NEW YORK

A Del Rey Book
Published by Ballantine Books

Library of Congress Catalog Card Number: 92-97047

ISBN 0-345-37714-1

Manufactured in the United States of America

First Edition: February 1993

Map by Chris Barbieri
Cover Art by Michael Herring

For J, P, G, & R

Who kept me from killing myself
once upon a time.

Thanks and love.

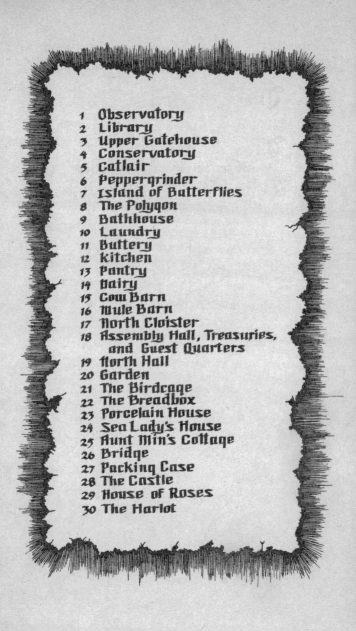

1 Observatory
2 Library
3 Upper Gatehouse
4 Conservatory
5 Catlair
6 Peppergrinder
7 Island of Butterflies
8 The Polygon
9 Bathhouse
10 Laundry
11 Buttery
12 Kitchen
13 Pantry
14 Dairy
15 Cow Barn
16 Mule Barn
17 North Cloister
18 Assembly Hall, Treasuries,
     and Guest Quarters
19 North Hall
20 Garden
21 The Birdcage
22 The Breadbox
23 Porcelain House
24 Sea Lady's House
25 Aunt Min's Cottage
26 Bridge
27 Packing Case
28 The Castle
29 House of Roses
30 The Harlot

And as for the wizards who use their power to further human ends, even ends which seem to them to be good, or who sell their skills, even such skills as they themselves deem harmless—they are but dogs who will feed from any master's hand. Such dog-wizards the Council of Wizards will neither recognize, nor teach its skills, nor protect from the haters of magic.

—ISAR CHELLADIN
Archmage of the Council
*Precepts of Wizardry*

# CHAPTER I

"IS YOUR FRIEND REALLY WHAT HE SAYS HE IS?"

There was a carefully casual note in Ruth Kleinfeld's voice that made Joanna hesitate a long time before replying.

"What has he told you?" she asked at last, cradling the receiver of the telephone against her shoulder to hit the SAVE key. As an afterthought, she punched through a save and exit, parked the heads, and took the computer down. Something in Ruth's tone told her this could get complicated. "And why do you ask?"

There was a pause. Ruth, Joanna guessed, was ensconced in the dingy gray office of her father's construction company in the cement wilds of South Central Los Angeles, painting her fingernails and trying to guess the amounts of the checks her father had written on the office account last week. The temperature down in her neck of the woods—Venice Boulevard and Hoover Avenue—would be hovering in the nineties. Up here in Van Nuys it was worse, and Joanna, clothed in her oldest jeans and a black Enyart's Bar & Grill T-shirt with sleeves and neck cut out, was wondering whether the air conditioner would make it till sunset, let alone till Thanksgiving, when the San Fernando Valley would finally cool off.

There was no question about which friend Ruth meant. It was just like Antryg Windrose, Joanna reflected, not to come up with an alternative to the unvarnished truth.

"He *says*," reported Ruth in a just-the-facts-ma'am tone, "that he's an exiled wizard from another universe."

*Why not?* Joanna sighed mentally. Antryg had been considered hopelessly insane by everyone who knew him in his former life. Why alter things now?

There was momentary silence on the line, something the girls had grown used to over the course of their years of friendship. On the other side of what had once been her Aunt Rachel's dining table, Chainsaw yawned and rolled over to a more comfortable position, all four feet in the air, on top of the pile of documentation Joanna was using to try—vainly, so far—to figure out why Galaxsongs Records' spreadsheet program refused to work. Chainsaw and Spock deeply appreciated Antryg Windrose's arrival on the scene last January, coinciding as it did with Joanna's decision to become a free-lance consultant and full-time dispenser of cream and catnip. It amused and interested Joanna that, although the living room had been transformed into a barely restrained chaos of papers, drawings, physics books, tarot decks, used teacups, animal skulls, dried and potted herbs, gutted computers, dismantled clocks, pinwheels in various stages of construction, and an artillery battalion of windup toys, the cats left most of Antryg's things alone.

After a moment Ruth went on. "Now, I mean, Antryg is definitely not from this universe . . ." Joanna could almost see her tap her forehead, indicative of her frequently voiced suspicion that Joanna's roommate hailed from the far side of the Twilight Zone. "Is he psychic?"

"Y-yes," said Joanna slowly. He wasn't, exactly, but it was one of the simpler explanations.

She heard Ruth sigh. "I didn't used to believe in it," she said. "But after you were gone last fall . . . I don't know. And there's something about Antryg . . . Maybe it's just that he believes it himself, until you get to believe it, too."

"There is that," Joanna agreed. She recalled Antryg's application for his bartending job at Enyart's. He'd seen no incongruity in listing "wizard" as a former occupation. "Not that I was ever paid for it, you understand," he had hastened to explain to Jim, the manager, who nodded and gave him the job. Jim had lived in L.A. a long time.

"The thing is," Ruth went on, "Jim says he sees auras—personal auras around people, that kind of stuff. And he says Antryg has the damnedest one he's ever seen. So I was wondering . . ."

She hesitated again, and Joanna felt, as clearly as if someone, something, had come up and laid a clawed hand upon her shoulder from behind, that she knew what Ruth was going to say.

And the cold fear of it shrank in her viscera, as it had one night two years ago, when she'd returned to the locked apartment and found a cigarette stub on the edge of the bathroom sink.

"The riverbed . . ." She heard the ghost-quick intake of Ruth's shaken breath.

"You've been there?"

Joanna shut her eyes. So Ruth knew about it. That meant it really was real.

She felt cold.

It hadn't been precisely a dream. It had come to her waking and in daytime, like the sudden recollection of something dreamed days ago, only she knew she had never actually dreamed any such thing. In a vision-flash of quasimemory, she had seen herself walking along the bed of one of Los Angeles' notorious cement-paved rivers, something she knew down to the molecules of her bone marrow she had never done and *would* never do. But the memory was so vivid, it nearly blinded her: the heat of the May sun beating on her tousled, too-curly blond hair, the scuff of her sneakers in the thin yellow-gray dust, the Hispanic graffiti on the concrete retaining walls that rose around her, and the pale pinks and greens of the sixties tract houses visible above them. One house, defiant heliotrope, stood out among them like a biker at a CPA convention.

The very clothes she'd had on at the moment of the vision—the slightly newer jeans and white tuxedo shirt, currently lying half-folded over the edge of the bed, which she'd worn to Galaxsongs' office that morning—had clothed her in the . . . dream? vision? *Please don't let it be a premonition* . . .

And more vivid than any of the rest was the memory of the fear that lifted like heat shimmer from the cement.

She couldn't recall what she'd been afraid of, though she dimly sensed it had to do with something on the ground: tracks, writing, something drawn among the dry, spreading rings of parching bull-thorns on the earthquake-cracked pavement of the wash.

But it was the fear that came back to her most clearly now, five hours later, sitting in her dining-room-cum-office on the phone with Ruth, the sun klieg-light bright outside the half-drawn drapes on the windows and the heavy, throbbing heartbeat of rising rush hour leaking faintly in from Victory Boulevard outside.

"Joanna?" Ruth sounded worried at the long silence.

Joanna took a deep breath, telling herself firmly that there was nothing to be afraid of in that ephemeral series of images which hadn't even been a proper dream. "I haven't been there," she said slowly. And then, "You mean you know where it is?"

"Sure." Ruth's voice, deep for a woman's, usually a sweet, slow, sexy drawl even when she wasn't turning on her charm for men, was low and hesitant now, and scared. "That's what spooked me so bad when I dreamed it last night. That's the Tujunga Wash just north of the Ventura Freeway. My parents live right over on Whitsett; my brother and I used to get in trouble all the time for playing down there when we were kids. And it's like that, even that crazy purple house up on the bank. On my way down to the office this morning, I drove by there.''

*If your dream was anything like mine,* thought Joanna with a shiver, *you're a braver lass than I am, Gunga Din.*

Or maybe she just didn't know what could happen.

Ruth hesitated, struggling with a truth, an admission, perhaps, of craziness that she wouldn't have made to anyone else. Then she said, ''Joanna, there's something weird going on down there. I didn't see anything, but I felt . . .''

She broke off, but it didn't matter. Joanna knew what she had felt.

The sense that if she had stood still and listened, she would have heard, in the empty, baked stillness of the morning heat, breathing other than her own. The knowledge that something was going to happen that had no business happening in the sane and daylight world of every day.

In a smaller voice, Ruth went on, ''I've been sitting here all afternoon wondering if I was crazy.''

''No,'' Joanna said quietly, and that something which had shrunk and shriveled within her tried to make itself a little smaller, tried to hide behind her sternum for protection—tried to tell her that if she ignored all this and went about her business, everything would be all right. ''No, you aren't crazy—unless we're both crazy. But I'll get in touch with Antryg. He'll know what's going on, and he'll probably know what to do.''

And she reflected, as she hung up, that that in itself was one of the less comforting aspects of the situation.

At this time on a Friday afternoon, Joanna knew that Antryg would be ''down at the shop''—a shabby twenties Spanish duplex up on Saticoy Avenue with a sign outside that said:

PALMS READ—TAROT—PSYCHIC COUNSELING.

The woman who owned the place had recently taken custody of her niece and nephew at her sister's death, and had cut back her psychic counseling to weekday mornings; she'd been happy to find someone willing to rent space afternoons and weekends. A Mazda Miata of a shade popularly known as give-me-a-ticket red sat in one of the two parking spaces in what had originally been the front yard; Antryg's bicycle was propped, unlocked as usual, against one of the splintery awning posts of the porch.

The bike was a good-quality Nishiki touring job, purchased with part of the spoils of Suraklin the Dark Mage's secret bank accounts shortly after Joanna had attempted to teach Antryg to drive a car. The neighborhood averaged five burglaries a week, but whatever it was that prevented Spock and Chainsaw from making free with Antryg's pinwheels in the apartment evidently worked on the local druggies as well. There was a parking place available, too, directly in front of the duplex, on a street whose proximity to a pre-zoning-law industrial park made walks of a block or more almost routine.

As she mounted the cracked brick steps to the jungle of the porch, Joanna heard Antryg's voice through the window screens, a brown velvet baritone like some mad Shakespearean actor's, the drop and flex of its intonations like the swirl of a stage villain's cloak. He was talking to a client, of course.

Joanna grinned inwardly. Another of her friends in Antryg's home world, the sasennan Caris, onetime sworn warrior of the Council of Wizards, once said of Antryg in scandalized tones, "He's nothing but a dog wizard!" Raised in the purest mainstream of Academic wizardry, Caris meant it as the basest of insults, for in the Empire of Ferryth the dog wizards were the semitaught free-lance mages who refused to take the vows imposed by the Council as a condition of teaching. Lumped into the same category were the outright charlatans who claimed powers they had not been born with at all, relying on sleight of hand to deceive their customers . . . men and women who used magic, or claims of magic, for gain.

The Academics, of course, were above such things, even had they not been forbidden by civil law and their own vows to use their powers to meddle in human affairs.

In a way, Caris and the Academics—who had chucked Antryg out of their highest councils when he was barely thirty—were right. Antryg Windrose *was* a dog wizard.

And in this world—in this city, with its scruffy palm trees and limpid swimming pools, its perpetual stink of exhaust and its shining glass high rises, all pretending like hell that it wasn't constructed on a desert and a dozen earthquake faults—fugitive and exile and unable to work the magic that was his in his own universe, he was making a fair living at it.

From the rump-sprung wicker loveseat in the porch's slatted shade, Joanna could see through the screen door into the room where Antryg talked to his clients. Mrs. Pittman would not have permitted another swami to use the same rooms she used, nor would Antryg have dreamed of doing such a thing—an assumption on both their parts that had gone far toward reconciling her to the whole deal in the first place. Instead they had cleared out what long ago had been the front bedroom of its years' worth of nameless junk, draped it with mysterious-looking hangings at $1.49 a yard from Fabric Champ, and set up Antryg's private sanctum. The plain wooden table and kitchen chairs lacked the elegance Joanna recalled from the house of the most famous dog wizard in Angelshand, the renowned Magister Magus, with its tufted carpets, black velvet drapes, and ebony throne . . . but then, Antryg was just starting out in the business.

She could tell by the pitch of his voice that his formal patter, as he laid out the cards, was done. The deep murmur of his words was interspersed by a woman's voice, soft and questioning, and her occasional laughter. After not very long she came out, beautiful in the same leggy, fashionable, well-cared-for style that Ruth epitomized, a style that always made Joanna unhappily conscious of her shortness, the prominence of her nose, and the fact that, at the age of twenty-six, she still had no idea how to put on makeup. In the presence of girls like the one leaving, Joanna always felt as if she had CAN'T COOK, EITHER printed across her forehead in large block letters. The absurdity of that image teased her into a grin in spite of herself as she pushed her way through the screen door and into the wizard's salon.

"My dear Joanna!" He looked up from the new spread he was laying out on the stained and mended silk of the embroidered tablecloth, his face breaking into the beaming grin of a slightly pixilated rubber doll. "Don't tell me Galaxsongs' programmers are more competent than their sound engineers and you actually were able to unwind what they'd done? Or have you come about the thing in the cement river?"

Joanna stopped in her tracks. *Of course,* she thought, *Antryg would know.*

He looked up at her, and behind the mischief sparkling in his eyes, she could see guarded concern as he studied her face. He wore, as usual, a faded and unwizardly T-shirt with the sleeves cut off—this one was green, and whatever rock-concert logo it once bore had long since flaked away to obscurity— and a pair of senile Levi's. A livid scar marked his bare left arm; just above it, fresh and blue, the Anheuser-Busch eagle was tattooed on his bicep, the result of an exchange of services with an artist in Long Beach. She knew that both still hurt. His hands, where they lay upon the cards, were large, bony, deft, and beautifully expressive despite the twisted fingers and swollen joints.

For the rest, Antryg Windrose could have been any age from his mid-thirties to his mid-fifties, though in fact he was forty-three. There was something oddly ageless about the beaky, mobile face, whose rather delicate bone structure seemed overbalanced by the cresting jut of the nose and the extravagance of the mouth. The round lenses of his steel-rimmed spectacles were thick as the bottoms of Coke bottles, and behind them his gray eyes, enormous to begin with, were magnified still further. There were people who attributed his habitual air of demented intentness to the glasses as well, but this, Joanna knew, was not the case. That was just how Antryg was.

Unkempt curls in the final throes of fading from brown to gray, mismatched earrings of yellowing crystal, and half a dozen strings of cheap glass and plastic beads in assorted garish colors around his neck completed the impression of an unreconstructed sixties flower child turned abruptly adrift in the steel-edged cyberpunk streets of fin de siècle Los Angeles; an impression, Joanna thought, not wholly inapt. Antryg had the definite air of being in the wrong place and time, though most people didn't guess quite how wrong. In his own universe, he had been a practicing wizard since the age of ten.

He laid down the cards—Joanna noticed the two of swords and the chaotic five of wands—and reached with one booted foot to hook a chair for her.

She said, "Ruth told me where it is."

"Ah." Something changed in his eyes.

Then he reached into the ice chest under the table for a couple of Cokes and, under cover of the motion, said with unimpaired cheeriness, "I'm delighted to hear it—I had visions of exploring the entire Los Angeles watershed system by bicycle, and that could take weeks, if I didn't die of thirst in the process . . . though I suppose I could cut my time down by running the location of all purple houses in the city through a computer."

"What's down there?" Her hand on his wrist brought his head up again—his first instinct when frightened, she knew, was to duck behind a screen of persiflage.

He widened his eyes at her like a befuddled Harpo Marx. "Nothing," he said, as if surprised she had asked. Then he handed her a Coke, flipped over the final card of the spread—a nine of swords—and swept all the cards up into his hand again with barely the flicker of an eyelid. "But it's east of here, isn't it? Southeast?" He turned his head as he spoke, like a man sniffing smoke on the wind.

"Did you have the same dream?" Her heart beat more heavily, almost painfully, at only the memory, and she tried not to recall any of it too clearly to her mind.

"Well," Antryg said carefully, "I don't expect it was precisely the same." He shuffled the cards lightly together, wrapped them in silk, and replaced them in their carved Indian box. "Whereabouts, exactly?"

"I'll drive you."

His eyes avoided hers. "That's extremely good of you, but . . ."

Thunderous knocking on the outside door interrupted him, followed instantly by a stampede of sneakered feet. Antryg rose with an odd, disjointed grace for all his gawky height as four small children barreled in, carrying between them a very grubby cardboard box bearing the legend CHUN KING SLICED WATER CHESTNUTS on its side. One of the children announced, "We got another one for you, Antryg. Zylima's mom, she says she got this one from a pet store down in San Diego five years ago."

"Her name's Ripley," one of the little girls added. Angling her head, Joanna saw that the box contained an enormous land tortoise. "My mom says she's a girl, but I don't know how she can tell."

"Here." Antryg gently lifted the tortoise out of the box and set it on the table. "Let's ask her." He laid his big, crooked hands on the mottled gray and brown shell, half closing his eyes as though listening. "Definitely a girl." From a drawer in a sideboard he produced a sheet of thin paper; rice paper, thought Joanna, watching in some bemusement: the sort of paper that antiquarians traveling through England use to take rubbings of tomb brasses with.

This was precisely what Antryg proceeded to do. He laid the paper very carefully over the tortoise's shell and, with infinite delicacy of touch, rubbed it lightly with red chalk, while all four children watched in fascination and Ripley retracted her head and limbs in resigned disgust. "One has to do this very carefully," he told them as he worked. "If you don't do it exactly right, it hurts the tortoise—they're really very sensitive, you know, and don't like to be picked up. Thank you for bringing her here in a box instead of your hands."

"Mom told us to," the older boy put in. "She don't let us pick her up at home." Then, "Antryg? Mom says she had this dream about you last night. About this place—this place where you was supposed to go."

"Did she?" Antryg removed the paper and held it up to the light, studying the lumpish pattern of squares on its surface with a critical eye.

"Yeah. She says it was like down this old riverbed—not a real river with water in it but like one of the rivers here. She said there was somethin' bad down there—she said it was pretty weird, 'cause usually she doesn't dream about strange stuff, just about going shopping and stuff like that. Do dreams like that mean stuff, Antryg?"

"Of course." Antryg smiled and returned Ripley gently to her box. She didn't deign to emerge from her shell, even when he touched the horn-hard carapace lightly and said, "Thank you very much, Ripley. You have contributed inestimably to the sum total of human knowledge. If your mother dreamed about it, Jemal, I suppose I shall have to go there. Thank her for me—and thank you. And Ripley, too, of course."

The children accepted the quarters he passed out to them and started to leave. The girl Zylima paused in the doorway, frowned up at him with narrowed, mahogany eyes. "You know where that place is that Mama dreamed about?"

Antryg's imp grin widened. "Of course."

"Course he knows, Zylima," the other girl said. "He a wizard, ain't he?"

And they were gone.

There was a curiously awkward silence as Antryg went to

place his newest tortoise-rubbing in the drawer of the battered old sideboard from which he'd taken the paper. He had, Joanna knew, at least two dozen similar rubbings in that maelstrom of papers at home. "There's really no need for you to come with me, you know," he said at length, as if speaking of a beer run. "If you tell me where it is, I have my bike." Thanks to Joanna, Antryg could drive a car after a fashion, but it was just as well, she thought, that he preferred an alternative mode of transport.

The memory of the vision was like the dry scraping of a knife along her bones, and she had to fight not to say, *Can't we just go have dinner and forget the whole thing?*

But she knew that Antryg wouldn't forget.

She took a deep breath. "I think we'd probably better both go."

For she had an awful feeling about what was down in that wash and knew that neither Antryg nor anyone else had any business going there alone.

Joanna's heart began pounding hard again as she braked her old blue Mustang to a stop on the service road. The white-yellow dust that lifted in a cloud around them settled slowly, soaked in the long brazen glare of the evening light. Daylight saving time had recently come into force, lengthening the tepid Southern California twilights far into prime time, and as usual for May, it was blazingly hot, a pretend-summer that got everyone in Los Angeles scrambling for shorts and tank tops, heading for the beaches and forgetting—as people invariably forgot—that it would turn cold and misty again in a matter of days and stay that way till the Fourth of July. Somewhere the cutting, unmuffled roar of an RV whined in the distance above the far-off rumble of rush hour going full-swing on the Ventura, yet about them, as Antryg swung one thin, jeans-clad leg out of the car, hung the baked and heavy silence of the desert. Los Angeles was full of these tiny patches of urban wilderness, minidomains of lizard and coyote that served occasionally to remind the Angelenos that theirs was, in fact, a City of Dreams, an unlikely mirage called forth against long odds from arid lands.

"I'm going to have to ask you to stay up here, my dear," Antryg said quietly, looking down into the wash at the bottom of graffiti-scribbled concrete cliffs, cement floor glaring like old bone under the harsh slant of the sun. "If you see anything happen to me, don't hesitate. Get away *immediately*. All right?"

"Happen like what?" Joanna touched his wrist, staying him as he started to rise.

A frown flicked into being between his sparse, reddish eyebrows; then he clambered out of the car, extracted an old railroad watch from one pocket of his jeans and a compass from another, and stood for a time comparing their readings.

"If I should turn into a toad, for instance . . . or get devoured by giant ants . . ." Antryg had been entranced by fifties science-fiction movies on the late show. Joanna rolled her eyes.

"Though I'd actually prefer being transformed into a tortoise, if it has to be some member of the reptile family. It would make asking other tortoises for rubbings much less embarrassing. They may even know something about why all the wisdom of the universe is encoded upon their backs, though I don't suppose that's at all likely."

Joanna sighed resignedly. "Well, if it happens, don't come around here expecting me to kiss you and make it better."

"My dear . . ." He leaned down to where she still sat behind the wheel, his lips brushing hers gently, with a kind of hesitant passion. As he started to pull away she caught him by the back of the head, her fingers tangling in his long hair, and drew him to her again, frightened for him in spite of his lightness—frightened of the stillness down below, of the terrible, oppressive exactness with which the view of the Tujunga Wash duplicated the flashing image of her own vision.

*Dammit, even the GRAFFITI's the same . . . !*

Ruth had been right, too, about the sense of nameless fear that hung over the place, the dreadful awareness of something, quite close but invisible, that had no place in this world.

He straightened up and turned to look down into the wash again, and she saw by the look on his half-averted face that he, too, knew or guessed what was down there.

But all he said was, "Now, in Elbertring they used to believe that all the wisdom of the universe was encoded in the patterns on peach pits, but the mages who were responsible for assembling it all died of beriberi. Interesting." He tucked watch and compass back into his various pockets. "No bees around here, either. I'll be back, my dear."

Glass beads glittering in the burnished light, he began to pick his way cautiously down the steep cement of the bank.

Prey to a sense of desperate protectiveness, Joanna watched him, and the dread grew in her, a scratching, sawing, sickened apprehension made no easier by the matte glare of the smog-filtered light. She would in a way have welcomed darkness, for in darkness her cold sense of waiting uncanniness would at least have been explicable. Down there the dirty daylight seemed to congeal, hot and still and filled with that terrible air of watching.

*What's wrong with this picture?*

Up here wind stirred the feathery curls of her blond hair, flattened the dark T-shirt against her ribs as she stood beside the car, a small, almost delicate-looking young woman, unobviously pretty. Mousy, people called her—people who didn't know her, or mice, very well. Antryg looked very small and solitary, kneeling in the midst of that winding ribbon of lizard-colored wasteland to sweep his fingertips along the cement, as if trying to read a message there in braille, and Joanna wondered if she shouldn't have detoured by the apartment for the rifle she'd bought in February.

It had been a revelation, after her adventures of the preceding winter, to find that she'd actually enjoyed something so alien to her previous experience as learning to shoot a gun.

An even bigger revelation was that she was willing to continue the study in the face of the disapproval of those few of her colleagues—mostly other hackers—who knew about it, let alone her mother's horrified and repeated lectures about the number of Americans who ended up being blown out of existence with their own firearms. But even as she thought about it, her mind trotted out her usual half-dozen reasons why bringing artillery on this expedition was out of the question, complete with scenarios of being pulled over by the Highway Patrol and she and Antryg spending the night in separate County lockups, or shooting Antryg while trying to take aim at the giant ants or whatever the hell else was going to appear . . .

And, she told herself uneasily, she could scarcely justify bringing a gun, because there really was *nothing* down in the wash.

But there was.

Antryg was kneeling in the precise spot, Joanna was virtually certain, where she had stood in the mind-flash of her vision; half closing her eyes, she tried to picture exactly what the skyline of the wash would look like from that angle. Pale houses, telephone wires waiting like unscored music paper against the polluted white of the sky, a defiantly purple gable end sticking up over a fence and SANTOS RULES in elaborate Olde English lettering standing out among the lesser spray-painted illumination . . .

His bent head almost touched the cement, dust, and bull-thorns underfoot; on his bare arms, dusted with reluctant sunburn, scar and tattoo stood out like a gash and a bruise.

What did he see, she wondered, on the cracked pavement? What had *she* seen, for that matter? But even trying to bring the picture back to mind frightened her, and she felt again the desperate wish that he would finish what he was doing and get the hell OUT of there.

He stood up, Coke-bottle lenses flashing, and though he did not move quickly at first, or dodge to either side, he backed from the spot for perhaps a dozen feet before turning and striding, now very fast, up the bank. Joanna was in the car and had the motor running before he reached her; he nearly ran up the last few feet of the embankment, threw himself into the front seat beside her, and they were rolling almost before he'd pulled the door closed. Dust boiled around them in a sun-shot cloud.

"What is it?" The dirt road back up to the street was steep and required careful maneuvering.

"Nothing," he lied.

Her glance flicked to him; he hesitated, then looked quickly away.

In an almost apologetic tone he said, "There really is nothing down there."

But he didn't, Joanna noticed, take his eyes off the rearview mirror until they were nearly a mile away.

"Can we have the truth now?"

Antryg looked up quickly from where he'd settled on the floor to receive the ecstatic welcome of Joanna's cats. After the irritating fashion of cats, Spock and Chainsaw had fallen desperately in love with Antryg at first sight and, at every opportunity, forsook the woman who'd fed them and paid their rent and medical bills for the past five years to fawn over this relative stranger.

Joanna stowed the leftover kung pao beef and fried rice in the refrigerator and turned, leaning against the square column that the designers of the apartment had installed at the end of the counter that separated kitchen from living room. In the slate blue twilight the apartment bore even more strongly than usual a resemblance to some undersea cave filled with strange jungles of life: computer cables and radio parts rambled at large, octopuslike, among the documentation on Joanna's desk and the madhouse of journals, specs, textbooks, and copies of the *National Enquirer* which heaped the trestle-mounted door that served as Antryg's worktable; the little windup Frankensteins and Godzillas, the pigs and dentures and hopping frogs glinted gently in the random glow of the Lava lamp like bizarre things recently emerged from holes in rocks. On their way to the Manchurian Panda-Date, Antryg and Joanna had picked up Ruth; now her high heels were clicking their way down the outside steps of the Chateau Burbank to her second-floor apartment directly below, leaving silence in their wake.

Antryg eased the cats from his lap and stood up; six feet three, his gangly thinness made him seem oddly fragile in the slanted yellow light streaming from the kitchen pass-through. His voice was quiet. "I was afraid you were going to ask for that."

She stood for a time looking up at him, torn between her morbid horror of being a nag like her mother and her certainty that Antryg and, possibly, she herself were in terrible trouble.

"There is nothing down there," he repeated softly. "Yet. And in any case it's nothing that need concern you anymore. They couldn't locate me by scrying-crystal, or through dreams, but they could send out a general Summoning to those close to me, knowing I would eventually hear."

His tone was explanatory and matter-of-fact, as if that made everything right. Like the old joke about *Oh, what you saw was just a UFO*, which was thought to somehow lessen the hideous shock of possible contact with an alien race.

" 'They' who?" Joanna asked quietly. "And what did you see?"

Antryg looked down at his boot-toes and propped his spectacles a little more firmly onto the bridge of his nose. Then he sighed. "Wizards' marks, written on the concrete. Marks of Summoning. Lady Rosamund's . . . Daurannon the Handsome . . . other members of the Council of Wizards. And one of mine."

"Yours?"

"To bring me there." He looked up at her, his gray eyes tired and resigned behind their protective wall of glass. "Which means they must know I'm alive." He looked away again and rubbed his hands, subconsciously trying to work the pain out of the badly healed breaks and dislocations the Ferryth Inquisition had left in its wake. In the pit of his throat, under the jackdaw beads, Joanna could see the round discoloration of the scar left by the Sigil of Darkness, like an acid burn on the thin skin. He had taken poison, she remembered, to avoid the Prince Regent's final sentence.

"Will the marks draw you there?" She came quietly around to sit on the arm of the rough green couch.

"Well, they certainly did this afternoon." He moved with nervous restiveness to the sliding glass door that looked out onto the balcony, opened it wide. The night air rolled in around him, warm as bathwater, bringing with it the incessant thrumming pulse of Victory Boulevard and the freeway beyond. "In this universe they shouldn't have that power, but there is power and power. The Council must have known that sending the dreams to you would bring me, if only to make sure that . . ."

He stopped himself, as if realizing he was saying too much, then shook his head.

"And you know, the terrible thing is that I'm curious. It takes a tremendous lot of power to open a Gate through the Void. Very few wizards can do it on their own. Having gotten rid of me once, would their hatred alone be sufficient for them to track me through it? Or is there some other reason?"

"Lady Rosamund wouldn't need another reason," Joanna said quietly. "You confessed to murdering the Archmage. That would be reason enough."

He shivered a little, though he stood in the open doorway, surrounded by the gluey warmth of the night.

"Antryg," said Joanna, her voice very small now, "don't go back there."

By his silence she knew he'd been thinking about it all through dinner.

"They'll be waiting, and they'll be ready for you. You won't get away from them this time."

*And I couldn't stand to lose you,* she thought. *Not again. Not so soon. Not for real.*

*Don't let me go back to being what I was.*

In a way she knew that she wouldn't, even were he to disappear. In some ways the past four months had been a roller coaster of new experiences; in others, they had the strange solidity of something she had done all her life. Like many shy women, she had regarded men as an incalculable and threatening alien species, though certainly nice for dating purposes, and had wondered why any sane person would want to live with one. She couldn't have phrased the answer in words, but it was obvious to her now, at least in this particular case. Following his easy friendliness with everyone, she had come out of her own reclusive shell; she had discovered that she could after all talk to people without the feeling that the minute her back was turned they'd roll their eyes and mutter *Jeez Louise!*

She would not go back to being what she was, but the thought of the road forward without him opened a core of sick pain down the center of her being, pain she hadn't known she was capable of feeling . . . or, if she had guessed it, far back in childhood, she'd been very careful not to put herself in a position to find out.

And above all that, she simply didn't want him to be hurt.

And they would hurt him, a lot, before they let him die. "I know." His voice was barely a whisper. "But it isn't only that, you see."

No, she thought. It wasn't only that.

A stirring of wind moved the curtain beside him, belling out around him like a pale, oatmeal-colored cloak and then falling slack again as if the mere effort had exhausted it; outside in the darkness the yellow lights twinkled—streetlamps, billboards, headlights, neon. Asphalt and hydrocarbons, the chlorine bite of the courtyard swimming pool and the sudden, nostalgic tug of charcoal smoke and chemicals as someone fired up a balcony hibachi. Somewhere in the building someone was playing "Sergeant Pepper's Lonely Hearts Club Band."

Watching the tall figure silhouetted against the jukebox glow of the city of lights—the City of Dreams—Joanna realized she had known for months, and the knowledge cut at her, that she could only distract him from his unhappiness, never wholly alleviate it.

For he was more than an exile. By the very nature of this universe, he was an artist blinded, a sensualist gelded, a singer whose tongue had been cut out. The studies he had undertaken here, the studies of physics and optics and computers and whatever details of the physical world he could get his hands on, though they delighted and fascinated him, were not enough. They would never be enough.

Her throat hurting with the wish that she didn't care so much, she said, "You'd never get away from them, Antryg. Even back in your own world, you'd never be able to work magic again. They'd track you through it, as they did before."

She saw his body relax, leaning against the doorframe as if with his breath he had exhaled the tension from his muscles, the very strength from his bones, leaving only grief behind.

She barely heard him say, "I know."

She felt the fear and the desperation in him later when they made love and, lying against his bare shoulder in the drifting aftermath, saw by the reflected glow of the driveway lights below her window the haunted look of hopelessness in his unprotected gray eyes.

"Antryg," she murmured drowsily as he got up at nine to make the late shift at Enyart's. "You won't do anything dumb, will you?"

He sighed but didn't pretend that he didn't know what she meant. "It might be best if I did."

"They'd only follow you further." She shook back the tangle of her thick blond curls, drawing on a rumpled pair of pajamas, as she watched him pull on his jeans. The beads he wore around his neck glittered against the fair, fine-grained skin of his throat. His arms were marked from elbow to wrist along the vein with a faded road map of whitening scars. They were nothing like a junkie's tracks: the flesh had been slit, torn, bitten . . . he had a few on his neck and chest as well. He'd given her a long and patently untrue story about attending a vampire convention when she asked him what they were.

"You may navigate better than they do in the worlds that lie in the Void, but you know they'll find you in the end."

*And you'll be lonely,* she didn't say.

*And I'll be lonely, too.*

A wry smile touched one corner of his mouth; he leaned down to kiss her hair. "Very well," he said softly. "I promise I shall consult you before undertaking anything dumb." She heard him lock the door, and half felt, half heard the creak of his footsteps as he carried his bicycle down the stairs. At least, she thought, in the Friday-night chaos of Enyart's he was unlikely to run afoul of wizards from other universes, whatever else he might meet.

Sleeping, Joanna dreamed of the Void.

Dreamed of running through it alone, of trying to cross it; her feet touched nothing, while its cold ate at her flesh and the blackness all around her whispered with the voices of the abominable things that slipped through its cracks when the Gates between worlds were open. Her breath came in gasps, her legs hurt with exhaustion, her chest burned . . . the dim speck of light she so desperately followed receded from her. She stumbled, frantic to reach it, to get out of this place before she was lost in its airless cold forever . . .

And above all else, the terror of the Void itself drowned her, darkness, falling, terror beyond all conception of terror; the terror she had felt, gazing down into the wash that evening, the terror of seeing the very fabric of space and air sliver open, split into a lipless mouth spilling out darkness . . .

It was coming at her, reaching to consume her, while the horrors of a cosmic wind streamed out over her flesh, to eat her unprotected bones.

She woke gasping, staring with huge eyes into the darkness of the bedroom. Antryg was gone. Somewhere in the building a faint pulse hammer of music still thumped, the lights from the driveway below still pooled their yellow reflection on the ceiling.

But they could not penetrate the vibrating darkness that had begun to grow—blotting walls, reflections, furniture, everything of the sane and normal world—like a grinning, all-consuming chasm of eternity in one corner of her room.

It is said that in the days of the Twenty Kings, the wizard Treegard Galsek had a house in the northern forests, on a great granite hill called Wizards' Tor. He gathered about him other wizards, and priests of strange faiths, and they would kidnap travelers, and enchant their minds so that, believing themselves to be moles, or asses, or beasts of burden, they labored for them, raising high walls and digging tunnels deep within the rock.

—FIRTEK BRENNAN
*Dialogues Upon*
*the Nature of Wizardry*

# CHAPTER II

"ANTRYG . . ." JIM HASSELART WAVED FROM THE INCONspicuous, lighted doorway at the far end of the bar. Antryg dropped maraschino cherries into the two banana daiquiris he'd been concocting, handed them to the Beautiful Kevin to deliver to table customers, and edged his way past the young waiter's tightly Jordached and much-admired behind to join his manager in the narrow galley among the crates of Corona and St. Pauli Girl. "Telephone."

It could only be Ruth, thought Antryg, with a glance at the clock. It was shortly before closing time, the sixth or seventh hour of the night—he'd just begun to get used to the time conversion in this world when daylight saving time had come along. There were, of course, talismans by which one could actually save daylight, but that didn't seem to be what these people meant.

"This is me," he said.

"Antryg?" It was Ruth, shaken and scared and nearly in tears. The Spell of Tongues by which wizards could understand and be understood—and which he had long ago extended

23

to cover Joanna—didn't work through electronic media, but in four months he'd mastered sufficient English to follow telephone conversations and most movie dialogue. "Joanna . . . she's disappeared."

Antryg closed his eyes as rage went through him like a wave of heat, smothering thought for a moment and leaving only cold behind.

For a moment the yammering of a thousand inebriated conversations beyond the door, the clink of glassware and the sweet, wailing song of what sounded like a male castrato faded from his awareness. They had dared. *They had dared . . .*

It had been years since he'd felt this angry, angry enough to take every member of the High Council of Mages by their scrawny necks and . . .

The aftermath was just as swift, an ebb wave of horror and dread.

*What had they done to her?*

Ruth's voice rattled swiftly on, speaking of a scream, of darkness fading away in a corner of the room, of something retreating along that darkness . . . a black cloak . . .

Or, he thought with a curious, terrible calm, the black robe of a mage.

They had taken Joanna.

He felt no real surprise. He had been waiting only to hear this, from the moment he had knelt to see the wizards' marks written on the concrete of the wash. In a way, he had been waiting for this since the first night he and Joanna had lain together in her apartment, she drifting off to sleep in the gladness that he wasn't dead, that against all odds he had come to her here in this bizarre City of Dreams.

And he, a little bemused that, all things considered, he was alive at all.

But all these four months he had spent here, he had kept an eye on the Void. And almost twenty-four hours ago he had sensed the Void's opening into this world, jolting him awake with a queer, oblique flash of awareness that had dissolved immediately; it was not until nearly noon that he had remembered the small-hours vision of Joanna walking down the dry riverbed, something seen as distant and very far away.

Ruth had had the vision. And Joanna. And Zylima and Jemal's mother, Luann. And Antryg was perfectly well aware that those visions, those dreams, were not merely to tell him, *Come to this place* . . .

*We cannot summon you, but we can certainly summon your friends.*

"It has something to do with that . . . that dream about the Tujunga Wash, doesn't it?" Ruth was saying, the frightened determination in her voice pulling his mind back from its lightning jumble of anger, thought, memory. "Do you know what's going on? How to find her, how to help her . . . ?"

"It's all right," said Antryg quietly. "I'll go down there."

"Do you . . . ?" She hesitated, torn between her loyalty to Joanna and her quite understandable terror of her dream. "Do you need help? Either just me, or I can get the two guys who live next door to Joanna . . ."

"No." Enough people, thought Antryg, had suffered through proximity to him in his run-ins with the Council—he still had periodic nightmares about the outcome of the Mellidane Revolts, that final piece of meddling which had gotten him imprisoned by his erstwhile colleagues. "But thank you," he added, realizing how harsh his voice had sounded in that one bitter word. "I know what's going on, and I should be able to take care of it."

"Trouble?"

He turned, as he hung up, to see Jim Hasselart leaning against the scarified molding of the jamb of the men's room opposite the telephone. Slightly paunchy and almost perpetually unshaven-looking even in the white shirt and tie of his managerial office, Jim had a certain watchfulness, a readiness for trouble, in his coffee-dark eyes.

Antryg hesitated, then said, "I'm afraid so." He untied and removed the black apron that covered his battered T-shirt and jeans. "Apologize to Kevin for me for not helping him close up—give him my share of the tips."

"Screw that. I never saw trouble yet that didn't need an extra hundred bucks. Take whatever's there; I'll make it good to him. Anything else you need?"

Antryg shook his head. "Not even the money, really. If I don't come in tomorrow night . . ."

"You phone me when you get back to town," finished Jim.

He was silent a moment, studying his erratic bartender; in a moment of silence between two songs a woman's voice said, "That's all very well, but it wasn't *my* underpants he had in his pocket . . ."

"You take care," said Jim, and let Antryg out the back door and into the warm blackness of the alley.

As he swung up onto his bicycle, Antryg remembered how close Joanna had come to being condemned as his accomplice during the brief time they had both been locked in the Silent Tower, the prison whose stones were dead to magic. He had only signed his second, and utterly damning, confession on the condition that the Council of Wizards release her and send her home. He knew he had misused his magic, had meddled again and again in the affairs of humankind against every command and precept of the Council, the Church authorities, and the law of the Empire. But that they should punish Joanna for his misdeeds . . .

And by coming here to be with her, by taking refuge in her world, he had exposed her once again to the Council's wrath.

But truly, he thought as he glided soundlessly down the rutted pavement between reeking dumpsters and illegally parked Porsches, he hadn't thought the Council would actually have stooped to taking hostages.

Emerging from the alley onto Matilija Street amid darkened apartment houses and the eerie turquoise glow of walled swimming pools, he turned right and, with headlights splashing across his back even at this late hour, headed north into the tepid night.

* * *

He reached the Tujunga Wash in the pearly thinning of the night. Even at this hour the freeway was alive, a few cars rushing by very fast with headlights staring, just beyond the graffiti-scribbled embankments; it amazed Antryg that people were still dashing around the streets so late—or so early. A search of the apartment had shown him nothing save that Ruth had fed the cats before going back downstairs to bed—he did not wake her. He hadn't expected to find any sign.

On the concrete of the wash he drew his mark, among the invisible spell-signs left by the Council, then stood back to wait.

The streetlamps above the wash laid their bilious yellow glow over the cement, and a coyote, trotting along the top of the bank, made a move to come down but then seemed to think better of it. Antryg had noticed that there had been no tracks, of cat, opossum, or even lizard, later than the inscribing of the marks.

*And they call animals 'dumb.'*

It crossed his mind again to wonder if it was his death the Council sought, or something else.

As he waited, the wind fingering his hair, he thought back to those strange stirrings within the Void.

He was, at all times, subliminally aware of activity in the Void, as he was subliminally aware of the weather, the movement of the stars, and half a dozen other matters pertaining to the energies of earth and sky. There was always activity of some kind taking place within that bizarre chaos which drifted between the parallel realities of the cosmos. So far as he knew, none of the other Council wizards—and, in fact, no one else he had ever met—had this awareness, including his ancient master Suraklin, who had taught him the ways of the Void.

For months now he had been aware of something odd happening a great distance away. It had come to his mind as a crimping or catching, like the snag of a stitch in flesh, but he had hesitated to investigate, knowing also that the wizards in his own world were, since the events of last winter, taking more interest in the Void.

It was perfectly possible that if there was some problem—someone from a third universe entirely visiting his home world, for instance, and letting through the sort of abominations that frequently slipped from one world to another when the fabric of the Void weakened in the proximity of the Gates—the Council would blame him, Antryg, for it, not understanding the scope and measure of the Void itself.

If that was the case, he thought wryly, he would have some explaining to do. And even if they did believe him, which he did not at all consider likely, they might decide to arrest him anyway, "on G.P.," as Joanna would put it.

But in a way it didn't matter. The fact that they were willing to take Joanna hostage to get to him told him clearly enough that his coming here had been a mistake, an act of selfishness that had endangered her inexcusably.

He should really have known, he thought wearily, that it would never work.

Before him, against the paling air, he saw darkness floating like a blossom.

Something—too many somethings—tightened in his chest, like a guitar string wound too straitly around its peg, and resolved into a sense of terrible regret. The night's cool had laid the smog a little, and though its metallic scent still clung in the air, with the stinks of dust and cement and sewage, still the crystal quality of dawn air came to him. All things around him—the world of the living—seemed momentarily new-drawn and magical, and every crack in the concrete, every poky line of all those pastel houses concealing each its own secrets, took on a brightness and clarity that was beauty itself.

He knew what wizards did to other wizards who had violated their laws as comprehensively as he had; for the last portion of his life that wouldn't involve spells of crippling pain he could, he thought, have wished for a better place than a cement riverbed in the heart of the San Fernando Valley.

But at least he could get Joanna off the firing line.

The air of the world split. Darkness swelled and spread like a cloud.

Far away, infinitely deep in the heart of the darkness, he saw the winds of chaos lift and swirl in black robes, dark cloaks . . . saw the glint of edged steel. All around him he was aware of smaller spots, rents, and ghosts of that same darkness, flickering in and out of being in the air—the fabric of the universe weakening, straining, all around the opened Gate.

*We'd better make this fast,* he thought uneasily. *God knows what might drop through.*

And then they were before him.

Framed in the gate of the darkness, their faces pale and tense with the shock of the crossing, he recognized the wizards who stood before him, his erstwhile teachers and colleagues. Some of them had been his friends.

The Lady Rosamund never had, of course. The tugging chaos of the Void swirled her raven cloud of hair; she was as beautiful as ever, the cold perfection of her features like marble and her green eyes nearly transparent in the dawn light. The purple stole of Council membership circled her shoulders, the staff of wizardry, of power, was grasped in one well-kept hand.

Beside and behind her he recognized Nandiharrow the Clockmaker—Nandiharrow the Nine-Fingered, he was called these days, after a particularly brutal brush with the Inquisition last year—big and solid and gray-haired, and beside him the wispy, androgynous physician Issay Bel-Caire. Both also wore the stoles of Council membership. *They must have elected Issay to the Council after Salteris' death,* Antryg thought. Nandiharrow, at least, avoided his eyes.

Behind them ranged the sasenna, the sworn warriors, the small band of trained and dedicated fighters who had given their vows, their lives, to the Council's will. There were nearly a dozen of them, some of them mageborn, youthful novice wizards in training, some of them not. They filed forth quickly from the darkness, surrounding Antryg in a ring of crossbows, pistol barrels, and swords.

"All right, here I am," Antryg said quietly. "You've proved your point. I can't protect my friends from you—I can only ask that you leave them alone. Joanna had nothing to do with . . ."

"So you wrote in your confession." Lady Rosamund's voice was like polished silver, as beautiful as her eyes, and as cold. "But we both know that she was an accomplice, not a victim."

"What I don't want her to be is a hostage." Looking at that aloof perfection, he felt anger again, the anger that this woman would have used her power against someone like Joanna, who had no defense. "She is . . . dear to me. And she never wanted any of this." The captain of the sasenna, a big, hard, red-faced man named Implek, stood close beside the Lady, holding in his hands a length of manacles and chain, marked with the runes of na-aar—thaumaturgical deadness—and twisted with bright ribbons of spell-cord that would also rob a wizard of his magic. Antryg held out his wrists to him, trying not to think about what would happen to him when they got back to the Citadel. "Just let her go."

Behind the Lady Rosamund, Nandiharrow and Issay traded a swift, startled glance, but her ladyship raised a quick hand for silence. Implek stepped forward and fastened the bracelets around Antryg's wrists, the touch of them hateful and cold, like the drag of a sudden nausea within him. He fought the urge to flinch.

"Bring him," she said.

Implek's hand closed around Antryg's arm, pushing him forward, and Antryg balked on the threshold of the darkness.

The cold of the Void breathed across him, chilling the sweat that had sprung forth on his face. "Rosamund," he said quietly, "I'm not hurting anyone here. I can't work magic—I'm an exile—I have no intention of returning. As far as our world is concerned, I *am* dead. Yes, I did . . . evil . . ." He swallowed, trying to push the memory of what he had done from his mind. "All I can plead is extenuating circumstance."

She looked up at him with cool eyes like the green ice floes that blocked the northern bays from winter into spring. "All dog wizards plead extenuating circumstance," she said. "It is the nature of dog wizardry . . . and the claim of all whores. Bring him."

She turned back into the darkness, and the sasenna closed him in. Antryg could sense the field of the Gate beginning to break up—Gates took a tremendous amount of the wizard's power to open, and even more to maintain—but even so braced his feet once more, and felt the prick of sword points through the thin cotton of his T-shirt. "You'll let Joanna go?"

Lady Rosamund paused within the darkness; the pallid glare of the streetlamps above the wash flaring across her face as she drew herself up. "Are you judging us now in terms of your own debasement?" she asked frostily. "We took no hostage."

The cold sank into him like black ice. "What?"

Her fragile nostrils flared with scorn. "We took no hostage. Did you think we would forget our vows as comprehensively as you have forgotten yours? Now bring him—we're losing the Gate."

"No!" With a quick twist of his arm Antryg slithered free of Implek's grip—one of the sasenna brought his pistol up, and Antryg used his manacled wrists to strike the man's hand aside. If the Council hadn't taken Joanna, someone had—someone powerful enough to open a Gate.

He lunged against half a dozen pairs of hands grabbing at him, hooked the feet out from under one guard with a sweep of his long leg and smashed another across the face with the manacle chain. He heard Rosamund shout something—probably about losing the Gate—as he twisted clear, ran two steps . . . If he could just get some distance, they'd never leave the Gate . . .

Weight struck his back, dropping him to his knees; he was trying to rise again when something hard impacted with the back of his head. He later remembered thinking he ought to bring up his chained hands to break his fall to the cement but had no recollection of whether he managed to do so or not.

Pain was the second thing Antryg became aware of as consciousness returned.

For a nightmare time he felt the implacable, mechanical drag of the rack at his joints, dwarfing even the agony of his crushed hands; heard the Witchfinder's whispered urgings, smelled sweat, ink, hot iron, and the acrid stench of the vinegar they'd used to bring him to.

Joanna had betrayed him. Suraklin the Dark Mage, dead-alive for twenty-five years, would devour the life and magic of the world as he had devoured the minds and souls of three men already, would go down the ages as a cold and silent vampire, invisible, untouchable, gloating in his chosen dark. And there was nothing he could do to stop him.

He tried to scream and the pain changed. His bruised arms smarted where they'd hit the pavement of the flood channel, and an egg-shaped lump of agony localized itself at the back of his skull. His hands hurt bitterly in the dawn cold of the room, an echo of the screws the Witchfinders had used seven months ago to dislocate the joints.

*Joanna* . . .

Anger swept back upon him, anger and fear.

Someone, somewhere, had Joanna, frightened and alone.

The first thing of which he had become aware, of course, was that his powers of magic were bound.

He moved his hand, half expecting to find himself still manacled. But it was only the braided silk knots of spell-cord, twined separately around each wrist. His fingers touched the worn softness of old blankets, and he smelled the unmistakable, fusty odor of a straw bed tick under his cheek.

Somewhere a bird sang, plaintive and sweet and achingly familiar.

Meadowlarks.

He moved again, to the muted creak of mattress ropes unevenly tightened.

The air was a threnody of spring foliage, of water, of spruce sweetness and the sour, acidic pong of bogs; of flat distances running untouched to the hem of wind-washed sky; of distant ice.

The Sykerst.

He was home.

The ache of it wrung him, obliterating all else in the hurt of nostalgic joy.

Shadow dimmed the nacreous dawn light that lay across his face.

"Daurannon?" He blinked up, recognizing the man who bent over him. The wide-set hazel eyes, the cupid-bow mouth, the straight nose and coal-black tousle of hair—Daurannon Stapler was one of those men who would look seventeen till the day he died.

"Drink this." The melodious tenor still had the soft underpurr of a lower-class St. Cyr accent. How many nights, Antryg wondered, had he heard that accent, in the years he and Daur spent studying together under the Archmage Salteris' tutelage? And after that, when he himself had been admitted to the High Council—the youngest mage ever to be so—and had been, nominally, Daur's tutor. He wondered, as he had even then, how much that had bothered the friend who had been only three years younger than himself.

With Daurannon it was always difficult to tell.

The bed ropes creaked as Daur sat beside him, helped him up with a strong arm beneath his head and shoulders; the cold stem of a metal goblet was pressed into his grip. As his lips touched the cup's rim, he smelled the bitter steep of phylax root in the water and drew back.

"If you don't drink it, I'm afraid I'm going to have to call the guards and make you," said Daur's voice behind his head. "I don't want to do this, but we've got to . . . now. They'll be in in a minute."

By the smell of it the concentration of phylax was very strong, enough to strip him of any ability to work all but the most minor magics for at least twenty-four hours. On the other hand, thought Antryg through the pounding pain in his skull, he had no doubt they'd hold him down and pour the stuff down his throat. That was what the Witchfinders had done, anyway, nearly drowning him in the process. With the spell-cord around his wrists, there was no real way he could fight.

Not against Daur, anyway.

Even in that split-second hesitation he heard the door open. He sat up quickly and drained the potion, almost throwing it up again immediately as his head gave a blinding throb. "Dammit," he whispered, his body bending under the reaction to the pain. Daurannon's hands, firm and warm and sure of themselves, pushed through his tangled hair to touch his scalp, seeking automatically the energy lines and pressure points; he felt the pain shunt away like fluid from a lanced sore, and with it, the worst of the aftertaste of his dreams.

After a few queasy moments he managed to straighten up a little. Around the low, coffin-shaped arch of the small chamber's door he made out the clotted wall of black that was all he could see of the guards.

But even without his spectacles he knew the room. It was the larger of the two upstairs chambers in the round stone house called the Pepper-Grinder, one of the several dwellings in the Citadel of Wizards traditionally given over to novices and Juniors. The lumpish, uneven window, and its sill and jambs of fieldstone, was half-obscured by encroaching ivy and weeds—clearly Bentick the Steward was having his usual problems finding enough village youths willing to help with the gardening.

The casements were open. The air breathed a delirium of dew.

He frowned up at Daur. "Is old Fred still the gardener here?" he asked, squinting. Most mages were able to control or arrest the deterioration of their own vision; he'd lost half his eyesight within a year of the Council's locking him in the Silent Tower. "He must have been seventy when I left, and that was nine years ago."

A faint, discontented stirring eddied the ranks congregated in the doorway; Antryg held out the cup upside down, a final droplet splashing to the worn, stained planking of the floor. "All gone," he assured the guards and put up one hand to gingerly massage the back of his neck. "I must say I'm tremendously flattered at your opinion of what a dangerous fellow I am, but I really wish you'd listened to a more realistic briefing about my abilities as a hand-to-hand fighter. Surely you could have informed them, Daur."

"I wasn't here," Daurannon said quietly.

He glanced sideways, meeting bland, deceptive eyes beneath their preposterous shelf of lashes. For all his choirboy charm, Daurannon had always been hard to read, and there was an opaqueness to him now, a wariness more pronounced than ever, that hid what lay inside.

"There was an abomination, a hideous thing, they said, at the Green King's Chapel in the forest beyond the village."

"Ah." Antryg turned his attention to picking at the knots that bound the crimson welt of the spell-cord to his wrist. "And was there? You can go, by the way," he added, glancing up at the guards who still lingered in the doorway. They started to obey him, then caught themselves. Daurannon signed assent, with only the slightest, annoyed compression of his lips, then turned back to his former fellow student.

"I saw nothing." He wore the purple satin stole of the High Council, Antryg noted—he had heard of Daurannon's ascension while he himself was a prisoner in the Silent Tower. A scabbarded killing sword was thrust through his belt. Like Antryg—like all the novices—Daurannon had trained as a sasennan during the first year of his schooling in magic. As of nine years ago, when Antryg had been thrown off the High Council for the final time and ejected from the Citadel for good, Daurannon had still kept up his training. They'd fought each other in hundreds of bouts, with split-bamboo training swords, up and down the long room on the top floor of the house called the Harlot. Antryg remembered that the excellence of his friend's technique, his speed and coordination, had nearly compensated for the fact that, in an all-out fight, Daurannon was basically a coward.

But unlike most cowards he'd admitted it and hadn't, as many cowards did, added bullying and lying to his lack of nerve. Antryg had wondered in later years whether this had stemmed from innate honesty or from the knowledge that nobody can hide on the training floor.

By the look of those broad shoulders under the fine dark wool, he hadn't let his training slide into abeyance.

"If you'd wanted me," Antryg went on after a moment in a reasonable voice, "you could have sent a letter, you know." He knotted the ends of the spell-cord together and began the preliminary loops of a cat's cradle over his long, crooked fingers. "The postal system in that universe is marvelous, really almost as good as the Angelshand penny post."

"Would you have stayed to keep an appointment if we'd written for one?"

"Well . . ." He shifted his fingers, but instead of assuming a new and pleasing shape, the spell-cord deteriorated into a sorry tangle. Antryg sighed and began again. "It would depend on how nicely I was asked. Lady Rosamund had years of deportment lessons as a girl. Somewhere in there she must have learned to write a very convincing letter of assignation."

Daur reached gingerly over and removed the silky crimson loops from among Antryg's fingers, handling the cords as if they were hot and setting them quickly on the floor beside the bed. "Some of the Council," he said, "seem to think that you might be behind it all." He reached into a pocket and produced Antryg's spectacles. The steel frames were bent where Antryg had fallen on them; he took them from Daurannon and straightened them carefully before putting them on.

"Behind the abominations that have been appearing, you mean?"

Daur's black brows snapped together. "Then you know about them."

"Well," pointed out Antryg reasonably, "you just told me about one, and since there's been a great deal of activity in the Void lately, it stands to reason there must be others." He shivered a little—the Citadel of Wizards lay in latitudes far to the north of Los Angeles—and rubbed at the ache in the crooked bones of his hands. "And I do get blamed for things of that nature almost as a matter of course. Was that what decided you to come looking for me?"

"In a manner of speaking," Daur said, getting to his feet. "Are you ready? The High Council will be waiting."

"At this hour?" Antryg readjusted the spectacles on his long nose and climbed stiffly to his feet. "I'm flattered that condemning me to death has risen in priority above Bentick's breakfast. And speaking of breakfast, do you think Pothatch would be up to getting us some coffee when we get there? Pothatch *is* still the cook here, isn't he? And muffins—the Manchurian Panda-Date makes very good kung pao beef but that *was* an awfully long time ago . . ."

"Don't flatter yourself," Daurannon cut in quietly, his voice suddenly hard. "You were condemned to death four months ago."

Antryg sighed. "Another pretension crushed."

"And in any case," the younger mage said after a moment, "that isn't why you're here."

The guards fell in around them as they emerged into the little gallery that bisected the Pepper-Grinder halfway up its tall interior. Spiraling iron steps looped down to the lower floor, half of which was occupied by the usual student clutter of books, crystals, dried herbs, and the endless lists that novices and Juniors had to memorize; the other half had been cleared for the practice of drawing Circles of Power. Second- or third-level Junior circles, Antryg automatically identified them, for minor spells of Summoning, drawn by a tall young woman of upper-bourgeois background from Angelshand who'd never been in love. Three steps led up to the little door; Antryg ducked his head, and his graying curls brushed the lumpish gargoyle carved upon the keystone. The guards crowded behind.

May dawn on the Wizards' Tor. More strongly than ever, the reminiscences of home. "*Is* old Fred still the gardener?" He looked around him at the jungle of wild grape and hardy taiga laurel that was, as usual, threatening to swallow the dozen or so little houses shared by the Citadel's Junior population. Against the gray-weathered wood and dark stone of the walls, the parakeet green of new-fledged rowan and birch stood out like fresh paint, sharply contrasting with the spruces' clotted darkness.

"No," said Daurannon. "He retired four years ago; his nephew Tom's taken over. And as usual, Bentick's not having any luck getting him help."

Antryg's boots, and the following feet of the guards, thumped hollowly on a short walkway of splintery planks across a sharp dip in the rocks to a half-dozen wooden stairs, and so up to the narrow, cobblestoned road that wound its way among the close-crowded labyrinth of buildings and trees.

Between the Juniors' houses—cellar to attic, where the hill was steep—ran a dozen little covered bridges, galleries, and staircases, all ramshackle, tiny, narrow, and needing paint. Nearly everything in the Citadel was connected. Antryg could have climbed from the pillared stateliness of the Council Hall up to the round marble observatory platform that crowned the Library's soaring bulk, six hundred feet above at the summit of the hill, without once going outside, had he cared to take a winding course through kitchen, laundry, cellars, and the bridges that linked nearly all the residences. And indeed, in the cruel months of the Sykerst winters, everyone at one time or another did precisely that.

But in spring, despite the glass-sharp chill in the air, and certainly through the short, soul-hurting magic of the muggy Sykerst summers, no one did so who had a chance to walk outside.

The little road, between its crumbling balustrades of field-stone, came clear of the trees just beyond the house called the Island of Butterflies, after a place in a fairy tale, and Antryg stopped, in spite of Daurannon's hand on his elbow pressing him on.

At this point the hillside dropped below them in a nearly sheer escarpment of granite to the pines clustering below. From here one could look directly across into the upper windows of the Polygon, the Citadel's main edifice, which rose in stately splendor from the easier southern slope: an incongruous-looking building whose lower floors and massive porch columns had been cut out of the living granite of the hill itself. The upper floors, above the columned dignity of the Council Hall, were a curious composite of later styles and materials, piled one on top of the other like a peasant wedding cake, the monolithic stonework and arcades of six centuries ago supporting garish Gothic arches and breezeways, galleries of carved wood weathered gray as pewter by the harshness of the northland winters, encrustations of jewel-like half-timbering, ornamental brickwork, and frivolous rococo turrets added by Pipin the Little, the Archmage who had immediately preceded Antryg's own master Salteris.

Turning, Antryg craned his neck to look up over the intervening walls and clusters of alder and spruce to the steep outcropping immediately above, where the foursquare bulk of the Library, the most ancient portion of the Citadel, loomed pale as old ash against the rising light. Its fortresslike slit windows had mostly been replaced by wide arches of glass, and along its eastern side, cantilevered out over the sheer granite drop of the hill, some nobleman anxious to win the wizards' favor had paid to install a conservatory, a ridiculous jeweled swallow's nest balanced on buttress and pillar, flashing in the new light of day.

Antryg smiled. As a forcing house for fruit trees, the Conservatory was absolutely useless, because it was accessible only through the Library, and hadn't been used for anything for seventy-five years, but the sight of that faceted absurdity always gave him joy.

As he and Daurannon resumed their winding course down the path, he inquired, "Does Seldes Katne still hang her stockings there to dry? Seldes Katne *is* still librarian, isn't she?"

Daurannon smiled a little at the thought of the stumpy, elderly woman who knew the location and contents of every scroll and grimoire that crammed those shelves. "I think she'll be librarian here when we're all dead and gone."

"There are worse fates." Antryg led the way along a raised-plank path over vine-cloaked, uneven ground to a side door of the Harlot: an enormously tall and narrow building faced on all sides with an extravaganza of multicolored ornamental brick and tile. "Chasing abominations and prodding 'round the Void on behalf of the Council with no guarantee of what I'll get out of it, for starters."

Daurannon halted in his tracks, his grip on Antryg's bare arm sudden and crushing. They stood in the doorway at the top of the Harlot's long stairwell, turn after square turn of sandstone stairs and galleries pillared in painted marble, flooded now with the first golden blast of the morning sun. High above them, the clash of feet and weaponry signaled morning sparring for sasenna and novices training under Sergeant Hathen's terrier-dog bark.

"You weren't told that!"

"My dear Daur, it's obvious I'm not going to be beheaded this morning," Antryg said. "If the Council didn't have some pressing need for my services, I'd have waked up in a cell on the bottommost level of the Vaults, not in one of the spare bedrooms, and you'd have dosed me with something considerably nastier than phylax root. I know there's been something amiss with the Void for months . . .''

''And how do you know that?''

''I just do. Partly, because you told me that abominations have been appearing. For how long? Just here? No, of course they've been seen in Angelshand, Parchasten, and Kymil, too, because the Citadel sits on a node of the energy-paths, and trouble here would cause faulting all along the Line. No wonder Bentick can't get villagers to cut the grass or sweep the stairs.'' He nodded toward the dried stains of crusted mud on the worn sandstone risers, tracks leading upward and down, some of them days old.

''And since my area of expertise *is* the Void, Lady Rosamund thought . . .'' He broke off, his mad gray eyes suddenly distant, a gangly, incongruous shape in jeans and T-shirt beside the younger mage's robed dignity.

''What is obvious to me,'' Daurannon said slowly, ''is that you know a good deal more than you should.''

''Oh, I always do,'' Antryg agreed cheerfully. ''And in fact knowing more than we should is the business of wizards.'' He turned and clattered down the stairs, Daurannon and his guards hurrying to overtake his longer stride.

''Nevertheless,'' Daurannon said, ''the summoning of abominations *was* in your confession.''

''Was it?'' Antryg glanced back over his shoulder as he swung around a marble newel. ''I didn't read the thing, you know. I'm surprised at you, Daur—hasn't anyone told you you shouldn't believe everything the Inquisition talks people into signing?''

''Not everything, perhaps,'' Daurannon agreed. They halted at the bottom of the last flight of stairs. Before them stretched the covered wooden bridge to the Junior Parlor on one side of the Polygon's upper floors. ''You also confessed to murdering my master, Salteris Solaris, the Archmage. Was that also something the Witchfinders made up?"

Antryg flinched, looking aside from the sudden naked rage, the pain of grief and loss, in those usually bland, agate-colored eyes.

"There was a reason for that."

"I've heard your reason."

Antryg started across the bridge. The hand Daur laid on his arm to stop him was trembling with anger. "Salteris was my master, my teacher, and my friend," Daurannon said. "He taught me everything I know and made me everything I am. I loved him. At one time you claimed you did, too."

Antryg sighed. Their footfalls echoed hollowly on the thick oaken planks of the bridge. Beyond it, the Junior Parlor was deserted, gray still with shadow, for it faced northwest, and filled with the smell of ashes from the unswept hearth. The crisscross patterns of its dragon-painted rafters seemed to murmur with all those conversations he and Daurannon had had there over the years, sitting up till dawn discussing spells and philosophy and the variations of plant life and insects; the notes of Salteris' porcelain flute seemed only just to have died away.

"If you've heard my reason," he said after a time, "you know why I killed him."

"As I recall it," the Handsome One said, his voice low enough to exclude the little knot of guards who trailed behind, "you claimed that your former master, the Dark Mage Suraklin, learned the secret of putting his own mind and soul into the body of another—in this case, Salteris. And for that reason you killed him. But it's an argument which cuts two ways, Antryg. And if Suraklin was capable of that, he was also capable of putting his mind and soul into *your* body . . . another very good reason to kill Salteris. And a good reason to summon abominations to plague the wizards who destroyed your own Citadel in Kymil—if you are he—all those years ago, and broke your power."

Antryg placed a staying hand on the doorway of the stair that would lead them at last, down one final flight, to the small round chamber where the High Council met. "Is that what you think?"

"Let's say it's something which has crossed my mind. Most of the others don't believe Suraklin had that power."

"Oh, he had it." Antryg shivered, thrusting other memories from his mind. "He had it. One more question . . ."

The guards had closed up behind them, pressing him on; through the open door he could feel the slow rising of warmth from the Polygon below them, the mingled odors bringing back to him all his own years as a member of the Council, sitting in that chamber at Salteris' left hand . . . candlewax and incense, the frowsty odors of old wood and ground-in smoke. Even now, even though he'd strangled Salteris— Suraklin—the mindless husk that Suraklin had left of his master—with his own hands, even now he half expected the old man to be sitting in his carved blackwood chair at the head of the council table, a cup of cinnamon tea at his elbow, making some joke about Antryg being late.

"Where's Joanna?"

Daurannon hesitated, his black brows puckering slightly. Then, "The girl from the City of Dreams?"

"Yes," Antryg said quietly. "She was kidnapped from her apartment sometime after midnight—kidnapped, from the description, by a mage. And because of the strength needed to open a Gate, it has to have been a member of the Council." Behind his thick lenses his eyes, usually filled with nothing more than a kind of amiable lunacy, had grown hard.

"We had nothing to do with that," Daurannon said after a moment. "With you as our prisoner, of course the Council has no need of a hostage. Truly, if something happened to her, it wasn't one of us."

He looked up at his erstwhile friend, his hazel eyes wide and slightly puzzled with the puzzlement of innocence.

But then, thought Antryg, as he turned down the last spiral of stairs, an appearance of slightly puzzled innocence had always been Daurannon's forte.

Of the Master-Spells, the spells of dominance by which the Archmage holds sway over all others of that kind, great or small, it is forbidden among them to speak.

—FIRTEK BRENNAN
*Dialogues Upon the Nature
of Wizardry*

# CHAPTER III

"WELL," ANTRYG SAID, BREEZING THROUGH THE GREAT bronze doors and into the High Council chamber, "you're probably wondering why I've called you all here."

Half a dozen pairs of eyes ranged around the worn and battered oak of the council table regarded him fishily. Only Issay Bel-Caire, newest member of the Council, sitting like a disheveled marsh fae down at the table's foot, could be seen to flick a hastily swallowed smile. For the rest, Nandiharrow only watched him gravely; Bentick, Steward of the Citadel, gave a little twitch and shut his eyes as if at some familiar inner pain; the Lady Rosamund's beautiful lips compressed in deepest disapproval. Down at the end of the table, near Issay, Phormion Starmistress twisted her square, delicate hands ceaselessly within the sleeves of her robe, and at the table's head Aunt Min—Minhyrdin the Fair, Archmage of the Council and eldest of the wizards—woke up, fumbled with her knitting for a moment, then peered the length of the room at the tall, loose-limbed figure in the paint-spattered jeans that had dropped so casually into the chair between Issay and Phormion.

At a sign from Daurannon, the squad of sasenna moved back, filing soundlessly out the door and shutting it behind them; the moment Minhyrdin lifted her head, Antryg was on his feet again, striding up the room to kneel before the old lady's chair. She had a footstool, he saw, its ivory legs retaining fragments of gilt in the carvings, so that those tiny feet of hers in their plain scuffed slippers would not dangle like a child's above the floor.

"Ah," the creaky voice murmured, and one withered claw reached out to touch his bent, graying head. "It's Suraklin's boy, that gave everyone so much trouble."

And there was a shocked muttering around the table at mention of the Dark Mage's name.

"Be fair, Auntie," smiled Antryg, raising his head, and his glasses flashed in the cool, shadowless light that flooded the round white marble room. "Salteris was my master, too, and the master I chose. Surely you won't hold my raising against me?"

"Badly brought up," she sighed, shaking her head. "Badly brought up, with all the wrong ideas . . . You aren't wearing yours emblem of office, the stole of the Council." Her pale eyes focused more sharply on him.

"I'm no longer on the High Council, Aunt Min," Antryg reminded her and straightened up to tower over the tiny bundle of black rags and knitting hunched in the great oak chair. His deep voice was gentle. "I was chucked off, oh, eight or nine years ago, for meddling in the quarrel between Lord Surges and the Imperial Governors . . . and you aren't wearing yours either."

"That," Lady Rosamund snapped witheringly, from her seat at the old lady's right, "is scarcely your place to comment!"

"I never know where that thing gets to." The Archmage dug aimlessly in her knitting basket, spilling yarns and needles in a wry-colored cascade to the yellowed marble floor. Antryg bent to pick through the hopeless snarl and produced a very much crumpled purple satin band, which he draped tenderly around the old lady's humped, skinny shoulders.

"There," he smiled. "Now we're official and all in print."

The faded aquamarine eyes narrowed to sudden sharpness. "And you were dead, too."

"Well," Antryg admitted, "that's another story and only partially true. There isn't a chance of getting a cup of tea, is there? Bentick, would you mind fetching tea? I'd go myself except that all those guards won't fit into the kitchen. And do you think," he added, as the Steward, tight-lipped with indignation, signaled Implek—the only non-mage in the room—to order one of his warriors to comply, "that you could borrow a jacket or something from the Citadel slop chest for me? It's appallingly cold."

Lady Rosamund opened her flowerlike lips to express her opinion of dog wizards who came to their own trials as if they owned the courtroom, but Aunt Min muttered something about dressing like a heathen savage and disentangled from her workbasket a huge shawl, part-knit, part-crochet, part-macramé, in an apparently random selection of spun and unspun hanks of silk and wool. Antryg slung it around his shoulders and settled himself in Daurannon's chair at the Archmage's left just as the younger wizard was stepping forward to take the place himself.

"Now," he said in a cheery voice, "how long after your first experiments with the Void did the abominations start appearing?"

Had he announced his candidacy for the position of Archmage there could not have been a more stunned silence in the marble chamber. Daurannon's eyes blazed with suspicion; Bentick and Nandiharrow exchanged troubled glances; but it was the Starmistress who spoke, her deep voice a hoarse whisper, and she stared straight before her as if she had not heard what he'd said.

"There was a Gate," she whispered. "Voices crying out."

"When?" asked Antryg, looking across at that stern, elderly lady who had always reminded him of a short-winged hawk. "Where?"

The librarian, Seldes Katne, spoke up. "Down in the Vaults. On the seventh or eighth level." She sat with five non–Council members present, their plain, bleached-pine chairs set in the gallery formed by a ring of pillars that circled the room a few feet from its white marble wall. With the exception of Seldes Katne and Implek, they were the very powerful Senior mages, in line for Council position: Otaro the Singer, whose round, brown face curiously blended jolliness and asceticism; the black-skinned, massive Q'iin the Herbmistress; and gentle old Whitwell Simm. "But that wasn't until months after the experiments began."

"We first started raising power to open Gates in the Void in February," Lady Rosamund said. "The abominations didn't start appearing until early last month. Nothing we did at that time differed from the earlier spells."

"What prompted them?" Antryg asked, propping his chin on his hand and regarding her with bright-eyed interest.

Her head lifted a little. "The knowledge that there were worlds, universes beyond the veil of what we know as the light and air of reality. The awareness, brought by your meddling in these matters, that there was knowledge out there waiting to be found."

"I see." Down at the far end of the table, Issay and Nandiharrow moved over to make space for Daurannon at Antryg's other side. The younger mage took the vacated chair, but his eyes, still sharp with wariness, never left Antryg's face. "I don't suppose it really matters where in the Citadel you made these experiments, given the number of energy lines which cross here; you could scarcely help shunting the power this way and that."

"We worked mostly in the hall on the North Cloister," provided Bentick. "I have the complete notes of those sessions."

"Thank you. Just out of curiosity, at what point did some one of the Regent's men inquire about how you'd disposed of my mortal remains? Which," he added earnestly, forestalling Daurannon's burst of speech, "is the only logical way you'd have of finding out that it wasn't the Regent's men who'd taken me out and buried me, as you'd probably thought."

There was a momentary, stringent silence, broken by Aunt Min. "The turn of the granny-winter it was, when the groundhogs come out . . . not that I've seen groundhog put his nose from his house any winter these thirty years."

"In other words," Antryg said, "around the first week of February. Was probing 'round the Void your idea, Daur?"

The Handsome One, who still appeared far from satisfied at the patness of Antryg's deduction, said coolly, "The matter was voted on in Council."

"And if our goal was to seek you out for what you had done," her ladyship added, "do you blame us?"

He widened his deranged eyes at her from behind the thick lenses of his spectacles. "Not nearly as much as you're blaming yourself, I daresay. I mean, it wasn't *my* doing that the abominations started appearing."

"Nor was it ours!" snapped the Lady, rising from her chair.

"Well, only one of us was messing about with the Gates, and there was no percentage in it for me, you see."

"Was there not?" Daurannon asked softly.

"The openings were done the same way last as first," Bentick added irritably, "and there were no ill effects—none whatever. We scried very carefully along the energy lines to make sure of that. It's all here in my notes." And he shoved the thick, leather-bound notebook he'd been cradling under one arm across the table with the air of a man refuting all possible contradiction. Of course, reflected Antryg, Bentick did everything, from lecturing on sublunary physics to tying his shoes, with the air of a man refuting all possible contradiction.

"So when *were* there ill effects?" Antryg inquired.

"Not for six, seven weeks." Lady Rosamund took up the tale. "Then abominations were reported, foul things, evil, unknown creatures. They were seen in Kymil, in Angelshand, in the woods near the village of Wychstanes here . . . and here. Monstrous things were seen in the mazes of the Vaults down below, strange mosses, vermin of other worlds. We began searching the Vaults, to see what might be the source of these evils."

"And there was a Gate." Phormion's huge eyes, rusty brown and, Antryg recalled, usually steady and calm for all their overwhelming intensity, shifted as she spoke; he had the impression she was fighting to keep herself from looking back over her shoulder for the memory of some terrible threat. "A Gate into darkness."

Phormion continued in the deep, almost masculine voice that was so startling coming from the fine-boned oval of her face, "I cannot say exactly where, now. I was searching, like the others. There were things down there, invisible as well as visible; the darkness was alive with their scyrrings and shriekings, like foul ghosts. I slew one creature which came at me." She shook her head; her brows, still auburn though her hair had lost its color years ago, pinched together, with pain or memory or the attempt to make sense of something incompletely recalled.

"I heard . . . voices. I think voices . . ." She raised a small, slim-fingered hand briefly to her temple and shook her head again. "A great voice called something which I have forgotten. There was a sound like the beating of wings, like wind in the reed beds along the river. I turned and there was a Gate, a Gate such as we had opened in the Void when we went into that other world to take you prisoner for your sins, Antryg Windrose.

"But the Gate was moving."

"Moving?" Antryg said, startled. "But they don't move.

They open and close, and when they do, they seem to be coming toward one, or going away.''

"No," she insisted quietly, "it was not like that." In her sleeves her hands were never still, scratching, searching, like mice in a sack. "I have seen Gates now. Seen them in the Vaults, some of them little, holes only. This one . . . it rushed toward me like a runaway cart in a city street. In the black maw of it, I saw moving lights, moving shapes . . . voices. It came at me like an ocean wave which curls down over the head, like a mouth opening to swallow . . .''

Her huge eyes snapped shut, and she turned her face away. Bentick's nervous white hand reached out to touch her wrist, and she flinched, startled, as if struck.

"I have searched the Library for any information concerning the Void," Seldes Katne said, after a time of silence. The diffuse, even light of magic that filled the windowless chamber did little to improve her round, heavy face, plain as a boiled potato; the tight braid of her hair, which lay across the black of her robe, was the color of fading iron, streaked with ashy gray. "I was in Angelshand when the manifestations started. There were riots in the dockside quarters; I think if the Regent hadn't banished all the wizards from every city in the realm we probably would have been torched out by the mob.''

"Banished you?" Antryg's eyebrows shot up with comic surprise.

"From every city in the Realm," Nandiharrow said, with a touch of bitterness in his deep, slow voice. "Every worker of magic, even some of the dog wizards.''

"Good Heavens, Pharos must be mellowing! A few years ago he would have arrested every wizard in sight and thrown the lot to the Inquisition. I'm pleased everyone got off so easily.''

"He would not *dare* . . .'' Lady Rosamund began indignantly.

"You don't think so? I can't imagine you know him better

than I do, but . . . Ah, thank you." A tall, rawboned, red-haired girl of about Joanna's age appeared at his elbow with a lacquered tray bearing teapot and cup, which she proceeded almost to spill over him. He caught the edge of the tray neatly, glanced at the chalk stains on her uncallused fingers, the shape and quality of the narrow ruffle of white shift collar visible above the edge of her gray Junior's robe, and the dried leaves adhering to the mud of her shoes. "Kyra, isn't it? My temporary roommate at the Pepper-Grinder?

"Chamomile," he added, pouring out the tea. "Pothatch remembered, bless his rotund little heart. Q'iin, did you ever succeed in making a cleanser for wounds from chamomile and fairy-paintbrush? I was saving fairy-paintbrush for you in Los Angeles—it grows there under another name—but . . ."

"*If* we might return to the matter at hand!" Bentick's rather high voice cut in like chipped obsidian, and a muscle twitched in his long, clean-shaven jaw.

"Terribly sorry." Antryg gave him his daft smile. "Would you care for tea? Kyra, my darling, we seem to be short of cups."

"Here," offered the Archmage, unexpectedly coming to life enough to dig into her workbasket and produce a delicate teacup of soft-paste porcelain, pale green and decorated with roses and a rim of peeling gilt.

"That's extremely good of you. Is this from Voort of Kymil's workshop?" He was turning it over to look for the maker's mark on the bottom—with Aunt Min peering over his shoulder—when Lady Rosamund slapped the tabletop like a gunshot.

"Enough of this foolery!" The edge on her voice was sharp enough to have jointed a deer. Then, more quietly, she went on, "Seldes Katne brought Salteris' books and notes back from Angelshand with her. For two days she has been searching, and so far she's found nothing in them about the Void, or about what could be causing the Gates to be opening and closing this way; nothing about a Gate which moves. We have all been patrolling the Vaults but have found nothing which seems to point in any direction but that of chaos. Nothing we have found in the library speaks of the Void . . .''

"Well, not a great deal about the Void was ever written down.'' Antryg shook an arm free of the shawl's folds to pour tea for himself and Aunt Min, then sat warming his crooked, swollen-knuckled fingers in the rising steam. ''Salteris learned what he knew of it from a dog wizard named Wilbron, who operated out of Parchasten and made most of his money smuggling. Did you know that one can temporarily disarrange the internal energy-paths of precious stones to make them pull a magnet, so they'll act like bits of iron as well as looking like them under a spell of illusion? To the best of my knowledge whatever books Suraklin had on the subject—and he was the one who taught me—went up in that bonfire you all built when you razed his citadel in Kymil. Rather a pity.''

"Whatever knowledge was contained in the Dark Mage's books,'' Lady Rosamund responded through gritted teeth, ''was offset by the fact that the things he touched were frequently found to be contaminated by his influence and power.''

"Oh, I'm not blaming you,'' Antryg hastened to assure her. ''Certainly not you personally, since you were still sewing samplers in the schoolroom at the time. Still, it *is* a pity. At a guess—and it's only a guess, because a Gate which actually physically moves, as opposed to appearing and disappearing, is something I've never heard of before—at a guess, I'd say the Gate was moving along an energy-track. With four tracks crossing here under the Citadel, the Vaults are stitched with them. It would help if you could remember where you saw it, Phormion.''

The Starmistress shook her head. ''I fled,'' she said simply, though her voice shook a little, and the cool light glittered suddenly on the mist of sweat that marked her upper lip. ''I think I must have lost consciousness at some point. I remember lying on the floor near the small downshaft on level five, near the Painted Halls, though I am sure that I descended past that level in my original search." Her eyes avoided his again.

Bentick's dark eyes met Antryg's challengingly. "She was exhausted and ill for hours after that. This was the day before yesterday, and it was at this point that your name arose in the discussions."

"In what context one can only guess," Antryg murmured, rising and pulling his long, sloppy shawl more closely around his bare arms. "I suppose the first thing I need to do is to take a look at the Vaults myself."

"No." The Lady Rosamund made a sign; Antryg heard outside the chamber the faint creak of sword harness, the movement of sasenna closing ranks about the door. "Given the old legends of objects of power which were said to be hidden in the Vaults, the first thing you must do, Antryg Windrose, is to surrender your powers to the geas of the Council."

Antryg's gray eyes widened with shock. He glanced toward Aunt Min, who appeared to have fallen asleep again, and then back to the slender, beautiful woman standing at the ancient Archmage's side. His voice was reasonable, if just slightly shaky. "Isn't it sufficient that you've poured enough phylax down my throat to fail every novice in the Citadel in their exams?"

"No," the Lady said coldly. "It is not sufficient. There were those on the Council who voted against your being brought here at all; those who argued that you cannot be trusted with power, as you have shown by your actions again and again. Phylax wears off in three days. All you need to do is go over the Citadel wall—and believe me, we have all heard of your escapes from the Silent Tower—and you would once again become a dog wizard meddling in affairs which do not and should not concern you, bringing the wrath of the Witchfinders yet more fiercely upon every mageborn soul in the land."

"And if I won't be a dog wizard in *your* pay," Antryg said mildly, "you'd rather I wasn't in anyone else's?"

Color flooded to the Lady's silky cheeks. Before she could

reply, Nandiharrow interjected gently, "The Regent hates us solely for what we are, Antryg. You're right—we were lucky to have escaped with banishment. We exist, to an extent, upon his sufferance, perhaps not for our lives, but for our peace: the peace to study, the peace to train others in the use of their true arts. The Council trained you in the proper use of your powers in exchange for vows not to meddle, and you have broken your vows, not once but over and over again. Surely you must concede our point?"

"I do concede it." Antryg sank back into Daurannon's chair, glanced from the big, gray-haired man's kindly face to his mutilated hands, and rubbed at the ache that never left his own twisted fingers. "And I was minding my own business—well, pretty much so—in Los Angeles. But you're asking me to do a job, and if there is something badly amiss with the Void—and abominations prowling about the Vaults are a fairly telling clue—I may need my powers on rather short notice."

As he spoke his eyes traveled from face to face, seeking a way out: Phormion still twisting her hands under Bentick's worried sidelong glance, Nandiharrow solid and grave as an oak, and Issay Bel-Caire like a sun-bleached bundle of weeds. His eyes touched Daurannon's and met there only opaque coldness and mistrust. At the head of the table Aunt Min snored gently. "I shouldn't care to have to reconvene this Council at three o'clock some morning in the face of an unexpected onslaught of fire-breathing caterpillars."

"He's right." Seldes Katne got to her feet, her round, potatolike face set in an expression of consternation. "Surely it would be a great mistake to take from him the very powers for which he was brought here."

"He was brought here for his knowledge and his experience." The Lady's gaze rested impersonally for a moment on the stout librarian, then moved to Antryg again. "You may call upon any member of the Council for assistance at any time."

"Oh, I'm sure I can." Antryg drained his tea and studied

the pattern of the leaves at the bottom of the cup. A house—ambition; fire—chaos and change; the rose that foretold a death; and everywhere the little three-legged track of danger. "The thing is, I'm not entirely convinced that it isn't some member of the Council who's responsible for all of this."

Had she still been the daughter of the Earl Maritime and not a mage theoretically equal with her brothers and sisters on the Council, Lady Rosamund would have snapped *How dare you?* and rung for a lackey to have him thrashed. As it was she only tightened her lips, but the unspoken words sparked in her eyes like pitch in a burning log.

"There are members of the Council who are not entirely convinced that it isn't *you* who is in some way responsible for all of this, Antryg Windrose," she said quietly. "And may I remind you," she added, her voice sinking still further, as if she and he were the only two in the windowless, light-flooded marble chamber, "that you do not have a choice."

"Antryg . . ."

He flinched from the soft creak of that ancient voice and kept his face turned away. But he could feel Minhyrdin's pale blue stare, and around his mind, like a tightening silver rope, felt the implacable force of her will. It drew at him, willing him to turn, an ancient power, rooted deep: a tree in the rocks, but a tree whose roots have melded with the roots of the mountain, taking strength from the fire deep within. She was bidding him to meet her eyes.

He kept his face averted for as long as he could, but the Master-Spells, the domination that the Archmage held over every wizard, drew on him, compelled him like the geared wheels of the rack, far beyond the capacity of human flesh to resist. Sweat sprang out on his face as he concentrated on looking down into his teacup, on looking anywhere but into her eyes, and he felt his hands tremble.

Then, through no volition of his own, he found himself facing those twin pale skies of faded aquamarine. Within them he thought he saw, not an old woman, but a girl in tawdry riches, scarcely taller than a child, with a dancer's muscular legs, a saffron tangle of hair heaped on her head and spilling in handfuls upon her shoulders, flashing with jeweled combs. And beyond that the image again of an ancient tree, roots locked to the living bones of the earth and drinking iron from them, so that the core of the tree had grown into steel.

The phylax he had drunk had numbed his ability to use magic, even as spell-cord did, but the power within him remained. He called upon it now, summoning his own strength from the chaotic, murky well of his being, trying to look away, to put the alien presence of her will, of the Master-Spells, from his mind. He tried to think of anything—of Joanna's cats playing, of Joanna herself, a prisoner and in danger somewhere . . . scenes from movies, television commercials, rock 'n' roll lyrics . . .

He couldn't let them take his powers from him, he needed them to find her.

But the steel strength of that ancient tree, twisted, black, incomparably strong, still gripped his mind. It was the strength of the earth, backed by the Master-Spells, the terrible strength of domination, and against the deep wisdom he saw in Minhyrdin's eyes he could not find anger to fight.

*I will not give in to you . . . I will not allow you to command me.*

His breath thickened, and though there was no pain—yet—he felt as if every muscle in his body strained and cracked.

*Joanna,* he thought, trying to summon back Ruth's voice, that panicked description of a vision glimpsed in shadow. A dark robe vanishing down a tunnel of night. *One of them has her . . . or all of them. They're lying to me . . . I can't . . .*

He clutched at the thought with the desperation of a man clutching the last tree root above an abyss, fighting not only gravity but the dragging of a whirlpool, pulling him down. Like a silver wedge driven in under his fingers, the Master-Spells plucked coldly at his loosening grip.

*Don't do this to me . . .*

If he could just turn his eyes away, plunge his mind down into darkness.

But Minhyrdin the Fair would be waiting for him in that darkness. And she'd be here, when he returned.

"Antryg . . ." The voice within his mind was not the scratchy, worn-out creak, but the bell-clear command of a wild-hearted dancer in her garish gown a century out of fashion . . . the voice of Minhyrdin the Fair, Archmage of the High Council in her later life, oldest and strongest. She was standing over him now, as he pressed back as far as he could in his chair; he was barely conscious of his body anymore, save that he felt deathly cold and could not turn his head away. He couldn't reply, couldn't release his hold for even the instant it would take to acknowledge. There was pain now, too, or something that read as pain.

"Antryg, you know that we can force your powers from you. I am within your mind now; in a moment I will bring in the others. They will strip you, break you . . ."

"No . . ." His breath came in sobs, fighting for darkness, for silence, for anything other than that terrible shining strength that cleaved his brain like a laser. He didn't know whether he uttered the word or only thought it.

"Surrender, child. It will hurt you less."

His mind was beyond framing words, beyond even the whisper of denial. It was naked before her, weaponless and paralyzed, overmatched and cut to pieces. Distantly he still remembered that if he let his powers be taken away from him he stood in danger of losing Joanna, of being stripped forever of that quirky, shy, and hesitant love and left anchorless in darkness . . . remembered that one—or all—of them had taken her.

But their dark presences hovered on the edges of his mind, waiting behind the small, shining angel of the Archmage's light. He felt their thoughts, like wolves closing on a blood-scent—shadows of enmity, hatred, fear, secrets . . . and somewhere, a glimpse of something else, something utterly dark and as filled with desperation as he was himself . . .

Even that brief awareness made his concentration slip and crack, and he felt her take another inch of ground. Whether his own eyes were open or closed he no longer knew, and it didn't matter. Those blue eyes, now sharp and filled with color like the killing sky of deep desert, burned like a watching tiger's in his soul.

"I will protect you, from the abominations and from them."

He was beyond reply, beyond breathing, dizzy and floating, chilled through in spite of the sweat that ran down his face.

"Surrender to the geas of the Council, Antryg; consent to its binding. I will see to it that your powers are later restored."

Hands touched him, slipping in over his shoulders, his throat, his scalp. The darkness of their power pressed in on him, pulling away pieces of his strength as they would have taken useless weapons from hands numbed by pain and shock, their own power glittering like white-hot knives. They would begin to tear him soon, dissecting his mind as the Master-Spells forced it open. Her awareness was burning light, but theirs would be calcining fire.

*Joanna* . . .

He managed to whisper, "Very well."

For a long time Antryg lay on the rock they called Melliga's Throne after some ancient Archmage or, perhaps, said some accounts, after a local deity of forgotten years—no one recalled which. Whoever she had been, Antryg thought detachedly, she had picked a good place to receive her petitioners or intercept intruders into the Valley of Shadows . . . or simply to lie, as he was lying, with the wind now and then stirring his hair, lifting and flattening the thin cotton of his T-shirt against his ribs, the thready sunlight slowly warming his flesh without coming near to dissolving the core of ice and pain locked into his bones.

His powers were gone. He was crippled, cauterized somewhere inside. He hadn't passed out—they wouldn't let him—and afterward he'd even managed to bow shakily and say, "I trust you'll all excuse me," as he left. He didn't remember much about leaving the Citadel, except hearing the Lady Rosamund's clear silver bell of a voice saying in the Council chamber behind him, "Let him go. He has to come back, you know."

Yes, he thought. He had to go back.

Here on the rock—the Throne—the pain had hit him, two long, shuddering waves an hour or so apart, as if lungs and spine and nerves were being ripped out in bleeding handfuls: greedy silver knives and long, clever fingers pushing apart the sutures of his skull to dig out portions of his brain. He'd blacked out the second time, come to weak and sobbing with a pulped exhaustion, the warm rock beneath his cheek and the shadows of the long weed stems lying far over on the granite's bleached breast.

Then he had only lain, like a rag on a beach, listening to the sigh of the wind in the endless sea of spruce and ghostly aspen that stretched out behind him and the soft chewing of the Crooked River over its stones below the high platform of the Throne. Listening, and knowing that if he hadn't yielded to the Master-Spells of his own accord, it would have been much, much worse.

Below him he heard a meadowlark's cry, lilting and joyous as the bird flung itself free of the earth. He fetched a deep breath, the air entering his lungs with that cold, startling sharpness that is neither taste nor smell, but rather a sort of awakening; there was a stab of pain deep inside him, as if he had incautiously rolled over onto something sharp, but not nearly as bad as it had been. After a time he struggled up onto his elbows, looking down and back at the Citadel and the country around.

He lay near the edge of the Throne, in reality a sort of natural platform, a blurred and misshapen square of granite overlooking the little break in the ring of high ground that surrounded the Valley of Shadows. The valley itself, an irregular, oblong dale two or three miles long by nearly two wide, was mostly open meadow and not shadowy at all, though the encompassing sprucewoods of the taiga encroached on its northern end and sent a long tentacle of trees down both sides of the Crooked River, which wandered in a series of twisting loops down its eastern edge. Boulders dotted the short grass; from Antryg's vantage point, he could see great patches of frail northlands flowers, lupine and anemones and gaudy, paperlike poppies, as if a gypsy had passed through and left colored scarves lying carelessly strewn in the grass.

There were stories that spoke of some local grand duke—back in the days before wizardry became respectable—who had marched his army against the Citadel in vengeance for some real or fancied slight. His men had camped around the walls of the Citadel for two nights, and on the third night (Bentick's version of the story said that the wizards in the Citadel had warned the attacker repeatedly to take himself away; Suraklin, recounting it to Antryg years previously, had said, *Without warning . . .*), the waters of the Crooked River had risen in roaring spate, mysteriously prevented from flowing out through the gap between the Throne and the granite hillock opposite, and had drowned the offending grand duke and all his train.

Looking down into the dale, Antryg believed it. Certainly the long fan of strewn rock below the gap in the hills spoke of floods in the past—not one, but over and over. The main wall of the Citadel itself, rising on its great jutting cone of gray rock in the midst of the vale, circled the granite hill just above the level of the surrounding ring, though these days the newer structures—the mule barn and dairy among their web of paddock and fence, the stillrooms and vegetable gardens—lay spread like a lady's train over the lowest slopes and among the clumps of spruce and alder on the valley floor.

Shaggy with its ancient trees, its moss-choked fountains and tiny gardens, the Citadel itself rose, buildings of every age and period clinging like swallows' nests to the steep rock. Suspended over the sheer northeast face, the Conservatory flashed dully in shadow, like a collection of dirty glass. Higher up, triumphant in the daffodil sun of afternoon, the marble turret of the observation platform shone white and blue with mosaicwork and flashed with threaded lines of gold.

"Study for the sake of study—*pah*." He could still hear Suraklin's soft, even voice saying it. He'd been buttering a scone—the scene was as clear to Antryg as if it had taken place that morning—the slant of early beams through the narrow lights of the sunroom window had turned his eyes and hair nearly the same color as the butter, the honey, the biscuit in his hand. "They like to pretend they have withdrawn from the vulgar world of money and politics and the petty groping for power. But let the Emperor cut one copper of his subsidies to them or try to appropriate the revenues of one of the pieces of property they own in every city of the Realm—let the Church step one inch over the lines they have drawn up for the Church to follow—and you'd see what they've been quietly studying in their peaceful bookrooms all these years. Why should they fight, when they've made the Emperor tamely give them whatever they wanted? Why take the trouble to police their competition, when the Inquisition will do it and let them pretend their lily white hands are clean?"

His own hands, very narrow and long-fingered, wielded the tiny silver butter knife as if he were dissecting a lizard in his workroom; when he was done, he handed the buttered scone to Antryg, who sat, a long, gawky, strange-looking boy of fifteen, at the other side of the pale-scrubbed oak of the little table. It was a gesture of curious kindness beside which the bone-stripping sarcasm, the hideous magics in which he called Antryg to participate, dissolved like shadows in morning sunlight and left Antryg even now—knowing everything that he knew—with the memory only of how warm that illusion of caring had been.

* * *

Antryg sighed and shook his head at himself. What a consummate vampire the man had been.

A shadow fell across him. Rolling over, with a little shock of residual pain in his bones, he shaded his eyes and looked up to see the librarian Seldes Katne standing in the long grass that grew from a split in the faded rock of the Throne.

"I've brought you a coat." She held it out to him—a ridiculous garment from the Citadel slop chest, clearly the former property of some actor or mountebank: broad bands of tarnished red and gold tinsel slashing the worn plum-covered velvet of its extravagant skirts. The small wind stirred its folds and moved Seldes Katne's black robe and ash gray braid. "It's growing cold."

"Thank you." He got unsteadily to his feet, Aunt Min's asymmetrical shawl sliding from his shoulders as he accepted the more substantial garment with hands that still felt oddly weak. But the first wave of nausea had faded, replaced by ravenous hunger. By the lay of the shadows, it would be nearly suppertime, and he felt chilled and empty to the marrow of his bones. "And thank you for speaking out for me. It was kind of you—good, too, to go against the Council. That couldn't have been easy."

Her round, homely face flushed unprettily in the primrose light. "I may not have much power," she muttered, "but I've been at the Citadel long enough, I should hope, to have a vote."

She sounded angry and shaken, and would not meet his eyes. For as long as Antryg had known her—which was well over twenty years—Seldes Katne had borne cheerfully the fact that she had only the barest minimum of magical ability. The Library was her bailiwick and the home of her heart, and though she was unable to accomplish three-quarters of the spells and cantrips, the great fields and Summonings and wielding-weirds recorded in its volumes, she had power enough to understand what they were and how they should be done by those who could. It crossed Antryg's mind to wonder whether it was this very mediocrity that had given her sympathy for him: having so little power herself, she had protested the casual violence with which they had ripped his from him.

Or perhaps, he thought, it might have been because they had been friends, partners in the wizardly greed for knowledge. But then, Daurannon had been his friend, too.

She went on gruffly, "I don't suppose that carries much weight with the likes of Lady Rosamund Kentacre or Daurannon the Handsome."

"Well," Antryg pointed out gently, pulling the shawl up over his shoulders again, "I couldn't actually disagree with them, you know, Kitty." And she smiled at the private nickname he'd given her in his novice days. "I *did* break my vows, and I *have* misused my powers . . . and perhaps that's the entire strength of the Master-Spells. To give the Archmage understanding of another wizard's mind sufficient to obtain that wizard's consent—be it ever so subconscious—to whatever spell she will cast. Suraklin did that sort of thing, too," he added, and shivered; the evening was cooling, and the coat she'd given him, for all its outrageous appearance, had been made for the gorgeous courts of Mellidane and the south.

Her dark eyes rested doubtfully, worriedly, on his face for a moment, and he could see she didn't really understand. "They still needn't have done to you what they did," she said after a time. "You're going to need your powers." She stepped closer to him, her small, square hand reaching out to touch his threadbare sleeve, and her voice sank to a frightened whisper.

"Antryg, I've seen it. I've seen that thing in the Vaults."

"Have you?" Antryg cocked his head, a curiously storklike gesture, and the slanting daylight flashed across his Coke-bottle spectacles like enormous, insectile eyes.

She nodded and withdrew her hand to clench it nervously before her. "I . . . I went down there after . . . after you left the Citadel this morning. The downshaft near the Painted Halls leads straight down to the eighth level. I thought if I could find it, I might be able to convince the others the danger was real, that you would need your powers."

"Well, I don't doubt they know how real the danger is; they're just not ready for that particular piece of logical elenchus. Does the Gate move?"

The librarian looked away from him and folded her arms closely; the wind, stronger now, soughed through the spruces along the river like the passage of a giant hand, bearing on it the knifelike bitterness of the ice-locked northern bays. The quality of the light had changed across the Valley of Shadow, as the brightness passed from the poppies and the lupine, and the first slow degrees of the long spring evening veiled the grass.

"Yes," she said slowly, "yes, it moves. I only saw it . . . distantly. That long reach on the eighth level. I . . . I heard voices, shouting something, I don't know what . . . saw lights flashing far away. But it was all coming toward me, rushing at me down that corridor. I ran down the nearest side tunnel—I was afraid it would come after me, but it didn't."

"Did you see it pass across the mouth of the passage you were in? See it sideways, so to speak?"

She nodded slowly. "Not . . . not clearly." She made a small rueful noise, and her coarse, dark skin reddened a little with embarrassment. "I pressed myself to the wall. When I looked up, it was just to see something like a cloud of darkness moving across the end of the corridor. I stayed where I was until the sound of it, the noise of beating wings, a noise like wind, had died away. Afterward I felt dizzy, but I can show you the place if you like."

"Curious," murmured Antryg. "Curiouser and curiouser. By all means, take me there. But first, let's see what Pothatch can get me in the way of dinner. I have the uncomfortable suspicion that it's going to turn into a rather long night."

In the days of the Six Kingdoms, a wizard was put to death by the Lord Caeline for trafficking with demons and lending his body to their uses. But as the wizard was possessed by a demon when he was slain, the demon also possessed his ghost, which bred into a monster, devouring all that it touched. No one could destroy this *tsaeati*,* for whatever power was turned against the demon, the ghost drank, and the demon was able to turn it against its wielders in turn. At last Berengis the Black, the greatest Court Wizard of the land, with his own body lured the creature into a piece of crystal the size of his hand, so that it became lost in the crystal's inner mazes, wandering forever in darkness there, unable to escape.

—FIRTEK BRENNAN
*Dialogues Upon the
Nature of Wizardry*

*tsaeati*—anciently, *devourer* or *glutton*

# CHAPTER IV

THERE WAS DARKNESS, AND DARKNESS, AND DARKNESS. Joanna didn't know how long she huddled in the corner where she found herself, her tousled blond head buried in her arms, shaking with fear and fighting off the urge to scream, to weep, to give in to the terror of what had happened . . .

And that was, she realized eventually, the point.

She didn't know how long. But it was long enough for her fear to give way to waiting—and the waiting to impatience, the perverse desire for *something* to happen, even something bad.

And eventually, it all gave way to boredom.

Because nothing happened. Only more darkness, and stillness more absolute than anything she had previously known; temperatureless black air lying against her face, utter silence hanging like a muffling curtain against the smooth glassiness of the wall against which she sat, the slick unseen floor.

A silence, a stillness, like a soundstage or the acoustical deadness of a radio broadcasting chamber—not an echo, not the hum of air conditioning, not the vibration of weight on some distant floor. Nothing—*truly* nothing—that elevated even the soft hiss of air through her nostrils to a distinct variety of note and pitch.

A nothing that never altered.

She didn't feel ready to shout—God only knew what might answer—but she uncurled herself from the fetal position she'd unconsciously assumed when . . . when . . . It troubled her that she couldn't remember the exact mechanism of how she'd gotten where she was.

She remembered jerking to wakefulness in her own bed, sitting up in disoriented horror to see the blackness of the Void materializing out of the corner of her room. She remembered screaming. As if half recalling a dream, she had the impression that for a moment she'd known what was going to happen to her, and that was why she'd screamed.

And then she'd been here, wretched and terrified and weeping in the darkness.

And then she'd still been here, bored.

Well, not bored, exactly, she amended, feeling in the darkness for the thing she vaguely remembered grabbing for beside her bed . . .

And found it, rolled like a lumpy teddy bear of Indian fringe and bunny fur in her lap. She thought she'd made a final snatch for her purse, which contained, among other things, her Swiss Army knife and a small can of Mace. What she really wanted was a flashlight. Her small, square hands sorted deftly through the contents with the ease of long practice till they closed around the short, smooth cylinder.

She drew it out and flicked the switch.

And nothing happened.

"Son of a . . ." She dropped the flashlight back and dug out one of her six boxes of matches.

It was when the matches didn't work that panic stole back on her, a chilly spot of something she didn't want to think about, as if she'd swallowed a neutron star the size of an apple seed and it lay there, ice-cold, heavy, tiny, and dead in the center of her chest. She shrank back into her corner—the join of two smooth unseen walls, facing God knew how large a chamber, occupied by God knew what—and wrapped her arms around herself, though the air was not particularly cold.

*Good thing,* she thought, with the oblique part of her mind not occupied by terror, bafflement, the helpless cry of *What the hell is going on*?!

*These pajamas aren't the warmest things in the world.*

But the bafflement and fear of knowing that neither the batteries in her flashlight nor the friction of the matchboxes worked here—wherever *here* was—wore off, too.

What was her Uncle Morrie's favorite proverb? *God protect us from what we may one day get used to.*

*Somebody will have to come for me eventually.*

And then, what felt like hours later . . . *Won't they?*

But they didn't.

After a time—*but how much time?*—she stood up, feeling along the corner toward a ceiling her fingers never reached. That didn't mean much, of course; at barely five feet she couldn't even get into the top shelves of her own kitchen cupboards—*unlike Antryg, the show-off*. Hunkering cautiously down to the floor again, she moved outward, passing her hands along the smooth surface in wide sweeps until they contacted another corner, this one the exterior, rather than the interior, of a square turn, meaning she'd been in the angle of an L-shaped room or hall.

*When you can't figure out everything, figure out the next thing.*

So far, so good.

She had groped her way a hundred and twenty of her own footsteps along the wall when she found another turn; feeling across in the darkness, she ascertained that the opposite wall was still there. Either a corridor or a hell of a long, narrow cell.

And still no light, no sound, no trace of either rescue or threat. No change of temperature in the lightless space around her, no movement of air . . . not even smells, she thought. No alteration of the smooth surface beneath her bare feet. Her exploring fingers had found no crack or irregularity to tell her whether the walls and floor were of stone or wood—or Fiberglas, for that matter. Her mouth quirked a little: Imprisoned in the Formica Dungeon.

Well, hell, she thought. If they're not coming for me, I'm going to have a look around. She had several granola bars in her purse, though she felt no hunger. The thought of water passed uneasily through her mind, but she pushed it aside: there was nothing to be done about it at the moment. Time enough to worry when she got thirsty. After a moment's consideration, she fished in her purse for a spool of thread and a roll of masking tape.

*Just call me Theseus.*

Hitching her purse more firmly onto her shoulder and hoping to hell she would smell or hear a minotaur before she stumbled over it in the dark, she set off to explore.

Suraklin the Dark Mage's greatest power lay in the fact that it was years before anyone, even his victims, realized that he was doing them harm. It would do to remember this in all dealings with wizards.

—SERGIUS PEELBONE
*Witchfinder Extraordinary of Angelshand*

# CHAPTER V

"IT'S QUITE TRUE THAT I WAS BADLY BROUGHT UP." ANTRYG leaned one shoulder against the rounded, uneven stones of the Pepper-Grinder's windowsill; the day's last brightness flashed wanly in the crystal dangling from his ear. He'd acquired a pair of much-discolored fingerless writing mitts to keep his hands warm in the silvery sharpness of the Sykerst spring; with his ragbag shawl and his age-darkened snake oil–peddler coat, he had the look of a dilapidated macaw in molt.

"And, as Aunt Min says, I was taught all the wrong things. But it wasn't entirely my fault. It's very good of you to do this for me, Kitty."

"I haven't managed to do anything yet. And you're blocking the light."

Antryg turned from the window, his spectacles gleaming like the eyes of a deranged tarsier. At the table, among a battlefield of ruined supper dishes, Seldes Katne angled the main facet of her scrying-crystal to the daylight. Beyond the window the shadow of the tor could be seen, an enormous cloak of slate blue silk, softening the contours of the Valley of Shadows

70

and blurring still further the dark spruces in their scrim of white river mist. Overhead the sky still held a chilly brilliance and would for hours to come, and though the air was sharp, already it breathed with the peculiar wildness of the wide steppe summer—life gorging itself on warmth against the knowledge of the long winter waiting.

"Perhaps if I'd been taken in by a Council wizard instead of by Suraklin," Antryg continued thoughtfully, "it wouldn't have come so easy to me to use magic against what everyone agrees was a gross injustice being done in Mellidane. And once I'd started . . ." He shook his head.

"There are those who'd point out," the librarian said, her attention still on the crystal before her, "that it was gross injustice to use magic against the non-mageborn, for whatever purposes. I sometimes think that's why we tend to live among ourselves, not going into the world much at all."

"Well," Antryg pointed out with a faint grin, "the rocks thrown at us in the streets, and the Inquisition, have a good deal to do with that, too."

She frowned, looking up at him with a kind of indignation. "Well, of course," she said. "But it's just too easy to take sides. And once a mage starts taking sides out of belief in the rightness of his or her own cause, how great a step is it to take sides for pay?"

"As great, I suppose, as the step to taking one's own side out of belief in the absolute priority of one's desires over everyone else's." He returned to the table and selected a strawberry from the painted clay dish Pothatch the cook had sent up with bread and stew from the kitchen. "First one's desires," he added quietly, "and, later, one's whims. Yes means yes under any circumstances, no means no under any circumstances . . . and the great problem with strawberries is that one is never able to dispose of the hulls gracefully. I wonder if Q'iin ever perfected her spells to ripen peaches in the wintertime? Nyellin the White was said to be able to produce any sort of fruit at any time of the year, including bananas and mangoes—she could have made a fortune in the fancy market of Angelshand, if her Council vows had permitted her to do so. And I'd accept the Council's judgment of me,'' he went on, veering back to the original topic with an insouciance that made Seldes Katne blink, ''if it weren't for the fact that one of them is lying.''

The stout librarian looked up in surprise. ''One of the Council?''

Antryg nodded, settling himself into one of the chairs and choosing another strawberry from the dish. ''I felt it, when they,'' his voice hesitated infinitesimally, then went on, ''when they put the geas on me. Some secret . . . some darkness, concealed from the others and from me. One of them took Joanna, I know that—only a member of the Council would have had the strength to cross the Void.''

He picked up the square of white pasteboard that had been under Seldes Katne's fingers as she'd scried in the crystal—one of Joanna's business cards, on the back of which was scribbled the start times of ''Karate Masters Versus the Invaders from Outer Space'' at the Van Nuys Cineplex 24. ''If you're trying to keep something secret from a wizard, it probably isn't wise to engage in theurgic gang rape; the victim is as aware of the perpetrator as vice versa. And perhaps that is why it is so seldom that such a geas is invoked . . . other than the obvious difficulty in getting the entire Council to agree and getting the culprit where the entire Council can operate in concert— something which hasn't happened for hundreds of years.''

Seldes Katne frowned, turning the small chunk of white quartz over in her fingers. ''But you have no idea who?''

''Not the foggiest.''

Through the open window the voices of the Juniors floated up to them as they returned from dinner in the refectory on the second floor of the Polygon. With the exception of the Mole Hill—the squat, shabby cottage where Issay Bel-Caire lived, buried save for its low door under an impenetrable tangle of honeysweet and taiga laurel—the houses on this spur of the tor were given over to the lesser members of the community. The Pepper-Grinder, the Cat Lair, the Cave, the Dungeon, the Isle of Butterflies, and the Yellow House were all connected by an interlocking maze of cellars, windowed galleries, covered bridges, and connecting stairways; in the wintertime, Antryg recalled, no one thought twice about hearing one's neighbors trot through one's downstairs hallway or across one's attic on the way back from dinner or class.

But now their footfalls thumped softly on the wooden steps that led up the sharp slopes from path to doors, or creaked on the jury-rigged plank bridges over the vine-choked gullies and drops. His red-haired housemate Kyra would be out at evening weapons-training—"Going dancing with Miss Maggie," the novices called it, Miss Maggie being the nickname for the garishly colored Harlot—or else drinking cocoa and talking till late with her friends in the Juniors' Commons. Antryg smiled, wondering if they still engaged in "practicing spell-casting in an emergency"—i.e., while falling-down drunk—as he and Daurannon had done on several memorable instances. Save for an occasional murmur from outside, and the soft, patient rhythm of someone in the Cat Lair playing beginners' scales on a harp, the round stone house was quiet.

"I'm sorry," Seldes Katne said as the daylight began to fade. "I thought that because this house is on the main Vorplek Energy Line I'd have a little more chance at this, but that doesn't seem to be the case." She put the crystal from her and did not meet his eyes; Antryg leaned across the table and put his big, bony hand over her fleshy, age-spotted one.

"What's more likely is that she's being kept somewhere that's spelled against observation." Seldes Katne's crystal, he recalled from somewhere, had belonged to the wizard Gantre Silvas two hundred years ago—the slip of rune-inscribed silver around its base had been added by that mage to increase its receptive powers. "God knows there are any number of places in the Citadel itself where she could be kept a prisoner un-known to anyone—any of the guest quarters above the Great Assembly Hall, or the attics above those, the clock-tower, one of the treasury rooms, the old South Hall. There must be a hundred places here where no one ever goes, and that,'' he added quietly, his voice sinking as he turned his eyes toward the window again, where he could see the Conservatory flash like an absurd diamond on the Library's granite flank, ''isn't even counting the Vaults. And I'm very much afraid that that's where she is.''

''It would make sense,'' the librarian agreed. Then she frowned again, her heavy brows pulling down over her nose once more. ''But . . . that's where the disturbance is centered. That's where the Moving Gate is.''

''It's more than that,'' Antryg said, getting nervously to his feet and beginning to pace, his movements restlessly graceful in his sweeping coat, like some bizarre wading bird. ''Most people believe that the labyrinth in the Vaults was dug as a defense—a place where, in the event of catastrophe, the wiz-ards might hide. But the Citadel lies on the node of four energy-tracks, at least one of them—the Vorplek Line, which runs through the Library as you know—extremely powerful. And while in the west, mounds at the nodes of such lines were frequently built with collecting chambers underneath them to hold and channel the traveling energies of the leys, in the east and north they used mazes.''

''I've heard that theory,'' Seldes Katne acknowledged, sit-ting up a little in her chair and putting back her braid, which had strayed forward over her shoulder again. ''But no one has ever proven that the mazes worked.''

''Perhaps because we have no idea *how* they worked.'' An-tryg leaned on the windowsill again, gazing out into the tangle of vines below. There was a murmur of voices from the win-dows of the Cat Lair, and someone else took the harp, calling the huge black-and-orange butterflies that had been feeding from the starlike blooms of the honeysweet to swirl upward into a drunken, dancing cloud.

Antryg fell silent a moment, listening to the sheer, glittering mastery of the music; Seldes Katne said softly, "That will be Brighthand—Zake Thwacker, Otaro's pupil. He has . . . great skill."

He glanced back at her downcast dark eyes, the sudden pinch of her thin lips. After her failure to scry Joanna's image in the white crystal, she could not bring herself to say, *He has true magic.* But the lightness, the delicate strength of the music, ignited the air above the butterfly jungle between the two houses; had he not been afraid of what was happening in the Vaults, afraid that Joanna might be imprisoned down there, Antryg could have easily slipped under the spell of it himself and spent the rest of the evening dreaming on the windowsill, until the last light faded from the northern sky.

"In any case," he said, turning back from the enchanted sharpness to the deepening gloom within the upstairs room, "I suspect that's why the mazes were dug, level upon level of them . . . their patterns are disturbingly similar to the garden mazes I saw in the east, and I know that glass, water, and bone were used by certain sects to further channel power—all things which have been found in the walls down there. And that's what frightens me about a Gate having been jammed open in the Vaults."

Seldes Katne startled so badly that she dropped the crystal. "Jammed open?"

Antryg blinked at her in surprise in the failing light. "Of course. Isn't it obvious that's what has happened?"

She said nothing, only stared at him, dark eyes wide with shock.

"That didn't occur to you?"

"I . . . I thought the Gates didn't remain open for more than a few minutes."

"They don't," he said simply. "And it takes a tremendous

amount of power to hold one open even for that long, which is as it should be, given the way the fabric of the universe weakens around a Gate. If one were held open even under ordinary circumstances, I'm not sure what the results would be; given the nature of the maze and the presence of the energy lines, the fact that the Gate is moving shouldn't come as too much of a surprise, though it will make it a beast of a job to track.''

He rubbed his hands absently, as if trying to massage old aches from the twisted fingers. ''At the moment it seems to be confining its ambulations to the Vaults, which is well and good. But the problem is, I can feel the situation is deteriorating. More Gates and wormholes are opening and closing, strange energies acting on the energies already moving through the Vaults . . . and I don't like the idea that Joanna may be imprisoned down there in the middle of it.''

She murmured assent and fumbled to pick up the crystal, which had skidded beneath the rim of a painted blue-and-yellow plate; then her eyes returned to his. ''I might try working in conjunction with a teles-ball,'' she said after a hesitant moment. ''Or you might, though I'm not sure how that will work with the geas. But teles can be used as power-sinks, as you know, and there are several very strong ones here in the Citadel.''

''No.''

The hard decisiveness in his voice made her look up in startled surprise. ''What's wrong with a teles?''

Antryg shrugged and resumed his gawky pacing, now more purposefully, hunting around for his shawl. ''I've never liked them. I know people use them for all manner of spells, from the summoning of elementals to the sending of messages to non-wizards . . . but I've never trusted them.''

She could only stare at him, baffled—rather, Antryg supposed, as Joanna would be by someone who refused to use the telephone out of a professed fear that such devices ate the souls of their users.

"They're only glass and mercury . . ."

"Glass through which magic has been channeled, in which power has been accumulated, year upon year, century upon century," replied Antryg, finding his shawl at last, wrapped around the teapot to keep the contents warm. The upper room of the Pepper-Grinder, though occupied by him for only a few hours, already had the beginnings of a formidable collection of books and scientific journals, stray flowers pressed for drying and at least two splendid, varicolored pinwheels set in a vase beside the window, turning like enormous sunflowers with the shift of the grass-scented wind.

"I know most of the academics consider it balderdash, but Brynnart of Pleth wrote that glass and mercury in combination have powers of their own, and I happen to believe him."

"Brynnart of Pleth was insane," Seldes Katne pointed out.

"So am I. That doesn't mean he wasn't right. And personally, I'm a bit leery of anything which has been imbued with that much magic over that long a period of time."

She gave an uncertain half laugh. "If you're going to suspect things that have had magic go through them, you might as well hold suspect the . . . the," she groped for an example of absurdity, "the stones of the Citadel themselves."

He paused in the act of slinging the slightly tea-stained shawl around his shoulders and turned enormous, deranged gray eyes upon her. "Oh, I do," he said. He plucked one of the pinwheels from the vase, large, delicately balanced, and of a brilliant red and yellow like a hallucinatory sunflower, and blew gently on its curving sail. "Daurannon should be in the Senior Parlor by this time, drinking his evening tea; I think it's high time that you and I had a look at the Vaults."

"As a theory it's preposterous," Daurannon had said. "The mazes in the Vaults were dug as a protective measure to guard the old wizard-lords' treasures against invaders, and their more dangerous secrets against the curious, the same way the very ancient lords built mazes into their castles. That's all those garden mazes mimic. And true or not,'' he'd added, seeing Antryg open his mouth to argue, ''the Council has agreed not to permit you to enter the Vaults without one of us as escort.''

Perched on the arm of the oak chair on the opposite side of the parlor fire, Antryg had experienced—and now, as the scene recurred to him through the smoky overlay of his dreams, experienced more strongly—a sense of odd and painful déjà vu. The Senior Parlor, on the third floor of the Polygon, above the level where the classical mass of that great building broke up into a stylistic jackdaw nest of additions and alterations, had been a home to him once upon a time. Asleep and dreaming in his borrowed bed in the Pepper-Grinder, even as his mind played back the scenes of the earlier evening, it tangled them with the memories of those other nights: hundreds of them, thousands of them, when he'd sat in the same fashion, perched, knees up, on the arm of that very chair, with Daurannon slouched comfortably in the opposite seat of heavily carved and age-blackened oak, stirring milk into his tea after the fashion of the lower classes on the western seaboard.

Even the people had been the same, as much a part of the small, cozy chamber as the linenfold paneling, the undressed stone of the fireplace, and the smells of herbs and candlewax. Bentick played piquet with someone, usually Phormion but on this occasion Nandiharrow; Otaro the Singer sat on the raised stone hearth, soft phrases and ribbons of melody flowing from his big old harp with the restful ease of conversation, while Zake Thwacker—Brighthand—a seventeen-year-old docker's son from the Angelshand slums in the gray robes of a Junior, sat at his feet. Pentilla Riverwych was curled up in a chair at the long table beneath the western windows, unconsciously plaiting and replaiting the end of her thick brown braid as she read from some obscure history that Seldes Katne had brought her down from the library.

Most of them had been Antryg's teachers, before he'd become a teacher himself. Pentilla, now a Senior, had been his student.

And he was an exile.

Even in sleep, deep in the dreams that brought the scene back to him, that hurt.

"But if my theory that the Vaults are an energy maze is preposterous—which of course it is," argued Antryg persuasively, "what harm can I do by going there alone? I mean, I'd have gone down through the kitchen—they connect up with the stores-cellar and the room where Pothatch keeps the flour— except it's locked up for the night, which I must say is rather hard, Bentick, on the poor students who just want a cup of cocoa."

"Considering the things abroad in the Vaults now," Nandiharrow remarked, judiciously rearranging his cards, "that cup of cocoa could be dearly bought."

"It isn't the energy from the lines of power that worries us, and I think you know it." Daurannon set his teacup aside— soft-paste china, white and yellow, from the finest workshops in Angelshand. Everything in the Citadel was that way—either exquisite gifts of past patrons, or rough local work of wool, terra-cotta, or whittled wood. "You know the records are full of rumors and hints and mentions of things that the old mages came up with, things of power that can no longer be accounted for. You know, and I know, that some of these are concealed in the Vaults. That was where you found the Archmage Nyellin's Soul-Mirror, which had been hidden away for centuries."

"If he has no power . . ." Seldes Katne began.

"Some of those tales speak of things that didn't need the power of a wizard," Daur replied. "Some of them, we don't know what they were, or whether they'd need a wizard's power or not to cause trouble with them. You know the Vaults better than anyone, Antryg, and I wouldn't put it past you to have located one of these implements in some obscure record and seek it out to lift the geas."

He got to his feet and collected the scabbarded sword propped against the side of his chair. "Believe me, geas or no geas, you are not going down there alone. It's probably better that you stay aboveground, Kitty,'' he added, as the librarian made ready to fall into step with them. ''Phormion's still shaken up from her brush with that thing, and it was two days ago; you can't be up to dealing with the abominations we're likely to meet down there.''

He spoke with a brisk dismissiveness that brooked no denial. Seldes Katne threw an anguished look at Antryg, then said stoutly, ''I didn't see it nearly as closely as . . . as Phormion did.''

''Besides, the more the merrier,'' Antryg said, who had absolutely no intention of descending to the Vaults with no company but his former friend. ''Nandiharrow can come to protect Kitty, can't you, Tick-Tock?''

Nandiharrow stifled a grin at the very old nickname; Bentick twitched as if his chair had become unexpectedly animate beneath him. ''Don't be ridiculous! For one thing, we're in the middle of the game.''

''Well, we *did* vote to bring him here for his knowledge of the Void . . .''

''With which Daurannon is perfectly capable of dealing. Besides, it's late.'' The Steward's long fingers fidgeted with the gold watch he wore on a chain around his neck.

''A perfect opportunity to observe the energy lines down there under increased influence of the moon.'' Antryg blew on his pinwheel, causing it to spin into a drunken kaleidoscope of color.

''Well, really.'' Bentick glanced at his watch again and laid down his cards, fretfully feeling at his belt for his ring of keys. ''All this trouble to escort a mere dog wizard . . .''

''They call us dog wizards.''

Like a thread of golden ribbon, the voice laced itself through the fabric of Antryg's dream. Deep in sleep he frowned, trying to escape it, as he had tried to escape it for years.

And for a moment, in his dreaming—in the dream parlor while Daurannon tried to talk Seldes Katne out of going with them and Nandiharrow folded up his cards with the slight clumsiness of one still not used to operating with fewer fingers than he had originally had—it seemed to Antryg that Suraklin leaned against the cobblestone of the chimney face, his long, light brown hair framing those narrow features, topaz eyes gently malicious in the saffron reflections of the fire.

And, as if the Dark Mage had opened the door to some infinite corridor of awareness, for a moment Antryg could see all the way down to the end of the dream and knew what it would be.

He tried to cry out, tried to wake himself, tried vainly to surface from sleep.


There was an old circular turret called the Rotunda attached to the Polygon, which it antedated by at least seven hundred years. An old temple, the ancient records said, though to what god was unknown. It lay on the crossing of three of the major energy lines under the Citadel, the Vorplek, the Brehon, and the Pensyk, and consequently the terrible sense of the Void's nearness was almost unbearable. Prowling back and forth in the brittle moonlight that streamed through the seven oddly shaped windows while Bentick knelt to unlock the square, iron-bound doors in the floor, Antryg had to fight the conviction that there was a Gate within a few yards of him—the Gate whose presence he believed could be anywhere on the Line. In the Library it had been the same, and as they'd descended through the corridor past the doors of the refectory, Seldes Katne had told him that others had reported such sensations elsewhere in the Citadel as well.

Daur and Nandiharrow bent their backs, lifting the iron-bound doors from their bed in the living rock of the floor. Bentick fiddled impatiently with his watch, his keys, his staff. Stepping back out of the range of the witchlight on the Steward's staff, Antryg ran quick fingers over the frescoed plaster of the Rotunda's walls, then, not finding what he sought, laid down his pinwheel and knelt to run his hand along the hewed granite of the floor.

As he sank his perceptions into the tight, igneous fiber of the rock, he could feel the silvery energy of the Vorplek Line, which joined the Polygon with the Library; like putting his hand into water and feeling currents of warm and cold, he sensed also the fierce, terrible strength of the Void's presence. There were other powers as well, locked within the granite, prickly and random but present, like ants crawling wildly over his flesh.

"Are you coming, my boy?"

"Considering the fuss you made about entering the Vaults at this ungodly hour . . ."

"Antryg . . . ?"

He scrambled to his feet, scooped up his pinwheel, and trotted to join them in a billow of coat skirts beside the square shadow of the pit that gaped now like the mouth of an open grave in the foot-smoothed floor.

In the real world—as opposed to the dream memory, which tightened closer and closer about him like tangles of colored vapor—the visit to the Vaults that evening had been of short duration. Antryg knew this and tried hard, in the ever-thickening mists of his dream, to steer his recollections to match the reality. The mazes wound, level below level, stairway, drop shaft, spiral, and chamber, deep below the Wizards' Tor in strangely rhythmical patterns that, when examined, turned out to be no patterns at all. All the members of the Council were familiar with their windings; Antryg was one of the few who had made the Vaults a subject of study, seeking explanations for every bricked-up door, devising theories to account for the inexplicable wells and basins, the rooms in which skeletons were buried beneath the flagstone floors or skulls were visible embedded in glass bricks sunk into the walls. Little as there had been to go on in the sketchy records of the most ancient times, the study alone had given him a sense of the Vaults as a whole. Now, following Seldes Katne's lead to the site of her own adventure, he was prey to a strong, uneasy sense of relationship between those half-perceived patterns, those bricked-up doors and unexplained painted chambers, and the places where the pinwheel's shifting marked changes in air pressure, where odd fields of magnetism caused the compass needle to flinch.

And everywhere, he felt the weight of the Void, a slow, nervous crackling along his flesh, as though the very fabric of reality were a breath away from bulging and splitting to let through some horror beyond imagination.

"Which is, of course, absolutely the case," he murmured to Nandiharrow, in response to the older wizard's question. "The Lines carry the sense here and there in the Citadel, as I'm sure you've noticed, but it seems to be everywhere down here."

"Then the problem might be somewhere outside the Citadel entirely? The energies could have been drawn here by something within the Vaults themselves? Maybe one of those 'unknown implements of power' Daur is so anxious to keep you from finding?" The Nine-Fingered Mage shifted his sword sheathe in his hand; by the way he held the hilt, Antryg could tell he'd gone back into training recently to relearn the precision and control governed by the grip. Seldes Katne, almost sheltering in Antryg's coat skirts like a little black hen, looked around her nervously, sweat gleaming on her face in the blue glow of the witchlight above their heads.

"It's a theory," agreed Antryg. "On the other hand, if *my* chickens were being eaten, the first person I'd speak to would be the man who keeps pet foxes." Daurannon, walking ahead of them with drawn sword, stiffened slightly but said nothing.

Only once had they been attacked by an abomination. A furred, eyeless thing of claws and teeth and lightning speed flung itself shrieking out of the dark of a side tunnel, slashing at them with razor talons. It hadn't gotten closer to them than a dozen feet—Nandiharrow had flung out his hand, lightning searing from his crooked, black-gloved fingers to bore through

the thing like spitting blue-white worms. The abomination—
Shriekers, Nandiharrow said the Juniors called them—was
flung back against the wall, kicking and writhing and voiding
syrupy greenish liquid from a half-dozen orifices. When they'd
gone back that way after a very brief exploration of the corridor
on the eighth level—which, as Antryg had guessed, did lie
more or less along the Brehon Line—they'd disturbed three or
four pale orange, sluglike things burrowing their way into the
corpse. At the gleam of the witchlight the things crawled hastily away into the darkness.

Antryg had seen abominations before, far worse than these
. . . that wasn't what troubled him. Dreaming the scene over
again now, he tried to follow Nandiharrow and Seldes Katne
back toward the main stair, as he had followed them in waking
truth.

But behind him in the dream's darkness he heard that soft
voice again, like molten gold and steel.

"They call us dog wizards . . ."

At the age of seventeen he'd run away in the night, knowing
that if that voice had asked him to remain, to give up his soul
and his life, he would have done so.

And now he turned back, as he'd known all along he would.

Suraklin stood under the inky curve of a tunnel which, in
waking reality, Antryg knew perfectly well didn't exist in that
part of the Vaults.

The pain of the geas, the shredding silvery agony of that
violation, flooded back on him: loneliness, bereavement, the
lightless, bottomless abysses of despair; the hollow horror of
a childhood that had driven him to slit his own wrists at the
age of nine; the gentle illusion of caring, the poisoned love,
that had saved his life.

"They call us dog wizards . . . they call *me* dog wizard . . ."

*I would rather have the pain. I would rather have the emp-
tiness, the darkness, the hollow inside . . . I would rather be
alone forever than return to you . . .*

But of course he went, following the darkness through the inevitable tunnel of time.

"A wolf wizard, perhaps," Suraklin said, smiling his gentle smile. "But then all men call 'dog' a wolf who will not serve them." They were now in the bottommost chamber of Suraklin's fortress, the room he and Joanna had entered, months ago, to destroy the evil wizard's final hiding place.

But the darkness there was yet undisturbed. The greenish glow of Suraklin's witchlight darted thinly on the waters of the central well. Like a sickly film of frost, it picked out corner and edge of the stained black altar at the end of the room. There were iron rings in the wall, chains . . . affixed to one by a tiny wrist was a child of ten or so, a blond girl, bought, Antryg knew, from one of the poor marshfolk who lived in brush shelters around the walls of the city of Kymil. He knew because he'd been there when Suraklin had bought her, suavely promising the child's mother that the girl would be taught good service, raised in modesty and propriety in his household.

The girl's face was hollow and pinched with the beginnings of a lifetime of want, even as her mother's had been. Standing at Suraklin's side—sixteen years old, awkward and strange-looking—Antryg had seen even then in the mother's eyes that she didn't believe but wished desperately that she could. In the little brush shack there were eight other children to feed. As the fifth of twelve himself, Antryg knew too well what that was like. In those days it was something he tried not to think about.

But it was those days. He was sixteen again, standing, as he had always stood, at Suraklin's side.

"Come," the Dark Mage said softly. "There are other magics besides those taught by the Council. There are possibilities beyond the defenses they establish—other sorts of fire unquenchable by their definition of water. But the power of that fire is too great for mortal flesh to withstand alone. My son, I will need your help."

Suraklin had never worn the robes of a wizard, dressing

instead in the tawny yellow coat and breeches, the crisp linen and silver-buckled shoes, of an old-fashioned bourgeois. He shed his coat, its rows of steel buttons clicking as he dropped it to the stone floor, and removed his shoes, his white-stockinged feet making no sound as he moved. Long and deft, his fingers rolled back the billowing sleeve of his shirt, tucked the ruffles aside. Those fingers were cold on Antryg's skin as he did the same for the younger man—the boy—exposing the arm to the biceps; and all the while the little girl watched with huge blue-green eyes, too terrified to speak or cry anymore.

With a ritually cleansed silver knife Suraklin drew blood from Antryg's arm, then his own, mixing them on the surface of a mirror and drawing figures in the mingled gore upon his own face and his pupil's. Then he pressed their veins together to complete the rite of blood-bonding—to insure that should his own magic, his own strength, the power of his own life, prove insufficient for what the rite would demand, he would have Antryg's to draw upon. He had done it before.

The rite itself was something Antryg had spent a good portion of his adult life trying with only middling success to forget.

He had a good memory for spells and ritual, his natural curiosity and adeptness trained by years of alternating drill and terror. Even now, nearly thirty years later, he could have accomplished from memory what his master had shown him that night, had he been morally bankrupt enough to want to do so.

As a man dreaming, educated in orthodox wizardry, he saw what the boy in the dream did not know: how different were the ritual patterns laid out on the stone floor from anything taught by the Archmage Salteris or any other Academic mage. Every curve, every line, harked to chaos, to darkness, to energies alien to the energies of earth and fire, water and stars and sky. And the latter-day student of physics and particle theory saw what even the Council-trained wizard would not have: energies to coalesce matter of reality other than that of this or any world—energies to spark the growth of a life, an entity, the metaphysical equivalent of an android, the simulacrum of a demon shaped in the image of the only soul Suraklin knew or could imagine.

The drain of the energy was tremendous, the drag of the magic needed to accomplish such an act of will far more than even the greatest of wizards could have borne alone. As the glowing brownish mists curled up from along the twisting ritual paths, Antryg could feel Suraklin's will and strength and magic bend to the Summoning, drawing upon his. When the brown flame began to flicker over the altar, he could feel the pull of it in his own blood and marrow; first tiny fingerlets flickering along the edge, then something no bigger than a hand, rising, glowing terribly, in the center.

Brown droplets of liquid began to form on the stone of the walls, to gather in tiny pools on the floor.

As a boy he had not known. As a man he knew and turned his face away. Suraklin had, as usual, chained him to one of the black stone pillars beside the door, distrusting not his courage but, Antryg realized now through the deeps of his dream, his sense of right and wrong.

The strength of the thing on the altar, when it began to realize its life, was hideous, as was its rage to destroy, not for anyone's will and bidding, but for its own delight. It fought the chains of domination Suraklin cast about it, its will cutting and thrashing like a flying cloud of razors at the strength of the man who sought to bind it—the man who did not realize that its hate, its wildness, its selfish frenzy for power were the clear and burning mirror of his own.

And the boy Antryg had been willed his strength into that slight, steely form of white and gold, giving him the strength of his blood, the strength of his magic, the strength of the love he bore. Had he been alone, Suraklin could never have had the strength to cross to where the little girl thrashed, screaming like a dying bird, against her chains. He would never have had the strength to drag her to the now-blazing altar without the strength that Antryg willingly gave.

The demon had eyes now, and teeth; it was dominated by Suraklin's magic and his will.

And just before it descended upon the shrieking child, Antryg saw the girl's face, changed by the dream from the face of the child it had been, tear-streaked and stretched with terror, to a woman's face . . .

*Joanna* . . .

His throat would not make a sound; he was too weak, his life too drawn into his master's, to do more than wrench futilely against the chains that held him to implacable stone. The demon's eyes were yellow, Suraklin's eyes. The girl's eyes were brown.

It was his own magic that had brought her there.

*"JOANNA!"*

Darkness shattered like a shell of bone, inside him or outside, he didn't know. He heard something metallic fall with a muffled clink to the wooden floor.

Blinking, he sat up in a tangle of sweat-drenched pillows, milk blue moonlight plashing over the linen of the sheets around him and glinting on something that moved near the foot of his bed in the Pepper-Grinder's upper room.

A knife. Someone rising from the floor, having picked up a dropped knife.

Antryg gave a yelp and flung the nearest pillow as hard as he could, but the black figure was already turning to flee. He tried to make a straight dive at it over the foot of the bed, but the tumbled sheets and blankets fouled his knees, sending him crashing against the bedpost. Even blurred with myopia—his spectacles were God knew where—his wizard's sight could pick out in the darkness the narrow opening of one of the house's several hidden stairs, just to the left of the fireplace; the dark form of his would-be murderer plunged toward it in a swirl of black robe and slammed it shut as Antryg scrambled in pursuit.

It opened, he remembered, by a lever on the other side of

the fireplace . . . damn whoever had built this house with half a dozen tricks like that.

Turning, he dove back to the side of the bed to snatch his spectacles from the nearby windowsill where he'd left them; it took a moment's groping, for unless he was wearing them he couldn't see the light frames of steel and glass and had to memorize where he'd set them down. By the time he pulled the trapdoor open, the intruder was well and truly gone. The stair was a seam in the Pepper-Grinder's stone wall barely wider than his shoulders, leading, if he remembered aright— he'd never lived in the Pepper-Grinder, having occupied rooms first in the Birdcage with Salteris, then in the Upper Gatehouse in the Library's tiny outer court—to the cellars, whence two other passages gave access to the Cat Lair's subcellar and the upper hallway of the Cave.

From there, he was perfectly well aware, the intruder could have fled anywhere in the Citadel.

"Are you quite all right?"

The deep, husky voice, like gravel and honey, made him turn; Kyra stood in the doorway, quellingly elegant in a brocade dressing gown that made Antryg highly conscious of his own knobby knees protruding from beneath the hem of his much-patched, borrowed linen nightshirt.

"Perfectly, thank you, my dear." Antryg hooked the final temple piece of his spectacles over his ear. "It's just that I think someone's been and tried to murder me, and I was wondering if I might impose upon you to see if you can get a reading of any kind from the frame of this door. I'm afraid he's taken his knife away with him. Or her, as the case may be."

"Good Heavens." She stepped swiftly into the room, dispelling the elegance of her appearance by tripping over her own robe hem, and, frowning, ran a searching hand over the jambs and threshold of the secret door. "I suppose it would be silly to ask who would want to do a thing like that."

"Thank you, my dear," Antryg said gravely.

"Well, I haven't heard those horror stories the Lady Rosamund, Daurannon, and Bentick have been telling about you all these years for nothing. I can't find a thing."

"Naturally not," Antryg sighed. "If my guest was a wizard, you wouldn't. Damn." He ran a weary hand through the tangle of his hair. "I'd meant to beg some kind of sleeping draft from Q'iin to keep the dreams under control, but I suppose that anything really effective is out of court if someone is trying to stab me in my sleep."

He put on his shawl and descended to the downstairs hall, Kyra parting company with him to return to her own bed. Then he built up the fire and located in the stacks of volumes on the table an account of astrological aspects upon spells that had not been in the Citadel Library as of his departure nine years ago.

"And no all-night movie," he sighed, setting himself into the chair. "I really must speak to Bentick about getting cable."

In the town where I was born
> There's ladies fair and sweet,
Like roses in the taverns
> On Algoswiving Street.
But out of all those lovelies
> There's just one all seek to win,
She'd raise the dead, she's a witch in bed—
> She's the dancer they call Min.

> A dancer or a vixen
> Or an angel made for sin,
> A fallen child or demon wild
> Is the lady they call Min.
> > —Old Angelshand broadside

# CHAPTER VI

THE COTTAGE WAS VIRTUALLY THE ONLY BUILDING ON THE Wizards' Tor not connected via a subcellar tunnel, or a shared chimney with secret passage, or even a covered arcade, with some other house. It perched on the one patch of more-or-less level ground on the precipitous southwestern slope of the hill, below the turreted rookery of Seniors' houses clinging along the northwestern face; Antryg had heard that it originally had been a potting shed in the midst of the vast herb garden which occupied that plunge of rock and soil. A little gate once stood between lichen-crusted stone posts at the turning of the cobblestoned road, but that was the last concession anyone had made to convenience with the garden. The paths that threaded at apparent random between the tiny beds of sassafras and lovage, high john and henbane, were unpaved, and only occasionally planks were thrown over the worst of the gullies. At the bottom a crumbling dry-stone wall balanced on the edge of the final drop to the upper courtyard of the Polygon, and against that wall, Antryg could see Aunt Min warming herself in the late-morning brightness of the sun, with Lady Rosamund sitting at her side on the low wall itself.

Antryg hesitated for a moment between the posts of the gate. Through his fingertips, bared by the writing mitt he wore for warmth, he could feel, when he shut his eyes and concentrated, that strange, crawling sparkle of energy deep within the stone. The threshold between the posts was yellowish sandstone, left over from the construction of the big arcade on the second floor of the Polygon and worn almost in half by passing feet. He knelt, sending his mind into the grain of the stone, but the energy there was fainter, softer; on a thought he hiked up through the hip-high jungle of sorrel, tansy, and garlic, to press first his hands, then his lips and the side of his face, against the worn wooden railing that surrounded the Cottage's narrow veranda.

The wood held no vibration of that energy at all, though several other sorts whispered to him through the fabric of the ancient wood. The door of the Cottage stood open, as it did all summer. Beneath the small table in the outer of its two rooms, he glimpsed one of the little footstools that were strewed around Aunt Min's dwelling wherever she frequently sat. Her big cinder gray cat Fysshe occupied it now; Paddy-winkle, her slate blue tom, dozed on the nearby chair. Two or three other of the Citadel cats sunned themselves on the veranda among a veritable jungle of potted poppies, geraniums, and spider plants.

Antryg moved along the side of the veranda till he found a patch of the bare granite of the tor itself and pressed his fingers to it; the rush of the energies was like the nibbling of tiny, carnivorous fish at his flesh.

"Curiouser and curiouser." Turning, he made his way down the twisty, dropping paths, the air about him heavy with borage and rosemary, garlic, eyebright, and serpent's sage.

"If you are trying to convince me you're too mad to be of any danger to us," Lady Rosamund remarked in her cool, silvery voice, "you can save your pains."

"Does one need to be mad to want to touch hewn rock and wood and the living bones of the hill?"

She folded up the small black book she'd been reading and laid it in her lap, shaded her eyes to look up at him. Beside her, Antryg could see that Aunt Min was asleep, her knitting a spill of untidy color over her knees. "If one is facing the danger of abominations swarming like rats in the Vaults—with God knows what to come—I suppose a little concern for the matter at hand is not uncalled for," the Lady conceded. "Unless there's something about the situation you know that we don't."

"Oh, I'm quite sure there is," Antryg replied cheerfully, settling on the parapet beside her. "I mean, the fact that there is, is the reason you brought me here in the first place . . . isn't it?"

Her green eyes met his. Tiny lines, feathering through the soft flesh around the lids, might have betrayed her age to a close—or a malicious—observer; her hair, braided away from her temples and lying loose at the back, was still the untouched sable of the hardest anthracite. Antryg remembered Daurannon telling him once that Lady Rosamund concocted her own ointments of sheep fat and rosewater with which she anointed her complexion nightly, though personally he couldn't see why that should be held against her, as the other mage clearly did.

"Of course."

"Nothing to do with revenge?" he inquired interestedly. "Or a desire to ingratiate wizardry as a whole with the Regent by locating a fugitive from his justice?"

"Wizardry," Rosamund said, in her most arctic upper-class accents, "has no need of the Regent's grace, nor of his approval, and it is our justice, not his, under which you stand condemned to death. And if there are social climbers on the High Council who seek to bring wizardry into fashion again in the circles to which they aspire, you can believe that the rest of the Council could not be cozened to such a plan. We are independent of the cities of the West."

"Well, scarcely that," Antryg remarked. "Most of the money that supplies this place comes from rental property, not to mention the subsidies."

She shook her head stubbornly. "It is money we can do without if we must. We have before this. They may have driven us out—scarcely a surprise, considering the attempt to murder the Regent by means of magic—but hardly the first time such a thing has come to pass. We will retreat, Antryg Windrose, but we will return."

"A month, I believe Nandiharrow said," Antryg murmured thoughtfully. "Since the abominations started to appear." He plucked a poppy from the clusters that grew wild at the foot of the wall, the sunlight through the delicate, pale yellow petals coloring his crooked fingers like privet-leaf dye. "I know there are those on the Council who blame me, but what possible object would it serve for me to be tinkering with the Void?"

"It would give you access to magic," she replied promptly.

He looked up from the flower, pushed up his spectacles, and smiled. "So it was you?"

Her cheeks pinkened, and she replied in a slightly constrained voice, "It was a possibility I considered. I and others. No magic exists in that smelly hell hole you've exiled yourself to—don't tell me you haven't hurt for it in the marrow of your bones."

*We are what we are, my son*, Suraklin once said to him. *You know in your heart that there is nothing we would not do—* nothing—*to realize our power. We give up everything for it— our lovers, our parents, our homes . . . the children we might otherwise bear, the people we might otherwise be.* There had been a wry glint in the amber deeps of his eyes, a kind of ironic amusement at his own self-pity, and his voice had flexed as if he had forgotten Antryg's presence and spoken to himself alone. *And we consider ourselves fortunate to be allowed by God to make the trade.*

When he'd been ten or eleven, those words had pierced Antryg's heart like a spear, bringing a sudden understanding of this most powerful, and loneliest, of mages. The knowledge that Suraklin, too, had his griefs and regrets, even he . . .

He always wondered afterward whether the flash of wondering pity and love he felt then had been his master's intent.

He shrugged and scratched the side of his long nose. "If I have, it's not an unfamiliar feeling," he said. "I was without power for seven years, locked in the Silent Tower, and I'm without it now, so whatever efforts I've made in that direction don't seem to have gotten me anywhere."

"But you are a man who hopes, even to absurdity. And there are those who contend that you caused this problem, knowing that we *would* bring you here and give you access to the Vaults and their secrets." Her haughty glance shifted from him to the tiny black bundle of knitting and straggly white hair slumped against the wall among the poppies. In the long silence three finches, chirping wildly, flung themselves in a brown, flashing kamikaze dive from the red-purple leaves of the nearby plum tree and plunged out into the brilliant gulf of the air. The cool hardness of her voice was like the smallest of dissecting knives. "Do you know what it cost her, to exercise the Master-Spells over your mind?"

"Well," Antryg replied mildly, "I know what it cost *me*." But he reached down with great gentleness to straighten the shabby old plaid shawl the Archmage had about her shoulders.

Rosamund struck his hand aside. Antryg sat back, startled at the contained fury of the blow—her ladyship met his eyes for a moment, then looked away. "I'm sorry," she said in a stifled tone. "I shouldn't have done that. But she . . ." She paused, looking down at the old lady dozing in the sun. "She has been ill a great deal of late." Her voice turned quiet, tender, and a little sad. "She is very old, over a hundred. She shouldn't have to be dealing with this. If she were anyone but the Archmage—if she were anywhere but this Citadel—she would have died at the turning of the granny-winter, when I brought her here from Angelshand.''

"When you decided to come after me."

The long, dark lashes lifted, unveiling emerald eyes that challenged him to debate what she had done. "It was not the only reason for our experiments, and I think you know it," she said. "In a way, we hoped to circumvent this situation by gaining knowledge of the Void ourselves." She reached down to draw up Aunt Min's shawl herself, and as she did so, she spoke without heat, or violence, or rage in her rose-petal voice. "She overtaxes her body, thinking it can bear the strain of her magic as it could when she was forty. She will not believe that battling your mind for dominance, or struggling with the wild magic of the Void, will do her harm. Believe me, Antryg," she added quietly, "if this does kill her, I swear to you that when she dies, and the Master-Spells pass to me, I will hold you responsible."

Antryg was silent, wrapping his aching hands in the trailing ends of his shawl. Though there was a certain division of opinion in the High Council as to whether the Lady Rosamund or Daurannon the Handsome would inherit the Master-Spells, Antryg himself had no doubt that they would pass to the woman now seated beside him. His mind and body still ached from the geas—he felt as if his flesh should bear the marks of it: slashes, bruises, burns. But the force that had left his mind a shredded ruin had been actuated, he realized, by no malice. Aunt Min had only done what she conceived needed to be done for the good of all concerned.

And Min, he had been aware even as the darkness had sliced and lacerated him to let the others in, had been trying quite sincerely to hurt him as little as possible.

Under ordinary circumstances he knew his own powers to be greater than Lady Rosamund's and guessed—though he was not entirely sure—them to be greater than Aunt Min's would have been, had she not been what she was. But the Master-

Spells that descended from Archmage to Archmage were not precisely a matter of strength. Few wizards truly knew what they *were* a matter of.

In any case, he knew that if he were still under the Council's geas—or for that matter anywhere within the Citadel—when Aunt Min died, he probably wouldn't like what would happen next.

"You love her a great deal," he said gently, and she looked up at him with a chilling bitterness in her sea-colored glance.

"I would love her," Rosamund said, "even were she not as good to me, as kind, as caring as . . . I would say 'as a mother' but in my case that would be a jest in exceptionally poor taste." She glanced aside, her face averted from him now and still as marble. "Perhaps I should say, as caring as the mother I dreamed about when I was doing stitchery with my fingers shaking from hunger because I'd been clumsy with my silks or talked impertinently to the music master and had been sent to bed without supper the night before. The mother I dreamed about when I was being trained to sit straight in my corsets for hours on end *doing nothing*, because the daughters of earls must learn to be idle gracefully; listening to my mother and her friends gossiping in the drawing room. Though I don't know why I call them 'friends.' They would betray one another's most intimate confidences the moment they thought they could amuse a superior by them."

Her chin lifted, her red lips set as if they were vermilion porcelain rather than flesh. The absinthe-tinted eyes stared out past him—past the tiny sandstone court spread out below them, visible beyond the roofs of the North Cloister and its hall, past the dark sweep of the forest, black and pewter and broken by rusty patches of bog, that stretched out before them to the milky ice of the horizon. In them Antryg could see the reflection of a young girl, stately and beautiful as a child queen, and cold within with a grief like frozen tears and mercury.

"I hated it," she whispered. "I used to sneak away and meet her by the kitchen door—she sold herbs to our cook. Even then she was very old, just a tiny old lady like a little black sparrow, always fumbling with her knitting. Later I would steal my maid's dress and climb out the window to meet her at night, to learn. One of the first spells she ever taught me was a sleep-spell, because the maid shared the room with me—a lady is never alone, *never*. And she . . .''

She looked down at the old lady dozing in the sun with her knitting lax under knotted little hands.

''I was a fledgling hawk in a gilt cage, with nothing but a linnet's seeds and fruit to eat. She fed me on my true food through the bars of my prison until I was strong enough to wrest open its doors.''

The green gaze flicked back to him, present again and angry, as much at what she had just told him as at anything to do with Aunt Min. ''You didn't need to fight her as you did.''

Something gray and swift flashed along the wall to their right; turning, Antryg saw that it was the cat Fysshe, followed closely by Paddywinkle and Issay's big red tabby Rufus. At the same moment a sudden, snarling shriek came from the courtyard below. Looking over the edge of the wall, he could see Imp, Lady Rosamund's huge black tom, bristling in furious challenge at Spooky Bob, the tailless charcoal tabby whose usual haunt was the kitchens. Half a dozen of the other Citadel cats—Otaro's geriatric calico Lady Dyna, Bentick's Silver, four more of Issay's, and several belonging to various Juniors—were prowling uneasily around the edges of the skirmish, hissing at one another and occasionally scurrying away, but never going more than a few feet. Spooky Bob, no hero, turned what tail he had and bolted but came up short as if at a barrier; turning back, he yowled furiously with an air of trapped desperation.

''What on earth . . . ?'' Lady Rosamund had risen to her feet, was looking down into the court, her brow a darkening storm of anger. More cats were arriving all the time. A couple of novices in their meal-colored robes had emerged from under the arcade of the North Cloister, and a gust of nervous laughter rose on the bright air.

"If it's one of the Juniors causing this I'll *flay* him!" Rosamund turned on her heel and strode off for the perilous little stair that led to the Cloister, and so to the court, like a gust of dark wind.

Antryg remained where he was, pulling the sloppy rainbow of his shawl more closely around his shoulders and watching the ragged mill of feline bafflement in the court below. Automatically, his eye traced the line from the stained marble turret of the Rotunda, just visible beyond the roof of the North Hall, out to a small chapel in the foot of one of the drum towers on the other side of the courtyard with its skirmishing knot of cats. Though the silver-gray trunks of the pines hid it, he knew precisely where an arrow-straight alignment of standing-stones lay in the forest, stumpy and eroded as broken teeth and stretching for miles out of the forest and on into infinity over the steppe.

"Eh, the poor things." Fingers like the claws of a chicken closed around his own.

Antryg glanced down at the top of that white-crowned skull, at the level of his knee, feathers of wind fraying its wisps of hair. "The Citadel's stood for nearly a thousand years," he remarked quietly. "Quite apart from spells the Juniors concoct for fun, there's a lot of very old magic locked in its stones, and not all of it was made by those who eschewed meddling in human affairs."

"And they brought grief down upon us all," creaked the old woman's voice. "And will again. Nyellin did spells with cats." She named an Archmage dead six hundred years, a woman rumored to have been addicted to taking cat-form herself. "And Feldchibbe used to call up demons out of the echoes made when he'd strike a silver ball. Did Rosie bring my posset? A honey posset . . . my old bones ache . . ."

"I'll fetch it." Down in the court the novices had scattered like terrified sparrows. Lady Rosamund was standing amid the cats, dispersing the spells that had summoned and kept them, releasing the nervous and frightened animals back to their accustomed ways. A gust of wind swirled the black skirts of her robe, made a velvet cloud of her witch black hair. The anger that enveloped her at whoever would do such a thing to defenseless animals was nearly as palpable and certainly as dark—a shadow guarding lightning.

Antryg shivered.

"Did you sleep well?" Aunt Min shifted her position a little, tugged his hand as he would have risen to go rattling off down the steps to the kitchens.

"Not very."

She made a little noise with what few teeth she had left, as if he'd been a novice who'd botched a simple illusion, and stretched out her hand. After a moment he slipped from sitting on the wall to kneeling before her, as he had in the Council chamber, so that her crippled fingers could brush back the graying curls from his temples.

"Old sorrow and old pain," she clucked. "Like the spells that fill this place, clinging to the teles-balls, clinging to the Vaults, clinging to every stone and kitchen pot. Why do the mageborn always grow up in pain? Why can they never let it go?"

Antryg thought about Lady Rosamund Kentacre, practicing the gentle arts of ladylike deportment and gossip; about his own nightmares; about the golden fifteen-year-old dancing girl they still sang songs about, nearly a century later, in the streets of Angelshand, never knowing what had become of her.

"Perhaps because it can never let them go?"

But at her touch he felt the bleeding grip of last night's horrors ease.

"'A flower sleeps in the earth,'" she said, "and dreams of color and sun. But when it blooms, the earth leaves no stain upon it. Maybe you only need to sleep a little longer in the City of Dreams."

She shook her head again and sighed. "Those things in the Vaults." She spoke as if the horror Nandiharrow had killed with lightning had been no more than a mouse that had slipped through the spells woven about the Citadel to keep it free of such vermin. "Sad little things, and no more to be blamed than the poor pussies. You really have to do something about it."

And putting her head down, she fell promptly back to sleep.

"And what will you do," Seldes Katne asked, out of sheer force of habit straightening the edges of the piles of books Antryg was sorting, "if Aunt Min does die?"

"Run like hell, I suppose." He glanced at the spine of a crumbling grimoire in the hard slice of butter-colored afternoon sunlight, set it in the largest heap. "Turn this one over to Nandiharrow's team—it has some mention of early wizardry in it, but I don't know how much bearing it would have on the current powers at large in the Vaults. The problem is that though she couldn't track me by scrying-crystal—geas or not, I *am* still mageborn—Rosamund knows I wouldn't go far as long as Joanna is a prisoner here."

The librarian glanced quickly at him across the heaped library table and started to speak, then stopped herself and changed what she was going to say to "You think the Master-Spells will fall to Lady Rosamund, then, and not Daurannon? I know Aunt Min favors the Lady."

It was a few moments before Antryg replied. To look at Salteris' books—to help Seldes Katne sort the former Archmage's water-stained miscellany of demonaries, catalogs, thaumaturgical cookbooks, and experimental notes from sorcerers long forgotten for anything containing reference to ancient magics in the Vaults—brought a yearning ache to his heart, a memory that was both hurt and joy. It had been less than a year altogether since he'd realized that Salteris was no longer alive in any real sense of the word, and less than six months since he had strangled the thing that was left of him.

He had taught himself to speak casually of the old man, when speak of him he must, only by thinking of him as someone who was still alive somewhere, someone he would one day see again—scarcely different from all those years imprisoned in the Silent Tower.

"It isn't a matter of favor, precisely," he said at last. "Nor is it invariably the strongest to whom they pass. Or perhaps it is, by some definition of strength other than the one we use. And of course, once the Master-Spells do pass to the new Archmage, the question of strength becomes largely academic."

"But it's always someone on the Council," Seldes Katne pointed out doubtfully.

"Well, I think that works backwards," Antryg said, flipping open a sheaf of notes—yellow and brittle as last year's fallen leaves—in Salteris' elegant hand and identifying the spells they glossed. "They usually fall to someone within a certain range of strength, and Council membership merely assures that those with that strength will continue the policies of the former Archmage. And they do seem to fall to whoever is most appropriate, though the Archmage doesn't *will* them to a successor. It's more accurate to say that to the Archmage, at least, the successor is obvious. And speaking of me skulking 'round the woods whilst Joanna is locked up in a tower here . . ."

"Quite." Seldes Katne carefully shifted a crumbling old tome on ophidiomancy to the sideboard behind her, to be sent down to the Juniors in the scriptorium for copying. "As you asked, I checked all the attics above here, and the subcellars below my quarters, though I really don't think anyone could be holding a prisoner there any more than they could hold someone in the Conservatory. They're just too close to my quarters for anyone to come or go unheard."

She turned back to him, wiping the dust from her hands and studying the stacks of books still on the table.

Every inch of wall space not pierced by windows in the great library chamber was already covered in an uneven crazy quilt of cabinets built on top of cabinets and shelves of all lengths and sizes, from the floor to the lower side of the gallery that circled the room at the height of twelve feet, and then again, above the gallery, up nearly to the curve of the ceiling. At some time in the distant past the three turrets that opened off the gallery had been used for study rooms, where novices could engage in their endless task of memorizing lists, laws, and songs—the work of every novice's first five years. Now they, too, were jammed with books, and the novices studied in their own—or one another's—chambers.

Seldes Katne was currently engaged in a losing battle to keep the scriptorium on the floor below from turning into an auxiliary library, arguing that the Juniors who worked there ought not to be disturbed by those in quest of what Tiamat the White had written about necromancy or Simon the Lame's ophthalmological spells, and so far she had held the encroachment to one wall. Below the scriptorium, half the Library's cellars, cut into the rock of the tor itself, were given over to the storage of paper, ink, parchment, and the like, while the remainder, built of granite blocks scarcely distinguishable from the native stone, constituted Seldes Katne's own quarters, onto which the absurd gothic gem of the disused conservatory cleaved like a pinchbeck-diamond codpiece set into battle armor.

"Thank you—it's very good of you. And I've put in about two hours this morning, when I should have been up here helping you with these, checking the Assembly Hall building from cellars to attics, including the treasuries and the clock-tower, and nothing to show for it bar a certain amount of evidence that some of the novices have been arranging assignations with the milkmaids in the guest chambers on the second floor."

Seldes Katne looked so shocked he could not forbear adding, "I deduce that it was the novices because, of course, the Seniors would have left no evidence at all . . . and I have it on good authority that when one attains Council rank, tumbling the milkmaids is beneath one's dignity. At least that's what Bentick was always telling *me*. This packet of notes contains probably the only thing Salteris wrote down about the Void, and it's only the spells of opening it, which he learned from Wilbron of Parchasten—nothing about its nature, or why some people can sense things happening in connection with it and some can't. As far as I know, Wilbron never wrote anything down about that, either.''

''You're sure it was the only one?''

He nodded, and she sighed. ''Salteris' house in Angelshand had already been looted when I got there, you see,'' she said, turning to set the notes with the others for copying. ''Not badly—not like the Witchfinders would have left it. But there were things missing. Books and a few magical implements—things the other wizards in the Mages' Yard said should have been there. And of course, while I was there the order came through from the Regent for all the mageborn to leave the city. I've only been back myself for a few days.''

Antryg frowned, thinking about that tall, soot-blackened old house in its quiet backwater court in the Quarter of the Old Believers—part of the numerous parcels of town property whose rents supported both the mages who lived there and the Citadel itself. Thinking of the years he'd lived there with Salteris and Daurannon . . .

''I hope to goodness they don't rent it to some idiot who'll try working magic there,'' he murmured. ''The situation's serious enough, with little enclaves of old spells and random fields opening *here*. Who were the mages who were actually involved in opening the Gate for Rosamund to cross the Void in search of me? I know Daurannon was off abomination-hunting . . .''

''Issay and Nandiharrow went with Rosamund through the Void, as you know,'' the librarian said, lowering her voice and glancing across the room to the table where the Senior mages were pursuing their research. ''Whitwell Simm, Q'iin, and

Otaro . . . Yes, Brunus?'' She looked up as a tall, fat, lunkish-looking young man in his early twenties, still wearing a novice's meal-colored robe, appeared at her shoulder. ''Excuse me . . .'' She crossed to the shelves under the north gallery that contained all the volumes of preliminary lists and spells. They stood for a time, talking earnestly. Antryg, watching them, noted the desperate urgency of the young man's gestures, and put that together with the color of his robe—novices had usually graduated to Junior status by the time they were eighteen—to deduce that here was another whose powers were small. His shirt collar and boots marked him as lower bourgeois, and the way he stood—even allowing for a fat man's slightly thrown-back stance—as a city boy. Countrymen were more relaxed as a rule. The loss of a son—particularly an only or eldest son—from a small business would almost certainly have caused family trouble . . .

That thought brought others, an uneasy spiral of free association that led him, as inexorably as last night's dreams had led him, back to the darkness of the Vaults.

To the dripping silences where niter-smeared blocks of stone were patched now in places with purulent mosses—red, black, or the slowly throbbing orange from which threadlike tentacles followed the movement of body heat; to the alien vermin with sightless, pale eyes and the quivery, hallucinatory thickness of the dark; to the cold ozone smell and all-pervasive weight of the nearness of the Void.

He could feel it here, through the energy line that ran beneath the Library itself. His instincts, his touch on the stones of the Citadel, told him that the situation was deteriorating steadily, but equally his every instinct screamed at him that he had no business down there—even on the upper levels—without massive physical and theurgic defense. Secret objects of power were not the only things rumored to have been concealed in those lightless mazes. Ugly magics had been done there, evil wielded by the Council's cold, implacable power; there were sealed doors in the Vaults, he knew from his own days on the Council, that hid things which could not die and should never have been permitted to live in the first place. From ancient records he suspected that there were things whose creators had taken care never to inform the Council what they had wrought, lest they fall under their peers' displeasure for dabbling in forbidden arts.

*Old sorrow and old pain* . . .

What had been bricked up down there, he wondered, by those who had subsequently pretended it never happened and burned their notes? What energies were being released, now that reality was fracturing along the shear-lines of the leys?

Yet he knew he could not take any member of the Council with him when he went to seek Joanna there. Even Nandiharrow and Issay Bel-Caire, who headed up the team of Seniors searching the most ancient Citadel records for mention of those ancient magics, might have their own secrets or might be allies in some unspoken double game.

Seldes Katne came back to him through the thick slant of the primrose light, her round face creased with concern. "Poor Brunus," she sighed. "He's failed the Junior exams twice already. He has a genuine feeling for spells, especially of healing. Just . . . very little power."

"You passed them on the third try, didn't you?"

She nodded. "I still don't know how. Probably because I couldn't . . . I couldn't see a life outside of this place. Outside of being a mage." Her square face was sad, and for a moment he glimpsed in her eyes the look of that long-ago girl, short and chubby and unpretty, clinging grimly to her dreams.

"Well, be that as it may," she sighed again. "He's gotten a little respite because Phormion was to have been his examiner."

"Ah, yes," Antryg said. "Phormion." He recalled the Starmistress' haunted eyes in the Council the previous day. "If Issay and Nandiharrow came with Rosamund, and they needed to get three of the top Seniors to make the Circles of Power here to keep the Gate open, and Bentick was off calming down old Trukild from the village . . ."

"How did you know that?" Seldes Katne demanded, her thick brows locking at the mention of the village headman's name.

"Well, it stands to reason if someone had seen an abomination in the Green King's Chapel ferocious enough for one of the top members of the Council to go chasing it, old Trukild would have been up here shaking his cane in Bentick's face and swearing he'd risk no more of his people by letting them come to work in this den of turpitude . . . though, if he didn't, God knows where he thinks half the village would come by its money for iron and salt and sugar at Yuletide."

"You," Seldes Katne said severely, "are going to get yourself into real trouble one of these days."

"I'm pleased you have sufficient imagination to consider powerless enslavement to two extremely vengeful wizards a bagatelle . . . to say nothing of the abominations in the wine cellar. Where was Phormion?"

"I don't know. Probably lying down, recovering from her encounter with the Gate in the Vaults. God knows that's what I did." She shivered and looked away.

"Interesting," Antryg murmured. "So we have Phormion and Daur unaccounted for, and possibly Bentick . . . and Min herself, of course. Odd how one tends to forget where she might be or what she might be doing. Just out of curiosity, where was Brighthand?"

The librarian glanced up at him quickly but said nothing; he saw in her eyes that she, too, had felt the boy's hidden power.

"He will be Archmage one day, you know," he said after a moment, pulling up one of the beechwood chairs and taking a precarious seat on the top of its back, his boots on the seat in front of him. "Probably not soon, but one day. He's so quiet I'm not sure how many people have noticed him, but the power is there. I don't know when I've seen a novice with that kind of power."

Seldes Katne did not reply. Looking down at the plump, doughy face with its suddenly closed expression, Antryg remembered that magic was not, and never had been, entirely a matter of study, of work, of diligence. Without all those, and unceasing mental labor, the greatest talent for wizardry would come to nothing, and over the years he had seen dozens of promising novices fail through laziness or overconfidence. But without inborn talent, the work—and the wanting—were simply not enough.

The librarian had dwelt in the Citadel for fifty years, working, memorizing, sweating, wanting . . . and was still one of the least powerful.

With the possible exception, he reflected ruefully, of the non-mageborn sasenna, Pothatch the cook, Tom the gardener, and himself.

"Well," Seldes Katne said after a time, "in the meantime, I don't really look forward to having the Master-Spells which command me being held by either a cold-blooded aristocrat or a slick little social climber like Daurannon Stapler . . . not that I'd ever be likely to have cause to feel their use. But you . . ."

"Oh, I don't know." Antryg smiled reflectively, leaning his elbows on his bony, jeans-clad knees. "Think what a tizzy there would be if Aunt Min should die and everyone wake up in the morning and find our Zake has become Archmage after all. Now, don't laugh," he added, looking down at her with mock gravity. "Precisely that happened in the reign of Tyron the Second. The old Archmage died and the Master-Spells fell on a chap who was working as a dog wizard in Kymil—well, a court wizard, since that was back in the days when it was more or less respectable all around for nobles to hire mages, but there must have been an amazing scene in the Council here, nevertheless."

"Beldock the Minstrel!" Katne laughed, recalling that less-than-respectable fragment of history. "Beldock the Unruly . . . and a very good Archmage he made, too, by all accounts." Her dark eyes sparkled at the thought of that old Council's discomfiture, as if its members had included Lady Rosamund and Daurannon the Handsome, and all those other, younger wizards whose abilities had surpassed her own patient, diligent, thankless work.

Antryg smiled a little, too. As scenarios went, it wasn't a terribly likely one . . . but it was certainly an improvement on the several that ended with himself being bricked up in a six-by-six pocket of darkness in the Vaults with his geas and a swarm of half-animate, carnivorous demons to keep him company.

He stepped down from the back of the chair and picked up yet another book—unfamiliar to him; Salteris must have acquired it after they had parted. "Good Heavens!" he murmured in astonished delight. "It mentions tortoiseshell readings. Listen! *'It is commonly known among the scholars of the South that all the wisdom and knowledge of the world may be divined in the patterns on the shells of tortoises, creatures whose age and wisdom is the reflection of this divine gift. Munden Myndrex copied these patterns for all the seventy-five years of his wanderings . . .'* Kitty, surely the Library has the papers of Munden Myndrex? He died here at the Citadel, didn't he?"

In a swirl of coat skirts he turned toward the shelves of massive, handwritten catalogs chained to the wall; Seldes Katne had to seize a handful of the threadbare velvet to stay him. "Antryg, why would Brighthand—or Daurannon, for that matter—kidnap your lady Joanna in the first place?"

"Well," he turned back to her, "that *is* the question of the hour." One corner of the long, absurd mouth hardened slightly, and for a moment, behind the thick spectacles, the mild daffiness of his gray eyes gave way to something else. "And though it's true we haven't been through all the hidden rooms and deserted halls aboveground in this place by any means, my guess is, she's in the Vaults. And that brings me to the subject of two favors I'd like to ask of you, and please don't slap my face because they're not that sort of favors."

"What sort of favors are they?" Seldes Katne asked warily.

"Quite easily granted ones, I assure you." He took her arm and led her over to a book-choked alcove between two of the wide windows. "Are you familiar with the construction of a Talisman of Air?"

She nodded, looking up at him. Beyond the open case-ments, the steep drop of the Citadel hill fell away to tangled clouds of dark spruce and bright-leaved larch and aspen, in-terspersed with tiny walled gardens of looserife and lady-fern, buttercup and poppies. Roofs of shingle and tile patched the dark of the trees, punctuated by turrets and stitched together by rickety galleries and stairs. Antryg identified every house and those who lived within them—the pink-walled Pavilion, the ornamental brickwork chain of the Four Brothers, the foliage-covered House of Roses . . . and above those, the gray towers and gilt-tipped roofs of the preposterous structure called the Castle, where Phormion Starmistress lived.

Seldes Katne's voice brought him back. "Of course," she was saying. "Opal, silver, the wing of a butterfly, spelled to hold air about it though it be plunged into water or fire . . ."

"Could you make one for me? This afternoon, I mean?"

She hesitated, as if asking herself why he wanted such a thing and whether Lady Rosamund would countenance putting even that small a device of magic into his unpredictable hands. "Mine were never very good," she said awkwardly.

"Well, they're certainly better than any effort of mine in that direction at present." Falling to his knees on the tight-woven straw matting of the floor, Antryg stooped to clutch the hem of her black robe. "Would you make one for me if I begged abjectly?" He kissed the hem; she pulled it from his grip, fighting unsuccessfully to smother laughter.

"You are absurd."

"If I promised to make you the finest pinwheels in all the land so that all other possessors of pinwheels would swoon away with envy at the sight of your shadow upon the grass? If I swore to bring you flowers at the first light of morning . . ."

"I can pick my own flowers."

"But not as well as I would. I'd sing for you, too." And throwing back his head he caroled:

*"In the town where I . . ."*

"Enough!" she groaned, stepping back. Antryg prostrated himself full-length at her feet and got in another quick kiss of her hem. Two Juniors, coming from the gallery outside, went over to where Nandiharrow and Whitwell Simm sat, nearly invisible behind a mountain of ancient scrolls, to ask a question. They'd all heard stories about Antryg Windrose.

He propped himself hopefully on his elbows. "Does that mean you'll do it?"

"I should have it for you by midnight." She shook her head as he collected his long legs and arms beneath him and unfolded himself to his feet. "What was the other thing you wanted?"

His voice sobered. "Could you find for me references to what teles-balls are now—and have been in the past—here within the Citadel? Who had them, and what they used them for, and what became of them? I'm afraid it's a little tedious," he apologized, seeing her look of startled alarm.

"For what? I mean, the research on some of them goes back a thousand years . . ."

"Yes, and unfortunately it's those I'm chiefly interested in. The very old ones, the legendary ones. I'll help you with it as soon as I can, but at the moment it is rather critical that I explore the Vaults as soon as possible, and for that I'm going to need a Talisman of Air . . . among other things. Will you help me?"

The librarian hesitated, her dark eyes raised to the long, ridiculous, bespectacled head, with its glittering earrings and graying curls. She was, Antryg knew, a woman who had spent her life in these bastions of Council orthodoxy, a perfect and conscientious servant of the Council for fifty years.

But she gulped gamely and stammered, "If . . . if I can."

There's no such thing as a wizard who minds his own business.
—BERENGIS THE BLACK
Court Mage to the Earls Caeline

# CHAPTER VII

ANTRYG PAID SEVERAL OTHER CALLS ABOUT THE CITADEL AS
the evening drew on. From the Library he made his way, over
plank bridgelets and fern-choked gullies and down long flights
of decaying wooden steps, to the plain little house called the
Breadbox, where Q'iin the Herbmistress was candying lemon
peel in the glass porch overlooking the sun-salted slope of the
herb garden. From that tall, beautiful, black woman he begged
a supply of jelgeth leaves, and her bright blue eyes narrowed
at the mention of the powerful stimulant.

"Staying up late to study for exams?"

"Something like that."

Her expression softened a little as she read the lines of sleeplessness the previous night had gouged into the corners of his
eyes. "You need help?"

He smiled and shook his head. "Only something to keep
me awake . . . and something to prevent dreams when I
sleep."

Emerging through the garden door with the two packets of
herbs in one pocket, a bag of candied lemon rind and half a

dozen hazelnuts in another, he climbed through lengthening pools of cobalt shadows to where Tom the gardener was patiently pulling weeds, an almost hopeless task in the Sykerst's short, lush seasons of growth. Already most of the garden lay in gloaming, though overhead the sky seemed to have soaked in enough radiance to give it back a good long while. Tom and Antryg sat together for nearly an hour, sharing the lemon peel and talking idly of this and that: of Antryg's years in the Silent Tower and how he'd managed to escape; of Tom's sister's newest baby and the furor in his family about her naming; of the rumors of abominations that had been rife all about the countryside for a month; and of the return of the wizards to the Citadel, exiled from their homes throughout the Empire.

"Nothing'll come of it, though," Tom remarked, lighting his pipe and following with huge, mournful blue eyes the swift-stitching track of a handful of swallows across a willowpussy sky. "The governors and police chiefs'll get tired of running down every rumor that this person or that is working magic, like they always do, and Issay, and Whitwell, and Pharne and them'll open up their houses again before Yule."

"Who brought word of the abomination at the Green King's Chapel the other day, by the way?" Antryg inquired, pulling a weed stem from Tom's sack and dissecting its leaves with his fingernails as he spoke.

"Henit the Swineherd saw it—Gru Gwidion and a couple of his hunters brought the word here. There's not many from the village'll actually come here these days."

"So it was something someone actually saw?"

"Oh, aye . . . well . . ." Tom scratched the north face of his enormous nose. "Henit thinks he did—my sister talked to his wife about it—but when he's been smoking moonweed, who knows? But that isn't what I've been meaning to tell you." He lowered his voice and sat up a little on the uneven log they'd been sharing as a seat.

"Rumor's going 'round in the kitchen this afternoon that the scryer in the tower's seen the Inquisition on its way here—the Witchfinders.''

"Is it, now?" Antryg murmured, lacing his bony fingers around his knees.

"Oh, aye. And her ladyship's fair waxed about it, too, blaming our boy Daur, and him denying he had anything to do with sending for 'em. So you want to watch yourself, m'lord."

"It appears I do." Antryg sighed and got to his feet, shaking the grass clippings out of his coat skirts. "Just what I needed."

On the top floor of the Harlot, where the half-dozen sasenna on night duty were waking one another up with a quite ferocious sparring class under Implek's bellowed orders, he found Sergeant Hathen, the troop's second-in-command. Hathen had always liked Antryg—the big, beefy woman had trained with him during his novice days, and they'd had a brief and enthusiastic fling the summer before she'd met the village butcher who was still her lover—and after a little flirting Hathen allowed that although she had been forbidden to give him a weapon, she might just mislay one in the Harlot's cellars sometime the following afternoon.

Much comforted by the knowledge, he then proceeded to the kitchen to beg dinner from Pothatch the cook.

Afterward, upstairs in the Pepper-Grinder once more, he brewed a little of the jelgeth-leaf tea, to hold off sleep and the oozing horrors of his dreams, and sat by the open windows breathing the dark crystalline spices of spruce forest and night. Music drifted from the candlelit windows of the Cat Lair, an old-fashioned kithara played with heart-tearing mastery that had to be Zake Brighthand's, while a young woman sang a thoroughly disreputable ballad about a unicorn and a sow.

By the light of his own candles, Antryg shuffled his cards, smiling a little at the sprightly voice next door as he laid down as significator the Queen of Wands. The academic mages, who had taken refuge in the Citadel to refine and perfect the study of magic away from the choices and prejudices of the cities, looked upon the cards as a dog wizard's tool, a trick for pleasing patrons with cheap and easy half truth. "They are seldom accurate," Salteris had told him once, looking dispassionately down over his shoulder in some low-raftered garret they'd shared in a hill-country inn long ago—not long after the old man had found him, in fact, and healed him of his first madness. "And the problem is that when they are accurate, you can't always tell it."

But on that night, and on so many nights thereafter, Antryg had continued to lay card on card, getting sometimes yes, sometimes no, desperate for an answer to the question that had in those days consumed his waking hours and stalked him like a grinning ghost in dreams—continued until he'd fallen asleep with his head on the gaudy layout, his question still unanswered.

It was a bad habit, he knew; and he'd seldom found the cards, even when they were being truthful, to be of any help.

His big, awkward hands quick as a faro dealer's, he laid four cards around the significator: the five of swords, the five of pentacles, the two of pentacles, the Mage reversed.

The Mage reversed? He turned the deck thoughtfully in his hands, looking down at the battered and enigmatic rectangles of pasteboard among the chaos of papers, pinwheels, and half-empty teacups littering the table's surface.

A reference to the geas that held his own powers in check? To the wizard who, for whatever reasons, had decided to kidnap Joanna? A Council mage? Someone using a teles as a power-sink? Or something else, someone else . . . someone who was the opposite of a wizard? Or was the message *Wisdom reversed*?

Five was strife, conflict, but it also indicated the crossover point at which the spiritual had absorbed too much of the material ever to go back to being what it was. And pentacles signified money—or craft. The craft of magic? Of music perhaps? The notes of Brighthand's kithara trailed through his consciousness like a line of crystal butterflies.

Pentacles was the sign of earth.

Deep earth, and the things of deep earth. Rock, clay, crystal
. . . enclosed darkness that has never seen light.

The Vaults.

He gathered the cards.

Joanna, he thought. Joanna would never forgive him.

When first he had escaped the vengeance of the Council and
the Regent's death sentence, he had hesitated a long time before
seeking out Joanna in her own strange, noisy, magicless world—
in the preposterous chiaroscuro of the City of Dreams. His friends
had suffered before through proximity with him, and she was a
woman who had her own life, her own priorities, her own needs
apart from him. He knew enough of her to recognize how the
emotional desert of her childhood had given her a need for sta-
bility, comfort, and orderliness that was as much a part of her as
her wry quick wit, her odd combination of bluntness and shyness,
and the calm intelligence of those brown eyes. He did not want
to bring trouble upon her.

But when it came down to the choice, he simply could not
bear the thought of not coming to know her better—of never
seeing her again.

Like a selfish fool, he'd hoped it would be all right.

It hadn't been, of course, he thought, laying down the significator of the Priestess and shuffling again. The Queen of
Swords, the King of Wands, the Dancer at the Heart of the
World . . . and the Fool. Outside, the novice Gilda's voice
tripped gleefully over the words ". . . *tie my ribbons 'round
your tail, my stockings 'round your horn . . .* ," and Antryg
muttered at the cards, "Tell me something I don't know, already," and gathered them up again.

And it might very well be, he thought, that he had lost her
now for good, whether he found her safe or not. If she was in
the Vaults . . .

He shivered at the thought of what he had seen there. In that
darkness there was no place that was safe, no place that was
even stable anymore, and it was getting worse as the pressures
on the fabric that separated the Void from its myriad of worlds

increased. Did her kidnapper know this? Did he—or she—care? And why hadn't they contacted him, why hadn't they made a demand of some kind? Why try to assassinate him in his bed instead?

Or had that been somebody else?

The significator Queen of Swords drew the four of cups reversed, the five of swords, the two of wands, and the Chain. The geas, he thought; the geas that lay upon his mind like a chain, the foul whispering of those waiting dreams. Or did the cold Queen of Swords, the dark-haired lady who bore all her ancient strifes frozen in her hollow heart, labor under some geas of her own forging?

"Tea leaves would probably be more helpful," he muttered, collecting the cards again and making a move toward the room's small hearth, where a pot burbled softly with water on the boil. At least tea would be comforting and would warm his aching hands, now that the evening air was growing sharp.

Damn the Witchfinders . . .

And they, too, were on their way.

*If there are social climbers in the High Council who seek to bring wizardry into fashion again in the circles to which they aspire . . .*

Would Daurannon have betrayed another wizard to win himself into the Regent's approval? A wizard who had murdered Salteris, perhaps, but a wizard all the same?

It was a week and a half to Angelshand by horseback. Daur would have to have known that far in advance that the Council was bringing him here. According to the Lady Rosamund, it hadn't been decided to bring him until a day or so, at most, before Ruth and Joanna and the children had started having visions of the Tujunga Wash. But whose suggestion had it been to fetch him in the first place?

On the other hand, he thought, dealing out, around the King of Wands, the five of wands ("All right, you've made your point!"), the reversed four of cups, the eight of pentacles

("Well, I knew *that*!"), and the doughty seven of wands, since the Citadel lay upon a major node in the ley-lines, the lines themselves could have faulted as far away as Angelshand. The Inquisitors might easily have set out to ask the mages a few questions about the sudden appearance of abominations in the streets of the capital. For a moment he stared down at the last card dealt; "Now what," he murmured, as he gathered them back like great flakes of colored fire, "is our Daur defending against all comers? His right to inherit the Master-Spells when Auntie dies? Or something else? Something in the Vaults, perhaps?"

He set the cards aside. Half rising, he began to search in the chaos of the tabletop for the little japanned canister of tea that Pothatch had sent back with him. Just in twenty-four hours, the table had become littered with books Seldes Katne had let him abstract from the Library, with papers and notes regarding the Void—she was still hunting, she said, for Munden Myndrex's notes on tortoise-rubbings—with maps of the Vaults he'd drawn to refamiliarize himself with its lower levels and with sketches of Bentick and Rosamund and the way the vines in the little garden below twined up around the windows of the Cat Lair . . . pens, inkpots, pestles; pinwheels in various states of construction and experiments with straws and bottles; prisms and chalk and magnets. At one end of the table, he'd pushed aside the litter to draw in red crayon a compass rose, over which he'd already dangled a pendulum stone; the stone had refused to move, meaning a) that Joanna was dead, b) that Joanna was neither north, nor south, nor east, nor west, but, in fact, virtually beneath him . . . i.e., in the Vaults, or, c) that as a method of divination, pendulum dowsing was a washout. Neither the ritual strewing of the hazelnuts he'd begged from Q'iin nor the construction of a feather-circle as he'd been taught by an old granny from the marshes of Kymil had yielded further information regarding Joanna's whereabouts. Divination with peach pits was supposed to work, but regrettably, peaches would not be in season until July.

Tea canister in hand, he turned back, deftly sorted his own significator, the Mage, from the pack and, laying it down, cut and flipped a card at random from the center of the deck.

For a moment he stood, regarding the skeleton on horseback bearing the black banner of the rose, where it lay in the molten amber pool of candlelight. Of course, he told himself, the Death card meant many things . . . change, transmutation, travel, passage to another world even.

"I really ought to stop doing this to myself." He folded the pack together for the last time and went to make himself a cup of tea.

By the time he was finished, it was close to midnight. Brighthand's music had ceased, but across the way in the Cat Lair, the novices and Juniors and a few of the younger sesenna were still talking, casting spells on one another for the sheer joy of it and shouting with laughter and triumph. The cats for which the place was named stalked moths and fireflies in the rambling carpets of wild grape, spruce needles, and fern, Pulling his sloppy rainbow shawl around his shoulders, Antryg descended through the great downstairs chamber where Kyra was supposed to be studying her lists but wasn't, slipped through a narrow door to the cellar steps and, from the cellar, passed through a rough-hewn entrance, up a tunnel in which he had to walk half bent over, and thence into the subcellar of the Cat Lair.

By attics, side stairs, more cellars, and a generally disused breezeway between the Pavilion and a tiny pear orchard clinging halfway up the tor, gritting his teeth now and then as he passed over an energy line and felt once again the stifling prickle of the Void, he made his way up to the scriptorium in the Library tower.

From the breezeway he'd caught a glimpse of light reflected through the glass panes of the Conservatory, like the far-off refraction of candleflame through an enormous, dirty diamond. The light would be in Seldes Katne's rooms, adjoining that ornate gothic folly. There was a rickety wooden stairway that stitched its way from the attic of the Pavilion, back and forth across the granite rock face beneath the Library walls, with a door at the top leading into the scriptorium. As Antryg ducked beneath the low lintel he saw wizard's marks written in a trailing scribble of faintly glowing magic on the stone doorjambs—Seldes Katne's personal mark. Across the room in the darkness he could see she'd so marked the door down from the Library above and portions of the floor as well.

Clearly, he thought, Kitty Katne was taking no chances on Daurannon or Lady Rosamund coming down here at this hour of the night and wondering why the librarian had been seized with the desire to make a Talisman of Air.

Dim lamplight gleamed suddenly on gold leaf and leather, picking out a leopard's eye, a skeleton's hand, carved on a pillar head. The marks had given their warning. The stout little form framed in the light of the opened doorway turned back for a moment to close it behind her; Antryg remained where he was, a loose-limbed shadow with his hands in his pockets, watching her as she hastened across the room.

"Here it is." She held out to him a rough ring of silver on a thong. Even in the darkness the two opals wired to it seemed to flash with inner fire.

"Thank you. Thank you very much." He took the thong and bound it around his head, centering the talisman on his forehead. "I shall be on your doorstep tomorrow with a bouquet of daisies and the finest and most beautiful pinwheels in all the land."

She swallowed a grin she knew was undignified and said gruffly, "Go along with you—don't be silly."

He regarded her with startled surprise, the talisman on his forehead picking up a thread of starlight from the window, flashing like a weird third spectacle lens. "Why not?"

The talisman was not a particularly strong one and would allow him at most fifteen or twenty minutes' extra air, but there was nothing he could do about that. Any of the stronger mages in the Citadel were ipso facto suspect, and any of the Juniors would not have been able to weave elements in this fashion at all.

"Are you going into the Vaults tonight?" Her voice sank to a whisper, and she glanced nervously over her shoulder, though not even a member of the Council could call the image of another mage in a scrying-crystal without the subject's consent. But this portion of the Library lay on the Vorplek Line, the main energy-track, and through it Antryg's own sense of the Void's instability had grown; here in the Library's foundations, it was particularly strong. "Will you . . . will you need help?"

"My dear Kitty, I should be delighted to have you," Antryg said earnestly. "But in point of fact I haven't the faintest idea how and where I'll be able to find my way into the Vaults, and in any case, when I do, I shall probably finish by having to run away from something very fast, and I'd hate to have to be gallant and slow down to let you keep up."

"Run away from what? And how . . ."

Antryg swung around abruptly and swept the talisman from his forehead; a moment later the door to the gallery opened, framing against the starlight outside a tall, thin, solemn-faced garden-rake of a boy in a Junior's gray robe—the boy whose harping could make butterflies dance.

"Me lord Antryg?" His voice was deeper than most boys' his age, settled already into a black-oak baritone with the soft, slurry drawl of the Angelshand slums. He was panting as if he'd taken the long stairs up from the Pavilion at a run. "Kyra said she'd seen you come this way. It's me master . . . Otaro. He's seen that thing in the Vaults, that Movin' Gate. The Lady and them, they say you ought to come."

The great problem with the creation of deathless elemental daemons to do one's bidding lies in finding a place to put them afterwards.

—PIPIN THE LITTLE
Archmage of the Council of Wizards

# CHAPTER VIII

*I'M GOING TO KILL ANTRYG WINDROSE. I SWEAR IT.*

Joanna sank against the wall, hugging herself as if with cold, though the tepid mildness of the dark around her had not altered. Nor was it hunger that made her shiver uncontrollably as she rested her head against the featureless smoothness behind her. Tears rose, a strangling heat in her chest and throat, and she fought them back. She was tired enough without hysterics adding to her exhaustion, and she had the hideous suspicion that once she gave way to them, she wouldn't be able to stop.

Ever.

Or was it, she wondered, that she knew that if she wept, when she did finally stop she would be precisely where she was now—sitting on a smooth floor in the darkness, with no idea where she was, or why.

Wearily, it crossed her mind that in a way, she had brought this on herself. If she hadn't been Antryg's lover—if she hadn't brought him into her life, knowing him to be a fugitive from vengeful mages in another world, knowing they'd eventually come after him—she wouldn't be here now.

*Wherever "here" is.*

*However long "now" is going to be.*

She had begun to be terribly afraid, not of what had brought her here or of what would eventually happen to her, but of how long they would keep her before anything did.

*If* anything did.

Ever.

Three times she had rewound the thread on its spool and returned to her point of origin, half hoping to find some evidence that someone had come looking for her . . . food, water, torture-droids, a human footprint in the sand, a Post-it note from her mother, a troop of armed orcs tracking her down the thread—*anything*.

The third time she had had to fight, as she was fighting now, to keep from sitting on the floor and crying with disappointment, loneliness, and terror.

What if they never came?

Antryg would rescue her, she told herself.

But in her heart she knew that the chief difference between the movies and real life was that the hero didn't always rescue the heroine.

Antryg, for all his blithe air of lunatic competence, could be dead.

Or locked up back in the Silent Tower.

*Stop it*, she told herself firmly. *You've quite obviously been kidnapped for a reason and the only reason I can think of is to gain some kind of leverage over Antryg. Being kidnapped at random by another wizard from some other place on the other side of the Void is stretching the bounds of probability.*

But there were bounds of probability regarding what had happened to her already that were beginning to make her profoundly uneasy.

Wearily, she got to her feet and, with the utter patience she'd used in conversation with recalcitrant DOS programs, hefted her purse more firmly onto her shoulder and began to rewind the thread on the spool once again, following it back to its source. Though her hands were shaky, she still didn't feel particularly hungry or thirsty—and her common sense told her that she must have been here for hours already. At times she'd been tempted to eat part of the granola bar she carried in her purse, more from boredom than anything else. But every time she returned to find nothing at the point of origin, she put it off.

*Besides, it would only make me thirsty, and I haven't come across water, either.*

When she'd hit the glow-in-the-dark button on her digital watch—also in her purse—and had gotten no result, the old panic that she might be blind had returned. But the matches still wouldn't strike—the problem seemed to be with energy, rather than her own vision.

*What the* hell *is going on?*

*Antryg,* she thought, pushing aside the wave of baffled despair. *If I wasn't involved with Antryg . . .*

*If I'd stayed what I'd always been, I might not have been as happy, but at least I'd be safe.*

*Is knowing him, loving him, having him in my life worth . . . ?* Her mind shied quickly from the first sentence formed, the sentence she didn't want to think about: *worth dying this way*? She changed it hastily to, *worth going through this? Is having Antryg in my life worth going through this?*

She wasn't doing to die. She told herself that several times as she walked. It would never have occurred to her to live with a crack dealer, or an outlaw biker, or a terrorist, or anybody else whose very life-style was a walking invitation to chaos— anybody whose enemies might seize upon her. But Antryg wasn't like that. The sound of his voice returned to her, that deep, flexible baritone that would be a part of her consciousness if she lived to be ninety, and the touch of his fingers along her arm. The way it felt to know he cared about what she did, and the knowledge that he'd back her up in whatever she chose to do. Gentle, considerate, careful of her feelings for all that he woke up at the crack of dawn to watch cartoons and sang in bed.

Something moving and cold like a stiff, membranous wing sliced at her face; a shriek like a steam whistle went off in her ear and claws snagged in her hair. With a scream of shock and terror Joanna slapped at the thing with both hands, springing back, crashing into the wall.

In the blackness her hands came in brief contact with something chitinous and moving—the only things that sprang to her mind were the hideous palmetto bugs that rattled 'round the porch light of her aunt's home in Miami on summer nights. Only this was vastly more huge, the size of a small child, bumping and crawling on her, grabbing at her hair and laughing.

Screaming, she fled, and it pursued her, vacant idiot laughter fragmenting from the walls. Sobbing, screaming, gasping, she ran on and on, bruising herself against walls and corners, stumbling down tunnel after tunnel, hallway after hallway, until somehow it was gone and she collapsed on the floor, hugging herself in the sudden silence and weeping as if her heart would break.

Wizardry lies in naming the true names of things—in knowing what they are, and what they were. Sometimes when one learns the true name of the thing one seeks to Summon, one loses all desire to meet it face-to-face.

—GANTRE SILVAS
*Annals of the Mages*

# CHAPTER IX

"I DO NOT . . . I DO NOT EVEN KNOW HOW I CAME TO BE down there." Otaro of the City of Cranes rubbed his round, brown face with one hand, small but broad and strong-looking; Antryg knew the fingers could flick and stop the gold and silver harp wires so that the sound of them danced like spring rain, stirring the heart to visions or the soul to the peace of sleep. In reminiscence of his distant homeland, the Singer wore his hair in long, oiled curls threaded with ribbons down his shoulders and back, and there were plugs of rose-colored jade in the lobes of his ears.

He sat on a bench in a corner of the Citadel's great kitchen. Around him most of the High Council had gathered: Nandiharrow looking flurried, Daurannon wearing a face of grave solemnity, and Lady Rosamund with a hint of grimness about the flowerlike nostrils. Bentick's expression was one of haggard, slightly nervous brittleness; his eyes moving warily, as Phormion's had moved in Council, his white fingers toying endlessly with his watch. While Otaro was speaking, Issay Bel-Caire came hurrying in through the pantry door—a secret

126

stair connected the pantry with the storeroom behind the baths, which was in turn connected, via a covered gallery and a stair up the outside wall of the Island of Butterflies, with the tangle of interlocking cellars that formed the subfoundations of the Mole Hill, the Pepper-Grinder, and the other dwellings of the Juniors' side of the hill.

"Nandiharrow spoke of having killed an abomination in the Vaults last night," Otaro said slowly, passing his hand across his face again. "I wanted to dissect it, to see what properties lay in its sinew and bones. He said it was on the second level. I entered through the stores-cellars here, under the kitchen."

"Those should have been locked up!" Bentick said indignantly.

"As they were," the Singer murmured. "Pothatch . . . I asked for the key from Pothatch."

The cook came over from the smallest of the three great stoves, a patented iron cooker sent by one of the Court's more practical-minded duchesses. A fat little man with a redhead's fair, freckled face, he handed the Oriental wizard a cup of tea; Otaro's hands shook so that he could scarcely hold it.

"I didn't see there was any harm in it, sir." The cook glanced worriedly across at Bentick, who had threatened him with transformation into one of the lowlier orders of amphibians at least once a month for the past twenty years. During his own residence at the Citadel, Antryg had frequently presented the hapless cook with jars of flies and bugs collected from the gardens, *Just in case.* "People have been going in and out to search."

After a moment Bentick shook his head and sighed. "No . . . quite all right . . ."

"I still don't understand what happened." Otaro set his cup down—the tea was beginning to spill—and ran stumpy fingers through his beribboned curls. From the shadows by the stove, Brighthand watched with concern in his coffee-colored eyes. "I was on the second level, and then suddenly I was . . . I was in an unfamiliar area of the Vaults. It took me some minutes to realize—I had somehow come to be on the sixth level, near the Twisted Ways. I know I did not lose consciousness."

Antryg, prowling along the kitchen's west wall and running his hands over the soot-dyed plaster, swung around in genuine delight. "Folded reality!" he cried.

Bentick glared at him. Seldes Katne, who had followed him down from the Library and now occupied a scullion's stool near the gaping hearth, merely looked baffled.

Otaro shook his head. "I do not know . . . if you say so. All I know is that suddenly I . . . I saw a darkness rushing toward me. A corridor, it seemed, or a gate, but a gate that seemed to move toward me, filled with crying voices, with sounds like wind, or the sea. I saw . . . I don't know what I saw. The voices . . ." He shut his eyes, his dark brow folding with pain. "I turned, I . . . I tried to flee. I ran down one corridor after another and it pursued me. Every time I looked back it was there, rushing at my heels, the voice shouting to me."

"I found him down the third level." Brighthand stepped forward and put a hand on his master's shoulder. "I'd got worried when he didn't come back. He was sittin' up against the wall, and his color was dead bad."

"Was there a smell?" Antryg inquired, tilting his head to one side like a bird.

"Roses," Otaro said slowly. "Sweet and heavy . . ."

Lady Rosamund started to speak, then looked impatiently at the faces around her. "Where is Phormion? She should be here . . ."

"The voices you heard," Nandiharrow moved over onto the seat beside the Singer, "were they human? Did you understand what they were saying?"

Under cover of Otaro's answer, Antryg stepped back to where Pothatch stood and asked in an undervoice, "May I borrow the key to the stores-cellars for a moment?"

His attention absorbed in the scene around the table, the fat man produced it automatically. Antryg slipped into the pantry, unlocked the stores-cellar door—the long, narrow hallway of a room was entered by at least five doors—and moved back to the kitchen with an unobtrusiveness surprising in a man six feet three inches tall and wearing a coat like a psychedelic orchid. "Thank you. May I take this?"

Pothatch nodded, not even looking at the enormous meat cleaver Antryg had removed from the chopping block.

The pantry was five or six steps down from the kitchen, part of the tangled complex of small brick-and-half-timber buildings set farther down the hill; from it a very long, very narrow flight of steps cut straight northeastward into the rock of the tor. Antryg had always suspected the big, low-ceilinged stores-cellar of being, in fact, the uppermost collecting chamber of the maze beneath. He threaded his way though the bins of potatoes and onions, and past huge sealed jars of millet, barley, and wheat, the musty odor of tubers and hanging garlic stirring about him and not quite curtaining the wet-stone breath from the archway that led down to the Vaults.

Here, as he had up in the cellar of the Library, he could feel the lowering weight, the terrifying nearness, of the chaos of the Void.

Another short stair, a wine cellar, a passage that turned and wound, descending . . .

And then he was in the Vaults.

The Shrieker, Antryg recalled, had been struck down just past the three-way fork near the downshaft with the brick threshold; all the old landmarks leapt clear to his mind. He pulled the Talisman of Air from his pocket and tied it again around his head, then hefted the cleaver and made for the place, listening, scenting, reaching out with all the hyperacute senses of a wizard that he knew would be his only defense. He did not pause, now, to check air pressure or magnetism; he knew he had little time here, and had to find some trace of Joanna, some clue to where in the Vaults she was hidden.

And there was something else he had to find as well.

Slightly more than twenty-four hours had passed since his first visit to the Vaults, but already he could feel the change. The energy seemed more dense; the strange, shuddery crawl of alien power in the stones, growing even in the rock aboveground, was nearly unbearable down here. He quickened his pace, seeking the place where the Shrieker had leaped forth at them.

And as Otaro had described, he felt a sudden shock of disorientation, the sudden awareness that he didn't know where he was . . .

Only he did.

He was on the sixth level, at the round mouth of tunnel that led into the tangled skein of isolated spirals known as the Twisted Ways.

Antryg flung out his arms and laughed aloud with sheer delight.

The maze behind him picked up the echoes, reverberating them into a dim, shuddering roar. Far off, chancy with distance and random reflection of sound, they were answered by a thin, alien, animal scream.

Antryg fell silent, his heart beating hard, remembering that he was not alone.

The corridor around him was knee-deep in ground fog that curled poisonously about his boots, the air above it weighted with sulfur. There were pits at this level, places where the floor dropped suddenly away or descended five or six steps for twenty or thirty feet only to reascend without apparent reason; heaving, shifting vapors lay like ghostly lakes in such places, shining queerly in the dark. Antryg avoided them, sidetracking around through dark capillaries in the rock where niter dripped from the walls. In some places he found the walls and ceilings thick with a moss that he was careful not to touch; in others, white and yellow things crawled sluggishly away from the sound of his boots or watched him, gleaming stickily, as he passed. Once he backtrailed up and down several levels to avoid a hallway—low-ceilinged, he remembered, and painted queerly over walls and ceiling with skull-headed serpents twining among roses and thorns—that was now entirely filled with greenish mist; in another place he did the same, though the room that lay before him, with its odd pattern of glass blocks set into the floor, was apparently empty.

He had no protection, save the minimal defenses of the talisman and the cleaver. He reminded himself of that and spent a good deal of his time glancing over his shoulder at the dark.

In a corridor that followed the Vorplek Line, he found Otaro's leather satchel, containing dissecting knives, tortoiseshell jars, oiled paper, and a magnifying lens strung on a ribbon, which he put around his own neck with the rest of his beads. As he stood up again, the satchel over his shoulder, movement caught his eye behind him.

It was high up, near the pointed arch of a narrow, sealed door. He flattened against the wall as a small ball of glowing blue light drifted through the crumbling bricks and into the corridor. It moved slowly, as if propelled by a wind humans could not feel, losing and gaining altitude a little like an errant balloon. Antryg held his breath, sweat starting on his face, as the light paused opposite him, hanging in the air at the level of his chest, and three or four other lights, some the size of his fist and others no bigger than walnuts, floated like a school of minnows down the corridor from behind him. Cold with sweat and fighting panic, he remained motionless, half guessing what they had to be, for some minutes after they had moved on.

"Joanna," he whispered, trying not to think of her imprisoned somewhere down here with those . . . and with the other things, material or immaterial or somewhere in between, that he knew would be moving through this darkness.

*Dear God, Joanna . . .*

He followed his ancient memories deeper into the maze: knots of tunnels that connected to nothing but themselves; tiny rooms with mirrored ceilings and walls; glass altars in niches; stairways descending a hundred and fifty feet to blank walls; pits and deadfalls and odd, fountain-fed basins. He passed through halls with strange things painted, half-obscured, upon their ceilings; cross-roads marked with pillars of glass or marble or iron; rooms whose floors were mosaics of tortoiseshell and bone. There were small doorways, long ago bricked shut and written over with spells of guard and oblivion; Antryg shivered, remembering what Suraklin had told him: in ancient times the Council had punished rebellious mages by sealing them into such places with restless spirits, things that would eat human flesh to the bones . . . but not quickly.

*They pride themselves on their famous rectitude,* Suraklin had said, his light voice a little shrill as he measured out his chemicals with his feminine delicacy of touch, the sunlight through the west-facing windows of his workroom turning his dust-colored hair to fire. *They are like painters, dabbing new colors over a canvas whose images are no longer the fashion. It was not mages bent on holding aloof from human concern who built their precious Citadel, and if ever you chance to visit it, my darling, bid them show you the lists of Archmages of old. You'll find gaps in the tale, of years they pretend to know nothing about.*

Ground fog swirled again around his feet. Passing a downshaft, he felt warm air rising against his face, smelled a curious odor like metallic flowers. Things scuttered distantly in dark, narrow ways, and under Antryg's fingers the granite of the wall whispered with the Brehon Ley's silvered strength; deep beneath it, he sensed the prickly, random energy of the stone itself. Knowing Suraklin, he found, altered one's perceptions of everything.

No sign of the Moving Gate. No sign of Joanna.

No sign of the other thing he sought, the thing he was almost certain had to be here—the thing he had to find if he was to make any progress in this puzzle at all.

In a long chamber whose corbeled ceiling barely cleared the topmost curls of his hair, something attacked him, something small and red that gave off a bitter, sugary stink when he chopped it away from his boot leather and crushed it under his heel. The walls here, he saw, were patched with fungi like human ears and fingers in colors that made him wonder what was considered camouflage in other dimensions; at the bottom of the pit in the room's center, white and yellow grubs seethed over something dead.

Clearly, Gates were opening and closing here all the time, now in one place, now in another. *Dammit,* he thought, *I could be down here for weeks and not run across the Moving one.* Something had to be keeping it open, something drawing the enormous power needed.

Distantly, he heard another shrill cry and wished he'd been able to talk Hathen out of a sword earlier this evening. In the four months Antryg had lived in Los Angeles, he had been able to keep up sword practice at a dojo in Burbank operated by a black kendo sandan and an old Japanese gentleman who taught iaido to those who understood and preferred that somewhat more esoteric art. Sensei Jones had looked a trifle askance at him when he'd explained that he'd been trained in a slightly different style owing to the circumstance of being a wizard in exile from another dimension—many people did—but several weeks ago Antryg had overheard Sensei Jones remark to Sensei Shigeta, "You know, I'm starting to *believe* the sucker?"

He paused by another sealed door, felt the ancient masonry, and shivered at what he sensed inside.

*Phormion didn't have this trouble finding the Moving Gate, dammit,* he thought, a little resentfully, as he moved on. *Nor did Kitty. Otaro practically walked into the thing. Perhaps I ought to pretend I'm here looking for mushrooms.*

*Phormion . . .* He recalled how her eyes had shifted, how deep the lines of strain had been on her gray and wasted face. He hadn't seen her all day, and, according to Kyra, the Starmistress hadn't taught any of her classes. Bentick said she was ill, but then, the fussy little Steward had always been Phormion's second in the Starmistress' long duel with life.

And neither Bentick nor Phormion had been present when the Circles of Power had been drawn to bring him through the Void. Which meant they might have been elsewhere, drawing Circles for an expedition of their own.

Daurannon . . .

He paused in the darkness, remembering the fresh-faced, handsome youth sitting next to him on the marble terrace of Salteris' house, listening to the old man's words with grave interest in his hazel eyes.

Always the one to get the last piece of cake on the plate, he thought, and manage at the same time not to seem greedy as he ate it.

It crossed his mind to wonder how Daurannon was dealing with the probability of having Lady Rosamund hold the Master-Spells over his mind. The two of them had never gotten on: *What can you expect of a boy who puts milk in his tea?* had been her dismissal of him at the beginning.

For that matter, how was Rosamund . . . ?

A flicker and a gleam in the darkness caught his eye, something like a thread of moving silk on the short flight of a half-dozen steps that lowered the floor of the level for no apparent reason. He turned back, springing up the shallow, worn treads.

And stood staring down at the thing he had seen, his heart shrinking cold within him.

It was what he had feared from the start.

It was a thread of running water.

"Oh, dear," he murmured and leaned down to dip his bare fingertips in it and bring them first to his nostrils, then to his lips.

Slightly salt, and filled with strange odors, strange flavors— alien and odd. He felt as cold within as if it had been the river Aa that souls crossed at dying.

On the seventh level he found water flowing again, a stronger trickle this time, smelling and tasting the same. It was there, too, that something attacked him, something that, even with a wizard's sight which let him walk in darkness, he could not see: a cold fluttering of air moments before he saw the sleeve of his coat open in three places as if slashed by a razor. A smell like bitter cinnamon surrounded him; he wondered if the thin squittering noise he heard was really there or only his imagination.

A cut seared open on his brow as he fled, a slash so quick he barely felt it; after he'd outrun the thing, whatever it was, he found the long skirts on the right side of his coat reduced by neat, parallel gashes to ribbons.

On the eighth level he finally smelled it. The shivery vibration of the opened Void, everywhere around him in these dark depths, grew stronger, and as he approached it, a strange and bitter pungency, coppery and rotted, scorched his nose and lungs. He touched the Talisman of Air on his forehead, and the silver warmed to his skin. The smell subsided; he quickened his pace, knowing that if he didn't find what he sought in ten minutes, he might not make his way out of the area of the poison before the breathable air held around his head failed. *Dear God, don't let Joanna's cell be anywhere near here.*

A short flight of steps that curved sharply in the middle, a high, narrow hall whose ceiling was painted in constellations neither he nor any other mage had ever seen.

Five minutes.

A branch in the tunnel. One fork led to a columned hall with a long basin in it, he recalled, the other down a blind lead. But the sense of the Void was strongest down that blind alley. Eight minutes. He was wrong, the lead was blind, and he turned back, cursing, his breath coming more shallowly now, and dizziness teasing at the edges of his mind.

At the next fork in the passage he halted, and with the back of the cleaver blade, he knocked on the rock of the wall.

Three strokes, and a pause. One stroke, pause; four, pause; one more, and another pause. Only silence from the darkness ahead, with its drifting suggestions of yellowish mist; the silence that had once filled a haunted church where first Joanna had used this signal, to reach the thing that he knew must come. Silence, and the growing sense that he had overstayed the time allotted by the talisman. Sweat stung in the forehead-cut left by the invisible attackers, mixing with the blood.

Five knocks, pause; nine, pause; two, pause . . .

And then, far off, echoing in the tunnels, an answering knock.

Six times.

Antryg rapped back sharply, five.

Three. The knocking drew closer, and with it, infinitely soft in the deadly hush, a kind of moist, leathery creak. It was now very difficult to breathe, the smell of the poison thick and all-pervasive. The yellow mist thickened; the Talisman of Air, which had been warm against the skin of his face, began to grow cold.

Five, he rapped out quickly and saw, far down the passage-way, a sickly corpseglow pallor bobbing erratically in the nightshade mists.

Eight . . .

A thing loomed suddenly from the darkness, a huge shape stooping under the seven-foot arch of the ceiling. Even the pallid light shed by the nodule that dangled, like a third eye, from the front of its platycephalic skull threw no more than a firefly sheen on the stretched, squamous green of its hide. Spider, dragon, and eldritch nightmare; chisel teeth glistened in the lipless muzzle; four long arms, four massive hands thick with claws between which writhed clusters of wriggling white tentacles. Those hands, Antryg knew well, could easily crush a man's skull. It raised one as it stepped forward.

"Do you have any idea," Antryg gasped, leaning against the wall for support, "what the hell is going on?"

"Not the slightest," the monster replied. "I've got an ox-ygen bottle and a gas mask."

"Ah." Antryg accepted the proffered breathing apparatus with hands that were shaking. "Thank you." He gestured back along the passageway with all the aplomb of a weekend lothario at Enyart's. "My atmosphere or yours?"

Limitations upon spells of forgetfulness:
—The boundaries of the field of the spell, both of area and of depth and height.
—The duration of the spell, for though such things wear away in time, yet some residue will linger unless the Caster returns to undo what was done.
—Whether the spell will be touched by daylight, wind, rain, the phases of the moon, and the rising and setting of the stars Vega, Aldebaran, and Spica, which govern matters of the memory and mind.
—The extent of what will be forgotten, for if the Caster be strong enough, passersby will forget their names and families, how to read or speak; some even will forget to eat, and so starve.
—The personages who will forget, whether it be one person, or all persons, or all living things.
—The duration of the forgetting, and whether anything that be forgot shall be learned again.
—Whether the Caster himself will remember what he has done.
All these things must be woven into the boundaries of the spell, before it be Cast.

—Isar Chelladin
*Upon the Casting of Spells*

# Chapter X

"So you had nothing to do with this . . . this glitch?"

"Glitch . . . I like that." LTRX2-449-9102-CF60913—who had first been introduced to Antryg some months earlier as the Dead God by villagers under the impression that the then-trapped transdimensional physicist was indeed that entropic deity—folded himself into a compact bundle of muscle and bone, arms wrapped about unimaginably jointed legs and the long, bony whip of tail coiled around one of the square basalt columns that ran the length of the narrow Basin Chamber, and emitted a deep, buzzing chuckle.

"And did you know to seek me here with this magic that you spoke of when last we met, wizardling?" Since the Dead God's organs of communication were not connected to his respiratory system, they had decided to continue the conversation in a section of the Vaults uncontaminated by the atmosphere of his world.

"Not magic, precisely," Antryg said, stashing the oxygen bottle behind a loose stone on the column head and settling down at the monster's side. "It was a reasonable supposition that you'd be somewhere here in the Vaults, considering that your specialty *is* the physics of the Void. At least, that's what got you into trouble in this universe the last time."

"So indeed it was." The tip of the Dead God's tail twitched, roving over the smooth stone of the floor like a hand seeking a grip for some unimaginable purpose. "My instruments were picking up heavy xchi-particle flux in Sector Eight-eighty; I went there half suspecting there would be a Gate opening. Reports were coming in of . . . strange things. Not only strange creatures, but strange effects, odd and completely localized spots of heat or cold or magnetism in places, or places where things would happen—voices would be heard, people would be spontaneously transported sometimes thousands of meters, or vanish entirely—reports of what sounded like Gates opening and shutting at random, sometimes hundreds of kilometers away from Eight-eighty." In Antryg's mind—since they were speaking mind-to-mind through the Spell of Tongues—Antryg heard the measurements, knowing them to be only rough approximations of the yards and miles in which he thought . . . which were themselves only rough translations of yards and miles as Joanna understood them. Sometimes, he reflected, the Spell of Tongues was simply not very accurate.

"The first thing I did when I entered this place—wherever this place *is* —was to bring through the components of the experimental xchi-flux generator I've been working on."

"That thing?" Antryg said, startled. "It filled three good-sized rooms when I saw it last."

"It isn't exactly small now," the Dead God growled. "I've never opened a full-size Gate with it—merely wormholes—but most of what you saw was guidance. The generator here is slaved to the main relay in my own universe, so with luck I should not be trapped here again. I've brought batteries—the thing needs an enormous amount of power—and spare air bottles. They are hidden in three different chambers, depending on whatever was nearest when the Gate opened. I have no idea where they are.''

''How do you know they're even in the same universe, if the Gate to your laboratory has opened and closed two or three times?''

The Dead God tilted his sleek, shiny head, the iridescent ocher lenses of his eyes glinting in the glow of his forehead-light with the expressionless stare of an insect. ''The appearance is the same, for one thing, as are the composition and pattern of the walls. The oxygen mix is virtually identical.'' He touched one of the instruments that hung on a bandolier over the ribbed, bony chest. ''That's how I knew I was in your world in the first place, though I had no idea where I was or what this place is. And the extent of the xchi-particle flux was the same at each reappearance. I have been searching for a way out of this maze.''

''There is one, but it's a bit complicated,'' Antryg said, leaning forward to study the long, thick rectangle of the sensory equipment with its dimly blinking lights. ''We're under the Citadel of Wizards. If you can give me a description of the rooms in which you left your batteries and air bottles and things, I could probably find them for you.''

''It would be a help,'' the Dead God rumbled. ''I could locate them with the multiscanner, but it would take a long while, particularly if they were far away. I carry spare air, but with a weapon, too . . .'' He reached back with one long arm, past the four curving tentacles of his breathing tubes, to where a device like a small bazooka hung on his back to the left side of his doubled dorsal ridge. ''It is all very heavy, and I may need to move swiftly. But you, wizardling . . .'' The light-bob on his forehead gave a little twitch, causing their shadows to reel grotesquely in the pillared gloom. ''How is it that I find you here? You said you were going into exile, to the world of your friend.''

''I did,'' Antryg replied, rather grimly. ''And lived as happily ever after as circumstances permitted . . . It's rather a long story. Have you encountered any other Gates in your explorations?''

"Four," replied the Dead God. "Also five fields of alien energies. None of them is stable—they appear and vanish at random. Everywhere I discover organisms with physiologies incompatible to what I know of your biosystem. Moreover, my instruments indicate the xchi-particle activity characteristic of Gates.'' Antryg was aware that the Dead God lacked the capacity to feel the sense of terror invoked in humans by the opening of the Void. "And they indicate also that this is increasing and the rate of increase accelerating.''

"I know that," Antryg said. "Something has to be done to stabilize it, and soon, to keep the entire Citadel from being swallowed in a maelstrom of all the magic done here in its past. Your instruments wouldn't happen to have registered a Gate which moves about? Not appears and disappears, but physically moves . . . ?''

The Dead God signed a negative with one huge hand; the snakelike tail shifted around the pillar's square base. "My instruments take readings at set intervals of time—they cannot track a single Gate from place to place or tell whether a Gate has opened first in one place, then another, or has moved from place to place without closing.''

"Damn . . ." Antryg folded his arms around his drawn-up knees, and rubbed absently at the drying blood on the side of his face. His right arm hurt, and looking down, he could see blood on his sleeve from the slashes dealt him by the invisible haunters. Far off in the darkness something howled, the narrow tunnels drawing out the sound into a shivery wail of terror and hate and hunger; moving air brought to him a whisper of ammonia and of water trickling in the dark.

"Listen," he said, recalling innumerable television shows, "can that sensor of yours find a human being? Or at least tell us if there *is* one, trapped somewhere down here in the Vaults?''

The Dead God tilted his head again, and the gleam of his bobbing headlight slipped wetly along the leathery breathing tubes that arched from his back to the flat, small gills of his chest. "How far do these Vaults extend around us? Sideways and down?"

"Two hundred, maybe three hundred, feet top to bottom; say a mile in diameter."

"Not large, then . . ."

"Relatively speaking, no. But five minutes isn't very long either, unless you happen to be under water . . . which," he added a little grimly, "is precisely the point of my inquiry."

The Dead God was already cradling the black rectangle of the multiscanner along one forearm while the tentacles of his palm reached around, like phosphorous-tipped worms, to manipulate its tiny toggles. On the round screen several lines of figures swam into view, followed by a succession of blank grids, glowing green lines laid over blackness. On one of them five glowing dots appeared, moving slowly.

"There. Five humans of your type, moving . . ."

"Search party." Antryg dismissed them. "Looking for me, I expect. We need a solitary, stationary reading."

The Dead God buzzed deep in the back of his skull, went on fanning through the grids. "Nothing." The tip of his tail moved a little with his thoughts, as if the nerves were wired to some independent circuit. "Unless the subject is in a room that is somehow shielded against a sub-meson-wave scan, which is unlikely, considering that requires electrophase polarization."

"Or magic," Antryg murmured thoughtfully. "Still, it isn't terribly likely a wizard would think to evolve a spell which prevents detection by microscanning . . . curious." He leaned back against the basalt column, deep in thought. The first sensation which swept him was relief so profound that it was almost exhausting—a sensation that everything was now solved, and he could curl up in a corner and go to sleep . . . definitely, he knew, not the case for a number of reasons.

But if Joanna wasn't in the Vaults, where was she?

In the Citadel itself? The pendulum stone seemed to indicate that, unless for one of the myriad usual reasons, the pendulum stone wasn't working.

And in any case—unless Joanna's cell *was* shielded in some way that excluded microscans as well as magic—his worst fears were momentarily allayed.

"Look," he said after a moment, "these xchi-particles of yours . . ."

Something flickered and moved in the darkness. The Dead God's massive head swung around toward it; Antryg's hand, like a crooked spider in its fingerless mitt, touched the heavy-muscled arm warningly, but the physicist had already halted his reach for his weapon, knowing he could not fire it in the close confines of the Basin Chamber. Light gleamed among the double line of square pillars that stretched down the center of the high-ceilinged, narrow room, but light that shed no shadows, that did not reach past the columns to the raw granite of the walls. For an instant the only sound was the faint, humming tick of the Dead God's equipment and the soft intake of Antryg's breath.

Down the length of the room a glowing ball of red light rolled, a few inches above the floor. Antryg drew back against the pillar; the Dead God seemed to gather in on himself, like a beast coiling for an attack, even his tail drawn close for balance. The light on his forehead died, and it seemed to Antryg as if darkness settled more closely around the dragon shape.

The ball of red light was similar to the ones he had seen before, roughly the size of a grapefruit; it paused above the waters of the small basin in the chamber's center, flickering a little, like the sun's corona in eclipse—paused again in front of the pillar where Antryg and the Dead God sat motionless, its pulsing ruby glow bloody in the Dead God's curved orange eyes, in Antryg's spectacles and earrings. The Dead God's hand moved toward the sensor on his chest, and again Antryg stopped him until the thing had rolled through a low arch in the middle of the opposite wall and away into darkness again.

"What was it?" The God's voice was soft, a barely audible buzz in the upper hollows of that weirdly shaped skull.

"I'm not entirely certain," Antryg murmured. "But my belief is, it's the animate portion of the residual energies vested in a teles-ball—a device wizards frequently use to hold or convert magical energy. Teles are generally felt to become stronger—better—with age; the magic used in conjunction with them becomes clearer and more precise. But there have been a number of cases in which for no apparent reason wizards have simply gotten rid of teles. In two cases that I know about by bricking them up down here, which, if the Vaults *are* an energy-collecting device, was probably not the most intelligent thing to do. There have been rumors that now and then teles become 'inhabited by spirits' nobody can get rid of— then they have to be buried or dropped in the ocean or something—but my theory is that the spirits were generated by the teles themselves. Quite a number of teles have dropped out of sight over the centuries—or had their names changed, which makes them a bit difficult to trace."

"And you believe the xchi-particle flux is . . . activating these energies?"

"Yes," Antryg said softly. "Yes, I do. And other energies down here as well. Energies that were bounded whose bounds are now being sheared and fragmented by the opening and closing of the Gates. These xchi-particles . . . are they a sort of random energy which is stronger in stone—and particularly igneous stone—weaker in metal and nonexistent in wood?"

The Dead God nodded.

"Is there a way of manipulating them . . . of freezing them, as ice freezes, or crystalizing them, so we could at least stabilize the field and keep the situation from getting worse? Not to mention finding the Moving Gate, of course . . ."

"If I knew what they were. Or how they work." The nodule

of his light twitched again, his eyes gleaming queerly iridescent in the glow. "But since they can't be polarized . . ."

"If they could be?" Antryg leaned his elbows on his knees, his long, crooked hands gesturing expansively in their shabby gloves. "If this energy, which seems to be activated in all the rocks of the Citadel, all the stone of the Vault, could be realigned to behave like ordinary electromagnetic energy . . ."

*"Realign the* behavior *of energy?"*

"Temporarily." There was a kind of mad matter-of-factness in Antryg's enormous gray eyes. "Of course, it would have a tendency to randomize itself after a period of time, but by then we'd have found the source of the problem . . . one hopes. Would you be able to create a stabilizing field under those circumstances?"

"Are you insane?"

"Yes. I have been for years, in fact." He propped his spectacles more firmly onto his nose. "Would you?"

The Dead God emitted a thin, buzzing whistle, the equivalent of a sigh. "I think so," he said after a moment. "With an oscillator and a series of field-effects transmission screens, provided the area of the field isn't too large."

"How large is large? Enough to cover the Vaults—could you establish the field within the boundaries of the outermost interface lines between solid and air? That should cover the deepest of the tunnels and will give me a perimeter for the energy-polarization spell as well. I'll need to establish the center point of my own spell directly above your machinery; as far as I know this chamber lies immediately beneath the lecture hall in the North Cloister of the Polygon, but I'll double-check—anyway, they both lie on the Vorplek Line. And the spell must go into effect the moment the energy field is activated, or there'll be a disjoin and the whole thing will have to be done over again. We can synchronize our watches, or at least you can synchronize yours . . . Joanna gave me one but I took it apart and hadn't put it back together again before I was kidnapped."

"I'll lend you one."

"Thank you." Antryg's expression of absentminded pre-occupation gave way to a smile of great sweetness. "That's very kind of you."

The Dead God made the gesture equivalent to rolling his eyes ceilingward, a brief outspreading of his lower left hand in petition to the Worm in whom his people no longer believed.

"I'll be back with the details and a map of the Vaults to help you find your equipment caches."

The Dead God shook his head. "I can run a microscan of the Vaults themselves to establish a digitalized map," he said. "What I shall need you to do is mark it for me. It will take a number of hours."

"It'll be hours before I can return anyway," Antryg agreed and yawned hugely. The jelgeth he had absorbed earlier had begun to wear off; weariness had settled, like a cloak sewn with plates of lead, upon his bones. The night was far advanced. He rose, shaking out his tattered coat skirts and wincing at the soreness in his arm. "I'll knock again. By the way, can you get me a pump-spray dispenser full of some kind of silver-chloride solution? And two more oxygen bottles and some kind of really good goggles?"

"Anything else?" The Dead God rose also, towering over Antryg's six-foot-plus height like a skeletal troll, unblinking golden eyes shining eerily in the bobbing fleck of the light from his forehead.

"Well . . . I don't suppose there's a good Chinese takeout in Section Eight-eighty? Ah, well . . . thank you all the same. I'll return to make arrangements as quickly as I can."

As the bobbing whitish light faded down the corridor, Antryg stood for some time, leaning one shoulder against the basalt pillar, feeling as if all the energy had drained from his frame. Somewhere, far off, he could hear the fragile, tittering squeak of the invisible haunters, and elsewhere a kind of blubbering slither, like tons of wet leather dragging itself over stone. He didn't even want to think about what that might be.

Farther off, the infinitesimal trickle and cluck of water came to him, flowing down, flowing into the lowest levels.

*Sweet gods of the Dark Below the Ground, I hope that microscan was right.*

All around him the Vaults seemed to be whispering, creaking as the building weight of the Void shifted, a vortex of darkness dragging at the fabric of light.

*Joanna,* he prayed, *I hope you're not down here.*

There were portions of the lower Vaults, he remembered, that were haunted. The moving lights returned to his mind, with a horrible breathlessness of almost-certainty. Animate magic without mind. Spells of evil, of pain, of death being released from their bonds . . .

Three mages had seen a Gate that behaved as no Gate he knew. There had to be Circles drawn somewhere, Circles of Power holding that Gate open. If he could only locate those . . .

Voices crying out. A beating sound like wings. A cloying scent like roses. The dark sense of secret desperation, glimpsed as his mind went down under a tidal wave of icy pain.

Why?

And, like a vise, the pressure of sheer weariness, of miles of tunnel walked, of evil dreams and incompleted sleep. He felt worn thin, his spirit holed like very old linen . . . holed like the fabric of the universe where the Void was breaking through. He really should sleep, he reflected. After all, it was only dreams.

He pressed his face to the stone of the pillar as a wave of trembling passed briefly through his flesh.

Only dreams.

"Put down your weapon." A quiet voice spoke from the archway behind him. "If you try to flee I will blast you out of existence where you stand."

He'd heard them coming down the tunnel behind him, quietly as they had moved. And in any case the Dead God had picked them up on his scan.

"Without Aunt Min's permission? My dear Daur!" He raised his head, slipped the cleaver from his belt and set it on the floor, then walked a few paces, his back to it, his hands raised. "Be careful how you handle it. It's Pothatch's best bone-chopper and he'll kill me if anything happens to it."

Swift footfalls padded behind him. A sasennan, he thought. Female.

"At this hour of the morning all I'm truly interested in is a hot cup of tea and some muffins," he went on earnestly. "You would have done better to have simply waited up in the kitchen for me, though it's very good of you to come looking."

The footfalls retreated, and he turned, his hands still raised. With Daurannon in the doorway stood Bentick the Steward, and three young sasenna with drawn swords, one of whom also had the cleaver thrust through her belt. None of them held a torch, by which Antryg guessed that the sasenna were all novice mages in their first year of training—certainly none of them looked over seventeen. Bentick bore a staff, a far deadlier weapon than a sword in the hands of a trained sorcerer; beneath his arm Daurannon carried a shallow lead box, written over with runes of power, of the kind wizards used to carry spell-cord or manacles written with seals that silenced magic.

"I warned them," said the Handsome One softly. "I warned them that it was all your doing, though before God, suspicious as I was, I did not entirely believe it myself."

"What was all my doing?" Antryg demanded indignantly. "Just because I happen to be friends with an abomination doesn't mean I caused the rip in the Void." With a quick move he swept the now-useless Talisman of Air from his head and tossed it deftly into the deep basin of water in the room's center. Daur made a move toward it and stopped—finding out who had made the talisman for him was not, at the moment, worth the trouble it would take to fish it out of fifteen feet of murky water.

Nevertheless, irritation flickered in his eyes. "Hold out your hands."

"That really isn't necessary," Antryg assured him. "I'm on my way back anyway to have breakfast."

The youngest novice, grim-faced and fair-haired, stepped forward, sword leveled a few inches from Antryg's breast.

"Don't be melodramatic, Gyrik, you can't possibly run me through without Aunt Min's say-so and you haven't proven me guilty of any wrongdoing."

"Not proven?" Daurannon retorted, as Gyrik lowered his blade and stepped back, an expression of embarrassed uncertainty on his beardless face. "We find you in conversation with a monstrous creature from the blackest pits of nightmare . . ."

"LTRX2-449-9102 is a perfectly respectable particle physicist and I'm shocked by your parochial attitude about his appearance."

"Whoever and whatever it is, you at least have obtained weapons and magical implements in secret, scarcely demonstrating either good faith or innocence. Whatever it is you're seeking here, it's clear to me you'd rather the Council didn't know of it. Now hold out your hands." The younger mage's hazel eyes glinted with a hardness that completely belied their usual facile charm. "As you know, I am perfectly capable of cutting off your breath to the point where you'd barely have the consciousness to be dragged after us, should you wish to accomplish this the hard way."

Antryg regarded him mildly from behind his massive spectacles. "It's a long way up all those stairs," he pointed out. "And if I'd obtained such a power from some lost secret down here, you wouldn't be able to do that anyway, would you?"

Daurannon opened his mouth to reply, then seemed to change his mind, and shut it again.

"Come on." Brushing aside Gyrik's still half-extended blade, Antryg put a friendly arm around Daurannon's shoulders and started back toward the reality-fold near the Twisted Ways. "It's too damp and cold down here to stand about talking and, as I said, I really would like some breakfast."

However, despite Antryg's protestations that the reality-fold would take them back up to the second level far more quickly, Bentick and Daurannon insisted on returning to the stair by which they had come. Bentick walked ahead, the tip of his staff unlit—Antryg wondered if the omission was because, being mageborn, they all could see in the dark, or from fear at what the light might attract—and the three novice sasenna followed noiselessly behind.

"And *have* you found anything in your searches?" asked Daurannon after a time, the echoes of their footsteps whispering after them up a short flight of steps, down a corridor whose walls dripped with yellow slime and stank of strange, sweetish rots. "Anything of this Moving Gate which Otaro saw, or of the powers which might account for its appearance?"

Antryg hesitated, remembering the drifting balls of red and purple light, and how they had hovered before him; remembering Daurannon's purported absence from the Citadel at the time of Joanna's disappearance.

"Or is that the reason you choose to seek that Gate—and to summon your . . . friend . . . alone?" Dark though it was, he could see his former comrade's eyes narrowed with suspicion; see how he carried the lead box of the spell-written manacles under his right arm, so as to leave his left arm—his fighting arm, in Daur's case—free.

"Would you like me to carry that for you? You're sure? Is it just that you're afraid I'll find some implement that will let me practice magic in spite of the geas, or do you still suspect me of being Suraklin?"

"I haven't dismissed the possibility."

"Not even after seeing into my mind to lay the geas on me?"

"Suraklin had great power," said Daurannon softly. "There was no accounting for what he might have been able to do—even as there is no accounting for you. Nandiharrow and Issay contend that with your powers bound, there is no harm in you walking the Vaults alone, but even were that so, I'm not so certain that whatever information you give us would be true."

Antryg sighed, shoved his hands deep into the pockets of his jeans, and looked around him at the walls of the chamber through which they passed—nearly black with mildew, but painted over with a pattern of snakes disturbingly reminiscent of patterns half-guessed within the labyrinth itself. "And I'm not certain at all that whatever information I might tell the Council wouldn't be used to the detriment of the situation by whoever's behind this—whoever it was who kidnapped Joanna."

"A convenient excuse for keeping things to yourself," sniffed Bentick. "Why on earth would a Council member stoop to taking hostages in the first place?"

"Perhaps because he or she feared that I could persuade someone—let's say Aunt Min for talking purposes, if they considered her to be getting a little foolish in her old age—to lift the geas and let me investigate as I pleased? Perhaps to get me to do their bidding against certain other members of the Council?"

"That's preposterous!" snapped Daur.

"No more preposterous than that I—were I Suraklin, that is—would engineer a rip in the Void smack in the middle of the Citadel of my enemies simply to disrupt their lives."

"Not 'simply,' " Daurannon said grimly. "The Citadel lies on the major ley to Angelshand and connects with most of the major cities of the Realm. I presume the Witchfinders are on their way here as a result of abominations that have appeared in that city."

"Oh, I shouldn't doubt it. They'd hardly be coming to talk about the Imperial government's subsidies to the Citadel."

Daurannon stiffened with outrage at the casual mention—in front of the novices—of links known only to the Council.

". . . or for the Council to set them on some dog wizard who's gotten too powerful."

"That's a . . ."

"Be that as it may, Daur, the fact remains that something— or someone—caused the experiments of the Council with the

Void to go dreadfully wrong; that the situation is worsening steadily . . .''

"*You* say," cut in Bentick's thin voice.

". . . and that somewhere in the Vaults a wormhole has opened through to some world whose atmosphere is water." They had reached the bottom of the upshaft, a stone chimney ascending three levels and entered by three small, crooked doorways. Quiet though they were, their voices reverberated up the long vent above them and back into the darkness spidering out behind, the darkness that was weighted with the uneasy vibration of the nearness of the Void.

Antryg turned to face Daurannon, and there was desperate intensity in his voice. "Daur, if it is you, or Bentick, who has kidnapped Joanna for purposes of your own . . ."

"How dare you!" the Steward gasped, and the young sasenna looked shocked.

". . . please, please, move her out of the Vaults if that's where she's being kept. Even without the—the things—that I've seen down here, it's only a matter of time before the lower levels flood." In the graying tangle of his hair his face was haggard and thin, smudged with blue beneath the eyes and streaked with a dried thread of blood from the cut on his forehead.

"Ninetentwo—my friend—said he couldn't get a reading of her presence in the Vaults, but there's always the chance of a shield of some kind around her cell, some spell that protects against *any* kind of detection. Like you, there are things about this situation I can't account for, nobody can. If she's here, Daur, move her . . . or organize a search for her."

"So that all the Senior mages in the Citadel—the ones who know the Vaults well enough *to* search—will be kept busy?" The younger mage leaned one shoulder against the rusty iron staples of the ladder, looked up into Antryg's face, the opaque suspicion in his eyes concealing whatever might lie behind. "We've searched before—for the Moving Gate, for clues—

and have found nothing comprehensible. What makes you think . . .''

Shreb, the tallest of the three novices, screamed, *''Look out!''*

Antryg and Daurannon swung around in time to see something huge and soft and dreadful come bursting out of the right-hand doorway into the upshaft, something that sprang with the horrible swiftness of a leaping spider but whose soft, billowing body spread like a jellyfish to reveal a ciliated mass of wriggling, saw-toothed tongues. It showed only for a second, yellow, filthy, wet, and virtually odorless—Daurannon slashed his hand toward it . . .

And nothing happened.

No lightning, no power, no help.

Antryg was ripping the novice Shreb's sword away from her even as the abomination fell upon Gyrik, wrapping the boy's body in an obscene billow of dripping flesh. The boy screamed, thrashing and tearing desperately—Daurannon was still staring in shock and unbelief at his hand. Bentick brought up his staff to hurl a bolt of power at the thing, a bolt of power whose destroying nimbus would have undoubtedly enveloped Antryg as well, had any such thing actually issued from the staff. But none did. The third novice, a young man named Nye, had sprung forward, sword flashing like Antryg's, to hack at the bulging membranes of the monster's body.

But the thing was tougher than it looked, and all the while Gyrik was screaming, shrieks of agony and horror passing over into blind animal howls, appallingly muffled in the sticky folds. Blood had begun to run down his legs, and an instant later he collapsed to his knees, Antryg and the two sasenna hacking and tearing at the heaving, clinging flesh of the thing while Daurannon and Bentick stood back, armed only with their magic, making signs that called no power from the black air, speaking words made nonsense by the agonized shrieks that greeted them.

Gyrik stopped screaming with a sobbing gurgle; the creature, its hide slit and shredded by its attackers' swords, backed and rippled from the prostrate body, and slithered away in long, shredded sections that moved independently, like flat, blubbery worms, leaving something that caused Bentick to go suddenly white and Shreb to turn away and vomit. Antryg knelt beside the eaten mess that was left of Gyrik's head and upper body, touched the stripped flesh of the boy's face. After two more sobbing gasps, Gyrik stopped breathing.

"See to Shreb, Bentick," Antryg said softly, as Daurannon dropped to his knees beside him.

"I couldn't even call fire." Daurannon's lips were gray with shock. "I couldn't . . . I can't . . ."

"Then I suggest we all get ourselves out of this immediate vicinity as quickly as we can." Antryg stood up—his hands, where he had touched the bloodied pulp that had been Gyrik's forehead, burned a little, and he quickly pulled off his mitts and wiped his fingers on his faded plum-colored coat skirts. "And let's hope this *is* just a small field effect, like the cat spell or that area of cold Tom told me about on the stairway between the Upper Gatehouse and the Library, or we're all going to be in a lot worse trouble than I care to think about when the Inquisition shows up."

By the time they had ascended thirty feet up the shaft, both Daurannon and Bentick were able to summon small feathers of burning blue witchlight to the air above their heads; in the phosphor gleam, the older man's high, smooth forehead glistened clammily and the younger man's graying black hair was stringy with sweat. Later the fabric of Antryg's coat skirts turned brown and crumbled in the streaks where he had wiped his fingers, and the following day his fingers were blistered.

But by that time the knowledge that pockets existed where magic's strengths were negated, or reversed, was the least of anyone's worries.

A young wizard named Truvas sought to play a prank on his master by setting up a spell that would cause him to get lost in his own house. The master entered the door, and after a week, young Truvas went in to seek him. Neither was ever seen again.

—*The Book of Tethys the Brown*

# CHAPTER XI

"CURSE HIM . . . OH, CURSE HIS NAME . . . CURSE HIM, OH, curse his name. Oh, dear God, send someone to get me out of here . . . oh, curse his name . . ."

The muttering whisper grew louder as Joanna felt her way along the smooth, featureless corridor. A woman's voice, droning and exhausted, low as if the speaker were huddled in some corner, rocking herself like a beaten child to this threadbare litany of despair. Joanna had heard it telling over and over to itself those same few sentences for nearly an hour, as she'd tried to get a fix on it through the darkness—drearily, monotonously—until she was ready to scream. Sometimes it would stop, but always it started again, not even filled with pain . . . filled with nothing at all. She had begun to suspect that the woman who crouched there in what could only be more corridor was insane.

But it was a human voice, the first she had heard. And maddening as it quickly became, she made her way toward it.

She had encountered other things besides human voices in her wanderings in the darkness.

154

She had lain weeping on the floor until she could weep no more, then had slept in her exhaustion and despair. Waking, she found the darkness as impenetrable as before. Neither flashlight, nor light-up digital readout, nor the matches in her purse would work; she still felt neither hunger nor thirst. Fear swept over her in a long, familiar wave, holding her sweating and nauseated for she had not known how long—fear of the clawing demons with their laughter, fear that she was now utterly separated from her point of origin . . . fear that these facts did not matter.

After a time—a nontime—she had gotten up and gone on.

Fear had come and gone ever since.

Some of it had been fear of meeting the demons again, or things like them: things that screamed at her, clawed at her, chased her in the darkness. This had happened once more, and now she walked every step in the stomach-clenching dread of the silence around her.

Once, turning a corner, she had encountered something else, something . . . She knew not what. Some vast, silent aura of waiting, some sound that was not a sound—as if something huge were holding its breath, a filthy, living silence. But a silence that drew her as if against her will.

As she'd stood there wondering if this was her imagination, if this was madness, she had felt a hideous sensation as if life, energy, her will, and the very electromagnetic heat of her body's chemistry were being pulled at—with a gruesome sensation of inner tugging, as if whatever it was that lay unseen in the horrible night before her wanted the life out of her flesh, down to its tiniest, most animal cellular energies. She had had a sense—and she didn't know why—of obscene vastness, as if she stood close to some enormous black yearning at whose center gaped a well that could never be filled, that would draw everything and anything into itself.

She had backed away, trembling, and in the dark before her, though she still heard no sound, she thought she could sense it move.

And she had run again, run and run and run, desperately turning and twisting in the winding corridors, queasy with the thought that she might have run in a circle and would stumble smack into it—or into something worse—from the other side . . .

And then she had heard the whispering, the dreary mutter of another human voice.

And had stumbled, seeking it, her mind conjuring scenario after scenario from the fertile fields of Hollywood horrors.

The dark thing, the silent thing, the energy-drawing thing, could mimic human voices.

Whoever had put her here had put a tape recorder here, too, with an endless tape loop—never mind why. Maybe just to hear her burst into tears of despair when she found it.

She'd find some haggard crone in rags who'd been rocking to herself, muttering to herself, for ninety years.

"Curse him, curse him, oh, curse his name . . . oh, God, please get me out of this . . . God, send someone to get me out of this . . . Oh, curse his name . . ."

"Who's there?" Her own voice sounded loud, queer, unreal in her ears.

"Who is it? Oh, who is it?" sobbed a voice—*Not a tape loop, anyway*—and a moment later there came a thick, heavy rustling of cloth, the froufrou of taffeta and a fusty smell of powder, perfume, and the slightly dusty odor of silk. A hand touched her extended hand, groping and fumbling in the dark . . . *Good. It really is dark. I'm not blind.* A woman's hand, soft and well cared for, with long nails and a bracelet of what felt like pearls.

"My name is Joanna Sheraton."

"Are you his prisoner, too?" she whispered. "Is your husband also one of his enemies? I know my husband will give him what he wants." The hands were all over her, clinging, pawing, patting, like an ill-mannered child's; grabbing handfuls of her hair, fumbling at her mouth, until Joanna seized them by the wrists and pushed them away. There was no resistance, and there was something very childish about that, too.

"When he talks to my husband—to my Gwimat—Gwimat will come to terms with him. His terms aren't so very unreasonable . . . it's only the waiting I can't stand. It seems so long . . . it seems like I've been here forever . . . oh, curse him, curse his name . . ."

"Who are you?" Joanna asked. She felt at the woman's arms in her turn, careful not to let her start pawing again, something Joanna hated because it reminded her of her mother's intrusive, fussy fingering and straightening of her clothes and hair. She felt plump, rounded arms in smooth, slippery fabric, the scratchiness of lace at the elbows. She'd worn dresses like that herself, when she'd been in Antryg's world under his protection. The woman threw her arms around Joanna, clutching her close, her face pressed to her shoulder—slightly taller than she, her long hair disheveled and spiky with jeweled hairpins.

"Oh, curse him, curse his name . . . I know it was he. I know he took me prisoner. It has to have been him." Joanna turned her face aside but suffered herself to be held. Only lately had she realized how desperately most people—herself included—needed to be held. Only, she realized, from the unself-conscious physicalness of Antryg's hugs and her own delight in hugging him in return.

"He knew my husband was working against him, you see; he brought me here, left me here, to blackmail Gwimat. And as soon as Gwimat hears his terms, of course he'll do as he asks to get me back. He'll do anything to get me back. It's just the waiting that's so hard for me, I never had any patience, never. God sent you, my dear, God sent you to help me bear this in patience . . ."

"Who *are* you?" Joanna asked again, gently disengaging herself. "And who put you here? And where are we?"

But the woman was already sinking to the floor in a vast billow of satin skirts and rustling petticoats, rocking and moaning and cursing the name of the man she would not name, clinging to Joanna with her perfumed hands and trying to make her sit, too. Try as she would—and she did try for some time—Joanna could get no sense out of her, only endless wailings and whispered mutterings, the same few sentences over and over that she had already heard repeated endlessly: her husband would come to get her out, her husband wouldn't allow him to keep her prisoner—she found the waiting so difficult.

After what felt like endless time Joanna extricated herself, not without difficulty, from the clutching grip and moved away into the sightless labyrinth once again. Her pajamas held the cloying sweetness of the woman's perfume, a reminder of her presence, like the mumblings fading behind her. When she was still within earshot she took another spool of thread from her purse and taped one end to the wall. She might in time, she reflected uneasily, become desperate enough even to long for such company and want to find her way back.

But as she unreeled the thread—that meticulous guide through the darkness of nowhere, a guide from nothing back to nothing—she wondered how soon it would be before she herself sat down against some wall and started muttering.

"Joanna!"

Startled nearly out of her skin, she swung around, flattening to the wall behind her, thoughts splashing through her mind—*the dark thing that drew at her life, mimicry of voices, how did it know my name . . . ? Why does the voice sound familiar . . . ?*

"Joanna Sheraton?" The voice in the darkness was known but unplaceable, male, a pleasant and well-trained light baritone. What made her think of an actor . . . ?

"It's me. Magister Magus. Is that Joanna Sheraton . . . ?"

"Magus!" she sobbed. "Here . . . I'm here . . ."

A hesitant hand touched her shoulder; she caught the wrist in a gesture that even as she made it felt horribly like the madwoman she had just left. The arm was cased in what felt like the sleeve of an expensively quilted and corded velvet dressing gown. *To hell with it,* she thought, and flung her arms around the slender waist and hugged the little dog wizard tight. He gathered her to him, as grateful as she for the human contact in spite of the fact that at their last encounter she'd been responsible for nearly getting his skull cracked for him. Against her temple she felt the scratchiness of his close-trimmed black-and-silver beard.

"My dear, dear girl . . ."

"Magus, what the *hell* is going on?" Her words came out as a sob. "Where *are* we, who the hell was that woman, what are we doing here?"

She felt his body relax a little in her grip, felt a kind of tension go out of him, his slender shoulders slumping. His breath escaped him in a sigh. "Oh," he said in a discouraged voice. "You don't know?"

*Dammit,* she thought, knowing what he was about to say. *Dammit, dammit, dammit . . .* "You mean you don't know, either?"

"Well," he said after a moment, "I know where we are, and I've got a good guess who that woman is. But as to why we were brought here . . ."

"Look, right now any information is better than stumbling around in the dark waiting to run into that . . . that thing . . ."

"What thing?" But by the uneasiness in his voice she guessed he'd felt its power, too. He had stepped back, but his hands still held hers; she felt the tapered fingers, forever innocent of manual toil, stroke the soft skin of her own hands.

"The thing that . . . I don't know. Something in the dark. Something that . . . it felt like if I got close to it, it would draw out my life, draw out everything in me."

"Ah," the Magus breathed, "so it wasn't my imagination. I was afraid . . ."

As ineffectual as this friend of Antryg's could be in an emergency, her delight in meeting him was unalloyed. Magister Magus might be a dog wizard, with a dog wizard's uncertain and frequently inaccurate training—he certainly was no more than a charlatan who made a royal living telling fortunes and peddling love potions, simple nostrums and fortune-cookie advice to the more superstitious members of the Regent's court in Angelshand—but in times past he had been a friend to Antryg and a friend to her when they were in need. Even had this not been the case, even had the Magus been a total stranger in this dark maze, he was, at least, sane and kind. And he did know something about the situation.

"What was it?" she asked.

"I believe," he said after a moment, "that it has to have been the *tsaeati* . . ." And the Spell of Tongues, whose aura still clung to her from long association with Antryg, translated the word to her mind from some archaic variant of an ancient speech as *devourer* or *glutton*.

"It was said to be indestructible. It devoured everything which came in its path and turned everything—fire, lightning, the magic of the wizards who fought against it—back upon its attackers, until Berengis the Black imprisoned it in a crystal called the Brown Star, where it is apparently technically impossible for anything to devour anything."

"And the Brown Star is where we are now?" Joanna asked. "I mean, it may not be impossible to devour something, but I certainly haven't been either hungry or thirsty since I got here, and I must have been here for days. And," she added, "the matches in my purse don't work, so there seems to be some kind of bar to the transformation of energy . . . technically, the sulfur of the match tip won't oxidize."

"Precisely," the Magus agreed, his voice radiating a scientific cheerfulness Joanna was far from feeling.

"That still doesn't answer what we're doing in the Brown Star."

She heard him sigh again, felt it through the arm he still held clasped around her shoulders.

"Well . . . Berengis the Black was a court wizard to the Lords Caeline, and the Brown Star, after hundreds of years, must have fallen into the hands of Suraklin the Dark Mage. At least, people disappeared whose very bodies were never traced—or, on the rare occasions when he did return someone he'd kidnapped, they could never tell where they had been or how long they had been there. That woman, whom I believe is Irina Siltrayne, the wife of one of the Dark Mage's enemies, seems to bear me out. At least, she disappeared literally days before the Council wizards and the Emperor's men descended upon Suraklin's Citadel. No trace of her was ever found."

"Oh, Jesus," Joanna whispered, horrified. "You mean the poor woman's been in here, waiting to be rescued, for *twenty-five years*? With those demons, and that . . . that *tsaeati* . . . ?"

"So it appears," Magister Magus said somberly. "I've tried to get some sense out of her several times since I've been in here . . ."

"Oh, God." Joanna shivered. "That long . . ." She was silent a moment, trying to comprehend and, when comprehension seemed imminent, trying not to. "But how did *you* end up here? And *me*, for that matter?"

"Well," the little dog wizard said after a moment, "that's rather a long story. You know that Salteris, the Archmage, disappeared—and later word reached the mages in Angelshand that he was dead. Some said Antryg murdered him, which is ridiculous on the face of it. He worshiped Salteris."

"No," Joanna said quietly. "Yes, he did love Salteris like a father . . . but it's also true that he killed him. I'll explain later."

Magus was silent for a time. Joanna led the way over to the wall and settled herself on the floor with her back to it, the dog wizard sitting at her side. As he did so his bare foot brushed hers, and the hem of what was almost certainly a very splendid bathrobe—she thought it was the black velvet one he'd worn in the mornings, the few days she'd stayed with him in his house in Angelshand six months ago, plush and luxurious with cuffs and collar of green silk trapunto that turned to emerald the light, clear green of his eyes.

At length he said, "Well, in any case word reached me that Salteris was dead. I had just returned to Angelshand after . . . er . . . a stay on one of Prince Cerdic's estates." He hesitated, the flex of his voice carrying the unpleasantness of the memory of being enslaved by the wizard Gaire—the wizard Joanna and very few others believed to have been in actuality Suraklin.

"In any event the mages were in a tizzy—they left the Mages' Yard, and one night I . . . Well, to make a long story short, I broke into Salteris' house in search of what I could find. I was in quest of books, mostly. I may be a dog wizard, but I do have some powers . . ."

"I know," Joanna said softly. "Antryg always said you would be one of the best of the Academics, if you'd consented to take the Council vows."

"And a lot of good they would have done me," grumbled the mage. "Swearing you'll never make a living off the one true talent you have in exchange for them teaching you, as if they were conferring a favor. Well. I . . . I wanted more. I wanted to learn, and I wanted . . . implements. Objects. Teles-balls, specifically. Salteris was said to own three. Things that would give me power enough to prevent being enslaved again or cracked over the head by impudent young sasenna who ought to have more respect for their elders."

"Have you seen Caris?" interrupted Joanna, ducking discussion of that last, disastrous parting in the Prince's house at Devilsgate Manor. "Is he well?"

"As well as a sasennan can be who's lost the use of one hand." In spite of his private feelings, Joanna could hear the genuine pity in her friend's voice. Then, more cheerfully, he continued, "He's training to be a healer these days, I hear. There have been rumors, off and on, about him and the Regent's wife, Pellicida, but he's so *very* stolid and she's so extremely pregnant, that I suspect they're not really much fun as a source of gossip, and besides, Pellicida seems to be the only woman the Regent likes or respects. Where was I? Oh, the Brown Star . . ."

He sighed. "The Brown Star was one of the things that I found at Salteris'. It was hidden in a cupboard with a catch and a spring—it must have been masked with spells as well, until Salteris died. He'd quite clearly picked it up when the Council broke Suraklin's Citadel . . ."

"No," said Joanna. "No, I think . . . It's a long story. But if Antryg was right—if Suraklin took over the bodies of first the Emperor, and then years later of Salteris himself, I think the Brown Star must have been something he brought away from the Citadel himself. But in either case . . ."

"In either case," Magister Magus sighed, "it fell into my hands."

There was momentary silence.

"I think," Joanna said at last, "that I can smell a bad case of Instant Karma in the making."

"As you say." His voice had a discouraged note. "I don't know how long ago it was—weeks, months . . . It could have been years; in this darkness it is impossible to tell. I was awakened by a sound in the middle of the night; I crept down to my study, where I had left the Star, quite well secured in a secret compartment of my own desk. And . . . I don't recall exactly what happened. Sometimes I think I remember a dark form standing by the desk, turning toward me. Sometimes I think that's only what I know must have happened. Then I was . . . here."

Joanna sighed and gave him an outline of the events leading up to her own nightmare awakening. "So you see, my being here has got to have something to do with Antryg. You . . . I don't know. I suspect you were just in the wrong place at the wrong time, and let that be a lesson to you about swiping magical implements that don't belong to you."

"You're starting to sound like that lunatic lover of yours," Magus said glumly. There was another silence, broken by the far-off shrieking laugh of demons—other creatures, Joanna guessed, that some wizard, unable to destroy them by any other means, had simply dumped in here, not thinking about what else might have been imprisoned in the crystal in the course of the years. She wondered if the *tsaeati* had drawn out poor Lady Irina's mind, leaving her mumbling in the remnants of what few memories were left; wondered if there were others, placed in the crystal by God knew who in the centuries of its existence and forgotten . . . others who had ceased to mutter, who only lay silently waiting.

"The one shred of comfort I can take from this," Magister Magus said after some moments, "other than the sheer pleasure of your company, though of course I wish that the meeting were in other circumstances, and I'm certainly sorry that you have been placed in this horrible position . . ."

"Not as sorry as I am, believe me."

He gave the ghost of a chuckle. "The one shred of comfort I do draw is that I have never known Antryg to abandon a friend. He loves you, Joanna—and he is a very powerful mage indeed. I have known him for years, and I know that he will attempt rescue at the cost of his life."

"It's inspiring to know that," Joanna said with a sigh. "But if he *does* attempt rescue, and it *does* cost him his life before he figures out where the hell we are . . . where does that leave us?"

"I wish you wouldn't say things like that," the wizard muttered, and they lapsed into pessimistic silence.

All magic is balance. The power which summons the wind and rain, which calls forth fire, which alters the random chains of circumstance, must come from somewhere: the energy of the stars, of the earth, of the blood and bone and life of the Summoner. Likewise all which happens, happens to something or someone—the rain which nourishes crops, floods streams and prevents messages from being delivered in time; the fire which warms, consumes the wood; the smallest trains of circumstance start other trains leading to goals that cannot be predicted. All this must be remembered by the mage.

—ISAR CHELLADIN
*Precepts of Wizardry*

# CHAPTER XII

THOUGH IT COULD NOT HAVE BEEN MORE THAN FIVE IN THE morning when a very shaken pair of sasenna escorted Antryg back to the Pepper-Grinder, daylight was already broad in the sky. He thanked Shreb and Nye and offered them tea, which they declined after a moment's confusion—it was not customary to offer sasenna food or drink while they were on duty, any more than someone would have offered them to a sword that stood in a corner or to a servant: sasenna were considered, by themselves as much as by those to whom they swore their vows, as a combination of the two. Once they had gone, Antryg collected his two finest pinwheels—a red one and an astonishing double spiral that turned in both directions at once—gathered an armful of looserife and poppies bound together with the trailing vines of honeysweet, and made his way up to the silent bulk of the Library tower to deposit the whole in the scriptorium before Seldes Katne's locked door.

That done, he fetched a clean shirt and made his way back down the tiny, zigzagging wooden stairways through ivy and raspberry bramble, to the baths stuck like a random half-timbered arm where the Polygon reared up against the southern limb of the hill.

He shaved and bathed and felt rather better, though tired to the marrow of his bones; descending to the kitchen, he begged muffins and tea from Pothatch and sat at the Juniors' table in the big, half-empty hall of the refectory, listening to the talk. There was shock and horror and a huge confusion of rumor about the death of Gyrik; briefly and quietly, he told the story to the half-dozen young people at the table with him. Gyrik had been a well-liked boy, but there was more than that; a nervous undercurrent of glances ran among them at the thought that magic itself would fail.

"I guess that's why Phormion isn't here," Gilda remarked, glancing along the plastered hall to the small knot of Senior mages at the upper table. "He was one of her best students."

"I don't know if that was the reason," Brunus argued, looking up from the lists he'd been studying even while shoveling down bacon, porridge, and fruit. "She hasn't taught the last two days."

"And she looked terrible that last day when she *did* teach," added Cylin, a tall, very serious young Junior from Senterwing.

Brunus nodded. "Not sick, but nervous," he explained, at Antryg's eyebrowed question. "She kept looking over her shoulder, though we were up on the observatory platform and the stair from the Library is really the only way up. She must have jumped a foot when Brighthand spoke to her from behind."

He frowned, earnestly stirring milk into his tea. He was another, Antryg noticed, of what Lady Rosamund, in her own novice days, had referred to only half in jest as "the milk brigade." The aristocracy, and those of the bourgeois who aped them, drank pale Oriental tea or thick bitter coffee black—*pure*, the arbiters of *ton* described it—or at most with tiny amounts of white sugar; peasants swilled honey-laced caravan tea by the tankard and chewed sugar afterward if they could get it, as Antryg was doing now. Cutting tea or coffee with milk was an urban trick, indulged in by low-class tradesmen at best.

Glancing around, Antryg noticed that neither Otaro nor Brighthand was present in the hall.

Nor were Q'iin or Whitwell Simm, Seldes Katne or Issay Bel-Caire or any of several dozen others, or the Archmage herself, for that matter. But still . . .

Kyra the Red and Cylin's featherbrained friend Mick joined them, to add their mite to the conversation: very early that morning all three of the Citadel dairymaids and Tom the gardener had gotten lost in the twenty yards of ground between the cowsheds and the stairs up to the back door of the kitchen, wandering helplessly among the weathered fences and sheds of winter fodder until Tom, by dint of a piece of string he'd had in his pockets, had managed to find his way out of the spell-field and summon Nandiharrow to disperse the magical confusion that hung over that spot. Two of the milkmaids had left the Citadel without even pouring the milk into settling pans.

"Well, one of the first-years might have done that," Gilda said, and Kyra brushed the suggestion aside with a wave that very nearly overset the teapot.

"I don't think even the youngest of them would play a prank like that on non-wizards," she said, as Mick and Cylin made simultaneous, rescuing grabs at the crockery. "It's too easy, for one thing. Really, Mick, you're getting very good at that. Now, putting down a field that would get a *Senior* lost . . ."

And there was momentary, contemplative silence.

"How would you keep from getting caught?" Mick asked, his blue eyes bright.

"You'd need a four-corner talisman system . . ."

"And some kind of a nonpersonal sourcing . . ."

"I think," Antryg said regretfully, "that this discussion had better remain academic, at least for the time being.''

They looked disappointed but nodded—Antryg guessed, however, that when the current crisis was over, there would be a time of more than usual navigational difficulties around the Citadel. He recalled the extremely localized rainstorms that had enlivened his and Daur's second summer here. No wonder there were fragments of odd old spells everywhere on the tor, floating back to life.

He made his way back to the Pepper-Grinder, the need for sleep weighing like a triple-thick shirt of mail upon his shoulders. Last night's concoction of jelgeth root had long since worn off; he brewed, on the tiny hearth, a tisane of the second packet of herbs Q'iin had given him, drank it, collected a pillow from his room, and made his way down the concealed stair in the wall to the subcellar. From there a tiny doorway let him, by means of a hidden passage, through into the attic of the Isle of Butterflies, where he made a bed of the contents of a trunkful of ancient coats beneath one of the corridorlike chamber's tiny dormer windows.

The tisane worked quite well, as far as it went; until nearly the end, his dreams were merely disquieting, filled with dripping darkness, filth, and insects, and a familiar voice whispering his name. Once, clear and heartrending, he saw himself walking hand-in-hand with Joanna down the sidewalks of Melrose Avenue through the garish neon darkness and blowing electricity of the Santa Ana winds, while she explained to him the unimaginable contents of shopwindows and they giggled so hard they had to prop each other up. But the dream melted, segueing into the face of a woman named Rheatha, with whom he'd stayed during the Mellidane Revolts—a woman who'd been killed by the Emperor's soldiers because she had sheltered him. He saw himself stumbling down a blood-trail in the Citadel Vaults, as he had stumbled through that looted house in the south all those years ago, finding a severed foot, a hand with the rings still bloodied on the fingers . . . a head lying in a huge pool of gore that matted its long, curly hair. He tried desperately to prevent himself from picking it up, from turning it to see whose face it was . . . He managed to wake up, gasping and shaking all over, before he saw.

Or, waking, he managed to blot the last second from his mind.

A skinny stick of primrose light stabbed obliquely down through the dormer window. Already the sun had shifted west over the peak of the Citadel hill.

"Well," Antryg murmured shakily, lying back again on the piled scratchiness of old velvets, plush, and braid, "we'll brew that tisane a little stronger next time."

Returning to the Pepper-Grinder, he collected the books he'd borrowed from Seldes Katne and settled himself in the bare, cleared expanse of the smaller of the two upstairs chambers. Starting, as was his custom, in a corner of the room, he proceeded to work out with chalk, first on the floor, later spreading to three of the four walls, the theoretical constructs of a spell necessary to deceive finite quantities of energy into believing that they should behave in one fashion rather than another. The geas, at least, had not hampered his adeptness with magical theory, and his study of optics and physics in Joanna's world helped enormously; still, at the end of the endless spring afternoon when he ultimately transferred the final procedures, patterns, and power-circles to paper, he felt as if he'd spent the larger part of the day getting himself pummeled to exhaustion in sword practice.

And no nearer, he thought, to locating Joanna.

"I looked for you earlier," Seldes Katne said, bringing him up tea and honey, bread and soft white cheese just as he finished; they sat on the floor of the upstairs gallery overlooking the small hall below. Kyra had spent the morning down there memorizing her lists but had gone off since to an astronomy lecture given by Pharne Pordanches, in Phormion Starmistress' continued absence. "I'm coming along on the list of teles, but it's slow. Individual mages make reference to them in their grimoires and histories, but no one's made a catalog of them, any more than they'd catalog the dishes in the dining hall.''

"The difference being that one doesn't use the dishes in the dining hall to work magic with,'' Antryg said, meticulously smearing cheese on a thick-crusted roll and acquiring long streaks of it on the tarnished gilding of his coat cuffs. ''At least, not as a general rule, though Daur and I used to get quite good conjurations using staghorn, nitrous salts, and powdered violets in those little bowls Pothatch cooks jam puddings in. It never seemed to work as well in the salad dishes. It is my eternal regret that nobody here has yet invented peanut butter; if I have time between avoiding the Inquisition, finding Joanna, and locating the power-circles which are keeping the Moving Gate jammed open—if the Moving Gate *is* in fact the source and not merely a symptom of the problem—I'll have to talk to Pothatch about it.''

"What do you mean,'' Seldes Katne asked slowly, ''*if* the Moving Gate is the source of the problem?''

Antryg regarded her with surprise. "Well, it may not be, you know,'' he said. ''It may simply be another aberrance. I'll be able to tell a great deal once the field is stabilized and I can locate the thing.''

He licked a drop of honey from his long fingers. Pothatch, who was also in charge of the baths, had bandaged his arm for him and patched the skirts and the sleeve of his coat, the squares of green flowered calico standing out glaringly against the plum-colored velvet.

"A pity you can't . . . well, use powers from one of the Gates themselves, from one of these other worlds, to get around the geas.''

Antryg hesitated for a long time, frowning into the shadowy spaces of the rafters opposite the gallery where they sat. ''It is something I had thought of,'' he admitted at last and looked sidelong at the stumpy little woman sitting beside him, her short fingers toying nervously with the end of her long, graying braid. He saw in her face what he recognized from shaving his own—the tired lines and bruised look about the eyelids, the mark of poor sleep or none. Her usual placidity had given way to a look of strain and nervousness, but that, he thought, was hardly unique in the Citadel now. With her quarters slap over the Vorplek Line, she must be prey to constant, low-grade spilloff from the pressure of the Void.

He did note that she hadn't worn any of the flowers he'd brought her, but then, he hadn't really expected she would.

"It wouldn't answer, you know." He set down his bread and honey, stared for a time into the mahogany depths of his tea. "I suppose magic *could* be brought from another universe into our own, though I doubt such magic would overcome the Council's geas on my mind. But even if I weren't afraid of further disrupting an already hazardously unstable situation, I would never try it."

"I thought you of all people . . ."

He shook his head. "There may have been a time—many years ago—when I might have. But, Kitty, we're already awash here in the effects of our *own* magic, which we don't understand. Magic from some other universe, some other type of magic, with different rules, different laws from our own . . . There are spells in *this* world that drive those who use them mad or have peculiar side effects like summoning cats or God only knows what. What would magic from another universe do?"

He drank off the tea—it was nearly as bitter as the jelgeth had been, but the caffeine, he reflected, would clear his head— and folded his arms around his knees in their shabby jeans, a scarecrow shape reminiscent of a curled-up crane fly, with his spectacle lenses flashing in the blue-gray dimness of the gallery and his earrings like chips of broken diamond in the tangle of his hair. "If it weren't for the fact that Joanna needs my help, I'd be inclined to agree with the Council in putting me under a geas, you know. I murdered six men and two women by means of magic—they were guards," he added, seeing the look of shocked horror on her face. "They had orders to kill us and we *could* not allow ourselves to be taken, not then. Too much depended on us . . . at least, if my perception of the situation was correct, it did, though from first to last it might only have been one of my delusions. But the fact remains that I did use my magic to take the lives of people who weren't expecting magic—who probably no more than half believed in it. I was desperate, but that's not really a valid excuse. Some people have very low thresholds of desperation."

His gaze returned to the shadows of the rafters; situated on the east side of the tor, the Pepper-Grinder was already settling into a soft blur of shadow, though through the windows the sunlight lay jewel-bright on the somber green-black of the pine trees far below and blinked like diamonds on the Crooked River's swift brown flood.

He sighed, not really wanting to admit what he knew to be true. "The thing is, the more I deal with magic, the more I come to the conclusion that the Council is probably right."

Seldes Katne said nothing, but he could almost feel her thoughts. *Easy for you, who have always had magic at your call, to say.* And there was nothing much he could say to her of that.

Pockets bulging with scribbled notes, Antryg and Seldes Katne ran Aunt Min to earth in the Council chamber. As they entered the round, white-pillared marble room from the gloom of the stairwell, Antryg recognized the voice of Trukild, the headman of Wychstanes Village, anxiously saying, "Be that as it may, my lady . . . all I'm saying is, if it keeps up, I can't be answerable for what may happen."

Of medium height, broad, square-faced and freckled under a beard like a holly bush, Trukild was a bigger version of his second cousin Pothatch the cook, done in brown rather than red. The ineradicable peasant stench of smoke and cattle emanated from his clothing and person and seemed to fill the room. Since the long *ibeks*—the barnlike dwellings occupied by three and four generations of Sykerst families plus Dutch uncles, hired hands, and remoter connections—were shared with the livestock down on the ground floor and filled with the smoke of the huge tiled stoves for the seven months of winter every year, this was understandable. Smoke was considered healthy and seldom allowed to escape, and Antryg had never lost his faint nostalgia at that particular pungent combination of stinks.

"It's not just they're afraid to come here through the woods, Lady." Trukild turned his shapeless felt hat 'round and 'round between callused hands as Antryg and Seldes Katne slipped quietly through the door. As before, the windowless chamber was bathed in soft, cool, shadowless light, picking out every thread of grain in the waxed oak council table, every frayed spot of the Archmage's worn robe and every wrinkle of that dried-apple face.

"What with the things that have been seen, out near the Green King's Chapel, and the filthy unnatural creature Gru and his hunters shot out in the woods near the Imp-Stones," he nodded back to where Gru Gwidion, the black-bearded chief hunter of the village, and two of his men, stood beside one of the circle of marble pillars that made an inner, headless colonnade around the walls of the room, "I don't blame 'em, but there's more than that. They're saying that your magics are the cause of it."

"That is ridiculous on the face of it," Bentick replied crisply from his post to the left of Aunt Min's big carven chair.

"The logic of your villagers overwhelms me." On Aunt Min's right, Lady Rosamund folded her arms, the fine wool of her sleeves catching a pewter sheen. Antryg noted, not for the first time, that the collar of the shift protruding above her all-encompassing robe was a plain, dark calico, while Daurannon's was white and finished with a modish ruffle. "The same people who have lived near us time out of mind, who have come and gone from the Citadel, whose holidays have been made cheerier by what we've paid them for eggs and milk and meat; the same people whose sons and daughters have worked here among us, who can testify that we cannot and do not tamper with human affairs *ever*—and I do not know how many village boys have plagued us over the years to sell them love-potions—they think we've suddenly decided to abandon six hundred years of teaching and precepts simply for the satisfaction of plaguing them.'' Her delicate oval face was pale with anger, making the black butterfly-wing brows, the sooty veils of lashes, stand out as if inked.

Beside and a little behind her, Daurannon said nothing, but those large hazel eyes, which looked so expressive and were actually such a perfect mask, flicked watchfully from one face to another.

Trukild eyed the Lady unflinchingly. "I'm not saying they're right . . .''

"Are you saying they're wrong? Saying it to *them*, I mean, when they talk about . . . what *do* they talk about doing?'' she added, her low voice, sweet as a struck jade chime, flexing with scorn. "Coming up here with torches? I hope they enjoy long walks in foggy woods! Or do they just plan on selling one another their surplus eggs and butter from here on out? I tremble!''

"Rosie, Rosie,'' Aunt Min murmured, raising her faded china blue gaze to her pupil, her head slightly cocked on the bent stem of her spine. "Can you blame them for fearing, when strange abominations are seen in the woods? They say things they could not see attacked children in the twilight near Gruddle Bog, and their cattle are being killed, bled white and half eaten alive. Can you blame them for turning upon that which they do not know?''

"I can blame them for attributing the matter to our malice, after all the years we have demonstrated our goodwill,'' her ladyship said in arctic tones. "Like the Emperor's Regent, who turned our people out of the cities, all for the deeds of one renegade dog wizard.'' Her glance cut viciously at Antryg, standing, hands in pockets, near the door. "What *must* we do, to escape blame for all the ills that people do not care to take onto themselves or attribute to impersonal Fate? Surrender our powers entirely? Go live in a place even more deserted than this, if there is one?"

Aunt Min held up her hand, stilling the icy passion of the younger woman's words. Then she turned, to hold out the twisted arthritic fingers to the big man in his crudely painted sheepskin coat who stood before her. Though her knitting basket of willow twigs, running over as usual with hanks of silks and wools spun and unspun, lay at her feet, she had not been working as Trukild had spoken; now she smiled at him, and in it was the echo of the warmth that had drawn nobles from an Emperor's court down to the taverns of the Algoswive quarter where, long ago in another century, another world, she had danced.

"You are good," she said in her katydid voice, "to come out and give us warning of how your people feel; I swear to you we'll do all to help that we can. Daur, my child . . ."

The younger mage stepped forward.

"Would you see to it that some of the boys and girls take weapons and go out to the woods, and hunt for sight of abominations, along the Brehon Line and out near the Imp-Stones, and near the Gruddle Bog? The Line . . . there'll be faulting all along the Line, out to the Green King's Chapel and beyond."

"Thank you, my lady." Trukild bowed clumsily amid a creaking of boiled-leather belts. "I'll do such as I can with the village men." Gru Gwidion and his two hunters stepped up behind him, preparing to follow him from the chamber. Their eyes, Antryg noticed, were hard with suspicion as they scanned the faces of the four wizards gathered before them in the Council chamber's white, sourceless radiance.

"You must pardon them," the headman added, turning back from the door. "But it's hard not to fear, you know. Yes, we've lived nigh the Citadel for generations, we know you and have heard all the tales from our parents and grandfolks. But you yourself know it's not something you can understand unless you're born in it, raised in it—like a city lady, begging your pardon, my Lady Rosamund, trying to understand us country-folk. We're like cattle grazing the banks, watching the dolphins in the sea."

"Much he knows of it," Lady Rosamund muttered, after the headman and his bearded hunters had gathered their cross-bows and blunderbusses and taken their leave. She touched the raven braids at her temples, the gold pins—the only reminiscence of her girlhood—glinting in the sable flood. "Cows may graze upon the bank, but they do not presume to pass judgment upon the dolphins."

"Oh, I don't know." Antryg unfolded his long arms and came forward into the room. "You're presuming a little about cows: have you ever asked one for her opinion about dolphins? Or anything, for that matter? I knew a Whisperer in Pretty Creek once who claimed to be able to converse with cows, though she said on the whole their conversation was extremely boring and morally unedifying . . . though not, she said, as unedifying as cats'. Aunt Min . . ."

He bowed to her, and she left off fussing about, trying to reach her knitting basket, to look up at him.

"Antreges." She used the softened diminutive as Suraklin had. "The abominations out in the woods . . . you should know of them."

"As it happens," he said, bowing in a great sweep of coat skirts and shawl, "I've been working at a way of stabilizing the field so the situation won't worsen—as it has been doing—and so all things will remain in place while a thorough search can be made, not only of the Vaults but of the Citadel itself and of the countryside around. The nexus of the trouble may be in the Vaults, but since energy is transmitted instantaneously along all the ley-lines—as Trukild was saying, abominations are appearing in the woods north of the village, so obviously . . ."

"No," Rosamund said, her voice like chipped flint.

"This is balderdash," Daurannon stated, after a quick glance through the papers he had snatched from Antryg's hand. "These aren't even real spells, the energy isn't grounded off . . ."

"What exactly are you looking for?" Bentick demanded in a voice that bordered on shrillness, and his long fingers quivered as they sought the watch about his neck. Though the Steward had been twitchy for as long as Antryg had known him—well over twenty years—since yesterday his dark eyes had acquired a haunted look, and he'd picked up the trick of glancing nervously around the room. The result of seeing a boy whom he'd taught slaughtered horribly before his helpless eyes? Antryg wondered. Of learning that his own powers could fail? Or from some other cause?

Antryg replied airily, "Oh, I'm afraid I won't know that until I see it."

"I daresay." Daurannon studied his face for a long moment, the sheaf of papers held so that their raggedy edges touched his cupid lips. Then Aunt Min stretched forth one shaky, blue-veined hand, and almost unwillingly, the younger mage passed the papers on to her. His eyes never left Antryg's. "And I suppose you're to head up this search and have access to everything that's found?"

Over Aunt Min's shoulder, Lady Rosamund said quietly, "I can't let you do this. I've never seen power-circles like those in my life, you have no idea what they'll do."

Antryg regarded her with limpid innocence in his gaze. "*I* do." He turned back to Daurannon. "Well, that *is* why you brought me here."

"The Council voted to bring you here," replied the Handsome One with icy precision, "for your advice on the problem, not to permit you to rummage through every secret in the Citadel's Vaults. There are things down there even the Archmage no longer understands—but that Suraklin, or his student, might well have been waiting for years to get his hands on."

"Come with me, then," Antryg said cheerily. "All of you come with me."

"I take it," put in Lady Rosamund, looking up from the scribbled papers like a queen cornered by a barbarian in a sacked palace, "that you came here to ask the Archmage to actually execute these spells of yours."

"Well," Antryg pointed out, "I'd be delighted to do it myself, but the geas has made that rather difficult."

"I should say rather," Daurannon murmured, "that some member of the Council should head up the search, and that whatever is found is reviewed by the Council as a whole before being passed along to you."

"An excellent suggestion!" Bentick said, rather too quickly, Antryg thought, but then, the Steward had always distrusted him and had probably been one of the original dissenting votes about bringing him here in the first place. "That way disruption could be kept to a minimum."

"Disruption?" Antryg's eyebrows vanished into the curly mop of his hair. "You don't consider novices being eaten by monsters in the Vaults sufficient disruption, to say nothing of everyone having to do their own milking and weed pulling? It is a splendid idea, Daur, except that it won't work. I need to be in the Vaults, and I need to see everything—*everything*—that is found."

"Because we have only your word on what is important?"

"*That* was the entire reason you dragged me here," Antryg retorted. "Because you *do* have only my word—my word or nothing. And personally, I would just as soon have this done as quickly as possible, because not only is the situation in the Vaults deteriorating, but the geas isn't the most pleasant thing in the world to live with . . ."

"You speak as if you feel you have some sort of right to be released from the geas afterward," Bentick said. His dark eyes, which had flickered back and forth from face to face during the discussion, with an anxiety very unlike his usual bossy self, turned cold and prim again. "As if you think that it will be your right to go free . . ."

*"THEN KILL ME!"* Antryg cried passionately, shaken suddenly with the cumulative effects of fatigue and dream-racked, unhealing sleep. The three wizards fell silent, moving back a step to close ranks against him, suspicious, hostile, and chill. Among them Aunt Min bent calmly over the jumble of notes in her hands, shuffling them and letting them fall from her grip to float like huge, lazy yellow leaves around her chair as if none of this matter concerned her. Not, Antryg reflected, that he was foolish enough to think for a moment that she wasn't paying attention to every word uttered.

After a moment he drew breath and went on, "But not until the field has been stabilized and the entire Citadel, from turrets to Vaults, searched. If the central Gate, be it the Moving Gate or some other we don't know about, is not located and closed, the situation will worsen until . . . I don't know what. You know that. I know you know it. If you want to kill me afterward, go ahead—in fact, if you're planning to leave the geas on me I'll probably reach a point where I'd rather you did— but *don't stop me from doing this*. And please," the deep, flexible baritone dropped almost to a whisper, "please let Joanna go."

"She isn't here," Daurannon replied, with equal softness, his face like some ancient mask of a beautiful god.

There was silence. Then, into it, like the chirp of an insect, Aunt Min murmured, "Hmmm . . . power." She shuffled the papers in her hands again, then let half of them slide off her knees to the floor while she blinked appraisingly up at the tall figure before her, like a shabby and degenerate iris in his purple coat. "Channeled . . . illusion . . . interesting. Was it Suraklin who taught you to see power in this fashion?"

Antryg bent quickly to pick up the drifted sheets from the floor. "No, actually it was Wilbron of Parchasten's studies of optics and refraction, and a mad kitchen witch in Pretty Creek who held conversations with the stones of her hearth.''

Aunt Min nodded interestedly, though Lady Rosamund's lips compressed with scorn and annoyance to cover her concern. "It will take all of a day," the Archmage continued. "Yes, the accomplishment of it must come at midnight, so that the power of the day will rise up into it. The North Hall of the Cloister here is on the Vorplek Line."

"It lies directly above the Basin Chamber on the seventh level," Antryg said. "The spell-circles need to be aligned with the Dead—er, with my friend Ninetentwo's machines in the Vaults in order to establish the field. I'll need to consult with him and establish the times exactly. The alignment needs to be precise. Everything depends on the spells' balance, or the whole thing will collapse before it starts."

"Yes," she murmured, rocking a little in her chair. "Yes, I see that." Behind her, Daurannon mouthed *nonsense* and Bentick fiddled with his watch. In the clear, shadowless whiteness of the Council chamber's light, Antryg was interested to see that a film of sweat had sprung out on the old man's high, balding head.

"I can't let you do this to yourself," Lady Rosamund said, laying a protective hand on the skinny shoulder before her. "The energy needed to establish these spells is too much for your body to bear. Let me do it. God knows, I understand what he seems to think are the principles . . ."

"You're willing to put that much of your power into a rite you don't even understand?" Daurannon's eyebrows shot up and he glanced, speculatively, across at Antryg again. "One of Suraklin's spells, most like?"

"Pish." Aunt Min slapped her pupil's hand dismissively, then, to take the sting out of it, patted it like a grandmother. "It has been a long time, Rosie, since I've worked a truly new spell, let alone a spell as great as this one . . . Now, don't argue with me! Always arguing . . ." She clicked her tongue and looked vaguely around for her knitting basket and cane.

Antryg picked up the basket, which lay beside her chair. She shoved the notes into it, dislodging a shower of yarn, needles, and crochet hooks that clattered on the marble floor. As Antryg collected them, Lady Rosamund handed Min her cane and began to lead her to the door, the old lady moving with painful, brittle slowness and leaning heavily on the younger one's arm.

They were still arguing about who was going to perform the unknown spells.

Nearly a century ago, the stories went, Minhyrdin the Fair had thrown a chamber pot at the Emperor's First Minister, who'd been sent to bribe her away from the then-Prince. Like a mad fairy, they had said; she had caused riots in taverns that spread through half the dock quarters, had accumulated one fortune by the age of nineteen and spent another.

And then one day she'd met old Tiamat the White, Archmage of the Wizards of the West.

Antryg reached under the carved oak chair for a last crochet hook; when he straightened up, arms full of balls of silk and hanks of unwoven wool, Daurannon still stood before him, arms akimbo and face smooth and unreadable as ever. "And I suppose," Daur said, "while we're searching the Vaults, and the Citadel, and all the countryside 'round about, you'd like us to collect tortoises for you, too?"

"Would you?" Antryg beamed. "I doubt you'll find many at these latitudes, but you know, that would be the first time I could assemble enough from a single geographical area to get some idea of how various segments of encoded knowledge are distributed—once I decode them, of course. Thank you. I appreciate that."

Turning from his former friend's disgusted gesture, he saw Seldes Katne, who had lingered all this time near the doorway, almost pushed aside by Bentick as the Steward hastened from the room. The old man's black robe billowed behind him, vanishing into the dimness of the hall as he passed the two women and disappeared at a run.

Once a thief broke into the house of Pipin the Little, Archmage of the Council, and stole a talisman of garnets, a golden chain, and a glass ball. But on that night, the thief's woman and several others at the inn she owned fell down deadly sick; and when the thief tried to prise loose the garnets from the talisman, the chisel slipped and cut his hand to the bone; and when he tried to melt down the chain, the crucible broke and burned him sorely, and set fire to the inn. He returned all the things to Pipin, laying them upon his doorstep and running away, and for long after that no thief in Angelshand would enter the places where the mages lived.

—GANTRE SILVAS
*Annals of the Mages*

# CHAPTER XIII

THE DEAD GOD WAS WAITING FOR HIM IN THE BASIN CHAMBER, a hulking shape that seemed to unfold itself like a skeletal flower out of the rock and shadows as he entered.

"There are fearsome things down there," Ninetentwo said, gesturing with two of his huge, clawed hands toward the doors at the chamber's far end. From the stairways beyond rose strange smells of wet stone, acrid mosses, and queer, unidentifiable, ozonous wildness. Another clawed hand touched the black loaf of the multiscanner. "Water is flowing down into the lower levels, seemingly seeping from the stones themselves in places. My readings show a sharp increase in the number of wormholes, energy fields, and Gates. I fear the randomization is accelerating still further."

"I've been working on that," Antryg replied cheerfully. "At precisely midnight tomorrow . . . Do your people have digital watches? Excellent! At precisely midnight tomorrow Aunt Min will put into being a spell to cause the xchi-particle energy in the stones of the Citadel to behave temporarily like electromagnetic energy, so that it can be polarized into a stable

182

field and we can finally search the place from top to bottom and see what we've got."

The Dead God made a rumbling noise of disapproval deep in his enormous chest but apparently found even the starting point, let alone the conclusion, of the argument too alien for quibbling.

"I don't suppose your multiscanner would register fields of energy as well as Gates in the Void, would it? It would save us considerable time."

"Some types it does, some it doesn't." Ninetentwo unslung the black rectangle of the sensor from one shoulder, and its small screen gleamed flatly in the pale light of his forehead nodule. "Personally, I should hesitate to trust my life to any information this gives once the Vaults are blanketed in a polarization field of any kind. I have moved my equipment through the Gate into this world and, I hope, sufficient batteries to run it should the Gate close again. But there are pocket fields wherein neither the batteries nor the equipment, nor this," he touched the massive weapon that hung strapped to his back, "will work at all. Should such a field manifest itself around me at the operative time . . ."

"Yes, that could get awkward." Antryg scratched the side of his long nose and viewed the masses of electronics stacked, like the basalt blocks of the ancient wall of Ygron, near the frozen black slit of the chamber's far door. In addition to the sword he'd found—conveniently abandoned—in the cellar of the Harlot, he carried a torch, more for a weapon than for illumination; its yellow light played uneasily over the hard edges, the sightless eyes of the now-darkened gauges and the blank, idiot faces of empty monitor screens. A dragon tail of cables stretched through the door and away into the impenetrable dark of the maze.

Slung over one shoulder he carried breathing equipment and the silver-chloride spray pump, which had, as he'd suspected, not only made visible but incapacitated the haunters that had attacked him again on the fourth level. He had left the hideous things flopping like gross, misshapen wasps on the stone floor and descended the switchbacks of the stairs, water trickling in a thin stream beside his feet.

"Pity about the multiscanner," he went on, turning to install the torch in one of the chamber's crude sconces. "We're going to have to act quickly once the field is activated if we're to have sufficient time to dismantle the balance between Circles of Power and the oscillators rather than let them fall into random decay. Given the energies at large in the Citadel, I'm not entirely certain what would happen, but it probably wouldn't be pleasant. Once your equipment is set up, we'll have to put a guard around this chamber."

"Not this chamber." The Dead God moved his great head, iridescent eyes flashing as he gestured toward the far door. "The water is rising: if the wormholes through which it is leaking are open when the field stabilizes, this chamber is too deep for safety"

"True enough," Antryg murmured, and his stomach flinched at the sudden image of Joanna, trapped in some pitch-dark cell, despairingly watching water trickle in under the door. He thrust the thought from him even as he felt the sweat start on his hands. *The multiscanner would have registered something.*

"The Chamber of the Glass Pillar, then," he said quickly. "It's on the fourth level directly above this—that will still put us immediately beneath the North Hall. How long will it take you to set up?"

"Three hours, four hours."

"Splendid! With both fields synched into the ley-lines . . ."

His voice must have quickened with his nervousness, or else the Dead God, usually cold-bloodedly phlegmatic, was more sensitive than Antryg had given him credit for. For after a moment's silence, the monster laid one tarantulate lower hand on Antryg's sleeve and said, "I have taken two other multiscan readings at different frequencies and from different points.

Never has human presence shown up that could not be accounted for by those who patrolled seeking you.''

Antryg drew a deep breath and let it out, trying to expel with it his awareness of dark waters rising and the poisoned images of his dreams. ''And I expect they'll be seeking me again as soon as our Daur realizes I've disappeared.''

''Here.'' With a thin shearing of Velcro, the Dead God stripped a timepiece from one of his arms and held it out. The maggotlike tentacles of his palm, wrapped around the square lozenge of black and gray, gleamed moistly in the torchlight. ''I had thought that we might synchronize electronically, but with the shifting of the energy fields, I find that radio beams do not always pass.''

''Marvelous stuff, Velcro.'' With a certain amount of difficulty, Antryg fastened the timepiece around his own far thinner wrist, his quick movements concealing the nervous tremor of his hands. The Dead God watched him with that great dragonlike head tilted a little to one side, the opaque eyes and rigid, leathery skin stretched tautly over the bones impossible to read.

''If I could figure out a way to manufacture it here, I should be able to retire from magic-working completely—not that I haven't been compulsorily retired, at least for the time being, but never mind. I suppose the High Council would never let me get away with it, or peanut butter, either.'' Antryg patted his pockets to assure himself that his spare oxygen bottle was safe and hitched the breathing tubes up over his shoulder where he could easily get to them.

''I will have the equipment ready and attached to batteries, at your hour of midnight tomorrow,'' the Dead God promised. ''Not that I have the smallest belief that it is possible for you to do what you say you are going to do, but I will do as you ask as if it were.''

''Thank you.'' Antryg took the torch from its holder and held it aloft, the Dead God's grotesque shadow curtsying hugely across the black faces of pillar and wall. "It is all anyone ever needs do."

After seeing the Dead God back to the slit of blackness that marked the Gate of his own universe, Antryg stayed until past midnight searching the lowest levels of the Vaults. In his heart, he suspected that the alien physicist was right and that Joanna was imprisoned elsewhere, yet he could not rid himself of the dread that he might be wrong. To his horror and grief, he had been wrong before.

In places the coiled black tunnels were knee-deep in water, the surface curling with faint ribbons of steam; in other places, waist-deep or deeper, where small stairways led randomly upward and downward, or the floors underfoot slanted, or gave way suddenly to unexplained pits and traps.

In a broad corridor, flooded shoulder-deep and thick with choking mists, he called her name outside a locked door written over in ancient runes, the flame of his torch sinking in on itself in the woolly vapors and his deep voice echoing across the broken yellow reflections of the water's surface. If a Gate opened in the cell with her, he thought, she might very well flee through to save herself, into God knew what other universe, and then she would truly be gone.

The mosses that padded the ceiling in a wet quilt of orange and purple seemed to pucker and shift at the sound of his voice; a moment later, a low, rolling bow wave lifted the slick surface of the water near him, and he felt something huge glide past his legs, the water bubbling thickly in its wake. He shuddered, wishing there were several of Joanna's favorite cinema films he hadn't seen.

In the end he had to be satisfied that Joanna was neither on the ninth level nor the eighth. He retrieved his coat, shawl, and boots, and climbed, dripping wet and bone-weary, up the spiraling vent shafts toward the stores-cellars far above. There was a little room downstairs from the main pantry where he could spend the night, cut into the rock of the hill's eastern face but open, save for a light lattice, across one side.

But even as he turned toward the minor stair that led there, another thought came to him.

It was well past midnight now—like most wizards, he could feel that in his bones. Carefully secreting his sword, spray gun, extinguished torch, and breathing apparatus behind some oil jars, he ascended noiselessly to the kitchen and began to work his way through the hidden byways of the Citadel toward the house they called the Castle, over on the north side of the hill, where Phormion the Starmistress lived.

The trapdoor between the cellar of the Castle and that of the Sea Lady's House—the tiny dwelling that Pentilla River-wych and old Idrix of Thray shared—was barely twelve inches wide and a yard high; a heavier man than Antryg, or a less limber one, could never have made it. The Castle's cellar ran deep into the hill and was filled, mostly, with bins of wood and coal whose fusty odor caught at the back of Antryg's throat. There was a huge brick furnace there, to warm the hypocaust beneath the floors during the bitter winters; a long, unrailed stone stairway ran up one wall, debouching, if Antryg recalled aright, into a sort of tiled hall between Phormion's rooms, Bentick's, and those of the two other mages who shared the place. Even occupied as it was by four Senior mages—pack rats by definition—the Castle, Antryg knew, contained half a dozen unused chambers, tucked away in turrets at the top of winding iron steps or reachable by spidery back stairs concealed in walls.

The trick, of course, would be getting up there. He could feel magic all around him in the cellar, spells of warning, ward, and guard. As far as he could tell there was nothing written on the trapdoor he'd come through; very few people knew of its existence, most preferring to use the passage that led through the lowest floor of Bentick's rooms in the north tower. Still, he supposed, pushing up his glasses onto his nose, the most they could do would be to lock him up for the remainder of the night and have Daur read him a lecture in the morning.

By clambering over the woodpiles, he was able to reach the foot of the stair without touching any of the ward-spells on the flagstoned floor. The ghostlike grayness of a cat poured itself at a startled run up the stairs—one of Bentick's, probably. Ascending undetected himself would be a more difficult matter.

With a faint clanking of the iron latch, he heard the door above him open. A moment later, a whisper of magic drifted upon the air.

Antryg's breath seized as if he'd been struck beneath the ribs by the thrust end of a massive pole; he gasped and caught the wall to keep from falling but felt his knees turn weak. His lungs felt numbed—pain like the jab of a dull knife seared his chest as he tried to fill them.

Darkness covered his eyes, his vision tunneling down to the few square inches of granite stair just before his face, but he heard a footstep at the top of the stair, smelled dirty wool permeated with stale incense and smoke. In the darkness of his blurring mind he heard a hoarse voice whispering death-spells.

Vicious little pains knifed his hands and feet like the bite of snakes as he tried to drag himself up the stairs. The power within him, bound and mute beneath the razor wire of the Council's geas, could have resisted those spells, could have thrown off the burning river of sand that seemed to be filling his lungs, could have flung back counterspells of life and light. His heartbeat sounded huge in his ears, a slow, bucking heave that hurt more on every throb. He had to reach the top of the stairs, he thought blindly. It was fifty feet, surely he could make it up fifty feet.

His arms collapsed under him; he barely felt the ragged pain of his cheek hitting the unrailed stone step. One arm dangled over the edge, and he was queerly conscious of the cold air moving around his hanging fingers. Though the whisper of the death-spells was now very soft, it seemed to fill his mind.

"Stop it!" Another voice, a whisper like the first, inconsequential as the squeaking of bats. The spell shifted a fraction, like a suffocating monster fidgeting its weight. A thread of air leaked into his lungs.

"Let him go!"

"She sent him. He is her cat's-paw. She brought him here that he might do her dirty work, that he might spy and probe . . ."

The spell locked down hard and Antryg cried out a little with the renewed pain. The specks of blinding fire swimming before his eyes blended into one huge slab of killing light.

"Then she'll know if he dies here! Let him go. I'll take care of him . . ."

Air in his lungs. Enough air—he would never, he thought, raise any objections to the smell of coals and mildew again. They were beautiful. Cold granite under his face was beautiful.

The voices were gone. He lay in darkness. He must have blacked out, he thought, gingerly gathering his arms beneath him. If so, he couldn't have been unconscious long, and the owner of the second voice would be back. *I'll take care of him* . . . Aunt Min's protection extended only over those who obeyed her command that he not be harmed, who feared her wrath. Quite clearly, there were those in the Citadel who did not.

Distantly, his straining hearing picked up returning feet, a voice whispering distraitly, "Oh, God . . . Oh, God . . ." He still couldn't stand but was past caring. Pins and needles racked him, seeming to originate somewhere in the marrow of his bones; every muscle trembled as he crawled and stumbled like an intoxicated rag doll across the cellar, dragged himself through the trap while the door at the top of the long steps was still shut. He fell repeatedly as he made his way through the dark byways, coming at last to open air—he barely noticed how he got to the little rock-cut chamber where he was to spend the night.

For a long while he could only lie there, trembling, as his muscles twitched and burned with cramp and his breathing steadied out to its regular rhythm again. It wasn't the first time such spells had been laid upon him—Suraklin had done so twice, the second time to the point where he'd gone into convulsions—but it was the first time he'd been completely unable to meet them with any magic of his own.

For what must have been nearly an hour he lay, looking out through the screen of lattice to the clear, blue-gray twilight that filled the land like an imbuing radiance. White mists drifted over the river; the taiga forest lay black and formless beyond, broken by the chipped brightness of streams; bogs and ponds reflected the queer glow of the sky in shining sheets. Beyond the trees the cleared fields of the village of Wychstanes slept, coarse and shapeless and gray; smoke rising from the long *ibeks* marked the settlement itself. And beyond that, deep in the woods of spruce and hemlock, was the Green King's Chapel, ancient shrine of the Lord of Animals, the Lord of the Trees, back when this whole area had been part of the estate of the Earls Boreal. Daurannon had been investigating reports of abominations there—allegedly—when Rosamund had conjured the power to pass through the Void.

Antryg pulled off his coat and wrapped himself in it, pillowed his head on Aunt Min's shawl. While he'd been in the Vaults, it had rained a little, and the warming ground gave back the smell and dampness, a thick sweet strength in the air. Clouds heaped the southern edges of the sky.

He supposed he ought to seek out Aunt Min immediately. At a guess it was Phormion who had tried to kill him, Bentick who had stopped her . . . But if Bentick was part of a plot with Phormion, why stop her? *Had* Rosamund actually brought him here for some ulterior purpose? It didn't seem terribly likely, considering how little she trusted him, but it might account for her having sent Daur away while she was doing it.

Or by *she*, had they meant Aunt Min?

It was a new thought, and not a comfortable one; and it

would account, he thought, for Rosamund's enmity toward him—not that that wasn't sufficiently accounted for already. But why would Min be using him as a cat's-paw against Phormion, if it was Phormion?

Far above him, against the dark bulk of the Library, a yellow glow of lamplight shone in the dirty glass walls of the Conservatory, marking where Seldes Katne still labored over her piled volumes, searching for references to the teles even as Nandiharrow and Issay sought clues to other magics in the Vaults.

And Joanna was somewhere, imprisoned in this maze of deadly secrets. His every instinct warned him that the longer she remained a prisoner, the more danger she'd be in.

He wondered if it was possible to get to Min's cottage at this hour. Rosamund would flay him for waking up the old lady.

But the ache in his body was like lead wrapped around his bones, and the thought of getting up and doing anything at the moment was more than he could bear. He shifted his head on his makeshift pillow and gazed out over the black pelt of the forest toward the Green King's Chapel again. At length he slept, and though he recalled no dreams, he woke up weeping, with the feeling that some irreplaceable thing had been taken from him during the night.

Tom the gardener found him at breakfast, hard on the heels of a near-riot in the refectory. Antryg, cautious now about dealing with any member of the Council, at least without several other persons present, was consuming muffins and tea in a corner of the kitchen after helping Pothatch stir porridge and cut bacon. Furious shouts drew them up the stairs to the pantry behind the serving-hatches.

Through the broad openings from pantry to refectory, Antryg and the cook saw Brunus, usually the most mild-tempered of men, standing a few feet inside the refectory and screaming at Zake Brighthand, who had just entered. Brighthand rounded on the older student with a perfect spate of amazing and barely comprehensible docker's cant, his thin face twisting with rage. Others—not all of them Juniors—rose from their seats at the long trestle tables and came to the open space before the door to fling themselves into the affray; Daurannon, sitting by the broad windows that overlooked the Polygon's main court, got to his feet and started to break things up but, within moments, was shouting at them all, a situation not alleviated by the arrival of Lady Rosamund on the scene.

"It's a pocket-spell, a field of anger." Antryg grinned at the cook and at Tom, who had just entered from the door that led into the drying-room. The voices were rising, echoing in the big room's scarlet-painted rafters. "Just inside the door, look . . ."

He gestured with his teacup. The Lady, usually frigidly polite to her colleague, was screaming like a fish-hag about "social-climbing little guttersnipes" and "slick traitors who'd sell us all to the Regent for an attic bedroom at Court"; Daurannon in turn abandoned his usual charming mask and made reference to "holier-than-thou aristos who can't stand anyone whose lives they can't run." Both opinions, Antryg was quite well aware, had been expressed privately at other times.

"My guess is it starts about three paces inside the door and runs to the corner of that table where Kyra's standing. Ah! Here comes Bentick. Now, is he going to fly into the fray or try to get them all out of there so the spell can be dispersed . . . ?"

"Will they come, though?" Tom inquired interestedly, folding his arms and cocking his head a little to one side.

Mage, cook, and gardener watched in fascination as the Steward of the Citadel, assisted eventually by Issay Bel-Caire and Sergeant Hathen, coaxed, called, and gestured the assorted combatants away from the open space and in among the tables, where the spell's field did not extend.

"Looks like our Bentick's had a bit of a rocky night," Tom commented, when the show seemed to be over and Pothatch had returned to his tea urns and muffin batter. This was true:

though immaculately shaven and prissy as always, the Steward appeared even more haggard than he had yesterday in the Council chamber and seemed to be scanning every corner of the big, raftered room for something or someone . . . probably, Antryg thought, himself.

"I shouldn't be surprised," Antryg murmured. "Did you happen to see if Aunt Min was about yet?" he added, looking back at the gardener. He knew Min was an early riser and frequently would sit on the terrace of her little cottage to watch the sun rise. If Bentick was here, dispersing the spell-field—which he was doing, assisted by Daurannon and Lady Rosamund, who scrupulously avoided one another's glance—it would be safe to duck over and discuss possible reasons why the Starmistress would want to assassinate anyone who entered the Castle.

Tom shook his head. "I haven't seen her. But there's something I heard, something I thought you ought to know of."

Antryg set his teacup down and regarded more closely the mournful-looking little man in his rough peasant smock and heavy boots.

"See, one of Gru Gwidion's hunters mentioned to me yesterday that he'd heard a woman's voice crying in the Green King's Chapel. When he went near it, he said, he was too afraid to go in. He said it was his instinct warning him that there was something unnatural there, but I know the mages do that: put spells of fear 'round a place if they want to keep us out—me, and the milkmaids, and Pothatch's kitchen help when he's got 'em. And I know you're looking for your lady."

"So I am," Antryg murmured thoughtfully. "The Green King's Chapel." He recalled the blue twilight on the dark woods, the glimpse of bleached stone like bone chips far off among the trees.

More people were coming into the refectory. Sergeant Hathen, posted in the doorway like an usher at a wedding, was warning them to edge around the wall to avoid the three mages at their rites of dispersal.

Out in the courtyard, the great bronze clock in the Assembly Hall tower struck seven. If Aunt Min started her conjurations at noon, thought Antryg, he would still be back in time to assist her throughout the afternoon . . . not that she actually needed it. For all her impersonation of senile vagueness, he had no doubts that she knew precisely what she was doing and would have no trouble following his notes.

And then, after last night's events, the thought of getting out of the Citadel for a few hours wasn't such a bad one, either.

"Kitty will kill me. I did promise I'd help her with the research into the teles-balls, and I've yet to do it. You'll let her know I was called away?"

Tom hesitated for a moment, as if that snagged some thought in his mind, then nodded slowly. "Aye. That is . . ."

Bentick, Daur, and Rosamund lowered their arms with an air of completion; the latter two turned promptly away to seek places at tables in opposite ends of the long room. Bentick made one last scan of the interested faces of the newcomers, then strode in a purposeful billow of black robes toward the serving-hatch to get his morning coffee. Rather hastily, Antryg gulped the last of his tea, shoved two rolls from one of the serving trays into his coat pocket, and said, "Thank you, Tom. You haven't seen me."

The long purple skirts of his coat flicked around the doorway leading down to the kitchen just as the Steward reached the hatch.

The road from the Wizards' Tor to the village of Wychstanes lay straight, following the track of the Brehon Line: on both sides it was marked with eroded and weed-shrouded standing stones of the sort that in more civilized portions of the Realm had been pit-broken or buried. For most of its length the road sank below the level of the surrounding land, rutted—typically for the Sykerst—with gluey runnels of foot-deep mud. Though winds moved the dark roof of spruces overhead, down in the roadbed itself the air was muggy and still, thick with the murky pungence of nearby ponds and the green shaggy scents of the moss that furred the alders and birch. Feathers of gold light played across Antryg's shoulders and face as he picked a way along the drier center of the roadbed between the ruts, the familiar dappling of warm and cool a reminiscence of home. Even the drag of the mud at his boots was a part of those childhood dreams.

*Home. After all these years.*

He had spent his childhood in a village very like Wych-stanes. There were hundreds of them, scattered among the endless forests and stony, rust red hills—villages wherever tiny pockets of earth could be found capable of supporting crops, and all of them much alike. Life in the barnlike *ibeks* could be incredibly crude—he remembered clearly helping his brothers dump fodder down the floor hatches to the animals who lived below and listening, through the long winter nights, to the murmurs, coughing, lovemaking, and drunken arguments of the sixty or so uncles, aunts, stepchildren, and thralls with whom he shared the place—but even as a pariah, he had felt a kind of delighted fascination with the complex life of the village itself.

He smiled a little, his gloved hands thrust deep in his pockets. Suraklin had almost scoured the skin off him trying to get rid of the stench of cow dung and smoke—at the time, he would have skinned himself, had it been possible, knowing the peasant smell displeased the old man. Ever afterward, when his master had been angry with him, he'd had the illogical conviction that the smell of his village clung to him yet—to his flesh, to the very marrow-bones of his soul—displeasing Suraklin still: the first of all the many things about himself that Antryg could never sufficiently change to meet the Dark Mage's standards. Even when, under Suraklin's tutelage of love and abuse, his powers had flourished so that he could call sand-demons to sit like birds on his hands or change the bread on a plate to nightshade from the other side of the room, or strike a man blind or mute or breathless with a word, he had never been good enough.

He shook his head. Coming back to the Sykerst had been like coming home. But as Joanna remarked upon the one occasion they'd driven out to Pasadena to visit her mother, childhood homes had a way of being haunted by the wan ghosts of former selves, and it was disconcerting to turn a corner and encounter them unawares.

But in any case, he thought, pausing to consider the broader sunlight of the village's open fields at the end of the enclosed tunnel of standing stones, taiga laurel, and overhanging trees, in view of Trukild's warnings it would probably not be a good idea to sashay down the main street. If the village still preserved its former patterns of crop rotation—and knowing villages, he would have bet an entire night's tips at Enyart's on it—they'd be plowing the south fields for the spring seeding and letting the north lie fallow. Thus it would behoove him to cut north through the woods around the far end of those fields rather than risk an encounter with potentially irate villagers at this point in time.

Ordinarily, of course, he'd simply have passed through the village under cover of a spell of illusion, and the goodwives washing clothes or plucking chickens in the yards would have mistaken him for the baker's wife with a basketful of loaves. But with the geas . . .

On top of the road bank beside him, a hare started, springing down through the blackberry brambles and away into the willow thickets on the other side of the road. A chaffinch flew up, chirping, and at the same moment Antryg heard the unmistakable stealthy creak of boot leather and the clink of a buckle against the pommel of a knife. A shape moved behind the screen of moss-thick alders . . . two shapes . . . a bead of sunlight glinted on the stock of a hunter's gun.

Out of sheer reflex Antryg formed the words of illusion in his mind, the illusion of a mangy brown tomcat; it had to be

Gru and his hunters, they'd know if there were an odd tree or clump of laurel just here.

He was crossing the road away from their path when he realized the geas still should have been in force upon his mind.

But none of them—and there were six in all, four of them with crossbows, two with old-fashioned, bell-mouthed muskets—did more than glance at him, and he knew by the angle of their heads that those who did saw nothing more than a cat. Even his boot tracks in the deep mud of the lane they saw as the light, rounded stars of cat pugs.

Then they were gone.

Antryg let out his breath, shaken with astonishment and, in spite of himself, delight.

For a long moment he hesitated, uncertain; then he held out one big hand and called to the palm of his ink-stained mitt a small ball of blue light, the lowest-level magic he could think of that did not involve potentially dangerous elements like fire or wind. When it appeared, he tossed it joyfully into the air, spun it on the tip of one finger, and slam-dunked it out of sight into the trees. He knew exactly what had happened.

He had walked into one of those small zones such as had formed within the Citadel, pockets where the Void had leaked the aberrant magics of other universes, universes where magic had different rules, different strengths.

The urge to call some greater magic, some wild pyrotechnic of joy, was almost overwhelming—it was like trying not to gasp in air after emerging from minutes underwater. But that, he knew, could be appallingly dangerous, particularly here on the Brehon Line; he only hoped the tiny dot of blue light wasn't triggering a field of darkness, or the spontaneous transportation of perfectly innocent people, elsewhere on the Line. Keeping the magic down to the smallest possible level, he called another tiny, heatless star to his palm, walked backward until it flickered desperately and disappeared, walked forward again—in a fair imitation of John Cleese's Minister of Silly

Walks—until it reappeared and then, in fifteen of his own erratic strides, sputtered and vanished once more.

Still no untoward side effects or, at least, none in his own vicinity. This pocket must be from a world whose magic operated much the same as it did in this one. Jumping cautiously over the cart rut and climbing the northern road bank in the scrambling track of Gru's hunters, he waded through the thick curls of buckler fern and bracken for perhaps another thirty feet before the glowworm brightness once again died.

He stood still, thigh-deep in a pool of blackberry brambles, hearing no sound but the whisper of the spruce and the pounding of his own heart.

It would take him an hour and a half to reach the Green King's Chapel, perhaps that long to return to the Citadel and find an unguarded scrying-stone of sufficient strength to get through whatever spells of guard had been established around Joanna's prison. Provided, of course, spells of scrying wouldn't result in fire or flood or lightning—though, if the magic of this field was similar, they should be fairly safe. And provided Daurannon or Bentick didn't take it into their heads either to stop him or accompany him back.

And on the other hand, Joanna might simply be at the Green King's Chapel.

"Dammit," he muttered, "this place might not even *be* here tomorrow." He glanced around him, taking note of the dead and leaning trunks of two alders—covered thick with shaggy green moss—that bounded one corner of the zone, and the zone's relation to three boulders he'd known from years ago, which he'd always privately described as Aunts Tilly, Milly, and Dilly Having Tea. As he moved off once more, northeastward toward the brighter afternoon sun beyond the pines, where the village fields lay, he held out his hand in a last futile effort to summon the star glimmer to his palm. But nothing appeared—only the sliding, illusory coin of wind-fluttered sunshine.

"Ah, well, easy come, easy go."

He heard the voices of the hunters again as he skirted through the elder thickets, haw, and horsetails that bounded the north fields: "It's laired near here—we've all seen its tracks."

"Splendid," Antryg murmured, propping his glasses on his nose and wishing he had at least enough magic to keep the mosquitoes off him. "Wolf or bear, I wonder? Or will I be really lucky and walk into the latest abomination?"

He spent the next half hour cautiously making his way through the thicker vegetation that divided the woods from the soft brown earth shawled now with a velvet of tender green. The mud in the fields would show his tracks if he cut across them; moreover, he recalled how Suraklin had sometimes put his own perceptions into the eyes of birds, as a means of looking for people—usually other mages—whom he could not track with a scrying-crystal.

Joanna at the Green King's Chapel.

The pentacle on the cards: the sign of earth.

A woman's voice crying.

Fear-spells.

*Whoever has done this to her . . .*

The Green King's Chapel lay silent and deserted in the dappled brightness of late-morning light. The ancient god of its dedication had been among the most popular of the old deities, and his worship had lasted long—indeed, there were places in the Sykerst where on certain nights the villagers still drove their livestock in procession down the long aisle of the witch-paths by moonlight, dragging the effigy of the Green King's sacrificed body upon a cart. The chapel itself, though long roofless, was a solid ring of stone, its eight high windows nearly obscured by the secondary wall of ivy that had grown over the original granite. Against the leathery green of last year's leaves, patches of new growth sparkled parakeet-bright; Antryg could have spread out his hand and not covered one of the larger leaves, and the twining stems were bigger around than his wrist.

There was no sound but a dove's soft mutter and the liquid reply of a cuckoo deeper in the trees.

Antryg moved in a complete circuit of the chapel, pausing frequently to shut his eyes and listen. No sound of human breath, no smell of human food or human waste . . . none of the uneasy silences that arise among animals when a human being is near. True, he thought, Joanna's prison was spelled against scrying, and there were ways of covering from nearer scrutiny as well.

He moved in for a closer look. His crooked fingers brushed the ivy, then worked through to the stonework beneath. The only spells on the building had been laid decades ago. They were fading now, with the scouring winters and thick-breathed summer heats, with the passage of beasts and insects to and fro: the scraping of the world's life against the counterflow of old magic.

And they had not been fear-spells to begin with.

Like everything else, the doorway was overgrown with ivy. Squirming his tall, skinny frame through, Antryg found himself in the open ring of the chapel's uneven floor, of which only a few moss-clotted tombstones remained. Salmonberry and fireweed were waist-high in places under the pallid sunlight; the granite of the altar had not seen sacrifice for almost three hundred years; the entrance to the crypt gaped to the sky.

"How very odd," he murmured, and picked his way carefully down the narrow, foot-runneled stairs.

Foxes startled and scrambled in the moist darkness of the crypt; an opossum shrank back among the ivy roots, staring at him with a white, pointed face and lunatic eyes. By the smell of it the Sacred Well still held water. The place would be a whining inferno of mosquitoes in less than a month.

But Joanna had never been here. Nor had anyone else, for years.

Antryg stood for a few moments, resting his hands on the crumbled lip of the well curb, the heavy earth smell of the place weighting his lungs, listening deeply and ever more deeply to the underground stillness around him and to the wild ringing of every alarm bell his mind possessed.

Tom had lied.

Or someone had lied to Tom.

Or someone had set up the illusion of fear-spells, the illusion of a woman's voice . . . Or someone had stopped Tom on the road this morning and touched his hand, looked into his eyes and planted there the belief that he'd talked to one of Gru Gwidion's hunters yesterday who'd given him that story.

It was something Suraklin had done all the time; Antryg had done it, too, and not only in the Dark Mage's service.

To get him out of the Citadel?

Quite clearly . . . So that he'd be well away from Aunt Min's protection and less likely to be found than he had been last night? Or simply so he wouldn't have a decent account of his doings and whereabouts for four or five hours?

"Dammit," he said aloud, his voice echoing in the deeps of the well. "I'm getting a little tired of . . ."

"A little tired of what?" demanded a cold, sweet voice from the crypt stairs behind him. He swung sharply around in a swirl of patched coat skirts; she stood in the bar of sunlight like an obsidian lily, her hands folded before the buckle of her belt. She'd tucked up the long skirts of her robe, revealing seven or eight inches of soft boot leather and the dark blue fringe of the undertunic beneath; her black hair was braided back for easier traveling, and without its usual frame of glossy curls, the exquisite bone structure of her oval face stood out more clearly. The light shining through the new leaves of the ivy was not greener than her eyes.

"Well," said Antryg, breaking into a smile of relieved delight, "of being followed, for one thing. I'm extremely happy to see you, Rosie. You didn't really think I'd run away, did you?"

"So long as the Council's geas lies upon you, no." She looked chillingly down upon him as he walked back to the steps. "I know that if you flee, you will perforce return."

"Well, for food, if nothing else," he agreed mildly. "Did you follow me for a tête-à-tête—or as they say in Los Angeles, a one-on-one? Or did you just not want to have breakfast in the same room with Daur, after your little altercation this morning?"

She stood looking down at him for a moment, her head silhouetted against the hard robin egg blue of the sky. Then she said, "I followed you to ask that you let me perform these rites of energy you have designed, instead of Aunt Min."

The steely coldness of her voice was a shield, and in it Antryg heard clearly that she would far rather have cut his throat than ask him for even the slightest favor. Softly, he said, "Ah," and then was silent for a time.

"I think the spells themselves are ridiculous and won't work—but they will draw a great deal of power. She isn't strong, Antryg. She hasn't been well." She handed the words to him like bleeding pieces of her own flesh and waited, green eyes watchful as cold stars, for his reply.

"Violets always grew well here, up behind the altar," Antryg said at last and ascended the stairs past her into the sky-circled arena of the chapel above. "The Duchess of Purlex used to candy them whole and make a syrup from the leaves which relieved kennel cough in her dogs."

Her ladyship at his heels, he sprang lightly up onto the lumpy dais, where the block of granite, its carvings hammered nearly away by centuries of winter, still stood under the ruins of its ancient canopy. Kneeling, he reached behind the altar, and found, as he had in years past, the shadowy space behind thick with them. "It's a bit late in the season for really good ones, but they say that if a girl places them beneath a young man's mattress at the dark of the moon and recites his name three times, he will be drawn to love her as the moon waxes—which gives her a clear two weeks to fix her interest. Presumably after the full she's on her own. Would you like some?"

He held out the bunch to her, queer little fairy-faces of plum and blue and white in their nest of leaves. She disdained to touch them, or perhaps to take any gift from his hand.

"No? I'll take them back to Kitty. Sometimes I think no one ever *did* give her violets in the spring, which is a great shame." He perched on the edge of the altar and fished in his pocket for a rubber band to tie the stems together. "I take it you came after me because Auntie told you not to be a mother hen?"

"They're your spells. You could find some reason why they would be better done by me."

Antryg braced his shoulder against the heavy trunks of the ivy in the chapel doorway, pushing them aside for the Lady with his free arm and one boot. She bent to step through, holding her skirts up. Though she had left the heliotrope stole of her Council rank back at the Citadel, she still moved through the woods like a cold-eyed queen.

"You think she'd believe me?"

His only answer was the bitter resentment in her eyes.

Catching one boot-toe under a pinecone and flipping it through the sunlit air, he said, "Rosamund, she wouldn't be who she is if she didn't revel in something new; in seeing if she couldn't make spells that are ridiculous and chaotic and against all the laws of physics and logic and orthodox magic actually work anyway. You know that."

"I know that *you* know that," she replied quietly. "And that you've always known how to charm her." Her rose-petal mouth hardened into a brittle line. "Or was that your intent?"

"What, to weaken my strongest supporter?"

"To weaken the linchpin of the geas."

Behind the massive lenses his rain-colored eyes were grave. "I think you're not giving either of us very much credit."

"Credit doesn't matter much to me in the face of . . . of losing her." Her voice shivered a little on those words, then turned sharp and silvery again. "And why aren't you back there helping her, at least?"

A wide grin split his face. "Because under the conditions

of the geas all I'd be able to do is get under her feet, and I didn't want to get thwacked with her cane. I came here looking for Joanna; I'd heard some rather curious news . . ."

"You still insist that one of the Council kidnapped her?" Rosamund cut in impatiently, lengthening her stride through the whispering lace of the bracken. "That one of the Council is behind the chaos in the Vaults?"

Antryg shrugged. "Well, I've tried hard to come up with a reason why Ruth would lie to me about seeing a wizard. She's generally a very truthful woman, Ruth—except, of course, when she's standing dripping wet with a towel about her telling someone over the telephone that she's just leaving the apartment that minute to meet them for lunch."

"Then why hasn't that person contacted you? Why hasn't there been some demand made, some threat, some exchange?" Her eyes narrowed in the fleeting splinters of the filtered sun. "Or have they?" she added softly. "*If* there is a renegade in the Council—other than yourself, that is—are you working for him already?"

Antryg paused and pushed his spectacles up onto the bridge of his long nose. The gleam of a knife in the moonlight returned to him, the retreating swirl of a long black robe around the closing door of the passage into the Pepper-Grinder's upper chamber . . . the crush of death-spells on his lungs. *She sent him. He is her cat's-paw* . . . And then there was the whole curious matter of Tom's story that morning.

"I'm not, of course," he said. "But that has begun to puzzle me. Even if my being under the geas put a glitch of some kind in their plans, one would think they'd at least use Joanna to discourage my investigations. And I may hear yet. But it seems a very awkward arrangement."

He moved off again, the Lady stumbling a little with her lesser experience of rough walking but drawing her hand aside from his offer of help.

"Holding anyone captive *is*, you know," he added. "Unless one has an accomplice, though of course for wizards it's easier because one can use spells to keep the captive quiet. I suppose it's conceivable that if our hypothetical kidnapper is on the Council, he or she is strong enough to transform Joanna into a canary, which would solve a lot of logistical problems. Has Phormion or Bentick recently acquired an unaccounted-for canary? Though of course I doubt it's possible to transform Joanna into a canary. A cat, on the other hand, would pass almost completely unnoticed.''

Lady Rosamund's mouth flexed in exasperation. "Can you truly see Bentick violating his vows so comprehensively? Or Nandiharrow? Or Issay, or Phormion . . . ?"

"Someone violated their vows badly enough to try to murder me last night,'' he said, and Rosamund's eyes widened with what appeared to be quite genuine shock.

"Who?''

"I don't know. I couldn't see. It happened beneath the Castle, so it could have been either Bentick or Phormion, but considering the number of tunnels which run through there it could just as easily have been our boy Daur. Whoever it was seemed to think . . .''

Like the stinging crack of a whipstroke, the heavy, flat roar of a musket smote the air, followed at once by the acrid stink of powder. Lady Rosamund cried out and fell, clutching the spreading patch of dark red wetness that splattered suddenly from the torn flesh of her thigh, and from the woods behind them a voice yelled, "There they are!"

Better to sleep among wolves than in a wizard's house.

—Sykerst proverb

# CHAPTER XIV

ANTRYG CAUGHT THE LADY IN HIS ARMS AS SHE FELL.
Though her eyes were shut, there was consciousness, if not
strength, in the arm she flung around his neck; he took a running leap down a broken dip of ground, ducked into a thicket
of moss-choked alder and blackberry bramble, then immediately slipped toward the shelter of a small outcropping of boulders forty feet away, running half-crouched in the waist-deep
jungle of fern.

"You see it?" yelled a man somewhere, and another replied, "Two of them, it looked like . . ." "That big gray one
with the three white paws . . ." "You see any blood? I swear
I hit one . . ."

"Stopping the bleeding . . . best I can," gasped Rosamund's voice, scarcely a breath in his ear. "Cold . . . dear
God, so cold . . ."

"Can you hold a cloaking-spell around yourself at the same
time?" Antryg shed Aunt Min's seedy old shawl for her to lie
on, slipped out of his patched, tawdry coat to cover her, and
hastily ripped a strip from its lining to tourniquet her leg. Ferns

and horsetails grew thick about the boulders, offering them minimal cover; with luck the men would beat the thicket and pass by this less obvious place.

The dark head moved against the dull rainbow of tangled color. Her lips already had a grayish cast; in spite of his makeshift dressing, she was losing blood. If she went into shock or lost consciousness, he thought, she was through.

"Hold on," he breathed and broke cover, darting through the ferns with the golden blades of late-morning sunlight sparkling on his earrings and beads. Another musket roared— they'd had time to reload—and with a snarling, woody twang the steel-and-hornbeam shaft of a crossbow appeared in a tree trunk inches from his shoulder. He remembered that, when they hunted predators, Gru Gwidion and his hunters put datura on their arrows; with no magic at his disposal it wouldn't take more than a scratch to kill him.

Another arrow flashed in the sunlight. Leaping like a scared deer, Antryg cut through the fern and spruce needles of the soft forest floor, the hunters in full pursuit. They knew the woods as well as he did—better, for their experience was fresh and not something half-forgotten for nine or ten years. In any case he couldn't think of losing them yet. They were still far too close to Lady Rosamund's hiding place.

Three spells, he thought, springing down a vine-choked streambed and scrambling up the other side. A major healing-spell to keep blood loss and shock at bay, a cloaking spell to turn aside the eyes of searchers, and a summoning to whomever she could think of in the Citadel . . . No wonder the Lady could spare nothing for direct action against her attackers. The musket roared again, and the leaves of the hawthorn brake into which he dived shuddered as if smote with a whip. *That'll teach her to put potential defenders under geas.*

He crawled through the thick cresses near the streambed as far as he dared, then showed himself again, drawing them after him; Gru Gwidion yelled something about ". . . big gray with three white paws.'' The identical repetition of the words snagged in Antryg's mind, as much as the words themselves.

"Damn," he breathed as he cleared the fallen trunk of an alder, half a jump ahead of another arrow, "I do believe someone's cast a glamour on them and they see me as a wolf."

Glamours were simple enough to cast. Completely illegal, of course, but Suraklin had used them frequently. Antryg recalled the young son of a Kymil merchant, who had shot his own father in mistake for a deer after the father had crossed Suraklin in a business deal . . . recalled another instance when the old wizard had disgraced a woman who had made a fuss about him speaking to her child, by casting a glamour on her that made her believe another man was her husband.

In both instances, Antryg recalled, he himself had helped, though he had known even then it was wrong—and that, he supposed, was a glamour of its own.

He remembered that both victims had later killed themselves. But Suraklin had robbed him even of the courage for that.

The undergrowth was thinner here. Antryg elbowed himself carefully from clump to clump of bracken, trying to stick to ground rocky enough not to show tracks. Had the hunters seen Lady Rosamund as a wolf also? *Glamours cast with a piece of the object's clothing often throw a field,* Suraklin had said, running through his slim fingers the old merchant's long black stockings, which Antryg had stolen from the laundry behind the painted wooden mansion. *People or objects near them become distorted in the subject's mind as well. So take care you keep clear of the old cheat. It's the commonest form of the spell, but crude. I prefer to use the perfume method, myself.*

The men behind him had gone quiet, but with the senses of his wizardry he could reach out and hear them, rustling through the willow thickets, their boots a heavy soughing in the carpet of spruce needles and fern.

Or had Lady Rosamund been the intended victim, himself merely the bait? Whoever had laid the first glamour on poor

Tom, it wouldn't have taken much to get Rosamund to follow him out to the chapel.

The bracken had thinned; the spruces grew thicker here, their needles killing undergrowth and at the same time holding his tracks. Swiftly, cautiously, he slipped from tree to tree, following the bare ground where he could or working his way along the more concealing vegetation that clogged the fast-running, ice-bitter streams. *That zone of magic,* he thought desperately, *had better still be in existence when I get there.*

He made it to within a mile of the rocks he'd called the Three Aunts Having Tea before the hunters spotted him. He'd heard them behind him all the way, now nearer, now farther; the rustle of their bodies in the blackberry brambles and laurel shrubs as they beat the thickets, the cautious, whistling bird-calls of their signals. Now and then, when the wind shifted, he smelled the cow-and-smoke reek of their clothing. So he was half-ready when the creaking snick of a crossbow alerted him and was able to duck and roll; the bolt took a two-inch gash in the leather of his boot, then he was on his feet and running for his life.

He was long-legged and knew the ground; ducking, weaving, clearing boulders and fallen trees like some grotesque gazelle, too taken up with trying not to trip to concentrate on the sounds behind him and praying one of them wasn't lying in wait to head him off. The musket roared, but he didn't see where the ball went, only knew it hadn't touched him. Sunlight on pine straw; squirrels pouring in fleet red streaks up the trunks of trees; a familiar shape of ground, a landmark tree . . .

He stumbled within a yard of the fallen trunk he'd taken as a landmark, and even as he struck the ground, he summoned like a thunderclap the spell for the breaking of the glamour. It crumbled like rotted wood from his numb mind, the geas tightening in smothering pain around his brain and nerves. An arrow caught sunflash like a huge wasp as he stumbled on toward the road, the whiffle of it brushing his torn calico sleeve; he gathered his strength about him and called the spell again.

This time it worked. He felt it, flung it back behind him like a glittering net, praying the magic would work as it should. One of the men yelled, "Son of a bitch!" and someone else, "What the . . ."

Antryg stumbled to a halt, gasping for breath as he dropped to his knees in the pine needles, sweat pouring down his cheeks and aware for the first time of the scratches on his face from holly and bramble, the rips in his shirt, and the bruises on his shoulders and knees.

"Dammit, don't shoot!" he yelled, throwing up his hands. Turning, he saw the men grouped behind him in the thin tangle of bracken, panting also and gazing at him with startled and frightened eyes.

"It's a wizard!" Gru Gwidion said, passing one leather-gloved hand across his eyes. "Lord Antryg . . ."

"*He* was the wolf." One of the hunters raised his crossbow to cover him. "He turned himself into . . . into . . ." His voice stumbled, hesitant. He lowered the weapon again and looked at his leader, puzzled, sweat trickling down his narrow, red-bearded face. "We . . . we was after a wolf. But there ain't been wolves around much this spring. Why'd we think . . . ?"

"No." Antryg got to his feet, brushing the spruce needles from the knees of his jeans, and shook back his long hair from his face. "And I'm sure if you count your sheep, nobody will find any missing."

"No, I—I know none of 'em's missing." Gru Gwidion came forward, uncertainly holding out his hand, his dark face puzzled and a little ashamed behind the tangles of his black beard. "We ain't even had 'em out to the far pastures. But . . . it's like we was all so sure this morning. Like we'd all talked about it yesterday but now, looking back, I don't see how we could."

The others wore that look, too: of men baffled by their own behavior, ashamed, puzzled, wondering how they could have

all done such a thing . . . and on the verge, Antryg knew—
like drunkards finding an ironclad justification for their
binges—of looking for reasons why their actions had to have
been right.

"You were under a spell, all of you," he said quickly. *God,
Daur will kill me for undoing six centuries of careful P.R.*
"You were deceived into thinking that there was a wolf in the
first place, and then, when I happened by—as somebody took
care that I would—into thinking that wolf was me. That's all.
Can any of you remember speaking to a wizard yesterday in
the Citadel?"

Gru scratched his head. Closer to, the smell of him was
stronger, but in an odd way it blended with the green smells
of the moss and the acidic pungence of the nearby bogs, disappearing into the general scents of the woods. "No, I . . . I
don't recall it," he said, looking up at Antryg. The suspicion,
and some of the uneasy, baffled shame, had faded from his
eyes; they were sharp again with the wary cunning of one who
lives by observation. "But if they was a wizard and out to set
a trap, I don't suppose I would recall. I'm damn sorry, my
lord, and in that," he added firmly, with a meaningful glance
back at his men, clumped together and muttering among themselves, "I can speak for us all. But wasn't there two of you? I
swear Cappy here brought down what looked to me then like
another wolf."

"He did," said Antryg grimly. "And she's still back there,
shot badly in the thigh. She was trying to summon the mages
from the Citadel but I don't know if she succeeded . . . ah!"

Distantly, down on the road he heard the swift clatter of
hooves. "Splendid. She'll be in the ferns behind those two
boulders near the first thicket you checked, where the blood
is . . . she may have a cloaking-spell about her and be hard to
see at first . . ."

"Davy, Crim, go on ahead," Gru ordered, signing to two
of his hunters. "There'll likely be some palaver, she needs
help fast."

The red-haired hunter and another shouldered their arms and headed off, flickering swiftly out of sight in the gloom beneath the dark trees. Antryg was already striding to the top of the road bank a few yards away, waving his arms. "Here!" he called out, his deep voice pitched to carry. "Over . . ."

And he stopped. For the riders down in the roadbed were not, as he had expected, Daurannon, Issay Bel-Caire, and a group of sasenna from the Citadel.

Most of them were sasenna, though their traditionally black uniforms were cut in a far more modern style than those of the Council's sworn weapons. Their coats were close-fitting, long-skirted, their black trousers knitted to move silently, easily, with the movements of their wearers. Among them were two riders in the long, blood-colored robes of hasu, Church wizards—Red Dogs—mages who had sworn their services to, and been taught their magic by, the small but powerful Magical Office of the Church itself.

Riding in the lead was a small, lean, broad-shouldered man whose strawy red-blond hair was fading swiftly to colorlessness, a man clothed in narrow-cut gray—coat, trousers, waistcoat—which also bore, small and discreet upon its collar, the many-handed red Sun of the True Faith.

"Damn!" Antryg ducked behind the screen of alder and hemlock even as the riders beneath him drew rein. In two or three bounds he returned to Gru and his remaining men, caught the chief hunter by the elbow and drew the others with a gesture close about them. "Lead them back to Lady Rosamund and get them to help her—they have mages with them—and take her back to the Citadel. She was hit by a stray musket ball when you were out hunting wolves," he added, with a small gesture collecting the magic which still hovered over the spot and casting it, a shining scarf of smoke, across their eyes and certain portions of their minds. "You haven't seen me at all."

*So much*, he thought with an ironic inner sigh, *for not messing about with alien magic, and for keeping one's vows.*

He was out of sight by the time the hunters had gone to the top of the road bank to call out to the riders below.

As a man who had had dealings with most of the representatives of the Inquisition in the Realm of Ferryth at one time or another, Antryg had easily recognized the leader of the party as Yarak Silvorglim, Witchfinder Extraordinary of Kymil and the Sykerst.

"So you weren't ever taught real magic at all?"

"Nonsense, my dear." Magister Magus' slim, velvet-clad arm shifted under Joanna's shoulders where they rested against the wall. "What is real magic? The Academics—the Council Mages—keep a tight monopoly on its teaching, and have for six hundred years hoarded every book and magical implement they can lay hands upon. But my magic, such as it is, is as real as theirs."

Hours had passed . . . days . . . Joanna didn't know. The darkness was unchanged and unchangeable, a black pressure cloaking them in hopeless stillness. Far off she could hear the mad, whispering mutter of the Lady Irina, but though their low voices must have been equally audible to her, she never made the attempt to draw near them. She herself never felt hunger, or thirst, though her throat was sore now from talking to Magister Magus for hours on end.

Yet still she talked. His presence was a lifeline . . . and his throat, she reasoned with a wry inner grin, had to be as sore as hers.

There was nowhere to go, and nothing to do, except talk. There was a kind of conversation even in their silences, an enormous comfort in the little diviner's arm around her shoulders, in the soft *hursh* of his breathing, in the smell of whatever scent steeped his dressing gown and the occasional pressure of his well-kept, slender fingers against hers.

The inaction nearly drove her crazy, but there was, literally, nothing to be done, and even moving around, Joanna guessed, would increase their chances of meeting the *tsaeati*, or something worse. Once, for no reason, she had cried, cried until she was exhausted—cried from terror, and hopelessness, and the certain knowledge that Antryg had met with something he couldn't deal with and would never get them out . . . cried against Magus' shoulder while he'd comforted her with the meaningless words he used to all those rich women who came to him for love-spells and abortifacients and talismans to give success in their endless high-stakes gambling at Court. Later, exhausted and a little ill, it had occurred to her that Magister Magus was probably just as scared as she was. But because they were not and had no intention of being lovers, the bone-deep conventions of the sexes forbade *him* from crying on *her* shoulder.

And so they had talked to keep from thinking about how much time had to have passed in the outer world.

She had talked about Antryg, about her mother and the California real-estate market, about being a nerd in high school, about rerigging an AI cube to accommodate CD-ROM, and about clients who wanted her to design coherent spread-sheets for antiquated CPM systems they'd bought used at Lou & Ernie's Kut-Rate Komputer Korner out in Simi. About the difficulties of incorporating *any* second personality into a life that had heretofore interacted strictly with books, cats, and bulletin boards, let alone something as alien as a man and as random in nature as a wizard.

"For a long time I lived . . . I don't know, very closed in," she said softly. "And I didn't like to be pulled out of that, let alone being kidnapped and having my life in danger. And after that, when I was getting ready to rescue him from the Silent Tower, I made myself learn all this stuff I never even *considered* learning before: how to shoot handguns and rifles and an assault rifle, for God's sake—I took a course in CPR and learned how to make a fire by flint and steel, which is a real bastard, and how to shoot a crossbow. I was just so scared. Scared of what I'd run into, and scared that I wouldn't . . . I wouldn't be able to find him. But the awful thing was—I liked it. But now . . .''

She shook her head. "I keep wondering if I should have done it at all. If knowing him—loving him—is worth . . . this. Risking this . . . this darkness that isn't even death. My life was good without him, I was comfortable and safe."

"My dear," the Magus said softly, "it sounds as if—and please pardon me for my presumption—you're looking for a reason not to need him."

"I *am*," Joanna said desperately. "That is . . . I *don't* need him. Not really, I mean . . .''

"You mean you don't want to need him."

She was silent, feeling by the tightness of her chest, the sudden hurt of her throat, that he spoke the truth. "Him," she said slowly, when she could again control her voice. "Or anyone."

The velvet arm tightened about her shoulders; the light, beautiful voice spoke from the dark. "Why not?"

"Because I'm afraid if I need him I'll screw myself up for him," she replied, with the perfect candor of weariness. "Because I'm afraid I can't think straight around him. Because I'm afraid I'm not doing it right—I'm not being the right kind of person. And mostly because I don't want to need him and then have him leave."

"Ah, Joanna," the little man sighed. "My dear child. Do you really consider yourself that foolish or that weak?"

She shook her head, her face pressed to his shoulder, the smells of orris root and velvet and spermaceti oil filling her nose. She whispered, "I don't know what I am anymore. Not with him. And I'm afraid I'm just acting out of—of some kind of hormonal insanity."

"If love didn't make us insane," the Magus said gently, "who among us would have the courage to step outside the walls we build to protect ourselves against life? I suggest that you not decide in advance. Just as no woman should make important decisions when she's under the influence of the moon, no one at all should do so when they're hungry, angry, lonely, or tired . . . or, I ought to add, in a situation as abnormal as this. When you have the choice again is when you should make it, not before. And then the choice will be obvious."

She sighed and raised her head. "I suppose," she said reluctantly. "But . . ."

"No buts."

She leaned once more into the comfort of his shoulder. "You know—I almost didn't expect it. But you're very wise."

Magus sighed deeply. "It's my job."

And they both laughed.

Doing what the Magus did for a living, his talk rambled from Caris and Pella, and the various mages he knew, to Court intrigue, to gossip about the Prince Regent—who was evidently growing madder, more suspicious, and more perverted by the day—and to tips on how to sound like you knew more about a client's personal problems than you did. "They're always terribly impressed when you come out with the name of their lover before they've told it to you, but all it takes is being on good terms with the Palace chambermaids, you know."

But beneath the charlatanry that made him his living lay the velvet undercurrent, not only of worldly wisdom, but of true magic, the magic he had been born with; the magic he had painstakingly studied, in bits and pieces, from an old card reader he'd apprenticed himself to in Kymil and from various dog wizards who, grudgingly or otherwise, consented to teach him a few tricks here, a few secrets there.

"Not that anyone's ever able to learn much," he added, with a curious mixture of longing and bitterness in his voice. "The Inquisition's sure to come down on any sorcerer displaying more powers than they like to see—a friend of mine in Kymil used to say the Council tipped them off. And you don't have to be a Suraklin or a Vorkhedne the Gray—he was another of the truly evil ones, my dear, long before my time— to be using powers to make a little money or give yourself and your children a decent life. But as I said, the Council makes jolly sure that every book of spells that gets confiscated ends up in their hands—unless the Magic Office of the Church gets them—and keeps a tight rein on such things as scrying-crystals and water bowls, *hemmerteyrne* and teles . . ."

"*Hemmerteyrne?*"

"Perceptual mirrors . . . artificial souls, some people call them. They're round and about the size of a one-crown piece . . . quite serious magic. They transmit the will. And the teles, of course, have to do with power itself."

"I know," Joanna said, remembering the circle of them around Suraklin's computer, the evil, glassy gleam of them, the sensation of being watched. "Antryg says they're dangerous."

"Well, of course they are, to someone who doesn't know how to use them. So is a gun. But mages have been using teles for centuries with no ill effects. Antryg is a little cracked on the subject, you know. The Brown Star itself is another one of those implements the Council would just as soon keep to itself."

"It sure did *you* a lot of good, didn't it?"

"I would never have been overpowered and imprisoned," the Magus said, with considerable dignity, "had I taken better pains to keep it locked up. The problem was with my study safe, not with any knowledge or lack of it on my part."

Joanna was silent. Far off, she could still hear the Lady Irina, moaning and weeping and cursing Suraklin's name. Somewhere even farther the shrieking laughter of the demons trickled to her like the ghost of mad wind. She wondered who had imprisoned those demons in the crystal and when, and for what purpose. Simply because they knew of no better way of getting rid of them . . . as the *tsaeati* had been imprisoned, and the Lady Irina, and this man beside her, and she herself? *And God knows how many others, over the years . . . over the centuries . . .* She clamped her thoughts down hard to prevent another attack of panic. How many others, imprisoned and forgotten as the crystal passed from owner to owner—how many owners forgot to mention to their successors the names, and the proper extraction-spells, for some of their prisoners? How many times had the crystal been stolen, as Magister Magus had stolen it, and the names of its prisoners simply lost, as if some file had been erased?

*Don't think about that,* she told herself desperately. *Antryg will get you out of this mess.*

*And when he does?*

*The Magus is right. Wait until you have the choice before you make the choice.*

"So tell me, Magus," she said, forcing lightness into her voice, "who was this Vorkhedne the Gray and what did he do that was so awful? And what did the Council do about him?"

"My dear," the Magus began, "some stories say that he wasn't even human; that he was the result of an unnatural experiment with a cat by a wizard named Czyram . . ."

When the forces of Crinias the Strong cornered the armies of the wizards and their allies against the cliffs of Stellith, the Archmage, Isar Chelladin, went forth to beg the pardon of Crinias and his troops, and to make what terms he could for the preservation of the wizards' lives . . .

—FIRTEK BRENNAN
*Dialogues on Wizardry*

After the daylong battle on the field before the cliffs of Stellith, Isar Chelladin stood at night above the battlefield, listening to the outcry of the wounded in the darkness. And he took pity on the forces of the Church, knowing that they would attack again in the morning and so be destroyed; and casting his cloak about his face he crossed to the camp of the defeated, to offer them a final chance of parley . . .

—GANTRE SILVAS
*Book of Isar Chelladin*

Then Crinias the Strong, general of the Church forces, had the defeated wizards brought before him in chains and said, "I will give you one final chance of life . . ."

—INQUISITOR BERON OF KYMIL
*The Defeat of Evil*

# CHAPTER XV

IT WAS SEVERAL HOURS BEFORE ANTRYG MANAGED TO WORK his way back to the Citadel again. He came in through the kitchens, climbing the old chuteway that had been established to haul building materials up for the construction of the Harlot and the North Cloister; Pothatch gasped warningly, "Lord Antryg . . . ," and Antryg shook his head and touched a crooked finger to his lips.

"You haven't seen me," he whispered, not as a spell—out of the pocket in the woods he couldn't have wrought a spell anyway—but as a request.

The little cook shook his head vigorously. "Of course, of course . . ."

Antryg perched himself cross-legged on the edge of the stone counter and helped himself to some oatcakes cooling on a platter there. Before slipping in through the pantry door he'd listened for voices but had heard none; only Pothatch's wheezy panting as he hurried from oven to sink to cupboard. "Scullions gone walkabout again?"

"Not a one of 'em showed up today. If it wasn't for Tom and Lady Q'iin, bless her, I'd be going fair distracted. But just as well, what with *them* here." His nod in the direction of the refectory doors—and by implication the Council chambers—took in the Inquisitor and his troops. He lowered his voice, as if the Witchfinder could hear through the stones. "They're most of 'em up in the Council chamber with Lord Daurannon, the other High Mages being off lookin' after Lady Rosamund. But their sasenna are in the hall, having lunch *and*, so Tom tells me, not sitting near our novices nor our warriors neither. And what Lord Daurannon and them others were thinking of, to let them find the Citadel in the first place . . ."

"They'd have to have been dealt with sooner or later," Antryg murmured, smearing jam on a fourth oatcake with his fingers and adding clotted cream to the mess. "Do they know I'm here?"

Pothatch shook his head. "Not to my knowledge, m'lord. Well, you know how the mages are about letting the Church know any more of our business than they have to. That Silvorglim, he was fratcheting on about abominations showing up in the streets of Angelshand before he even got through the gates, but you? I think they still think as how you're dead."

"Well, let's hope no one disabuses them of that notion. The death warrant the Regent has out for me was fairly detailed and quite unnecessarily nasty. Leave a door unlatched for me tonight, will you?" He uncoiled his long legs, put his feet on the floor again. "Something tells me I'm going to have to turn into a kitchen wight for a time, stealing food where I can."

He headed for the door of the scullery, a long, narrow room where knives and boots were cleaned and the painted earthenware dishes stored between meals. A smaller door led from it to a stairway cut through the Citadel rock up to the subcellar beneath the Harlot, whence he could make his way back to the hypocaust under the North Hall. In the North Hall, he was certain, regardless of incursions by the haters of magic, he would find Aunt Min. On the threshold Pothatch laid a round, heavily knotted hand on his wrist, staying him, and looked up into his face with worried hazel eyes.

"You all right, m'lord?"

Antryg sighed and rubbed a hand over his face. "Fine," he said, though he didn't feel it. His bones still ached from the death-spells he had so narrowly avoided; moreover, the effects of exhaustion, of too little sleep, of troubled dreams and the geas' continual, grinding, low-grade pain were beginning to tell. "That is, I'll be fine." He hooked a handful of dates from the painted wooden bowl that stood on a cupboard and disappeared through the pantry door.

As he had suspected, Antryg found Aunt Min in the North Hall, forgotten by everyone, calmly drawing up the preliminary field to a major conjuration. As he slipped through the rivet-studded oak of the great double doors from the Hall's vestibule, he noted that she'd marked out the field in about three-quarters of the long chamber, leaving open the space in front of the door, so that people could enter and leave without automatically violating the limitations and destroying the energies which would later be worked there. The other doors into the room—a small postern and a semisecret panel in an alcove at the back—had been barred from within. Ten feet or so into the room from the main entrance she had drawn the first of the boundary lines, leaving a ritual door, a break in the lines through which others could enter and leave the field up until the time when it was "sealed," when the true conjurations would begin.

For a moment Antryg folded his arms and stood by the cluster of narrow sandstone pilasters of the North Hall's doorway, only taking pleasure in watching the tiny old woman lay out the cornering-spells and preliminary alignments. Every line, though drawn freehand, was as straight as if ruled; the circles might have been made with a compass. Shaky as the old Archmage's hands were at other tasks, each rune, each sigil, each seal was a minor work of the calligrapher's art.

"You took your time," she muttered as she finished the northwest corner and turned to look at him; he had entered soundlessly, and as far as he could tell she had not moved her head. Maybe she really did have eyes in the back of it, as all the novices claimed.

"I'm afraid I was unavoidably delayed."

She fumbled about, collecting her cane and the overflowing twig-basket of her knitting, and came doddering across the length of the light-washed room. Aunt Min always doddered— she'd doddered nearly thirty years ago when Antryg had first seen her, when she'd visited Suraklin in Kymil. But there was something in the careful slowness of her step now that twisted a knife of dread inside him, something in the fallen, weary lines of her delicate-boned face. He shivered—after the warmth of the kitchen the North Hall was chilly, and he'd left his coat and shawl in the woods with Lady Rosamund—and made a move to go help her but stopped himself; the ritual "door" was shut. To have crossed the scribbled line of runes that marked its threshold would have condemned the old lady to another two hours of careful remaking of spells.

Though he could see the knife of meteor iron nesting among the tangled chaos of her knitting, she made no move to open the spell-field and admit him, only stood on her own side of the lines, looking up at him sidelong, her white head cocked a little on its bent spine.

"I don't need you here." The high, shaky voice was like a piping child's. "I understand well these spells you've made, to fool the very stones into thinking they're what they're not, and I can work well by myself, *and* bring it all to its proper fruiting at the very turn of midnight." Pale blue eyes glinted up at him, defying him to offer help. "Nor do I need you to sit with your eyes on *that*," a finger like a bent twig moved in the direction of the Dead God's watch, still wrapped around Antryg's wrist, "like a timekeeper at a footrace, to make sure when midnight is, as though I couldn't feel it in the breathing of the earth and the moon.''

"Well," Antryg said apologetically, "it would be terribly bad manners of me to shove the spells at you and run away to play.''

"As you did with poor Seldes Katne," Min grumbled, relenting a little and fumbling in her basket, dropping a ball of purple yarn and a packet of herbs to the smooth-scrubbed oak of the floor. "Like a mole she's been, combing through notebooks and memoirs and catalogs of wizards long dead and forgotten, looking to see any mention of which teles belonged to who, and where they got it from . . . *and* you needn't tell me why. Always fidgeting and digging, you are. Not that she hasn't been digging, searching, combing like a woman who's lost a pin in a loft of hay, long before you came among us again . . . as she's been digging and searching all her life, poor soul. It's her you should be helping, or be making yourself useful by going back to Pothatch and washing up the dishes.''

She traced the proper signs with the iron knife, unsealing and opening the door. Antryg stepped through, and she closed it once again behind him.

"Here." She handed him her basket. "It's a long Making we're to be doing today, drawing up the great circles and signs of power from the leys, and from the maze beneath us, and running the power down through the Line itself, to the chamber in the maze below. I'll need a boy to go censing after me, and marking the curves in chalk while I conjure. You'll do for that.''

"I'm honored." Antryg smiled.

"More than you deserve," the old lady muttered. "A troublemaker you always were. 'Twill keep you out of trouble with the Witchfinders in any case. Mind you don't step on the lines.''

The long bands of sunlight that fell through the clerestory windows shifted; on the whitewashed plaster of the walls the cinder gray shadows of the lattices shrank from exaggerated gothic spears to lozenges and at last to squares, alternating with squares of light that burned almost too bright to see. To Antryg's account of the events of last night, Aunt Min only shook her head, and muttered, "There now! If it's not one thing it's another, and it's something to be looked into, when all's said and done." And then, Antryg knew, put the matter completely from her mind, returning all her concentration to the spells she wove on the North Hall's sandstone floor.

Late in the afternoon Antryg heard footfalls in the vestibule outside, entering from the North Wing's stone colonnade; since by then he was sitting in a corner where Aunt Min had ordered him while she executed the delicate paths of power along one of the field's great curves, he left off putting her knitting basket in order and got to his feet, guessing who it might be.

Daurannon entered quietly, carrying, almost absentmindedly under his arm, Antryg's garish coat and shawl. These he dropped in a heap beside the door and walked to the boundaries where Antryg waited.

"I thought I'd find you here." His voice was barely a whisper in the big chamber's hush, and in the floating gray-blue shadows his eyes were grim.

"Will she be all right?"

The younger mage nodded, but by the way he stood, Antryg guessed it had been a near thing. "The hunters say they shot her in mistake for a wolf—an odd sort of mistake to make. They can't tell quite how it happened."

"There was a glamour on her," Antryg said impatiently, "a glamour on us both. She followed me out of the Citadel."

"I know. Is that why you led her?"

"What? So I could point to her and shout at the hunters, 'Oh, look, there's a wolf!'? It's all I could have done along those lines, as you should know."

"I know nothing," Daurannon said quietly, "when it comes to your schemes. The hunters said she was the only one they saw, yet your coat and shawl were found near where she lay."

"I left them with her. She was going into shock, she needed to be kept warm."

"She could have found them herself and made the dressing from the lining."

"I take it she hasn't regained consciousness, then. When she does, she'll tell you."

"She came 'round for a few minutes, Issay tells me," Daurannon said. "I've been with the Witchfinders all afternoon, trying to rebuild sufficient goodwill so they'll stop talking about ransacking the Citadel from top to bottom and arresting the lot of us."

"You didn't offer to buy them off with my body?" Antryg folded his arms casually and blinked across at him.

Daurannon glanced toward Aunt Min, rocking on her knees like a child, whispering as she drew along the lines of power the long interlocking fretwork of sigils, knotting light like an artist crocheting silk. Then his eyes returned to Antryg, a glint of resentment in them at the reminder that Aunt Min would not have stood for such a betrayal.

"She asked after Aunt Min," he went on, without answering the question. "It was the first thing she said: 'Don't let her hurt herself. Antryg's conjurations will kill her.' " He folded his own arms, the movement a challenge.

Antryg was silent.

"Or was that your aim?"

"To make Rosie Archmage while I'm still under the Council's geas, you mean?" And he saw Daurannon stiffen indignantly at the suggestion that the Master-Spells might fall to his rival rather than himself.

"That might have been in your mind."

"Or yours."

The hazel eyes darted quickly away, then returned, catching and holding the gray. For a moment the two wizards stood on opposite sides of the ritual bounds, graying-haired men who had known one another since they were teenagers, Antryg in a tawdry glitter of cheap beads, crystal earrings, round-lensed glasses flashing where they caught the late slant of the sun, Daurannon somber and elegant, the straight black fall of his robes broken only by the killing sword scabbarded at his waist.

"You know the Master-Spells might just as easily fall on Bentick."

Daurannon waved off the suggestion impatiently. "He hasn't the strength."

"He has more than you're giving him credit for," Antryg said. "And in any case someone lured me out to the Green King's Chapel and set me up to be attacked; and when she comes 'round, Rosamund will certainly tell you that I got her away from the hunters and lured them from her."

"Or simply went off with them," Daur returned. "And disappeared at a convenient moment, which argues for at least the ability to work more magic than the geas should allow. Why haven't you been sleeping in your room in the Pepper-Grinder?"

Antryg tilted his head inquiringly to one side. "Why have you been watching the place?"

"Because you're our prisoner." Daurannon's gaze lingered for a moment on the brown mark Antryg bore in the pit of his throat, the mark left by the accursed Sigil of Darkness. "And because you are not to be trusted."

"I don't sleep there because I'm afraid I'll wake Kyra with my dreams," Antryg replied gently, and Daurannon looked away.

"Then where do you sleep?"

"Oh, tut, Daur, that's not a question one gentleman asks another." Antryg grinned and propped his spectacles up onto the bridge of his nose. "As for the Witchfinder, I should say that within twenty-four hours we should have the problem more or less in hand. His sasenna might even come in useful for searching the Citadel. I'll want a marked map of every passage and chamber, from the bottom of the Vaults to the top of the observatory platform, with the locations and natures of every Gate, wormhole, spell-field, reality fold and patch of alien moss, once the whole business is stabilized and they aren't appearing and disappearing.''

"Why the Citadel?"

Antryg blinked, surprised. ''Why not? The more information we have, the likelier we are to come to a correct conclusion. But I shall need it done quickly.'' He nodded back over his shoulder to Aunt Min, who had moved a few feet along the curve, still rocking on her heels and muttering, like a woman tying intricate, invisible bows of light one at a time along some mighty fulcrum beam.

''The Citadel is built on a conjunction of the ley-lines, on top of probably the biggest collecting-maze in the western world, though I'm told there's a cave system in Djovangg that's been worked up into a bigger one. They shelter sheep in it these days, for of course the fortress it was once a part of is long in ruins and forgotten. But with that kind of energy to draw upon, once the balance is established between the magic circles and the electronics of the stabilization field, I'd rather not give that kind of a double-feedback loop too long to build up.''

Daurannon sniffed. ''And you really think that nonsense you wrote will have any effect at all? Other than getting poor Aunt Min to half kill herself pouring her strength into the kind of thaumaturgical rathole you invented?''

''Kill myself? Kill myself?'' Aunt Min tottered fiercely over to them, ruffled like an offended hen. ''You think I am no judge of my own strength or of another wizard's spells? You think because I'm an old lady, I can be deceived to my harm by a young man's pretty eyes? Pssh!'' She made shooing motions with her hand and cane, waving Daur toward the outer doors. ''Go away, you tiresome boy! Smile and be nice to the Inquisitors, since your teeth are so white. Come back at midnight, when this shall be accomplished. Go.'' She waved her cane again, like a farmwife chasing ducks. ''Go.''

Daurannon went, nearly colliding with Seldes Katne in the doorway. The librarian got hastily out of his way, clutching a sheaf of notes to her heavy bosom; she looked after the Handsome One as he crossed the vestibule and passed through the outer doors to the arcade outside. Thus only Antryg saw how Aunt Min's face changed, drooping from anger into sudden lines of exhaustion as she groped with her free hand for the support of his arm.

He caught her quickly, but an instant later she shook him off as the librarian came into the room. "No," Aunt Min hissed, pulling free of Antryg's grip. "No, I am well; I only need a little rest. A little rest. Here . . ." She fumbled the knife from where it lay beside the ritual entry to the field and with a hand that trembled unmade the seals. "Go out and speak to her. I only need a little rest." And she stumbled back to where her knitting basket lay and sat down beside it, abruptly, as if all the remaining strength had gone from her legs.

Doubtfully, Antryg stepped outside the field and crossed to the doorway where Seldes Katne, notes still clutched in hand, waited beside the heap of his coat and shawl.

"I've brought you all I could find so far," she said, as he slipped gratefully into the threadbare velvet. Though sunlight still blazed in its concentrated frieze of squares high on the wall, the plastered stonework left the hall far from warm. The wet, heavy heats of the Sykerst summer were still some weeks off, and in the badly mended bones of his fingers Antryg could feel more rain on the way. "It isn't complete, by any means."

"Hmmn." He thumbed quickly through the overwritten palimpsests of Seldes Katne's tiny, orderly writing. "Otaro has two, Issay one, Nandiharrow one . . . 'said to be that owned by Spurentas the Blind . . .' But Spurentas' was the one called Wolperth, which was allegedly 'inhabited by a purple spirit,' and vanished at his death. Nandiharrow's, I believe, was the one called Varverne, which used to belong to Berengis the Black and could call around itself the illusion of its owner, which could talk to people who came to his rooms and even do magic for them. Now Malvidne the Herbwife, four centuries ago, had one which had similar powers, though it was smaller than Berengis' by all accounts—and that, I believe, was the one they walled up in the vaults during Tiamat's time because fires tended to break out in the rooms where it was stored. And as far as I know, Bentick has two, and there's no mention here of Vyrayana, the one Phormion got from Simon the Lame. Curious—Vyrayana was one of the most powerful, but perhaps Phormion had it walled up somewhere; it was always the old ones that became unstable. And I recall some rather queer stories about Vyrayana. Still,'' he added, smiling reassuringly down at her dismayed face, ''it is a start, and considering how many volumes you've had to go through to get the histories of these, it's amazing you've gotten so much. The seven that Suraklin had, by the way, we can discount—I know what became of those. I'll write it down for you one day when I have time, if Daurannon doesn't sell me to the Inquisition first.''

Her dark eyes widened with alarm. ''Will he?''

''Not as long as Aunt Min's alive.'' He glanced back over his shoulder, to see that the old Archmage had taken a loose wad of yarns and silks from her basket and, laying it down as a pillow, had curled up and fallen asleep on the floor among the sigils and curves of power.

Antryg sighed. He knew exactly how much concentration, how much raw power, was needed for the conjuration to be done that night, and there was a grayness to the old woman's face that made him deeply uneasy. By the height of the sun patches on the wall he knew the afternoon was drawing on; the long Sykerst twilight wouldn't fade until less than two hours short of midnight itself, and after that, he reminded himself, there would still be the search to do. At least, he reasoned, it was a good excuse not to go to sleep.

''Kitty . . .'' She spun as if startled. She, too, had been looking at the Archmage. ''Could you bring us some bread and honey and coffee—strong coffee—from the kitchen, and maybe a little brandy for Aunt Min?''

"Of course."

"And if you see Captain Implek or Sergeant Hathen, could you arrange for guards to be placed in the vestibule here, and around the Rotunda, and the stores-cellar entrance to the Vaults? Once midnight passes and the Circles of Power link with Ninetentwo's stabilization field, I don't want anything breaking the balance."

After she closed the great oak doors behind her, he could hear her heavy, rather clumsy tread going off across the little vestibule and the almost-soundless creak of the iron hinges as she let herself out into the arcade. Wearily, Antryg sank down to the floor, his back to the slender pilasters beside the door and his head tilted to rest against the stone behind him. Whatever happened, he thought, it was going to be one hell of a long night.

In about an hour Aunt Min woke up. By that time the lattice shadows were fading. Light still lingered broad in the sky outside, but it no longer streamed into the hall. Min and Antryg worked in gathering gloom, for the Archmage was unable to spare the concentration to summon light; the only illumination came from the phosphoric blue flicker of the light-circles drawn by the old woman's finger. These spread out like shining concentric ripples among the other Circles of Power—the Circles of Water, of Smoke, of Silver and Earth and Blood— weaving all together into a glowing maze, eerily reminiscent of the maze of darkness far beneath their feet. The magic that seemed at all times to hang whispering in the air of the Citadel thickened, like the scent of hay on a hot night, and now and then Antryg could see veins of light beneath the plaster of the wall or gleaming like streaks of niter on the pillars and in the wood grain of the door.

Power was drawn down, called up, summoned forth from the leys that crossed the earth and from the patterns of the stars overhead. Power spread out, slowly, through the stones of the Citadel itself, through sandstone, tile, and granite, through terrazzo, marble, and glass, thready silver webs of it impregnating the igneous bedrock of the tor itself. Deep in the Vaults below, Antryg knew, Ninetentwo the Dead God would be checking his equipment, wiring oscillators, field generators, backup batteries and resonating screens, aligning them as if there were energy present that could be polarized, matching them to the strange patterns of the maze, the sparking points of long-buried glass and bone. In his mind, or in some corner of his senses, he could see the immense, bony form, like the mummified skeleton of a dragon, more hideous than the most insane tale-weaver's imaginings, moving among the banks of dark metal components, the orange eye-blink of lights glittering on breathing tubes, weapon fittings, and the alien, glossy hide.

Power reached out to power. Fingers of lightning readied themselves to touch.

In the vestibule, those sasenna who were also novices of magic could feel it. If he closed his eyes and listened, Antryg could hear their voices mutter and whisper. Farther off, by reaching out his senses to the whole of the Citadel, other sounds came to his mind, other whispers: Silvorglim the Witchfinder saying, "It is abominable! Abominable!" Brighthand's voice: ". . . hasn't eaten in two days and won't touch what I bring him." A thread of a whisper murmured in darkness: "Dear God, what am I going to do?" And, somewhere deep in the Vaults, a thin, despairing shriek. Around him in the hall the darkness deepened, the sky beyond the lattices the strange, holy blue that seemed deeper even than night's starry darkness. Min's face by the foxfire glow of the runes appeared to thin into a strange little skull, framed by the flaring white halo of her hair. The bent old fingers drew at the power, knitting it, as she knitted yarn, into a glowing net, and in his mind Antryg saw again the ancient tree of her soul, its black steel roots the roots of the mountain, drinking iron strength from the iron heart of the earth.

Outside the first stars gemmed the night. Somewhere in the Citadel he half heard a thick, guttural muttering about poison, plots, and death—then it was gone like smoke when the wind turns. In the vestibule Kyra murmured, "Can you feel it?" and though Antryg himself felt the coming of midnight in his heart and bones, still he glanced at his watch, counting down the seconds as he hoped the Dead God's instruments were likewise counting them down.

Aunt Min, he thought, were she not so absorbed in the horrendous effort of summoning and directing power, would slap his hand for looking.

In the trained, piercing shriek of a wizard's power the Archmage cried out, rising to her knees and spreading out her skeletal arms, power funneling down around her like glowing smoke, sparkling like a queen's treasure of jewels. At the same moment Antryg, his hands, bare for once, spread out on the stone of the wall, felt the energies within the stones shift and change . . .

A deep shudder seemed to pass through the very stones, so profound as almost to frighten him. The next instant he jerked his fingers away as a new energy, like fine-drawn, fast-moving wire, seemed to slice his flesh.

With a sensation of crushing, of dark weight redoubled, he felt the lowering presence of the Void.

In the courtyard beyond the Cloister, the clock finished singing out its twelve tiny chimes.

As for the ancient practice of exposing children at their birth, it is utterly forbidden upon pain of anathema that any parent shall cast out, or cause to die, any child of their bodies, from the day they first enter the world.

But it is understood that if the child be monstrous—that is, given to perversions, or to base and abject cruelty to other children, or to the torture of animals, or if that child be found to be mageborn—then, should the parents cast the child out, or cause it to die, anathema shall not be pronounced.

—Inquisition of Kymil<br>Advice to local priests

# CHAPTER XVI

"THERE IS SOMETHING BEING HIDDEN IN THIS CITADEL, I TELL you—some great plot or secret, whose evil weights the very air."

At the sound of the Witchfinder Silvorglim's voice, Antryg slowed his steps. "What on earth are you doing up at this hour of the night?" he breathed, a sound no louder than the droning wing-flutter of the giant brown moths that beat themselves on the window frames of the Polygon's turret stair behind him. "You ought to be in bed like decent folks."

He tiptoed forward, a disjointed rustle of velvet and beads, to the concealment of one of the archway's heavy wool draft curtains that had not yet been taken down for the summer. By angling his head, he could look down the hall and see into an amber-lit corner of the Steward's office.

The entire Polygon was dangerous territory for him. The darkness of its stairways and passages would give him no concealment from the hasu, the red-robed Church wizards in Silvorglim's train, and it was at least even odds they'd know who he was. The Bishop of Kymil had changed guards in the Silent Tower frequently enough that half the Magic Office would recognize him, by his height and his spectacles if nothing else. Despite the rather elaborate procedure of breaking, skinning, slicing, and disemboweling detailed in the Regent's warrant for his death, he suspected that Silvorglim would simply settle for slitting his throat on sight, rather than risk his escape on the way back to Angelshand and a formal execution. An unpleasant thought at the best of times, he reflected, but with an artificial energy field building up on top of the looped feedback of a collecting-maze, were he not around to supervise its dismantling before disintegration set in, the results could be disastrous.

Even through his shoulder, pressed to the linenfold panelling of these upstairs halls, he could feel it a little. Resting his fingertips on the wood, sinking his mind through to the sandstone underneath, he could feel it still more: the searing cold, as if his flesh were being scored by a thousand razors moving too swiftly for pain, and beneath that, a gathering heat.

A search had to be organized, and soon. That Bentick obviously had done nothing in that direction—or, if he had, was concealing it from Antryg—was enough to make him take the risk of bearding the Steward in his office, despite the danger of being seen on the way.

"The Citadel is a place of secrets," Daurannon said, his light, pleasant voice smooth with reassurance. "That was the reason of its establishment—that secrets too heavy for the untaught, the uninitiated, might be kept in safety, sparing humankind their misuse."

In the saffron rhombus of candlelight he could see them: Bentick at his tall, slanted desk, upon whose polished surface every inkpot, every quill, every pricker and pumice stone and candlestick ranged like neat-uniformed guards at attention, winking in the starry glow of the lamp overhead; Daurannon standing beside him, his gestures as refined, as expressive, as an actor's. And Silvorglim, taut suspicion in those fox-colored eyes.

"A fine lot of good it has done," the gray-clothed Witchfinder snapped. "Witches and sorcerers still haunt every large city of the Realm."

"Dog wizards only," Daurannon replied easily, "who call themselves sorcerers out of envy of the powers they cannot touch without our teaching."

"But wizards still." Silvorglim's arms were folded tight over his broad chest, and his gaze darted sharply over the books that ranked the circular room floor-to-ceiling, neatly arranged in their curving shelves. They were, Antryg knew, only the Citadel's ledgers, but it was clear from the Witchfinder's expression that to Silvorglim they were volumes of arcane secrets, forbidden learning lying in wait like those balls of dough-coated nightshade that professional poisoners dropped down wells, waiting to go to work when the culprit himself was long gone.

"But this," Silvorglim went on, "this evil, these creatures which have been appearing, abominable and terrible . . . you cannot claim this is a matter brought about by those without power. And now your Archmage refuses to see me, you refuse to give me proper accounting of what is taking place within these walls . . ."

"Within these walls," Bentick cut in crisply, "we owe you no accounting. After the Battle of the Field of Stellith it was agreed that you of the Church would go your way, and we would go ours, not attempting to meddle with humankind."

*"On our sufferance!"* Silvorglim's voice grew softer rather than louder, but with the contained rage in his voice, the words might have been a shout. "On our sufferance, and by our leave, were the Council's wizards allowed to depart."

"There was no such . . ."

"Gentlemen . . ." Daurannon raised a hand, then went to the Witchfinder's side and dropped a friendly pat on the wide, stiff shoulder in its close-fitting gray coat. "It's late in the night to be arguing about who said what to whom one afternoon six hundred and twelve years ago, you know. And it's certainly late to go calling on the Archmage.'' Antryg saw his eyes move, touching Bentick's, then returning, with casual naturalness, to Silvorglim's. ''She'll be asleep, if she's finished with her studies and meditations.''

''Studies and meditations!'' The deep voice, so at odds with the spare smallness of Silvorglim's frame, tightened like the steel bands of an Inquisitor's screwed boot. ''Something is going on in this Citadel. Some power was called forth at the hour of midnight—Elberard and Tobin, the Saved Ones who accompanied me from Angelshand, have sensed it.''

''Of course.'' Daurannon widened those expressive eyes, as if surprised that the Witchfinder needed to make a point of the matter—he did it, Antryg thought, quite well. ''Anyone here would have told you that the powers of the universe's balance can be brought to bear on the accomplishment of great magics, usually at the hour of midnight. But I promise you it has nothing to do with any affair of humankind. Certainly nothing to do with the purposes of your visit. Come . . .''

He put a friendly hand on the back of the Witchfinder's arm—as he had, Antryg recognized with a smile, on his own arm that first day—and steered him with the same coaxing pressure to the door.

''The Archmage will make it all clear to you in the morning.''

*Not if Rosie has anything to say about it*, thought Antryg, slipping deeper into the concealment of the curtains as his old friend guided Silvorglim into the hall.

''She had better.'' Silvorglim had taken one of the five-branched bronze candelabra from the top of Bentick's desk as he'd left the room, in spite of the white cone of glowing light Daurannon had politely summoned over both their heads. The Witchfinder's eyes, pale brown almost to yellowness, flashed in the glare like those of vermin in an outhouse. ''Does she not, I warn you now that I will order my troops to tear this

Citadel to pieces, to find what it is that you are hiding from us.''

"Look," Daurannon said in a lowered voice, "if she doesn't, I can promise you that I'll give you all the cooperation you need. I know this Citadel's secrets better than any, and I promise you that whatever happens, you shall have the truth.''

*Or at least a convincing sop to stop you from asking awkward questions*, thought Antryg, watching the master-wizard's back framed in the arch at the far end of the hall, the bobbing glow of the candelabra diminishing in the wider stairs at that end. From his position in the curtain Antryg glanced back, to see Bentick, still sitting at his desk.

The old man had lowered his face to his hands, the high, bald curve of his forehead catching a spot of the lamplight's sheen; after a moment he drew a long, thick, shaky breath, like a man steeling himself against sobs. He gripped it as a man would grip a lifeline—then let it out, measured and controlled, as he measured and controlled all things.

Dark robe billowing about him, Daurannon returned down the hall.

"Has she gone to her house?" Bentick spoke without looking up, barely audible through the constriction of his throat.

Daurannon nodded. "I saw them crossing the gardens together just after midnight. I would have intercepted him the minute he'd left her, except that Silvorglim came up to me.''

"Damn." The Steward's long, nervous hands snapped into fists as his head lifted with a jerk. "And now we've lost him.''

"I've sent for the guards," Daurannon said quietly. "One thing that stabilizing field will mean—*if* the thing actually exists, after all this—is that we won't have to worry about a Gate opening in his cell and letting him disappear again. But of course," he added, as Bentick started to speak, "chains and drugs, nevertheless.''

The old man nodded, satisfied; Antryg noted with interest how his hands trembled as they fussed with the golden watch, how his dark eyes darted to the younger wizard's face and then away. "And Rosamund?"

"She's asleep; she won't be up for days, especially if I report to her that everything's going well. The Witchfinders will be gone before she knows anything."

"Daurannon . . ." Bentick caught his sleeve as Daurannon turned to go with that same natural air of conclusion with which he had ejected Silvorglim.

Daurannon's brows arched inquiringly. Antryg could almost hear him saying, Me *pinch the cakes, Pothatch?*

"You aren't by any chance going to turn him over to the Witchfinders, are you?"

"With the field stabilized," Daurannon pointed out in his most reasonable tones, "we don't need him. We know what we're looking for, now: Circles of Power involving a teles. And what with the abominations that have appeared in Angelshand, we may need some kind of spectacular favor to sweeten the Regent's temper."

"You're not going to go ahead with the search *NOW* ?" Bentick demanded, horrified. "With the Witchfinder's men pecking about the place, ready to pounce on the first indication of something amiss?" His voice stammered a little, and as he turned his head again to avoid Daurannon's suddenly inquiring eyes, Antryg could see the silvery glitter of beard stubble on the long, usually immaculate jaw. He went on hastily, "We . . . we'd have them running roughshod through every chamber, every workroom, every study and hallway, disrupting everyone's studies and experiments."

"Then we won't search until they're gone," Daurannon said agreeably. "And if we give them Antryg, you see, they'll be gone all that much sooner."

Bentick started to stammer something else, some other protest; Daurannon shook his head. "We have to buy our peace in the coin of the Realm," he said softly. "Quite literally, if you like: you know as well as I do where the money comes from to run this place, and the Regent and the Inquisition could do a sight more damage to us by confiscating rental properties and cutting off donations than they'd ever do by rack and wheel. I don't like turning one of ours over to the Inquisition any more than you do—it sets an awkward precedent— but he isn't one of ours anymore, really, is he? Only a dog wizard.'' The younger mage smiled a little, the cupid-bow mouth flexing with a bitter little quirk, and laid a suave hand on Bentick's wrist. "And don't worry," he added gently. "I know Antryg well enough to make sure that when they take him, he won't be able to talk."

Avoiding Daurannon's patrols—at this point, mostly the night-watch sasenna anyway—it took Antryg slightly more than an hour to rally as much of a search party as he could. Tom and Pothatch he found asleep in their respective alcoves off the dark cavern of the kitchen; Q'iin the Herbmistress and her novice Gilda, in the herb garden at the bottom of the tor, gathering arnica by the light of the late-rising moon. Kyra and Nye he found on guard duty in the vestibule of the North Hall, Cylin and Mick swilling tea and passionately arguing spell-casting technique in the otherwise-deserted Junior Parlor. Brunus was raiding the kitchen, and Brighthand, his gaunt face hollowed still further with weariness, sitting awake over a pile of books in the darkened downstairs chamber of the Island of Butterflies.

With these ten Antryg searched the Vaults until dawn, marking the locations of every Gate into darkness, every strange anomaly of time and space, every cul-de-sac where alien moss grew thick, every field of coldness, or strange vapors, or the tingling sense of unknown magics. Water was flowing now down two of the main stairways, lapping with uneasy whispers and curls of strange-smelling steam in the downshafts. The weight of the Void pressed heavy everywhere, a constant presence, an unseen stalker waiting in the shadows, chained now, but patient.

On the fourth level, Antryg introduced Cylin and Mick to the Dead God and left them guarding the round, painted chamber where he had set up his oscillators and reflecting screens by the pallid glow of four small lumenpanels wired to the glass pillar in the chamber's midst. "We'll be back with other patrols later in the morning," he promised, leaning against the jamb of the room's low doorway, his face gaunt and his eyes black-circled with fatigue in the sickly light. "No one must be allowed to disturb your machines here, Ninetentwo, nor must they be allowed," hc added, looking back over his shoulder at Kyra and Nye, "to enter the North Hall, or tamper with the Circles of Power that keep the magical end of the equation in balance."

He reached uneasily to touch the granite of the chamber's wall. Under the smooth plaster, and the queer, garish scenes of judgment, torture, and death painted upon it, he could feel still more strongly the sear of the channeled energies and the slow, building heat of power—from the leys, from the maze, from the Void itself—trapped and growing within.

"Have you ever played ring-of-roses?" he asked quietly, looking from the looming, insectile form of the Dead God to the faces of the young people grouped in the passage behind him. "Do you remember how it all works, the circle spinning faster and faster, until someone lets go? We've brought the power up, and stabilized it, and we can bring it down again."

"What happens if it breaks?" Brighthand tipped his head a little to look beyond him, fascinated, at the cold columns of glowing machinery in the chamber's shadows.

"The problem is that we can't be completely sure," Antryg said, and scratched the side of his long nose. "Let's just be certain that it doesn't."

Before he slept in the hayloft above the mule barn, to which he earnestly hoped he hadn't been followed, Antryg scanned through the crude sketch maps his Irregulars had drawn for him of the portions of the Vaults they had patrolled. Some of these had registered as dark blurs on the Dead God's multiscanner, others—reality-folds, cold spots, places where strange clangings could be heard—did not, though whether this was due to a flaw in the scanner or to ancient fields of magic in the walls, he did not know. Since he knew now that it was possible anyone in the Citadel, not merely the members of the Council, might be at the bottom of the problem—and there was an outside chance that it was someone like Pothatch or Tom—he knew the possibility existed that one of the maps was false. Still, with a dozen of them searching, and all but three of those unlikely to be deceived by illusion, the odds were good that these maps were reliable.

He frowned. No sign yet of the Circles of Power he knew had to be holding open a Gate—perhaps the moving one, perhaps not. True, it might be down on the lower levels, filled with water now, the enchantments still holding in the haunted dark.

Neither had anyone reported the cloying smell of roses, which all of them had been instructed to flee at once—to flee, and to fetch him. And though four minor Gates—wormholes two or three feet across at most—had been sighted, held by the stabilization field in uneasy stasis in the blacker dark of the twisting maze, no one had reported anything like a Gate the size of the one the librarian, Phormion, and Otaro had seen, nor had anyone heard the confusion of voices and cries all three had witnessed in conjunction with that Gate.

*A voice crying out,* Phormion had said. *I heard someone shout something . . . I do not remember what it was, but I remember the fear.*

Was it significant that both Phormion and Otaro had forgotten?

It crossed Antryg's mind suddenly that he hadn't seen Otaro lately.

He shuffled to the next map, noted a reality-fold between the tunnel that led to a minor spiral on the fifth level and the long stretch of tunnel on the second where a line of pillars ran down the center. The searcher—Tom, by the laborious and ill-spelled handwriting—had not actually been able to search that spiral on the fifth level. And a small, localized area of thick fog near there, knee-deep.

He shook his head, fighting against a sudden, blinding wave of tiredness. In the barn below, a mule whuffled in the thin light of dawn already filtering through the great windows of the loft. At the far end of the long, low-raftered chamber a cat picked its way over the hay bales, dainty and disdainful—not in quest of anything to eat, Antryg knew, as spells against mice and other vermin ringed the Citadel's outer walls, obliging the feline population to hunt in the fields beyond. There had to be a pattern, some answer to the riddle.

His eyes ached and he took off his spectacles, laid his forehead on his crossed wrists, though part of his mind protested at the folly of so tempting Sleep. And as he had feared, Sleep emerged from the shadows like an assassin with a club and took him unguarded, and he subsided like a broken and garish scarecrow into the hay.

"Can we even know how much time has passed?" Joanna asked, raising her head from Magister Magus' velvet shoulder, where it had rested in silent exhaustion for . . . how long? Minutes? A year and a half? She closed her eyes, too tired now for panic or anxiety. "I mean, if this place is . . . is an energy-stasis of some kind, years could pass outside. Aren't there any stories about this thing?"

"It is mentioned," the wizard said cautiously. "But then, the stories generally concern those whose friends and families *did* eventually get them out."

"After how long?"

"Well . . . I don't remember, really," he hedged. "Most stories are about things that were simply imprisoned here for good, like the demons."

Joanna sighed. "Things I'd really like to hear are somewhere in the dark with me. Dandy. And I suppose . . ." She felt a momentary stirring of the old anxiety, but it was too worn to surface. "I suppose I don't really want to know about people who were locked up here for twenty years, either, really. It's sort of like cruising your boyfriend's house to see what cars are outside when he tells you he's got work to do that evening—knowing's worse than not knowing, but you don't know that until it's too late.''

In the ensuing silence Lady Irina's endless, half-heard ramblings drifted like the meaningless purl of a stream. A muscle in Joanna's jaw flinched as all the old questions crept out of the dark: How long would it take for Ruth to give up on her and stop paying her rent? For her friends to move out of L.A.? For the knowledge by which she made her living to become obsolete? What would she return to, if she spent even a year or two in this place?

*STOP IT, JOANNA! It will be all right. And if it's not all right, there's not a damn thing you can do about it and unless Security National Bank collapses in the interim, you're not going to come out of this with no place to go and no money—your account's going to pick up all that much more interest if you can spend the next fifty years here rent-free, so STOP WORRYING.*

*Worry's not going to help. There is nothing you can do.*

She hated that.

Something, not a sound, but a feeling, like a cold dragging somewhere within her chest, made her raise her head, and beneath her shoulder she felt the Magus' rib cage stiffen.

There was silence, terrible silence, and the slow sensation of some dreadful vortex drinking at the very heat of her blood.

''The *tsaeati*.'' Sweat started on her face, on her body beneath the thin cotton of her pajamas. ''It's moving this way.''

*It can't hurt us,* she thought. If this place was an energy-stasis, it could not draw the lives from them, could not absorb either the electrochemical flickerings of their thoughts or the substance of their flesh.

But still she took Magister Magus' hand, and the two of them got to their feet and moved off silently into darkness that had no end.

* * *

"I'm sorry," the little man said in the doorway, "but you can't stay here for free, you know. We have at least four hundred applicants for the twenty-five rotating openings, and we simply can't afford to turn one of them out for a nonpayer. You understand."

Antryg sighed and nodded, though he was exhausted and, even in the dream's altered perceptions, very hungry. The wide, straight street behind him was jammed with pedestrians, who brushed the mended skirts of his tattered purple coat, and the air was thick with the peculiarly acrid smell of cheap polyester permeated by old body-sweat, mingled with the chest-burning weight of a third-stage smog alert. In spite of the smell, everything in the dream was very brightly colored and rather pretty—bright pink and yellow polyester tunics, gaily colored neoprene sneakers, green and yellow stucco and paint on the crowded walls of the buildings. Only, upon closer inspection, everything was very dirty, and whirlpools of trash eddied along the edges of the sidewalks with the scuffing of the passing feet or pooled thick and sodden in the damp gutters. The bright red-and-blue buses that rumbled among the crowds belched clouds of black diesel smoke that were barely seen, so thick was the air already with it; most of the people who moved past him, not looking up at him or at one another, didn't seem terribly healthy, coughing or sniffling or rubbing their eyes.

He said to the man in his dream, "Is there some place where I could stay for the night? Or some place where I could find work? I'm really quite respectable, you know."

"I'm sure you are," the man said, in that same half-polite inflection, still not looking at him, and shoved into his hand a stapled sheaf of papers on which a list of unreadably tiny government agencies had been printed in a language he could not have deciphered even had the list not been a sixth- or seventh-generation photocopy; the door shut in his face. In the moving mob he was alone and tired, so tired his flesh hurt on his bones and he could barely get his legs to carry him away from the shut door. In the dream he was aware that he had been alone and tired for a long time now, constantly moving, unable to find a place to rest.

The turgid swirl of people swept him on.

The dream changed and blurred, breaking into a series of impressionistic fragments: himself standing in line after line to be told that he hadn't the qualifications for anything except shaling, whatever shaling was . . . or fleeing, dodging through those bright-colored, weary, unwashed crowds to escape something or someone that filled him with dread. Once, he glimpsed his own face in the grimy reflective surface of a shopwindow and saw that he was old. Dirty and ragged and unshaven and old, with a look of defeated hopelessness in his eyes. Why he didn't open a Gate and exit this world he didn't know, only that it wasn't possible—either because the Council would find him if he did, or because it was simply not possible in this world, or because he had lost the ability. Or perhaps because in his heart he knew that the next world he entered would be worse.

There was no one who would speak to him, no one who would touch him, no one who would be his friend. Struggling feebly to escape the iron weight of sleep, he sensed in his dream that he had been thus alone for years. Everything he had once known had faded behind him, like a light in a black tunnel, with no light ahead, nothing but age and blind weariness and the slow, creeping onset of pain.

In an alley he glimpsed something brown and curved behind a trash bin where men and women as old as himself were scrounging for food. They snarled at him like half-toothless dogs, warning him from their territory, and he stepped back, but not before he'd seen that behind the bin lay the broken shell of a tortoise, shattered and turning to dust.

*Joanna* . . . he thought, wanting her more than he could ever remember wanting anything. Wanting to touch someone, to talk to someone . . . it had been years since he had talked to anyone, save polite civil servants like the man in the door. But Joanna was dead. Like a leaf in the wind, graying away to rot, he moved on, an eternal prisoner of his own flight.

One of the strongest supporters of wizards during the first two centuries after the Accords of Stellith was King Plugard II of Senterwing. He invited them to his court and freely endowed them with gifts, and from his own privy funds built, in their northern stronghold, the barracks of colored brick which now houses their sasenna.

When Plugard's nephew Bardelys organized a cabal of reactionary nobles and overthrew him, the exiled King appealed to the mages for support against his supplanter. To this the Archmage replied, "It is against our vows to use our powers for good or for ill in the affairs of men. We shall give you shelter among us for as long as you require it, but we cannot assist you in reclaiming your throne."

For this reason, when Plugard did rally popular support (for Bardelys was not only oppressive, but vicious and much hated among the people), he cast out of his kingdom all the mages, even such as had been his dear friends, and afterward it was many years before any wizard dared return to Senterwing.

—GANTRE SILVAS
*Annals*

# CHAPTER XVII

ANTRYG WAS AWAKENED, FAR LATER IN THE AFTERNOON than he had intended, by the flashing scamper of a cat bounding across his shins. He moved a little and groaned, aching with the weariness of bad sleep; the light in the loft was opal-colored and diffuse, and rain drummed softly, steadily, on the thatch a short distance above his head. The crooked bones of his hands hurt from the dampness—it was the pain that had carried into his dreams.

He groped around for his glasses, finding them by memory mostly, and sat for a moment, picking the hay out of his hair and listening to the rain. The cat he identified as Fysshe, Aunt Min's big gray tom. There was, by the sound of it, one hell of a mouse hunt going on among the hay bales that filled the long, low-raftered space above the stalls.

Smiling a little, Antryg sat back, undoing all his former

efforts of picking the hay off his coat. The rain smell wandered among the bales like a heartbroken ghost in search of half-forgotten memories, trailing in its wake the nostalgia of his own childhood. He had almost forgotten how much he had loved this country, with its crushing, empty silences, its cool woods and the hot, muggy, mosquito-ridden magic of its summers.

Not, he thought, leaning back into the pillowing clouds of hay, that mosquitoes would be permitted within the Citadel's bounds.

Then he sat up, frowning.

As well as mosquitoes, the Citadel bounds were, of course, spelled against mice.

So what was Fysshe after?

Suddenly deeply curious, Antryg got to his feet, hay clinging to his coat like burrs to a dog. Standing, he could see over the nearby wall of baled fodder, and realized why the cat was making so much noise. There were, in fact, four cats: Fysshe, Ru, Paddywinkle, and Littlekitty, all darting and springing among the hay in quest of . . .

Tiny abominations? Antryg hooked an elbow over the nearest low rafter and watched until Paddywinkle flushed her quarry and went pelting across the floor after it.

It was the illusion of a mouse. Moreover, there was something different about this illusion: the fur was longer and softer, and the color was more like that of a black-and-white cinema film than the slatey bluish brown of a field mouse's coat. Its smell was stronger, too, a pungence of blood and mousiness and . . . catnip?

He realized then that the illusion was being cast *by the cats*.

Paddy sprang past Antryg's booted ankles, pouncing with both forepaws . . . and the phantasm-mouse vanished. The cat skidded to a halt, cocked her head, then turned back to where the other three were still leaping madly around the hay in pursuit of their illusory quarry. Her long tail lashed . . . and the phantasm-mouse appeared once more, skittering wildly away—they certainly had the movement exact—with the hunter in hot and savagely joyful pursuit.

Antryg smiled, delighted, and stepping forward, held out his hand. No dancing simulacra of Fred and Ginger graced his palm; he shrugged and said aloud, "Well, it was worth a try." Evidently, in whatever reality that was the source of this field, cats could work magic and humans couldn't.

"And let's just hope there aren't side effects from *this*," he muttered, as he collected his shawl and last night's maps from the hay. Somewhere in the Citadel there *had* to be a field, however small, which would permit him to at least, very cautiously, work a scrying-stone.

He glanced through the big window at the rain pattering steadily down, drenching the maze of corrals and dairy yards into a sea of yellow mud. By the light it was midafternoon . . . he should have wakened hours ago, though he felt that the uneasy slumber had done him little good.

Who was guarding the vestibule of the North Hall? he wondered, raking the last straws from his curls. And had Aunt Min recovered enough to see Silvorglim before the Witchfinder succumbed to either a coronary or the temptation to institute a pogrom? The Archmage had been exhausted beyond speaking, bent and fragile, when he had taken her back to the little cottage in the gardens at midnight and put her to bed. Fortunate, he thought wryly, that Lady Rosamund was still in her own bed under Issay's care and hadn't seen how badly the old lady's strength had been sapped. With any luck Min would be on her feet before her heir was; if not, Antryg supposed, clambering down the ladder from the hayloft, he was in for a bad time.

There was a well in the corner of the big barn, a deep shaft descending far into echoing rock and darkness; twenty feet down, a tiny door let into a passage connecting with the storage cellars beneath the kitchens, reached by footholds cut into the living granite of the wall. Pothatch nearly jumped out of his skin when Antryg stepped silently through the narrow doorway of the pantry and tapped him on the elbow.

"Save us, Lord Antryg, I was afraid they'd got you!" He glanced swiftly over his shoulder as he pushed Antryg back through the narrow slit and into the pantry again. "That Silvorglim, he's been in a terrible bate all morning."

"Why? What happened?" Antryg put out his hand to touch the wall, where the granite of the tor itself underlay the plaster, and the heat of the energy running through it almost seared his fingers. Coming down the narrow well shaft had been nearly unbearable. The rest of the investigation had to be conducted and the field dismantled quickly, he thought with a shiver. Polarized as it was, there was simply too much energy building up where the leys ran through the labyrinth . . . the Witchfinder's hasu had to have noticed. The suffocating pressure of the Void's nearness had half the cats in the Citadel walking on pins, the other half retreating to the fields or the barns.

"I don't know, rightly." The cook scratched his thinning red hair. "But he came down to Lord Daurannon this morning screaming as how he had to see my Lady Min right that second—and of course the Lady Rosamund had dragged herself there, leaning on a crutch and looking like death, and got into it with him proper."

"He stumbled through a magic-field that gave him power." The pantry door slipped open and Brighthand edged through, his thin face seeming even more gaunt with weariness; streaks of purple beneath his eyes showed how little sleep he'd had. *Why?* Antryg wondered. Surely not from patrolling the Vaults last night?

*"Silvorglim?"*

"Aye." A wry, tired grin revealed a brief flash of teeth. "He wouldn't say where it was, but it must've been in one of the tunnels goin' up to the subcellars of the library, 'cos it was dark enough they were carryin' torches. One of his lads tripped on the stair, like, and dropped his brand and caught the skirts

of his coat on fire—Silvorglim damped it out without thinkin'."
Brighthand used the word *gn'iya*, the technical term for those
acts of crude magic born of panic and reflex, "and then went
into a dither when he realized what he'd done."

He grinned again. While he was speaking, Antryg noticed
that he was, in the most matter-of-fact fashion possible, slipping rolls, apples, and cheese into the pockets of his robe.

"No idea where the field was?"

The boy shook his head. "Just that he came down ravin' to
Daurannon, lookin' like he'd seen a ghost and carryin' on like
the field turned him into a eunuch instead of a temporary
mage."

"So Silvorglim's been searching the Citadel?"

"Well, sort of patrollin'. But Seldes Katne's got keep-out
spells across every door leadin' into the Library, and Bentick
has 'em across all the ways into the Vaults."

In spite of the urgency of the matter, Antryg grinned at the
thought of the little Witchfinder's face when confronted with
such spells of ward and guard. It wasn't likely that whatever
magical barriers Seldes Katne might raise across the entrances
to the Library could withstand the greater magic of Silvorglim's two hasu, but Bentick's spells guarding the Vaults would
be another matter.

"And no patrols from our side have been organized yet?"
he asked, a little grimly.

Brighthand finished his casual pilfering with the appropri-
ation of a small crock of honey. "Only the ones they got out
lookin' for you."

There were two ways to get from the kitchens to within
striking distance of Aunt Min's cottage, discounting of course
the direct route through the refectory, along the North Cloister, up the steps, and among the winding and overgrown beds
of the garden. One of them involved several flights of back
stairs through the Polygon, a secret panel beside the fireplace
in the Junior Parlor (which everyone in the Citadel knew about

except the dairymaids and Silvorglim), and thence across the bridge to the lowest floor of the Harlot; the other, a connecting passage between the Polygon's boiler room and the hypocausts under the Great Assembly Hall, and a succession of trapdoors and minor staircases through the subcellars of the Senior Mages on the northwest side of the hill.

Though the route through the Harlot was more direct, Antryg knew that the odds against both the Junior Parlor and the bridge being deserted at this time of the afternoon were astronomical, particularly since the Council sasenna—now directly under Daurannon's command—were actively searching for him. *Of course, chains and drugs*, Daurannon had said casually. Antryg encountered only one party of them, in the low-roofed, shadowy maze of columns beneath the Great Assembly Hall, and was able to pass unseen, crouching in the brick mouth of the tunnel until they'd gone.

Having no desire to encounter whatever spells Phormion might have in the cellars of the Castle, Antryg came aboveground by means of a narrow stair leading up from beneath the Sea Lady's House, and stood for a time in the shelter of the little area dug out beneath that house's kitchen, studying the long, overgrown slope of the gardens under the whispering patter of the rain. He could see no sign of life under the peach and apple trees that half screened his view of the little cottage at the garden's top; all the cats in the Citadel, nervous as they were, were doing their edgy prowling indoors or had retreated in disgust to the barns. But he knew that Daurannon would, of all things, want to keep him from getting to Aunt Min's protection. After a few moments he dug in his jeans pocket for a rubber band—not a very good one, since the ones he had were the small, thin, red sort that came around supermarket fliers—and, fitting one of his divinatory hazelnuts to its improvised loop, let fly into the thick beds of rosemary that made a gray-green screen across the garden's center. But he watched the clumps of laurel and hawthorn nearer the cottage, and sure enough, at the sharp rustle of the missile in the foliage he saw movement in two places and, under the leaves, the momentary glimpse of a black sleeve.

"Damn." With infinite care he slipped back down to the cellar, and thence, via a disused well in the subcellar and a trapdoor behind a cupboard full of old crockery, down to the Porcelain House, where Lady Rosamund lived.

The Porcelain House had been so named for the slick-glazed white tiles of its downstairs entryway and for the delicate chinaware capitals of that entryway's slender columns, capitals which also appeared on five of the seven columns supporting the arcade of the little house's balcony. They were intricate pieces of artwork, brightly colored—cardamom, cobalt, daffodil, and white—and wrought in the shape of griffins and chrysanthemums. Antryg suspected they had originally been ordered by some nobleman who had changed his mind about the design and donated the rejected samples to the wizards in the hope of some kind of favor; in any case they were the sort of work that had been intensely fashionable a hundred and fifty years ago in Mellidane, before softer shapes and colors had supplanted the bright.

The latticework doorway leading in from the balcony was open, and Antryg slipped soundlessly inside. For a moment, seeing the Lady asleep on the room's plain, narrow bed, he was afraid Daurannon had talked Issay into drugging her. It wouldn't be difficult, considering the shock she had suffered and the blood she had lost. But the black cat Imp, curled like a dropped muff in the hollow formed by the Lady's leg beneath the coverlet, raised his head and regarded Antryg with a solemn gold gaze, and at the movement Rosamund turned a little on her pillows and opened her eyes.

"What do you want?" She sat up a little, wincing. Her nightgown was plain red calico, faded with washing, and against it the black braid of her hair was long and thick as a man's forearm. "How long have I been asleep?"

"Imp . . ." Antryg turned to the cat. "How long has your roommate been asleep?"

"Don't make jokes," Rosamund snapped crossly. "Where's Daurannon?"

"I haven't the slightest idea—looking for me, I expect, or having tea with the Witchfinders. And if you're going to put a geas on me against joking, I really *will* die of it. I need to see Aunt Min, and Daur's posted guards in the garden."

"I posted them there." She pushed the tendrils of her hair back from her cheeks. Even pale and haggard with the loss of blood, her eyelids smudged blue with fatigue, still the beauty was there, the song of her bones. "I saw to that, first thing this morning. I won't have her disturbed: not by these Witchfinders, and certainly not by you. You've done enough. And what Daurannon was thinking of, letting the Witchfinders through our defenses . . ."

"What he was thinking of," Antryg said, turning to the room's small, tiled hearth to check the earthenware teapot being kept warm near the flames, "is how to restore wizardry to acceptance in the Realm by doing some ostentatious favor for the Regent, a favor that's probably going to involve my head and a silver plate. He *was* asking Pothatch for the silver polish, now that I think of it. Tea?"

"That's nonsense." Her hands were a little weak as she took the plain red cup from him, but her glance had all its old imperious flash. "You are the Council's prisoner, and he is far from being the head of the Council. And the very idea that he would turn a Council mage over to the Inquisition . . ."

"Our boy might not be the head of the Council," Antryg remarked, picking up a second cup from the hearth, sitting cross-legged on the hearthrug to wipe it clean with his shirt-hem and pouring tea for himself, "but the Archmage is unconscious and you're rather conveniently laid up. Oh, I don't see Daurannon as having engineered the attack on us for that reason . . . At least," he added worriedly, "I don't *think* I see it . . ."

He got to his feet, took the empty teacup from her hand and studied the leaves for a moment, then sighed with relief and shook his head. "No. But he's opportunist enough to have seen his chance. And between Daur wanting me out of the way so I don't have access to whatever old secrets might be in the Vaults, and Bentick's determination not to conduct a search while the Witchfinders might poke their noses into things, no search of any kind seems to be scheduled for the forseeable future." He set the teacup down beside the bed when Rosamund shook her head at the offer of more.

"The stabilization field has been in place for nearly eighteen hours already." Behind his spectacles, his gray eyes were deadly earnest as he seated himself on the edge of the bed. "Our time is limited. Within a day or two at most, the spells that altered the reactions of the energy within the Citadel's stones will decay, and long before that happens, the entire metaphysical construct of spells and polarization field will have to be dismantled with the utmost care, to prevent an unbalance causing God knows what kind of energy backlash. This Citadel needs to be searched and all anomalies charted from turrets to bedrock, no matter what the danger is or who might see the results. If I had my way I'd have the surrounding countryside searched as well, at least along the ley-lines."

He leaned forward, the chill gray light from the open balcony doors catching a pewter glint in the beads around his neck. "Rosamund, we can't fool around with this. At the rate the decay was progressing before the stabilization field went into effect . . ."

In the hall below, a door thudded, and boots creaked the oak of the stairs. Dimly, Antryg heard a deep voice saying, "Don't lie to me, witch, and don't palm me off with excuses! There is an abhorrence being wrought here, an evil plot to cast the Realm into chaos."

The voices were in the upper hall already; Antryg turned to flee out onto the balcony, but Rosamund lifted a finger, warning . . . in any case, he knew, the guards in the garden would see him. Her hand made a quick gesture, and Antryg stepped back into a corner and did his best to look like a lampstand as

Daurannon, Bentick, Silvorglim, and one of the red-robed Church wizards strode through the door.

"And to what," Lady Rosamund demanded, sitting up straighter in bed and flicking her dark braid back over her shoulder, "do I owe the outrage of this *extraordinary* intrusion?"

Her voice was like a physical slap; all of them stopped involuntarily, even Silvorglim—even Daurannon, who had spent over twenty years taking great care not to be impressed with her queenly hauteur. Antryg saw the hasu's gray-blue eyes linger briefly on him and then wander away; Bentick and Daurannon, far more powerful mages, did a double-take so perceptible that it might well have given him away had not Silvorglim claimed center stage by striding to her ladyship's bedside in a swirl of rain-mottled gray coat skirts.

"Last night I was told that the Archmage, and only the Archmage, could and would answer my questions regarding the propriety—the legality—of what is being done in this place." His deep voice was low and level, but there was a shivery edge to it, and his pale eyes glimmered in the wet light with the anger of a man badly frightened at unimaginable betrayal by his own flesh. "This morning I was again fobbed off . . ."

"She sleeps still," Lady Rosamund cut in coldly.

"*As* I told your Excellency," Daurannon added.

"Her . . . meditations—" Rosamund's ironic inflection, Antryg knew, was aimed at him. "—of last night were more than a woman of her years should have to endure." Flaked jade could have been no more cutting than the glance that sheered briefly to him where he stood in his corner, then away. Daurannon and Bentick traded a look, but it was more than either dared to do, to violate the Lady's protection.

"As the guards pointed out." Daurannon stepped forward to the Witchfinder's side conciliatingly. "They had their orders."

"*If* the Archmage will not—or cannot—see me," Silvorglim's voice dripped sarcasm like a snake's venom, "perhaps it is time that the Council delegated another to speak. I have been fobbed off, lied to, even as the Regent, the nobles, the Church, even, put aside our advice and ignore our warnings."

"Look," Daurannon said reasonably, forestalling Lady Rosamund's frigid rejoinder and Bentick's almost-spitting outburst of rage, "if we wished to tell you lies, certainly we'd have done so more believably than this."

"You are a people of lies," returned the Witchfinder, his yellow gaze hardening to a pin-bright glitter of hate. "Your power is the stuff of lies, the outspewing of devils designed to tempt human souls to their destruction with the illusion of a power which is and can be the province of God alone."

"God?" Lady Rosamund drew herself up still further, pride and rage smoking from her like the vapor that breathes along a mountain of ice. "Don't you mean God's Church, which grudges to see any wield power but itself?"

"Nor should any," the Witchfinder replied calmly. "The Church, and the Church alone, speaks the will of the Sole God. All the others you have corrupted, even the Emperor. So don't argue semantics with me, you apostate whore, and don't pretend to me that an evil isn't going on here in this Citadel, an evil to tempt and twist true men from what is right. You will find that such a temptation is unavailing, such a twisting impossible." But his eyes, paled to the color of dead leaves, flicked from face to face with a nervousness that belied his words, and Antryg thought, *Were you tempted, then?* Outside, under the balcony, boots scuffed amid a muted creak of dagger belts and harness leather, where more of the Witchfinder's guards awaited. The hasu, standing with folded arms behind Silvorglim's shoulder, was gazing idly in his direction; Antryg felt the crawl of sweat on his forehead, making his scalp itch and his spectacles slip down his nose.

"I demand to be given the freedom I need, the freedom which my charter grants me, to investigate . . . ."

"No!" Lady Rosamund cried.

At the same moment Bentick snapped, "There will be no search of the Citadel save that conducted by the Council!"

"Take care, then, that I do not return with the full might of the Church . . ."

"*You* take care," Bentick shouted, "should you be fool enough to . . ."

"Please!" Daurannon interposed his body between the Witchfinder and the Steward, who looked ready to seize one another by the throats. The hasu also stepped forward from his post in the door but hesitated—quite sensibly, Antryg thought, considering he couldn't be more than a medium-strength wizard, certainly no one to take on three members of the Council. Though he knew that to move would shatter the spells of misdirection that cloaked him, Antryg saw his chance—their attentions all looked fully engaged, and the door was now clear. Stepping softly, he slipped past the red-clothed wizard's shoulder and out into the hall. Daurannon and Rosamund were both too occupied with the shouted recapitulation of the Concordances of Stellith to stop him as he tiptoed down the stairs and paused for a moment in the shadows of the lower hall.

Through the door he could see the Witchfinder's sasenna clearly now, gathered under the balcony to get out of the rain. Across the garden, Antryg could see Seldes Katne leaving the Polygon, a sheaf of notes clutched under her arm; she paused at the turn of the path up to the Library, peering out from beneath the protection of her oiled-cloth hood as if scanning the waist-deep wet jungle for sight of someone . . . probably, Antryg thought, himself.

He could, he knew, work his way on up through the cellars to the Library and intercept her there, to learn whatever it was she had come down to tell him. But the doorways into the Library would be barred with her spells, and even the ward-words of so slight a mage as Seldes Katne were sufficient to keep him out . . . or to trap him against them, as against a locked door, should either the Witchfinder's or the Council's sasenna close him in from behind.

Moreover, with the graying of the afternoon the sense had grown upon him of lost time, of minutes ticking away—of the growing pressure of the energies within the field and of the Void itself. So he turned his steps downward, edging back through the cellars of the Breadbox and the Assembly Hall, through the hypocaust, and so to a downshaft from the cellar of the Island of Butterflies that had escaped Bentick's notice. His hands didn't stop shaking until he was safe in the darkness of the Vaults again.

Down on the fourth level, Mick and Cylin still mounted guard over the Chamber of the Glass Pillar. They both looked tired and rather shaken by the things they had seen and heard slipping through the blackness of the maze all around them. They would feel, too, Antryg thought as he listened to their account of the night, the growing weight of the Void, the rising shudder of the powers of the leys fed through the collecting-maze, polarized, turned back on itself in an eternal loop like the reflections of an endless mirror.

Nevertheless, neither of the young men would return to the Citadel above, offering instead to continue the charting of the middle levels until they were too exhausted to go on. "It's very good of you," Antryg said, emptying his kitchen loot from his pockets and dividing the rolls, cheese, and fruit with them. "If you smell anything like roses, call a spell of winds around you as fast as you can and get out of the vicinity at once. Find me immediately and let me know where it is. And if you meet anyone on the Council—or any of the Council sasenna—you haven't seen me. I don't like this," he added quietly to Ninetentwo, as the two young men vanished around the corner of a twisted staircase and the dark of the Vaults swallowed them up. "I don't like it at all." Reaching out, he touched the wall beside him—the energy felt stable to the bare tips of his fingers but dangerously hot.

"Nor I," the Dead God buzzed softly. "That Moving Gate your mages described—the longer I consider it in the light of all my experiments with the mechanics of the time-space continuum, the more aberrant it sounds. According to my computers, it should not even be possible."

"Well, to use a quite hackneyed example, for many years the flight of a bumblebee was considered to be contrary to all laws of aerodynamics, but it was eventually discovered that not all factors had been taken into account. Saint Vespaluus, as I recall, is the patron saint of honeybees, but for some reason the bumblebees have their own patron saint, Saint Olpo, to whom one also prays to have one's garden delivered from plagues of rabbits. Everything else peaceful?"

The tall arachno-dragon nodded, but his hands, huge and skeletal, shifted unthinkingly along the thick duraplast of the rifle slung over one shoulder. "According to my readings the sixth level is deep in water that is still rising."

"Damn." Antryg threw a nervous glance at the chamber's far door, wondering if, somewhere in the darkness beyond it, he had glimpsed a flicker of moving light. The dim green lumenpanels wired to the pillar shed a cold, feverish gleam over a small pyramid of spare equipment, extra air bottles, first-aid kit, and what he dimly guessed to be a portable computer, and the pillar itself refracted chilly shards of the light across walls and ceiling, touching with ghostly highlights the edges of generators and screens.

"The Gate to my own world is up one level from here." The air hoses flexed like obscene musculature as the Dead God gestured toward the fat hawser of cable that vanished through the door. "I've run a line up to it, to save the batteries for emergencies. Each battery is good for one hour, as we reckon hours: roughly two of yours. I've got a com-cable hooked through, too, and the bulletins I hear from my own world are disquieting."

Antryg shivered, thinking about the cold, floating, half-formed sentiences of the teles-balls that had over the years "gone bad" drifting through the charged mazes of the Vaults; about the power he could sense, almost palpably now, streaming through the fibers of granite all about him; about the dark, straining strength of the Void twisting at the magic that held it in place. The exhaustion he'd felt in his dream seemed to have carried over into waking: he felt more tired than he could remember being in years, the pain of the geas a constant, slow gnawing at his bones.

But somewhere in the sightless mazes of the Vaults, somewhere in the labyrinthine tangles of pits and traps and doors that led nowhere, lay the answer: the Gate from which issued the scent of roses, the darkness in which voices cried out words that were afterward forgotten . . . and the Circles of Power that held the thing open.

*The answer,* thought Antryg wearily, and his bones cringed from the thought of more wandering through this haunted underworld of filthy mosses, unseen demons, drifting ghosts of fog. The answer would be there. It was the question he had begun to worry about.

"I suppose," he said at length, "that eventually I shall have to go abovestairs again and try to see Aunt Min. By that time I hope Rosie will have called the dogs off me and convinced Silvorglim and his myrmidons to go elsewhere—at least, I hope she manages to do that before it comes time to dismantle the polarization field, because it's going to take all the strength the Council can raise to do so safely. And I'm beginning to experience a sort of academic curiosity about what they're going to do with me once this is all solved."

The opaque golden iridescence of Ninetentwo's eyes gleamed at him as the Dead God tilted his head. "Perhaps they wonder that, too."

Pothatch and Tom were just putting the last of the supper dishes away when Antryg emerged from the Vaults again. It was almost full dark, and still raining, the sound of it a soft, steady drumming on the tiled roof above the clumsy rafter shadows. Supper was long over, but the sasenna who would ordinarily have filled in for the absent servants were still out walking uneasy patrols. Tom dished up leftover lamb stew that, for once, Antryg was almost too exhausted to eat while Pothatch slipped out to puff his way up the hill to the Breadbox to beg more dream herbs from Q'iin. In the deserted bath-house, with its smells of wet stone, herbs, and soap, there was sufficient hot water in the boilers for Antryg to bathe and shave and wash his hair; afterward he climbed a ladder in the back of a stores cupboard to the attic, to sleep for what remained of the night.

Better a whore than a wizard, for at least a whore'll give you summat for your coin.

—ELLIE BRUE (Mistress to King Pharidon II and one of the most notorious prostitutes in Angelshand)

# CHAPTER XVIII

"LET ME ALONE . . . GO AWAY . . . I SWEAR TO YOU I NEVER killed you."

Suspended inches, it seemed, above the poisoned seethe of dreams, Antryg opened his eyes and listened. Up here under the roof tiles the rain was very loud; the air smelled of wet dust where leaks dripped through and of herbed steam and soap from below.

He heard nothing more for a time, but, reasoning that anything was an improvement over what waited for him on the other side of the wall of sleep, he got noiselessly to his feet and pulled on his coat. As he crept to the top of the ladder, he heard a soft bumping, the scrape of furniture as weight caught at it, and a broken voice filled with terror and grief.

"Please . . . *please* . . . I didn't mean it. I never meant you harm."

Otaro's voice.

Antryg slipped down the ladder, put aside the hanging that separated the closet, with its shelves of terra-cotta crocks, from the main length of the baths.

The Singer of the City of Cranes swayed like a ghost in the middle of the big stone room, holding a corner of one of the tables for support. He wore only a yellow calico nightshirt, baggy over a frame that had visibly lost flesh in the past three days; the long black curls hanging down over his shoulders were matted and filthy. He swung violently around at the scuff of Antryg's boots on the flagstoned floor, hand raised. "Keep away from me!" he screamed in a voice shrill with terror.

Antryg froze, seeing the blind panic in the older man's dark eyes. Mages were drilled to use defensive spells of lightning and fire if attacked—if he moved, he'd be a pile of greasy ash long before he could reach either Otaro or the door. The Singer's face was pouchy and gray with fatigue, grimed with beard stubble, and wet with sweat as if he'd dunked it in one of the tubs; his breath labored in the rain-drumming darkness.

"I'm not here to harm you, Otaro," Antryg said in a low, friendly voice. "I just found your seeing-glass in the Vaults, that's all." Moving very carefully, he slipped the magnifying lens on its ribbon from around his neck and held it out. "And I knew you needed help."

The little man backed away, trembling, hand still upraised. Antryg wasn't sure who or what he was seeing through those fear-stretched brown eyes, but, at a guess, it wasn't the bathhouse. "I don't need help."

"Of course not," Antryg agreed soothingly, the voice of a healer's spells. "I'm here to protect you, Otaro—to protect you so that you can go to sleep."

He lowered his voice still more, recognizing his own dreams, his own fears, his own madness in the Singer's frightened stare. "You're quite safe, you know, and as long as you have your seeing-glass he can't come for you—he can't come near you. He'll stay dead and underground where he belongs." That kind of fear, he knew, came only from seeing in dreams one who by all rights and reason must be long rotted to dust. "Let me give it to you, and then you'll be quite safe."

A lie, of course, he thought—he himself had never felt safe—

but a lie for which the little Oriental reached as hungrily as he reached for the promise of sleep. The brown hand lowered tremblingly, and Otaro hugged himself like a beaten child, black hair hanging down over his face, catching only the ruby glimmer of the banked embers beneath the boiler; in the bloody light Antryg could see him tremble.

"I'll never be safe." The magic beauty of the voice was a cracked whisper of despair. "Nowhere. Never."

"You'll be safe as long as you wear this." Antryg edged closer, holding out the magnifying glass on the end of its ribbons. Even the smallest thing, he knew, could act as a talisman to a mind unhinged with exhaustion and terror.

"Here," he said comfortingly, "let me give this to you and get you back to your room. You'll be safe there."

"You didn't know him," Otaro whispered, still clutching himself, still not looking up. "I was his only son, his only child. He expected . . . so much of me."

"Yes," Antryg breathed, remembering the glint of tawny eyes. "Yes, I know."

"The money I took was his savings. But I had to be free of him. I had to come here, to study, to escape. He would never have let me. Later I sent it back to him, sent it over and over . . ." Tears crawled down the sunken brown cheeks, like droplets of blood in the ember glow, to lose themselves in the iron gray stubble of beard. "He cursed me. He said . . ."

"I know what he said." Antryg held out one hand, the magnifying lens dangling by its ribbons from one crooked finger in the ink-stained woolen mitt. "You don't need to tell me. I know."

"I thought I had fled from him," Otaro whispered, "all those years ago."

*But you never can flee from them,* thought Antryg. *Not when they're alive in your mind.*

"It was your father's voice you heard, wasn't it," he asked gently, "coming from the Gate?"

The chubby mage nodded brokenly, seeming to shrink further and further in on himself. He snatched the lens from Antryg's hand and clutched it to him, hugging himself while Antryg put his long arms around those heaving shoulders. "I heard it again, saw it again, and again . . . every time I shut my eyes. The Gate, opening in my rooms, rushing at me, pursuing me, swallowing me. And then it was gone. But it would come back . . ."

Turning convulsively, he clutched at Antryg's sleeves, plucked the shabby shawl with hands that could call music to make birds weep and draw clouds down to listen—gripped him with bone-breaking strength, as if fearing some rising flood of blackness would sweep him away.

"Oh, Father . . ."

Then he doubled over, his hands flying to his temples as if he would smash his own skull like an eggshell, his face ghastly with pain.

Hoping to hell Rosamund had managed to call off Daurannon's orders for his arrest, Antryg half guided, half carried the sobbing, stumbling little man out of the baths, along the darkened North Cloister, and up the tiny stone stepway at its end, between stands of dripping birch and then through a door and a cellar and up another flight to the cellar of the Pavilion, the house on the northern side of the hill where the Singer lived. Though he was fairly certain Otaro was mad, Antryg searched the rooms nevertheless for any sign that the Moving Gate had indeed manifested itself there but found none. Which didn't prove, he reflected, that it hadn't been appearing there at every chime of the clock for the past three days; the house was situated on the Pensyk ley.

During his search Otaro only sat in a corner, twisting like a nervous child or clutching at his head, sweating and whimpering in pain. But the big downstairs study and the smaller loft where he slept above smelled fusty, shut up, frowsted with long habitation and little air. The sheets on the bed were sweat-damp and twisted, the scrolls and papers on the desk scattered, crumpled, torn. Not from a search, thought Antryg, turning them over in his long, gloved hands. They'd been hurled about by an angry arm, torn because they'd been there to tear.

In his own days of madness in the Silent Tower, his papers had frequently looked the same.

"Master . . ."

Antryg looked over the loft's carved rail. Zake Brighthand stood in the open doorway, gray robes freckled with rain.

"He's upstairs." Antryg clattered swiftly down the narrow twist of oaken steps as the boy came into the room, looking around him at the tumbled papers and scattered books. There was shock and grief in his fatigue-hollowed eyes but little surprise, the expression of a man who has finally nerved himself to open a door behind which he has smelled blood and death. "When was the last you saw him?"

"Yesterday." Brighthand shook his head, his long hair slapping wetly against his cheeks. "He swore he was well, said there was a plot among the wizards of the Council, that his life wouldn't be safe if I went to any of 'em. I could see he looked bad and begged him to see Issay or Min or one of t'other healers. Then when I came back with food for him last night the door was locked, spelled shut. I didn't know what to do."

"He's gone mad, you know."

Brighthand turned his face aside, biting his lips; Antryg guessed that this was knowledge he had been fighting against for some time. "That Gate?" the boy asked after a moment.

"Maybe. I found him in the bathhouse . . ."

"He swore he was well," the Junior repeated, his slurry docker's drawl breaking a little with desperation and strain. "I been comin' back every few hours to check, try and get him to eat or sleep. This's the first the door's been open. If it hadn't been, I think I'd have disobeyed him and gone for help, and hell with what he said. I just didn't know what to do."

"Stay with him now," said Antryg softly. "I'll send Issay over."

His hand on the cellar door, Antryg added, "He's in pain,

and panicky—he may hurl lightning or fire at you, so be ready.''

Brighthand nodded; Antryg could see him mentally going over defenses. He might still be a Junior and a new one at that, and his technical knowledge slender, but for all his quiet, his strength was such that Antryg had little fear of his being hurt.

''He spoke of seeing the Moving Gate here, in his rooms, which may have been a hallucination—or not. By the way, you don't happen to know if Mick and Cylin came back from the Vaults, do you?''

''Oh, aye, hours ago.'' Brighthand paused on his way up the steps. ''In time for dinner, anyway.''

''Lucky bastards.'' Antryg sighed and went down the cellar steps at a run, making his way via attics and cellars and nameless little stairs and bridges around the western side of the hill toward the Mole Hill, where Issay Bel-Caire lived.

The Silent One was still awake, spell-weaving a tisane designed to restore strength badly depleted; the whole floor of the Mole Hill's single room was a labyrinth of power-circles, chalked spirals, sigils of light and silver, with the little physician sitting cross-legged in the middle, long gray mare's tails of hair braided back over thin shoulders and the archaic glass amplification tubes that no one else ever used capping each spidery finger.

After a rapid conference in which Issay warned him of the patrols and demanded to know about the alien energies that whispered now in every stone of the Citadel's ancient bones, Antryg dispatched the Silent One to the Pavilion to look after Otaro. As the slight figure flitted up the vine-choked outer steps and into the rainy darkness, Antryg leaned for a moment against the doorframe, wondering exactly how he was going to assemble sufficient force for a rapid, surreptitious shakedown of the entire Citadel without letting either Daurannon or Silvorglim know what was afoot.

It had to be done soon, and it had to be done quickly—with the energy buildup running dangerously high, the stabilization field should not be permitted to continue more than another twelve hours.

Yet Bentick seemed determined not to let it take place as long as the Witchfinders were present in the Citadel. Antryg thought about that as he made a quick search of the Mole Hill for a jelgeth tisane—as he'd suspected, Issay had concocted one for the conjuration. They were frowned upon by the Council, but all the wizards used them. Exactly what was it that Bentick—or Phormion—feared would be uncovered? Old secrets in the Vaults? Daurannon could screen those from the Witchfinders as he'd certainly screen them from Antryg.

And yet, he thought, his boots thumping hollowly on the enclosed staircase between the subcellar of the Isle of Butterflies and the attic of the laundries, if Bentick or Phormion was behind all this, why not play their trump card and threaten Joanna? Why try to murder him? He'd told Min of two attempts on his life—one in the cellar of the Castle and the other at the Green King's Chapel—but the second attempt might just as easily have been directed against Rosamund, with himself as bait.

As he swung through a trapdoor into the laundry and scrambled down a drying-rack to the floor, he glanced toward the three massively shuttered windows, wondering whether he ought to risk getting to the Porcelain House tonight to warn Rosamund, or try cutting through the garden to wake Min.

And what, he wondered, rattling down a twisted iron stair to the boiler room between the laundries and the baths, did all this have to do with keeping the Moving Gate open in the first place?

Unless, of course, someone had panicked.

Having just dealt with one panicky wizard, he shuddered to think of what could happen to such a wizard's helpless prisoner.

As he descended in the silent warmth of the boiler room, the sound of lowered voices arguing came to him from the baths, the soft-footed rustle of many bodies, the muted creak of belt leather and and the clink of weapons.

"This is outrageous!" he heard Nandiharrow fulminating.

"Be silent!" snapped Silvorglim's deep voice, and Antryg, knowing full well he should head in the other direction as fast as he could, nevertheless stole softly to the open archway that separated the boiler chamber from the long bathhouse with its curtained tubs. "I have received evidence that the Council is harboring a condemned wizard, an outlaw ousted by the Council and turned over to civil justice."

"*No* Council mage is *ever* turned over to civil justice," the nine-fingered clockmaker began hotly, but Daurannon, who stood quietly beside the Witchfinder as the red-robed hasu led a dozen Church sasenna up the closet ladder to the loft above, said nothing, and his choirboy face was enigmatic and still. A small group of wizards and novices clustered behind Nandiharrow, those who had been awake at this hour and had come to investigate the commotion: by the flickering light of the sasenna's torches Antryg recognized Whitwell Simm, Q'iin and her student Gilda with robes pulled on over their nightdresses, Seldes Katne, Kyra the Red, and, with smoke almost visibly coming from his ears, Bentick the Steward.

"Considering that the Council lied about his fate four months ago . . ."

"It was not a lie!" Bentick snapped furiously. "We were deceived when he made his escape."

Feet thundered in the loft overhead; through the sound of the rain it was difficult to tell, but Antryg thought he heard more sasenna passing down the pillared arcade outside, sword harnesses creaking softly. He wondered if he had been betrayed or simply followed when he left the kitchen. Anyone could have trailed Pothatch earlier in the evening when he went to Q'iin's for the tisane.

"No one up there, m'lord . . ."

"Enough of this!" Silvorglim swung around, his pale eyes blazing with a kind of haunted glitter; Antryg could see he was almost shaking with suppressed nervousness behind his rage. "From the moment we entered these gates we have met with nothing but deceptions and lies. Captain—have your men search the Citadel. Top to bottom, every room, every chamber . . ."

"By what authority?" Nandiharrow stormed.

"You can't!" Seldes Katne gasped.

"I forbid it!" Bentick snapped. "There are places which ought not to be disturbed."

"If you know what's good for you, you'll stay out of the Vaults," Daurannon added reasonably.

"Do you mean, if *you* know what's good for you, you'll tell us to?" the Witchfinder retorted, turning to stab a finger at the Handsome One. "What is it that you are hiding, besides a man who murders the innocent by magic? Some plot to tempt and twist the minds of every man who . . ."

But Antryg had turned already and was headed for the stair shaft back up to safety. He was halfway there when the almost-unheard whisper of fabric made him glance back; Bentick had slipped through the curtains that guarded the archway and, gathering up his robe, was also striding for the stairs at close to a run. He saw Antryg and stopped, momentarily non-plussed; Antryg was lifting his finger to his lips in a soundless plea for silence when Daurannon appeared in the doorway behind him.

"There he is!" Daurannon shouted, and Antryg bolted for the stairwell like a startled deer. "He'll be making for the Vaults."

Antryg swore, silently but mightily, as he ripped open the tiny plank trapdoor under the stairs and dropped down it into the vine-choked web of struts and pilings which supported that end of the baths above the steep drop-off of the hill. As he pulled the trap shut above him he felt the wooden floor of the little shaft shudder with the jarring weight of men streaming up the stair; nimbly he swung to the heavy Y-fork of wooden braces below him, and so dropped seven or eight feet into the tangle of vines. This end of the baths, with its little turret and the makeshift covered stairway leading up to the subcellar of the Island of Butterflies, projected out over the drop of the hill. The ground was steep, the night pitch black, and lightening rain pattered briefly on Antryg's long hair and the shoulders of his coat as he scrambled along the outer wall of the buttery, making for the wide windows of the kitchen.

Even as he plunged across the huge, darkened stone cavern with its smells of sugar and batter, it occurred to him to wonder where, exactly, Bentick had been bound when he'd slipped away from the Witchfinders. To report to Phormion? Footfalls thundered in the refectory as Antryg slammed through the pantry door, down the narrow stairs to the storage cellars . . .

And stopped, gasping with a sickened wrench of pain and fear, on the threshold of the steps that led still farther down into the Vaults.

He knew the fear he felt was only Bentick's spell. He could see the Steward's marks glimmering in the utter dark, fussy and neat along the jambs and lintels of the little door that led to the subcellar—marks of torment and terror, marks of ward and guard . . . marks that it was impossible to pass. Sweat stood out on Antryg's face; through gritted teeth he whispered, "This is only a spell, only illusion . . ."

But something inside him seemed to dissolve at the thought of putting so much as his hand, let along his entire body, through that doorway. It was a fear that bypassed the mind entirely and centered in the gut, the flesh, as if it had been the door of a furnace, radiating a bone-stripping heat. A simple counterspell would have dusted that fear away, but the geas bound him, and it did him no good to simply tell himself that the pain would be illusory, the blinding certainty of death and worse than death illusory.

He simply couldn't do it, any more than he could have brought himself to grasp the blade of a running chainsaw with his hands.

Men's voices sounded in the stairway behind him. There

was every chance they'd have hasu with them; four strides took him across the room to the square entry-hole of the disused shaft through which building materials had once been hauled up from the courtyard below. The door on it looked old and splintery but was still stout, and it opened inward into the room; drawing it shut after him, he could get his fingers behind the cross-brace and hold on, keeping the door fast with the weight of his body at the same time that he kept himself from sliding down the steep shaft to the foot of the Citadel hill.

The shivery burn of energy all around him was stifling in the granite of the narrow shaft. His eyes closed, he listened in the darkness to the soft, swift pad of footfalls in the storeroom, the rattle of drawn swords, the arguing voices as they searched. Once, they tested the shaft doorway but, finding it would not open, assumed it was locked, not that it was being held shut from the other side. He heard one of the hasu say, "No one has passed these signs," and in time, the footfalls faded away up the stairs again.

The well shaft in the mule barn, Antryg thought. It went down deeper than the storeroom tunnel, and it hadn't been spelled shut. He had to reach the Chamber of the Glass Pillar before the Witchfinders did, to keep them somehow from interfering with the Dead God's machinery there. With the amount of energy perilously balanced between the magic circles in the North Hall and the oscillators and reflecting screens of the polarization field in the Vaults, the mere thought of what could happen if one or the other side of the equation were knocked away turned him cold. As he slipped out of the shaft and up the kitchen stairs again, moved like a flitting shadow across the empty refectory and out into the darkness of the North Wing's Colonnade, he reviewed his options.

If nothing else, he supposed, he could always listen for their coming, or watch for it on the Dead God's multiscanner, and if they came too near the Chamber let them see him, lead them away into the mazes he knew far better than they. His bones ached at the thought of another game of hide-and-seek, especially in the

Vaults, but there was not time even to think about it now. In time one of his friends had to come down to the Vaults, had to deduce that that was where he would go.

But as he strode swiftly down the foot-worn pavement of the North Cloister, he saw something that made the entire question—and most of his other concerns, not to mention the concerns of everyone else in the darkened Citadel—utterly academic.

The rain now drummed the tiled roof of the arcade and glittered dimly with the reflection of the lights in the Polygon as it ring-pocked the standing pools in the courtyard and dripped in a sparkling curtain from the arcade's gutters. Beneath the arcade, the pavement itself was dry, save for a single line of wet footprints, crossing where someone had cut through the courtyard itself—footprints leading to the opened door of the North Hall.

Long coat billowing behind him, Antryg ducked through into the Hall's vestibule. The steady yellow glow of the lamp high on the wall showed him two guards in the black clothing of the Council's sasenna, slumped on the benches at either side of the room; a third lay close to the huge, iron-strapped doors that led into the hall itself. Their faces were peaceful—the stillness whispered with the deep breath of sleep. The wet footprints led between them, to the closed inner doors.

Cold shock sinking in on him, as if all his veins had been suddenly opened, Antryg ran to drag at the massive iron of the handle. The jar of thrown bolts on the other side mocked him. Flattening to the three-inch oak slabs, he could hear, with the hyperacute senses of a wizard, the insectile scratching of broomstraw and holystone beyond, the whisper of a voice speaking words of dissolution, of breaking.

*"NO!"* His fists slammed the door with a force that nearly broke the bones. "Damn you, don't do it! Don't . . ."

He kicked the panels desperately, reached with his mind to throw the bolt aside, and felt even that simplest of spells crumble to smoke under the geas' black cold. "Stop . . . !"

Even as he cried the word he heard behind him the creak of

sword belts, the wet squelch of booted feet crossing the vestibule at a run. He dived for the dropped sword of the nearest sleeping guard, but didn't make it. Hands seized his arms, dragged him backward; someone twisted his shoulder to drop him to his knees.

"Break down that door!" he commanded, and such was the authority in his voice that three of them moved to obey before Silvorglim cut them off.

"Hold on to him, you fools! You won't deceive us that way."

"Dammit, get that door open!" Antryg ordered desperately. "The spells in that room are the only thing holding the Citadel in balance with the flux-spells on the Void."

"Keep hold of him, dammit!" the Witchfinder snapped, striding into the room through the outer door, raindrops glinting in his fading red hair.

Antryg twisted frantically against the grip on his arms, tried to get to his feet; someone behind him changed the angle of his hold on his wrist, and the pain turned his knees to water. "Please," he said rapidly, his voice level now and very quiet as he looked up into the Witchfinder's face. "Get in there and stop them."

"So this is the heart of the secret evil being done?" Silvorglim's pale eyes flickered to the doors. "The center of the Council's plot . . ."

"No . . . Yes . . ." Someone grasped a handful of his long hair and jerked his head back, and he felt the razor edge of a sword against the thin skin under his jaw. "It's not a Council plot but if the person in there disrupts those circles the entire Citadel may be destroyed!"

The Witchfinder turned back from the doors with a momentary start of surprise. "Is it so indeed?" he whispered, as if to himself. Then, "A small price to pay, if you speak the truth." His eyes moved from the shut doors to the eyes of the man behind Antryg with the sword; he gave a quick nod of command. "Do it."

Antryg felt the guard's muscles stiffen, the first thin stroke of pain—he cried "No . . . !" more in fury at their stupidity than fear of his own death.

What happened then in the room was impossible to describe, either then or later. Not a sound, nor a wind, nor a change of light or darkness, save that the flames of the torches held by the sasenna and the small lamp burning high on the wall altered somehow for a moment.

There was a change of pressure, slamming shut the outer door to the colonnade. But it was not immediately noticeable amid the thing, the event, the clap that was not a thunderclap, the reverberation which struck each person in that room as if with the sound of an echoing explosion within his or her mind, and within the mind alone.

The sasennan behind Antryg dropped his sword and loosed his grip on Antryg's hair, jerking his hands up as if to cover his ears. In the grip of the other guards who still held his arms, Antryg flinched, shuddering, knowing it was too late . . . he scarcely felt the hot thread of blood running down his neck from where the vein had been barely nicked.

If the man had gone through with it and slashed his throat to the neck bone, he reflected an instant later in that first, terrible, endlessly echoing silence, it would still have been the least of his or anybody else's worries.

In the silence there was not even the draw of breath for a count of fifteen, as each person in that room save one wondered what had happened, wondered what was different.

The rain smell, the earth smell, the smell of wet grass and sky that had seemed to breathe even through the shut door was gone.

The pounding downpour on the roof was gone.

It was Silvorglim's voice, thin and very calm, that broke that dreadful stillness. Quite levelly, he asked, "What have you done, witch?"

But when Antryg, still kneeling among the guards whose grip on his arms was slowly slacking as they realized—as well as they *could* realize—what must have happened, did not reply, the Witchfinder's own sword seared from its sheath in a single slash of hysterical rage, the point coming to rest in the pit of Antryg's throat. *"What have you done?"*

Antryg disengaged his hand from the guards' nerveless clutch and pushed the blade aside. Then he climbed slowly to his feet, wiping at the trail of blood from his neck with a corner of Aunt Min's shawl, and walked to the vestibule's outer door. Shaken and shocked, Silvorglim reached to open it again, and Antryg said softly, "Don't do that, Yarak." After a long moment the Witchfinder's square, red-furred hand dropped to his side.

"Tobin . . ." Antryg gestured to the hasu who stood, chalk-faced, among the sasenna. After a moment's hesitation the man stepped forward and placed his hands upon the door.

In the meantime one of the guards had gone to the vestibule's single small window and stood with face pressed to the glass. "I can't see a thing out there, my lord," he said, twisting and angling his head. "I can't swear to it, but from here we ought to be able to see the lights of the refectory."

The hasu Tobin fell back, his hands shaking and his face paler than before, so pale that the brown age spots on his shaven scalp stood out as if painted in the shuddering torch-light. Reaching out to touch the iron handle of the door, Antryg found it cold as ice.

"There's nothing out there," the hasu whispered, and his eyes, as they moved to the ungainly wizard in his beads and purple coat, showed a rim of white all around the iris. "Nothing. . ."

"No," Antryg agreed quietly and turned back to face them: Silvorglim with his sword still in his hand; the Church wizard, trembling all over like a whipped horse, at his side; the Church sasenna in their long-skirted black coats; and the Council's three guards, waking now, drawing together as if for protection against some terrible threat that none of them could see.

In a quite reasonable tone of voice, Antryg went on, "Any member of the Council will tell you, Yarak, that it is impossible for me to do anything with magic under the conditions of the geas. On the other hand, I am going to suggest to the Council—if we can *find* the Council—that they remove the geas from me as quickly as possible, since I would say just offhand that we're all in terrible trouble."

Face ghastly with shock, the Church wizard whispered, "What has happened?"

"Well," Antryg explained calmly, "whoever it was who disrupted the circles holding together that spell-field in the other room unbalanced a rather critical equation of forces between the magic which made it possible for the Void-energies to be polarized, and the stabilization field set up by the Dead God's machines down in the Vaults. I did tell you to break down the door and stop him, you recall." He wiped at his neck again and regarded for a moment the smudge of blood on his fingers before looking up at them all again.

"I'm very much afraid that the result seems to have been to precipitate the Citadel into the Void."

It is said that Clovis II, the present Emperor's grandfather, was in his youth much given to scandal and riot. Indeed, when he married Nerri d'Arrantsan, daughter of the King of Trusand, during the wedding fete a notorious seventeen-year-old tavern dancer whom he had been keeping in the City drove her sporting carriage up to the great fountain before the Palace steps, and in full view of the wedding guests—including the bride's father—threw into the fountain all of Clovis' coats, shirts, and breeches which he had kept in her apartments.

—VYRLAINE
*Imperial Chronicles*

# CHAPTER XIX

"MAGUS!"

"Joanna!"

"What the hell was that?"

In pitchy darkness hands groped for hands.

"There's movement," Joanna said, after a long, breathing time. "The air is moving; can you feel it?" After the utter stillness—heatless, coldless, soundless, endless—even the faint drift of breeze was like the falling down of dreadful walls. The soundlessness had changed, too, altering in some fashion too subtle for identification, but it was as if, Joanna thought, what had been utter nullity had suddenly been made somehow finite, defined by ambient echo.

"Come on!"

She sprang to her feet, then turned back impatiently when she felt the drag of the dog wizard's unwilling weight. Without stopping to argue, she hauled him up by his wrist, pulled him determinedly after her in the direction of that soft, drawing breeze. "What's the matter?"

"Do you want to walk into . . . into whatever it is?" Even his voice sounded different with the change of air pressure.

"Do you want to stay where you are and keep poor Irina company?" The newness of the air was an intoxicant; Joanna felt suddenly, glitteringly conscious of the texture of the velvet sleeve under her hand, the silk trapunto of the cuff and the cording that edged it. The loose, soft cotton of her own pajama sleeves against her skin seemed new-made, new-textured, as did the cold smoothness of the floor underfoot, the flutter of her own loose blond curls against her cheeks. The very molecules of the air against her skin seemed alive in the changed air pressure. It was all she could do not to run, waving her arms and shouting in the dark down the endless turnings, following the stream of moving air.

Half-drunk with hope, she flashed from wild joy to horrible forboding. *How long? Ten years? A hundred years? Please, God, don't make it have been a hundred years. Don't make everything be different. Don't make me be alone again.*

Shaky terror overwhelmed her, and for a moment, she wondered if Magus might not be right. Never knowing might indeed be better than finding out . . . it wasn't so bad, once you got used to it, if you stayed away from the demons.

Far, far off, she saw light.

Tiny and dim, the round spot of ocher had a wavery quality, like fire- or torchlight, but it was so bright after the long darkness that her eyes hurt with it. Her hand tightened on Magus' and she began to run, the thud of her feet on the floor jolting her bones, her purse slapping heavily against her thigh. Once, as the light strengthened, she looked down and saw its topaz reflection on her own pumping knees, but it wasn't until she stepped into the room at the end of that long tunnel that she dared look around behind her, to see her companion's white, thin face, with its trim black beard and startlingly green eyes.

Then she looked around her, at the place to which the light had led them.

It was no bigger than the minuscule dining-room-cum-office

of her apartment. Shelves lined the walls, filled with neat rows of books; a scrubbed plank table upheld a tidy assortment of terra-cotta pots containing herbs, plus a few gardening implements. A knitting basket, wrought of twigs and overflowing with varicolored yarn, rested on a rough chair, and in a corner a small loom crouched like some kind of bizarre wooden robot, while beside it, tall and angular, stood a spinning wheel.

On a shelf a pair of tiny pink silk dancing slippers sat, frayed and covered with dust. Coals burned on a tiled hearth no larger than a good-sized washbasin. A red teapot, a white cup.

Beyond the window, blackness as utter, as complete, as she had known in the halls of her prison. All around, broken only by the tiny cracklings of the fire, silence as dreadfully profound.

"A mage," Magus whispered behind her. He had picked up the solitary book which lay among the potted plants on the table and was turning over its stiff yellowed pages. "And in my own world. This is written in old High Trebin."

The stillness was horrible, the stillness of death. Joanna tiptoed across the room to push back the heavy white cotton curtain there. The chamber beyond was even smaller, the wooden walls likewise banked floor to ceiling in shelves of books. In a little alcove a single bed was half-hidden by white curtains. Cats prowled uneasily; the largest pushed its flat-skulled gray head at Joanna's calf and miaowed softly, as if it, too, feared to violate that dreadful hush.

Dim firelight showed her the face of the woman lying in the bed, tiny, pink, and wrinkled, incredibly old in the thin fan of white hair spread about the pillow.

"It's Aunt Min." She spoke barely above a whisper, not wanting to wake the ancient Archmage. She felt half-afraid, by the stillness of the little dried-apple features, that the old lady was beyond waking. A deep sadness seized her, for old Minhyrdin the Fair looked so tired, so ancient, so isolated from all the world she had grown up in, a time traveler in her own body, far beyond everything she had known as a girl.

"Good," Magus said, and at the briskness of his voice Joanna turned around, startled. "Well," he reasoned, "if she's still alive we can't have been prisoners for so very long. *Is* she still alive?"

Joanna leaned down, wanting to touch the claw twisted with arthritis and no larger than a child's. But when it came to it, she didn't dare. "I think so," she murmured. She raised her eyes. A cat jumped onto the bed, kneaded with soft paws at the old woman's thigh. Through a small window to one side of the bed alcove—through all the odd-shaped windows of the little room—was only blackness, impenetrable, silent, and terrible. "There's nothing out there," she asked softly, "is there?"

Magus had gone to a larger window, looking out with the night-piercing eyes of a mage. "No," he said softly. "Nothing . . ." He turned back to her, his face struggling to remain calm. "So this really isn't a way out at all."

"Then that means it can't be where the draft was coming from," Joanna pointed out. "When we came in sight of the light, we quit following the air current—all we have to do is go back to where we were and pick it up again." She turned around. Past the half-opened curtains she could see into the other room, and beyond that, to the narrow slit of darkness that seemed to hover a few feet in front of the opposite wall: an eyepit into Hell, a crack opening to the haunted abysses from which they had so newly escaped. Resolutely, she walked back into that room, and selected the two largest balls of yarn from the knitting basket. She tied an end of one to the leg of the table; the other ball she secreted in her purse.

"Come on," she said bracingly, seeing Magus hesitate, torn between the certainty of imprisonment in this lighted cul-de-sac and the possibility of escape through the darkness once more. "There has to be another way out."

Most of the mages had already assembled in the refectory by the time Antryg, Silvorglim, and the Witchfinder's guards reached it. Antryg's hands were bound behind him, the steel of the Witchfinder's manacles laced with scarlet spell-cord despite Antryg's repeated assertions that under the geas it was impossible for him to work magic of any sort. "And I certainly have no intention of running away, you know," he added as he strode along in a swirl of coat skirts, the littler man scurrying in an undignified fashion to keep up with his longer strides. "Turn left here, and a stair will take us down to the main cellars of the Polygon. For one thing, where on Earth would I go?"

"For that I have no surety," Silvorglim gritted, and his fox-colored eyes glinted dangerously in the torchlight. "Nor will I trust what you say you cannot do, or would not do, given the chance." It was only with the greatest of difficulty that Antryg had talked Silvorglim out of cutting his throat in the vestibule after all, the Witchfinder reasoning that if he brought his quarry back into contact with the other mages, he would probably be prevented from doing so.

But he had faced opposition, not only from the three Council sasenna but, unexpectedly, from his own warriors as well. "He knows this Citadel like the back of his hand, sir," their captain had said, glancing uneasily at the vestibule door as if he could see through it the dreadful, shifting darkness beyond. "And he knows what may be going on. And," he'd added, jerking his scarred chin in the direction of the tall wizard still standing in a thorned circle of drawn steel, "we can always kill him later."

"That is my point," Silvorglim had said softly. "If we give him his life now, we may not be able to take it later, as our warrant permits and the safety of the world, I am now convinced, demands. These wizards all plot with one another, and this man is the worst. I know him."

"Oh, fiddle-faddle." Antryg had widened his huge gray eyes at him behind his spectacles. "We've met exactly twice and I challenge you to find an etiquette master in the country who'll grant that putting red-hot irons to a man's feet constitutes anything more than a nodding acquaintance.''

Silvorglim had ignored the remark but in the end had had to give in. At Antryg's behest the Church wizard had finally used his spells to slip the bolts of the North Hall's inner door, by which time, of course, the Hall itself had been vacant. One of the small doors on the far side of it had been unbolted, opening into the maze of cellars, communicating tunnels, and tiny stairways that could lead anywhere in the Citadel; of the Circles of Power themselves, nothing remained of the curving galaxy of chalk trails and spirals into which Aunt Min had poured her power save scuffed and muddled fragments here and there upon the smooth sandstone of the floor.

And everywhere, as Antryg led the way through the back ways of cellars and tunnels to the Polygon, he could feel the shattered energies of the polarization field, the flickering lightnings of power, darting uneasily through the stones of the Citadel or flashing with a queer, shining, half-visible deadliness in the close-crowding shadows. Broken from their field, scattered everywhere under the built-up pressures of the past twenty-four hours, the energies that had been raised and redoubled and then released, undispersed, from their bounds were far from spent. Their crazy backlash had precipitated the Citadel into the Void; its pressure and influence still operated on the swirling bits of spell-field that remained. Even the non-mageborn sasenna of the Church felt it, and as Antryg led them through boiler rooms and hypocausts and disused staircases, they kept looking behind them as if subliminally aware of the random stirrings Antryg could so clearly see moving in the gloom that closed in behind.

For all his appearance of calm, Antryg himself was badly shaken, seeing now and then the lightning crawl of bluish glow that ran down certain cracks in the walls and hearing the low mutter of strange sounds in places where no sounds should have been. There were few places in his life he had been gladder to reach than the long, prosaic refectory with its carved hammerbeams and cold stone hearth, and few people whose faces he had welcomed more than the furious, beautiful woman who came limping across the room toward him, black robes swirling like storm cloud around her, staff clicking on the stones and eyes blazing like green Samhain fire.

"If this is any doing of yours, Antryg Windrose, I swear to you by the Horns of Hell I'll . . ."

"You'll have to stand at the end of a rather long line, I'm afraid," Antryg told her reasonably. "And by that time I'm sure there will be very little left except soggy bits. Someone got into the North Hall," he added more quietly, looking down at the Lady, who appeared ready either to order his execution or box his ears. "I tried to stop them but they'd bolted the doors . . . the guards had been put to sleep with a simple Good-Night—anyone could have done it. Do you think you could get them to unchain me, by the way? It's tremendously uncomfortable, and I'm certainly not going anywhere."

"Release him," Lady Rosamund ordered shortly, and, when Silvorglim opened his mouth to protest, she commanded, "Do it!" in a voice like silvered steel. "Sentence of death or no, we need his knowledge, his services, for the remainder of this crisis."

"And if he is the man who caused the crisis?" the Witchfinder demanded, his whole creased little face seeming to tighten, like a dog's before it snaps. "How can we judge what he tells us is truth and what is lies?"

"*We* can judge," the Lady retorted haughtily, "because *we* know something more of magic than the propaganda dribbled forth by magic's foes. Now let him go."

"Thank you . . . there isn't a great deal of time to waste." Antryg rubbed his wrists where the chain had bruised them, his gray eyes already going to the group of Junior mages gathered beneath the great chandelier in the center of the hall. The waxlights on that massive triple hoop of iron and chain had not been kindled; instead, half a hundred shreds and fragments of bluish witchfire clung to the cold wicks, casting soft, strong, wavery radiance on the faces of those gathered around the table below.

Kyra the Red was there, and Mick and Cylin; and Q'iin the Herbmistress' student Gilda was tallying something on a long piece of paper. Scrying-crystals flashed and shimmered like chipped ice in the pallid light; Antryg could hear Cylin saying, ". . . trapdoor into the hypocaust will get you to the first level of the Vaults at the far end of the buttery, from there you can get into the kitchen."

"Who's that?" Gilda asked quietly. "Nye?" And at the tall man's nod, she checked something off on her list. "We still haven't heard from either Bentick or Phormion."

"Zake Brighthand checked in," Mick said, glancing up from his fragment of yellow tourmaline. "He's in the Pavilion—Otaro's with him, and Issay. Otaro was taken sick, he says."

"Otaro, Brighthand, Issay . . . can they get here from the Pavilion? Implek and his patrol haven't been heard from—that other hasu of Silvorglim's seems to be trapped up in the Juniors' side of the hill, he doesn't know where he is."

"Well, you scarcely need a crisis for that," Antryg remarked. "It happens to novices all the time."

"Brunus, can you hear me?" Kyra was murmuring, cradling her lump of pale blue topaz in her palm. "Brunus, answer . . . Brunus, look into your crystal," while in another part of the room, Daurannon was speaking quietly to a sizable group of black-robed Senior mages gathered around a table as far as possible from the dreadful darkness of the tall windows that had looked out upon the court.

"Antryg, why?" The Lady Rosamund brushed aside the tendrils of hair from her cheeks—it was the first time he could recall seeing her when she hadn't dressed her hair. Strands of cobweb clung to it, to her sleeves and the hem of her robe— she must have come here through the hypocaust under the

North Cloister, as he himself had. "Why would someone destroy the circles? Never mind whether they believed that disturbing the balance of the spells would do . . . this. I didn't believe it myself. But why would someone want to disrupt the spells that were holding the situation stable? Why prolong the confusion? It was obviously a wizard, who presumably knew . . ."

"It was an act of panic, I think," Antryg said softly. "An act to prevent the Citadel from being searched at all costs. We'll go into who might have done it later. At the moment it's imperative that I check the situation in the Vaults—Silvorglim is welcome to send as many guards with me as he chooses; in fact, I rather hope he will. We're going to need to move the Dead God's machinery up here if the flooding is getting worse."

"The Dead God?" Silvorglim's thin face paled a little, and his topaz eyes flared wide at the mention of that uncanny deity. "What pagan lies are these?"

"Not the real Dead God, of course," Antryg explained rapidly. "But he was originally introduced to me in mistake for the Dead God and you know how first impressions stick. His name is actually LTRX2-449-9102-CF60913 and I hope you won't be prejudiced by his appearance. His machinery is probably the only reason the Citadel didn't dissolve completely when the balance between the two spells was broken, and if anything happens to it, we're likely to be in real trouble."

"And are we not now?"

Antryg paused, startled, his big hands in their stained and ruinous gloves arrested in midgesture; then he smiled. "Well, it depends on your definition, of course. I spent twenty-five years not knowing whether I was in real trouble or not."

"As did the rest of us," Daurannon murmured, coming quietly up to join them with an ashen Seldes Katne and a couple of Council sasenna in tow. "Rosamund, we need you in the Circle of Spells . . ."

"And if you think," Silvorglim added, pushing his way

forward into the conversation with a gleam of half-comprehending malice in his eyes, "that I'm going to let you slip away into the Vaults, dog wizard . . ."

"No, no . . . by all means, come with me and bring at least a dozen of your stoutest fellows. I think I may need one or two of the Senior mages with me as well, if they can be spared. Goodness knows what's down there now."

"I'll go," the librarian offered at once.

Antryg hesitated, then said gently, "Kitty, thank you—because I know you know how dangerous the Vaults are now. But I'm going to need someone of near Council rank."

Poorly put—he knew it the moment he'd said it, knew it as she turned away, her lips pressed tight, blinking back tears of rage and frustration. But there wasn't time, and he couldn't risk someone whose powers would be unequal to what they might meet. Through his feet on the stone floor, through his bones, through the air, he could feel the slip and shift of the Void just beyond the Citadel walls, the movement of terrible energies through the stones themselves, the trapped and tangled fragments of the disjointed leys, the powers of earth and stars. In the Vaults, all the gates would be shifting, opening and closing, appearing and disappearing, giving access to God knew what bizarre worlds.

"Rosie," he added softly, turning to drape a familiar arm around the Lady's shoulders, "a word with you in private. Excuse us," he added as Silvorglim tried to press closer to hear. "I'm going to propose marriage to this woman and we really do need a few moments alone.

"Is there any chance, any chance at all, of getting the geas off me?" he whispered, as he drew her aside into the shadows of the room's great eastern door, which led, through the serving-hatch, into the kitchens. "I—we all—are going to need my powers if we're going to get out of this."

She looked warily up into his face. Even the strongest of healing-spells could not completely eradicate the effects of a gunshot wound, and she'd dragged herself here unaided; the stress of it, and the responsibility for the Citadel itself, made her features like something pared from bone.

"Look, I *swear* to you I haven't precipitated this situation to force your hand."

"I believe you." She drew back a little from him and disengaged his arm from her shoulders with a motion she had to have learned as a debutante.

"Good Heavens!" Antryg murmured in surprise.

"Don't widen your eyes at me, dog wizard, and don't play the fool for my benefit," she continued icily. "You're devious enough to have created the illusion of precipitating the entire Citadel into the Void in order to gain your way, but if this all had been illusion, I and all the Council would have known. I've been scrying through every inch of this Citadel, trying to get in touch with everyone—novices, Seniors, sasenna, servants—in its farthest reaches, and I know the extent of the danger we're in. And I don't think you capable of such a baroque ploy."

"And here I thought you considered me capable of anything."

"Anything except a straight answer."

"Well," Antryg smiled, "there is that."

"So I'll give you one. No." Her hand tightened on the ebony of her staff, and her voice shook a little though her eyes were like cabachon gems. "Aunt Min and I could remove it, but Aunt Min . . . has not been found." She shook her head. "Or the rest of us in concert could do it. But I don't think Daurannon would consent."

She glanced toward the Handsome One, who had returned to the group of Seniors—Nandiharrow, Q'iin, Idrix of Thray, Whitwell Simm, and Pentilla Riverwych, in fact, every available mage of any degree of power. By the patterns chalked around them on the floor Antryg saw that they were raising spells of stabilization to strengthen the Citadel's boundaries against the dragging dark of the Void. "And I know Bentick wouldn't, even if he could be found. Neither of them trust you . . .''

"The feeling's quite mutual, I assure you. I told you at the outset that the geas was a bad idea.''

"Don't jest with me, Windrose.'' Her voice, so low as to be barely audible, was level again but cold as an iron ax head in winter. "For the time being I acquit you of malice, and I never truly have believed Daurannon's contention that you are really the Dark Mage. But as for your sanity, and for your responsibility for this entire situation, I make no allowances. I don't know who can be spared from the stabilization spells here. I'll ask.''

"I shall kiss your hands and feet at a time when we'll both have the opportunity to properly relish the experience,'' he promised. "Until then there's no time to be lost. By the way, has Pothatch checked in?''

"He's on his way. He was in the old drying-room with Tom, it's cut off from here.''

"There's a trap up to the attic, that connects to the subcellar of the baths, and from the boiler room he can get into the buttery. When he gets here, you might suggest that he put on water for tea. I think everyone would benefit from that. And muffins if he has batter standing. Silvorglim!'' He turned and snapped his fingers, raising his voice as if summoning a butler. "Come along, man, bring your men and don't dawdle. You're always dawdling.''

And with the infuriated Witchfinder at his heels, trailed by a dozen sasenna of both Church and Council and old Whitwell Simm with his flowing silver hair, he strode through the east door of the refectory and into the kitchen, and so down once again into the darkness of the Vaults.

Below the third level, sanity ended. Alien energies ran like blood down the walls of the ancient collecting-maze and whispered in the darkness of its endless, curling spirals; strange winds flicked at Antryg's coat skirts and hair as he led the way down passages echoing with hideous sounds. Twice he turned aside from the quickest route and led his party on long, circuitous detours down forgotten stairways and rusty ladders of spikes in fog-choked vent shafts to avoid places where the darkness seemed thicker than it should, or where some sound or smell in the shuddering air lifted the hair on his nape without ever becoming clear enough to identify.

The pressure, the presence, of the Void was everywhere, as if a layer of skin had been stripped from him and his every nerve lay exposed to the shivering vibration of its fear. Niter and mosses gleamed on the walls; here and there he could see places in the darkness where the very fabric of the universe seemed to thin, showing through the more dreadful blackness that lay beyond; the air was filled with strange smells, trace elements and gases, curls of mist, twinges of static. He wore slung around his shoulders the tubes of the oxygen mask he'd left hidden on the first level, and Whitwell Simm, walking at the back of the party, had orders to stand ready with spells of wind and air at an instant's notice, but Antryg had studied in Joanna's world long enough now to know that this might not be enough.

And directly behind him in the juddering torchlight, Silverglim walked with drawn sword and eyes growing grimmer, more angry with the frightened anger of the self-righteous at every step. Once one of the Church sasenna cried out in hysterical terror, holding out her two hands and screaming, then doubling over, clawing at her face, and Antryg, pulling the woman's hands away, saw that the bones were already beginning to lengthen and deform, the skin to sprout coarse, gray animal hair. As the other guards stared in frozen terror, Antryg caught the stricken sasennan by the back of the neck and shoved her, dragged her along the passageway at a run, until she stopped screaming and clung panting to him, gritting her teeth against the pain.

"It was a pocket field, that's all," he explained, when they stopped and the woman sank, nearly unconscious but a woman once more, to the floor beside him. "In whatever universe that bulge or bubble of reality came from, this woman would have been a lycanthrope, a werewolf, just as in some other enclaves some of us wouldn't have had power at all, and others of us, who haven't it here, would."

Kneeling at the side of the shaken warrior, he looked from face to face, seeing the fear in the eyes of the sasenna—mostly young men and women, though several of them, the afflicted woman among them, were tough middle-aged troopers, scarred like fighting dogs. One or two were surreptitiously looking at the backs of their hands. "That's all," he added. "That's absolutely all. It has nothing to do with our world, our reality . . ."

"So you say." Torchlight gilded the jump and twitch of the hard muscles around Silvorglim's mouth. "And you—all of you," his glittering eyes flicked to Whitwell Simm, keeping quiet guard on their rear, "have taken us out of our world, our reality, haven't you? So that you might do this to us . . . and other things."

The sasennan beside Antryg ran her hands hesitantly over her face, finding the sprouting hair there had vanished and the bones and teeth resumed their normal shape, though Antryg guessed the flesh would bruise horribly and the woman would ache for days. One of the younger Church warriors stepped forward and held out a hand to help her to her feet: "We always did say you were a wolf bitch, didn't we, Gandy?" and the woman slapped his hand aside with a returning grin and got to her feet by herself.

"So what're we going to do when we walk through the field that turns *you* into what you really are, Venk? Buy you carrots?"

"Guard your virtue . . ."

They walked on, the sasenna trading filthy and speculative bandinage to cover the aftermath of their fear, but Antryg could feel Silvorglim's eyes on his back.

Once, when they passed a downshaft that plunged the depth

of the Pits, Antryg looked down and saw black waters roiling and tossing far below, but not as far, he thought, as the seventh level would be. Something long and gleaming reached up from the depths, like a faintly shining segmented worm, ending, not in a head, but in a small coal black hand that groped along the stone of the shaft's side, then withdrew once again to the water below.

The Dead God was waiting for them in the Chamber of the Glass Pillar. Knee-deep ground fog had filled the tunnels in this area, cold vapors flowing like water through the archways and pouring sluggishly around the shining monoliths of the oscillators and pickups, rising in wisps to veil the monstrous shape of the God himself and glowing with the movement of the light upon his masklike head. With a silvery rustle a dozen swords were drawn.

"Oh, put those away," Antryg said briskly, striding forward through the mists with his hands held out. "Ninetentwo my dear chap, I'm delighted and relieved . . ."

"I am delighted and relieved that a field hasn't settled upon this room which is inimical to electricity," the Dead God retorted acerbically, turning upon him golden eyes as unwinking as those of a shark. "Not to say astonished. I cannot imagine how the batteries stayed in operation through the first shock."

"Hence my merry men." Antryg swept his arm back at the nonplussed sasenna grouped behind the Witchfinder and the stunned Whitwell Simm. His glasses flashed in the phosphor lights of the lumenpanels and the beads on his neck glittered cold and strange, a curious, gawky entity nearly as alien as the creature standing before him. "The worst of the energy flux, as far as I can tell, is centered in the Vaults; if we can get the field generators upstairs, we may have a fighting chance of keeping the Citadel itself stable long enough to find the Moving Gate—or the power source which is keeping it jammed open—and rectify the whole situation by shutting it down. You, you, you, and you . . . start carrying those backup batteries to the refectory. Whitwell, go with them and lead the way. How much time will those give us?"

"Two hours apiece . . . as hours are reckoned in my world. Antryg, what happened?" Two of the clawed hands shifted the weapon slung over his shoulder, and the glowing nodule on the Dead God's forehead flicked back and forth like a cat's tail. "The power cable I had stretched through the Gate to my own world was cut off cleanly, as if with a laser . . . no surge, nothing. Just dead. My sensors show me Gates opening and closing, strange things, things I have never seen, energies and concentrations of heat and cold, moving all through the Vaults."

"Oh, peachy," Antryg sighed, lapsing regrettably into language picked up from his colleagues behind the bar at Enyart's. He ran a weary hand through his hair. The decoction of jelgeth he'd nicked from Issay's house was beginning to wear off, the exhaustion coming back on him worse than before, the usual result with repeated doses of the herb.

"God knows what's going on elsewhere here, but I'm sure I'm going to be blamed for it. Someone deliberately disrupted the circles holding the energies of the Citadel's stones in alignment. There's been a steady buildup of energy from the feedback loops through the leys—you know that."

The Dead God nodded. "But why on earth would . . . ?"

"Why would anyone dismantle the ecology of their planet in order to produce TV trays and hair spray? Or assassinate a national leader at the outset of a ticklish phase of reconstructing the country after disastrous civil war? Or marry a person with whom they've been fighting like cat and dog for five years, or go out and get blotto drunk the night before a critical business meeting? Because it seemed the appropriate thing to do at the time. If I knew precisely why, my friend, I should probably have a flying guess at who . . . or would if I wasn't so tired I can hardly stand up straight."

Across the room, a voice called out, "ANTRYG!" and he

swung around, his eyes wide with shock and astonishment, all weariness, for the moment, forgotten.

Joanna and—of all people—Magister Magus stood framed in the narrow black archway that led from the deeper Vaults.

It is said that the wizard Simon the Lame lived for five years in the dungeons of the Duke of Dreghan, coming and going as he pleased to his studies while his guards believed him to be imprisoned in his cell. It was only when the Duke encountered him in the public marketplace that the Duke realized that the Archmage had been his guest rather than his prisoner.

—Gantre Silvas
*Annals*

# Chapter XX

For that first instant, Antryg was all she could see—thin, gawky, and very tired-looking, a seedy purple coat hanging loosely over his faded jeans and decrepit green calico shirt, and over that a shawl which looked as if it had been knitted for him by a spider on bad drugs. She didn't even feel terribly surprised . . . *Of course he'd be here*.

The relief was like the curious, dizzy high that comes from the cessation of a blinding headache.

She hadn't realized how worried she'd been about him.

Beyond that she had nothing more than an impression of swirling mists, cold over her bare feet as she crossed the room at a run: torchlight, men standing around with swords, looming pillars, and the eerily steady pinpoints of green and amber light from the hard, black shapes of electronic components. Then he swept her into his arms, his longer stride covering more than half the distance, her feet leaving the chilly flagstones and his grip crushing her tight . . . the taste of tea and honey and bitter herbs on his lips.

She was safe.

*Well, no,* she decided a moment later, still locked in his embrace, on tiptoe now to reach up his loose-jointed height. The shifting, nightmare darkness of the Vaults all around them, the floating lights and distant screams and the terrible, growing presence of the Void told her that. *Not* safe, *exactly . . .*

But Antryg always gave the impression that he knew what was going on and could salvage any situation.

"Dear God," he whispered, his angular, bespectacled face stricken with sudden guilt. "You were down here after all?"

She remembered she'd had distinct doubts about ever wanting to be involved with this man again and wondered momentarily why. She looked past the baggy, smoke-smelling folds of his coat to the room beyond him. In the glow of half a dozen torches she saw sasenna in the trim black uniforms of the Church, pausing in the act of picking up electronic components with great care so as to not break the connections between them; saw, a few feet behind Antryg, a diminutive man in the close-fitting gray garb of a Witchfinder, drawn sword in his hand and baffled fury in his hard face; and, beyond him, haloed in stirred vapors that caught the glow of the electronic eyes all about it, a looming black silhouette hideously reminiscent of the monstrous construction of rotting flesh which had attacked them once, in a deserted chapel in the Sykerst.

"Is that . . . the Dead God?" She looked sharply up into Antryg's face. "What the *hell* is going on?"

"Ah . . . well . . ." He pushed up his spectacles to rub the side of his beaky nose. "I'm under arrest—all those gentlemen are my guards. Joanna Sheraton, Mr. Yarak Silvorglim, Witchfinder General of Kymil and the Sykerst."

In something of a daze she shook hands with the red-haired man not much taller than herself; like Caris, her sasennan friend of former days, he offered his left hand, not releasing his grip upon the drawn sword in his right. He had eyes of yellowish hazel, unpleasantly cold and watching her now with narrow suspicion.

"And Magister Magus! My dear fellow, I never expected . . ."

"I assure you," the little dog wizard said, drawing himself up and pulling more firmly closed the silk lapels of his exquisitely cut velvet dressing gown, "the lack of expectation is absolutely mutual."

"Antryg . . ." The Dead God's voice was a deep, buzzing whine, the words resounding in Joanna's head with the familiar echoes of the Spell of Tongues that Antryg had bestowed upon her. "We need your help in keeping this field straight while it's moved."

"Absolutely . . . Joanna," Antryg continued earnestly as he strode back toward the ring of stabilization oscillators, his arm about her shoulders, "I did search for you, I swear I did, I searched every inch of the Vaults."

"I wasn't exactly in the Vaults." She checked quickly over the connections between the backup batteries and the oscillators and generators rigged in series around them. The configurations were unfamiliar but clearly along the same lines as those of her own world. Same-to-same and inny-to-outty connections were clearly marked, and it took only a few minutes' study to figure out how they linked up. "Is this an auxiliary jack to the same circuit? If so, we can keep the connection going while we replace with a longer main link."

"Right, but we need to keep these three in their current configuration."

"There's an internal backup," the Dead God hummed. "Connection can be broken for up to five seconds while it's altered without anything going down. The important thing is not to let these alignment indicators slip out of phase."

"According to Magister Magus, we were in something called the Brown Star, which he got from Salteris' study."

"Dear God!" Antryg whispered, spectacles flashing as he drew back to look at her in surprise. "So that's where . . . I wondered what had become of it." His long, crooked hands in their fingerless gloves were working neatly as he spoke, unhooking cables and rewiring, while the Dead God, his maggotlike palm-tentacles wriggling like infinitely tiny fingers, occupied himself with resetting the gauges. "We're going to need something like a litter to carry these on if we're going to keep the configuration stable."

"I have an antigrav lifter . . ."

"But how did you get out?"

Joanna shrugged. Near the chamber's central pillar, Silvorglim and the one of his sasenna not occupied with scut work stood in postures of armed guard over the unfortunate Magister Magus, the only other person not required for the assembling safari of electronic goods.

"I really don't know. We just . . . got out. There was a change of some kind and . . . and Gates opened."

"When the stabilization field buckled, at a guess," Antryg said, poking his long nose back into the tangle of wires. "I always suspected the Brown Star of being the Gate to a pocket dimensional enclave. It must be somewhere in the Citadel, and the shock of the field breaking down just . . ." He paused, then drew back to look at her, his gray eyes wide with shock. "You mean that Gates into the Brown Star are just *standing open*?"

"Yeah . . ." She thought about that a moment. "Oh, cripes."

From the archway through which Joanna and Magus had first entered the room came the sudden, shrieking laughter of demons. Antryg was on his feet and headed for that door almost before Joanna could draw breath, unslinging from his shoulder something that reminded her strongly of an old-fashioned bug-sprayer, a pump and canister apparatus that he aimed into the darkness as he braced himself in the frame of the arch. When the demons appeared—and Joanna was horrified at the swirling, moon-colored shapes, with their flying spiderweb hair and raking claws—Antryg pumped the contents of the canister at them, a shower of fine, blackish mist that set them screaming, cringing, clawing at their own flesh and one another's as they blundered back into the eternal night of underground.

"What is that?" Joanna asked. "Exorcist in a Can?"

"Silver chloride," the Dead God explained, coming up behind her with a sonic extractor in one hand and a coax cable in another, light nodule flicking nervously over the shining bulk of his head. "He claims that most ab-material manifestations are allergic to it—I would not know. Such things are unheard of in my world."

"Not even in legends?" She looked up at his tall bulk, hung with tools, sensors, weapons and with the gleaming weight of breathing tubes. "You have extra air tanks, by the way?"

The huge, bony skull inclined. "Your concern is appreciated. The antigrav lifter is now refusing to work. It may be that it simply cannot, in this dimension—or it may be that, being cutting-edge technology, it has malfunctioned for reasons of its own." The end of his tail lashed with annoyance, like a cat's; Joanna wondered what bizarre biosphere had selected for his ancestors.

"How long does it take to get a repair person out?" They began, with the help of the three Council sasenna, laboriously to transfer the oscillator/generator configuration to a makeshift litter improvised of halberd poles, hampered by the swirling mists that concealed kelp beds of now-useless cables underfoot. "Not to here, I mean, but usually . . ."

"Forty days. The only service center is in Six-ninety."

"Yeah, the company that makes my CD-ROM drive sends its techs out on foot, too."

*I should be in hysterics,* she thought calmly, *instead of standing here discussing repair problems of first-generation technology with something that looks like It, Terror from Beyond the Stars.*

She supposed, as the safari got gingerly under way, that her mind was simply refusing to believe that this creature—this man—this thing with its shiny green-gray skin, its light nodule, skeletal tail, and cold, orange, insectile eyes—was not in fact some kind of special effect. Probably, she thought, she was still subconsciously looking for a zipper up his back.

*Well, what the hell. None of us really needs for me to have hysterics now anyway.* Mentally she resolved to schedule a bout of them later, after a meal, a shower if possible, and a change of clothes into something more dignified than baggy blue cotton pajamas.

Antryg came striding back through the dark archway, spray gun clutched in one hand and his face, in the torchlight, pale with shock and strain. The greenish, cloudy brume of ground fog rose around him and emitted a faintly metallic, carrion smell as he moved. "There's no time to lose," he said, glancing back over his shoulder at the dark archway and the tunnels beyond. "We have to get out of here and get out quickly. For if what you've told me is true, Joanna, we're in much worse trouble than I thought."

"That's *possible*?" she demanded, aghast.

And Antryg smiled, though the nervous horror still lurked in the back of his eyes. "Alas, anything is possible." And he looped the strap of his weapon over his shoulder and bent to take part of the litter of components.

And that, Joanna supposed, was why she ought to be still seriously considering having nothing more to do with this man—always assuming they made it out of the present crisis alive.

*So why is it that every time I look at him, I smile?*

"More slowly." Antryg held up his hand, then licked one fingertip and raised it, as if testing the wind, while looking at his watch.

Joanna heard Silvorglim mutter savagely, "This is absurd," but for the most part, the huddled line of sweating sasenna watched the wizard's face with strained concentration, knowing that he, and he alone, was sufficiently familiar with the mazes to get them out.

Nearly an hour had passed. The sense of danger, of chaos,

of shifting and pulling in the darkness all around them had increased. Sometimes Joanna wondered if it was a problem with her own perception, or if the floor itself was tipping, the focus of gravity slowly moving itself through the dark rock of the walls. She wondered whether this would be possible at all without the spells of the wizards in the Citadel above, holding the fabric of the universe together like masking tape. Once Antryg, who had moved up to the front of the line, ordered the entire party to back up thirty or forty feet and detour through a spiral of blind alleys thick with moss like dripping purple velvet before returning to their original course; another time he had led them through a windingly circuitous side trip only to emerge at a stairway they had seen, down a straight stretch of corridor, fifteen minutes earlier. Joanna guessed that either the entire energy field was bending and shifting with the movement of its center point and Antryg was making allowances to keep it as stable as possible, or that he perceived dangers, or possible dangers, invisible to the others. But the sasenna muttered among themselves, burdened under the weight of batteries and the long litter with its oscillators and field generators, or struggling to maneuver the unwieldy reflectors and screens that had to be borne upright and at a certain angle. In the fitful glare of the few torches still alight, the sweat-streaked faces were taut with fear and stress.

"Dear God," whispered Magister Magus, who had been pressed into service carrying one end of the litter and was walking near Joanna, as far from the Dead God as he could get. "Dear God, I think we were safer in the Brown Star."

"Oh, you were," Antryg informed him cheerfully. At his cautious signal the entire safari moved on again but with slow care. "A great deal safer. D'you think you could find your way back to it?"

"Like a shot from a gun, my dear Antryg, had I a sizable bodyguard to escort me."

"I shall see what I can do to arrange that."

A high-pitched shriek ripsawed the blackness behind them.

Antryg swung around, and looking back over her shoulder, Joanna could see down a long reach of corridor the gleam of torchlight on bared and slime-dripping teeth. There was no gleam of eyes, but something in the darkness bounced and rocked as it ran toward them—*A biped*, she guessed dizzily—and dimly, beyond it, she sensed some darker movement, a kind of wet glister and a rotted, poisonous stink of fish.

"Shoot it!" Antryg yelled to the nearest of the few unburdened guards. "NOW!"

The thing was still a good hundred feet away. The guard, a middle-aged Church sasennan whose lips and nostrils were swollen with plum-colored bruises, whipped up her crossbow and let fly at the flickering gleams that were still all of the thing Joanna could see. It was one hell of a shot, she thought.

There was the soft skidding thump of tumbling flesh, an alien, acrid stink that must be its blood. Joanna strained her eyes to see in the darkness beyond. Surely that irrational sense of the floor moving was a trick of the light.

"Magus!" Antryg caught the little dog wizard by the back of his robe, pulled him away from the litter pole he was carrying. "A spell of misperception, of illusion—quickly! Across the end of this corridor . . ."

"What? But there's nothing . . ."

"Of course there's something there—granite, water, mud, and dead flesh among other things, so weave the illusion, there's a good chap—anything to prevent something at that end of the corridor from knowing what's at this end."

"Prevent *what* . . . ?" But Magus was down on his knees already, fumbling in his pocket. Silently, Joanna produced chalk from her purse and handed it to him.

"Mind you," Antryg said hastily, "make it as strong as you can—truly as strong as you can, against perception of any kind. Gandy, my pearl of delight," he touched the arm of the sasennan who had fired the crossbow, "do you feel up to staying with Magus until he's finished? You'll get him safely back to the refectory, won't you? Thank you. Magus, I'm terribly sorry we can't remain."

The dog wizard looked up with a protesting squawk, but the sasennan only grinned and saluted; Antryg was already herding his little train of bearers on up the corridor, glancing alternately at watch and compass, sniffing the air, studying the darkness all around him with the skittish preoccupation of a demented bird dog and now and then reaching out a hand to pat the stone of the wall, only to jerk it back as if the contact burned his fingers.

"What was it?" Joanna whispered to the Dead God, as the narrow, randomly twisting corridors gave way to a succession of dusty cellar chambers filled with jars of oil, barrels of dried fruit, bins of potatoes, and rows of herbs in clay pots. Antryg was now walking behind them, nervously listening, his absurd bug-sprayer his only weapon. The only one who would not accept this rear guard was the Witchfinder Silvorglim, who insisted on walking at the wizard's back, drawn sword in hand. "Did you see anything on your sensor?"

"Not when the creature was alive and moving, no," Nine-tentwo replied, bent easily under the weight of his end of the litter and carrying his own weapon, like a lightweight minia-ture bazooka, now at the ready in one of his other hands. "It happened very quickly; by the time I keyed in," he gestured with the thick rectangle of the sensor in his fourth hand, "the animal we saw was dead, and the reading purely residual syn-aptic reactions. In truth, there are so many strange energies moving about the Vaults now, it is difficult to calibrate."

"Is something following us now?"

He held the sensor up on his broad palm, the long fingers and two clawed, stumpy thumbs hooked over the edge to show her the screen as they waited for the sasenna carrying the clumsy reflectors to maneuver through the doorway at the top of a short flight of steps ahead of them. The little white manipulator-tentacles slithered around the edge of the sensor to work the two dials; Joanna could see distance-calibration rings traced on the fine-grained plastic, and the indistinct whitish blobs of the body energies of the carrying party, fading out as the dials moved on through the spectrum of possible energies. Colors wavered and moved on the screen. Once, horribly, a whole river of blue plasma seemed to come into focus, oozing through the walls all around them, but the tentacles edged the knob calmly past that.

"You see it is difficult to tell," the Dead God said. "Nothing animal."

Looking back at Antryg's scarecrow shape against the blackness, seeing the worry in his eyes, Joanna was unable to take as much comfort in that information as perhaps it warranted.

Torchlight flickered over an enormous black iron stove, an open hearth redolent of meat dripping, the flashing eyes of nervous cats. An arch, some shallow steps . . . the blue-white, eerie glow of witchlight streaming through another archway, and a door guard's voice calling out, "They're here."

Then they were in what appeared to be an enormous dining room, illuminated by the spooky flickering of balls of witchlight like stray balloons about the intricate rafterwork ceiling, and occupied by small clusters of black-clothed sasenna, young men and women in gray or mealy brown, and wizards.

So these, thought Joanna, stretching aching shoulders as she set down her end of the litter pole near the stack of backup batteries at one end of the chamber, were Antryg's colleagues. His jailers, his friends, his enemies . . . the people with whom he had spent most of his life. The people who knew him as she, perhaps, never could.

Some of them she recognized vaguely, from the briefest of encounters at the Silent Tower four months ago: Whitwell Simm, kindly faced and white-haired; the stern and haggard Nandiharrow, black gloves covering deformed hands. Others she knew about only from Magister Magus' descriptions in the endless hours of their imprisonment. She certainly knew the Lady Rosamund Kentacre, who strode across the long hall with a decisiveness unmarred by the staff upon which she leaned so heavily, her storm of black hair hanging half-braided on her shoulders and her movie star–perfect face icy and grim. At the sight of the Dead God she stopped, fist going to her lips in quick shock, but she paused only an instant before going to Antryg. She had been well trained, Joanna smiled to herself, in the etiquette of not commenting upon people's appearances.

"We've had word from most parts of the Citadel now," the Lady said as the last of the sasenna carried their burdens over to where the Dead God was already setting up shop. Several teenagers in brownish homespun robes and a little man in the blue smock and clumsy boots of a civilian were moving tables back against the wall to make room; another civilian, a fat little red-haired man in an apron, was dispensing tea and muffins whose warm scent hung like an incongruous blessing on the air.

"We've established what spells we can to stabilize the Citadel's boundaries, though God only knows how long those will last. We're still scrying for Implek; he may have been down in the dairies, outside the Citadel entirely, looking for you. Pordanches and Selim and Shippona—you remember Nandiharrow's student? the little girl with the braids?—seem to be trapped on the upper floor of the Four Brothers; there are creatures of some kind in the hall below them. Pordanches has tried half a dozen spells to get rid of them and they have no effect. No word yet from Bentick or Phormion; Kyra has gone out to search."

"Damn," Antryg whispered.

"Joanna," the Dead God said, and she turned. "I need your help, or the help of someone who understands electronics."

"Well," she said, crossing to the pile of backup batteries,

oscillators, and screens, "I can program a VCR and get a computer to run."

"Good enough. You remember how the jacks hooked together? These three need to be relinked in parallel."

"Do we need to readjust the ports?"

Someone considerately sent a floating galaxy of witchlight to hover just beneath the rafters above the pile of backup batteries, shedding a cool, even glow on their work. Several of the mages not occupied with the stabilization spells came over, wearing either the black of masters or the shorter gray robes of Juniors, to study the equipment minutely, hands tucked carefully into their sleeves to keep from touching. One stoutish little woman in her sixties, no taller than Joanna herself, with her graying hair skinned unflatteringly back into braids, was neatly copying onto a wax tablet the arcane symbols written on the equipment's sides—presumably, Joanna thought, serial numbers, voltage information, and brand names.

Voices floated behind them. "My dear Silvorglim, I was . . ."

"Don't you try to cozen me, Daurannon Stapler!" Silvorglim spat. Joanna looked up to see the wizard to whom he had spoken, a tallish man with gray-flecked black hair and the cherubic features of an aging choirboy, draw back before the venom in the little Witchfinder's eyes. "I have seen enough of the evils that you have summoned to convince me that you and all your works here are utterly pernicious! You say you have no contact with the affairs of humankind, but if that is so, what is that man doing among you?" His finger stabbed viciously toward Magister Magus, who had just entered and slumped on a bench, to be given tea by the fat man in the apron. "He is the lapdog and adviser of every heretic at the Court, cringing around the Regent's heir Prince Cerdic, trading lies and illusion for table scraps . . ."

"See here, now," Magus protested, raising his head in feeble indignation.

Daurannon's wide hazel eyes flared wider. "What on earth are *you* doing here, Magister Magus?"

"Believe me, my lord, had we several hours and an atlas of the world I could list you all the places I'd rather be. Thank you, one lump of sugar, if you have such a thing."

"Don't feign innocence with me!" Silvorglim said, his voice low and deadly. "I can see now the link between . . ."

"Have you heard from Brighthand and Otaro?" Antryg was asking, ignoring this byplay as he accepted a cup of tea from the mournful-looking little man in the clumsy boots. "Thank you, Tom."

"There's a . . . a fold, a crease, as you described it, in the bridge which leads across from the cellar of the Pavilion to the House of Roses," Lady Rosamund said. "Brighthand and Issay have twice tried to bring Otaro across and both times found themselves up in the Winter Solar. They're working their way back to the Library to bring him over the bridge into the Junior Parlor and down from there. Issay dosed Otaro with poppy— he's been raving about the Moving Gate following him, says that his father is controlling it, his father is coming to get him."

Antryg's voice lowered still more. "And Aunt Min?"

The silence made Joanna look across at them, in time to see the silver-hard brittleness freeze in that beautiful face.

"I saw her," Joanna said suddenly.

Both Lady Rosamund and Daurannon turned toward her, startled. She stood up, wires trailing from her hand.

"Magus and I . . . when we were wandering through the Brown Star. There was a . . . a flaw, or a Gate, that led us into these two rooms. Aunt Min was sleeping."

"It's true." Magister Magus stepped around and away from Silvorglim and came over to join the other mages, still carrying teacup and saucer, his dressing gown of sable velvet like an elaborate parody of their dark robes.

"You're sure she was sleeping?" For the first time, Joanna saw human concern break the flawless perfection of the Lady

Rosamund's face. The fear in her eyes, the desperation and the hope, was painful to see.

"I checked," she said, a little awkwardly. "And the cats were nervous, but not . . . not like anything had happened to her. This was . . . I don't know. Maybe two hours ago? It's hard to tell time."

"It hasn't been much more than three hours since the binding-spells were destroyed," Lady Rosamund said quietly. "If she is still in the cottage . . ."

She drew a deep breath and suddenly turned away, pressing her fingers to the inner corners of her eyes as if to still the throbbing of a headache, but Joanna guessed it was so that the gesture would cover, for a moment, whatever expression was on her face. But when she turned again, the jadelike hardness was back, forbidding any to touch. "Will you guide me there, Joanna? Do you remember the way?"

"It's out of the question." The Dead God rose from behind his oscillators, resting all four hands like a row of huge green spiders along the top of the generator. "I need someone who understands electronics. There remains at least an hour's worth of adjustments to be done."

"You'll have no problem once you're inside the Gate," Joanna said. "I kept track of it with yarn. But it was Magus who guided us in the Vaults."

"Well," the dog wizard modestly said, not seeing his danger, "someone—by all appearances a novice mage—had very recently passed that way and left wizard's marks all along the walls."

"And I'm sure he'll be delighted to guide you back, Rosie." Antryg draped a friendly arm around Magister Magus' shoulders in time to keep his friend from bolting like a startled hare for the nearest doorway.

"And what gives you that impression?" Magus demanded, struggling discreetly. But Antryg, for all his peculiar appearance and the fatigue worn visibly into his beaky face, was very strong.

"Because it is now imperative that the geas be removed from me," Antryg said, his demented pleasantness fading and his eyes growing suddenly grave. "And without Bentick, Phormion, or Issay—nearly half the Council—finding Aunt Min is now our only hope of accomplishing that before what remains of the energy-polarization field fades out of the stones of the Citadel and we are torn apart by the forces of the Void."

"How did Magister Magus know that it was the Brown Star in which you were imprisoned?"

Joanna looked up, a little surprised, from the two-color split screen of data she was comparing—right half to left with an overlay capability whose exactness more than compensated for the fact that she hadn't any comprehension of what those characters meant—to see the handsome Council mage Daurannon hunker down at her side.

Running on an internal battery, the Dead God's portable computer was about the size of a first-generation laptop with massive capacity. Ninetentwo had hand-sketched a sample keyboard in chalk on the floor, and Joanna, sitting cross-legged on the floor within the shadowy ring of oscillators and flux capacitors, had jotted copious notes about exactly which keys—only they were tiny levers that flicked with the quick pressure of finger-picking a guitar—to press to run the alignment programs on the oscillator's eight transmission screens.

"It was his crystal." She grinned a little at the recollection of the Magus' indignation at his brush with karma. In addition to a pair of old breeches and a faded calico shirt from the Citadel slop chest, Pothatch the cook had brought her tea and oatcakes, but she still had a headache, which, when she thought about it, was scarcely surprising. It occurred to her that with all these wizards around she could probably get it cured. Even in her own magicless world, Antryg could do that.

"*His* crystal?" The black eyebrows pinched sharply down, and a whole network of lines sprang into being around those calculatedly melting eyes.

She sipped her tea, smoke flavored and almost as strong as coffee, but very good. "Well . . . he sort of swiped it from Salteris' rooms."

"*Salteris'* rooms?"

On the other side of the long refectory, Silvorglim and his sasenna were clumped together in a little island of smoldering torchlight, muttering and whispering. The Witchfinder had protested volubly against Magister Magus leaving his custody, not to mention Antryg, whom he still spoke of as his prisoner, and had been roundly ignored. The mages, for the most part, had returned to the round table directly beneath the chandelier's eerie glow, hunched over their crystals like freezing men about a fire in their efforts to guide back those who had been stranded in the farther-flung corners of the Citadel. The murmur of their voices was a fragile surface smoke, floating on the fearful silence of the night beyond the doors.

After a long moment Daurannon said, "He told you this?"

She nodded.

"I wonder why he never . . ." The words were murmured as if to himself; then he drew a deep breath and shook his head. "I suppose Salteris found it in the sack of Suraklin's Citadel. But in that case, why did he not tell the Council?" His eyes remained troubled, as he tried to work out in his mind where and how his master could have acquired such a thing. "There cannot have been two . . ."

"It was Suraklin's, all right," Joanna said softly and told him of Irina of Kymil, whispering to herself in the dark. Daurannon settled back, leaning one shoulder against the smooth, faintly gleaming side of the oscillator behind him, chewing his lip a little with thought. The smooth sangfroid he wore like a well-tailored suit had been put aside, and Joanna found herself more at ease with the uncertainty that lay hidden beneath.

"I don't understand," he said after a moment. "If Salteris had found the crystal at the sack of Suraklin's Citadel, why didn't he free this woman then? They all knew she'd vanished."

"Maybe Salteris didn't find it?" Joanna turned quietly back to her computer screen and carefully inserted the next test wafer. Rather to her surprise, the left side of the screen wiped obediently to the new data; she studied her notes for a moment, then keyed in the instructions for an overlap. In spite of the warmer clothes she'd been given, she still felt cold—over the past half hour, she had begun to wonder whether it was her imagination or whether the temperature was dropping.

"Maybe it had been hidden, and only after Suraklin took over Salteris' body and mind did he dig it up again?"

"You believe that tale of Antryg's?" The bitterness of betrayal in his voice made her look up. In the soft lambence of the witchlight, she could definitely see his breath.

Her eyes returned to the screen to avoid the steely anger in his. "I believe that all the mannerisms, all the speech patterns, of the man I knew—briefly, I'll grant you—as Salteris later turned up in a man I knew well, who'd never had them before. I believe that all the computer programs of information, of personality transfer, were written by Suraklin as part of his plan to live forever."

"I know nothing of these *computers*." Daurannon used the English word, there being no equivalent in the Ferryth tongue. "But I do know that Antryg—like his master before him—can be stunningly persuasive. Witness how he's achieved the goal for which he's been striving since his arrival and has gotten Rosamund to consent to having the geas lifted, giving him the power he seeks again. Witness how he's gotten you to shelter him."

Joanna looked up again, her brown eyes hard. "Completely leaving aside the fact that I love the man—which I know can happen to anybody and with anybody, God help us—Antryg saved my life, rescued me from the Inquisition, protected and sheltered me. And it was Salteris he spoke of as his master." Her own words startled her, her tone of voice more so—she tried obliquely to remember the last time she'd argued with a man in authority, a man with power. Certainly in the past she had had to be very angry indeed to argue with anyone, without immediately following up with half an hour's worth of mollifying apologies.

Rather to her surprise, Daurannon didn't point out her stupidity at falling for Antryg's lies but only said, his voice unbending steel, "Whom he murdered."

"If that was Salteris." Her hands, resting on the keyboard, were quite steady; she felt she should have been coming unglued under the pressure of his rage and his will but, curiously, felt very little but a kind of hot lightness in her chest. "And if it was Salteris, don't you think, in the sixteen years he was Antryg's teacher and friend, he would have been wise enough to recognize Suraklin? To guess if that was what had happened?"

"Antryg is mad." There was a doggedness to his answers now, a stubborn anger. Matched, she supposed, by her own stubborn determination that it was *his* friend, not hers, who had harbored the evil wizard's disembodied mind. "Has always been mad, and more so when Salteris first found him. It's a good cover."

"All right," Joanna said reasonably. "Then answer me two things. First: How close were you to Salteris those last four years, between the time when the Emperor went insane—since it's Antryg's theory that Suraklin spent most of his time hiding in the body and brain of the Emperor—and Salteris's own death?"

"Salteris was in Angelshand those years," Daurannon replied coldly. "I was here. And he was changed by the death of his wife." He used the Ferryth word for an unofficial wife, far stronger, and with far different connotations, than *mistress*, but lacking the sanction of the Church. "But those few times I saw him, I could swear he was the man I knew."

"And second: Where did Salteris get the Brown Star?"

Daurannon was silent for some time. In fact, Joanna never did find out what he would have said. For as he drew in his breath to reply, from the darkness beyond the room's north doors came a sudden, drawn-out cry, a shriek that resolved itself into a man's harsh voice shouting "No! NO!" and the splitting crack of what sounded like a thunderclap, echoing in the enclosed halls. Footfalls thudded, running, stumbling; the two sasenna guarding that door called out, and light flooded into the passageway beyond, the bright, cold glare of magic. Silvorglim and his guards whirled and started for the doorway at a run, swords winking in their hands. The Council sasenna, clumped around Sergeant Hathen, ran also.

Daurannon sprang to his feet, crying, "Bentick!" as an old man, white hair streaked with blood that ran from it down a face scarcely less pale, stumbled through the doorway and collapsed sobbing on the floor.

If you pay a mage to summon Darkness, be sure to have candles on hand.
—BERENGIS THE BLACK
Court Mage to the Earls
Caeline

# CHAPTER XXI

"SHE IS MAD." BENTICK'S LONG, INK-STAINED FINGERS trembled around the cup Pothatch had to hold to his mouth. "God help me, I tried to heal her. When she tried to murder Antryg in the cellars of the Castle, I knew she was mad, and I tried to heal her. And then the Witchfinders came."

There was shocked whispering among the half-hundred sorcerers and warriors clustered around them, the old man huddled like a broken doll, the younger mage kneeling over him, the fat little cook with his tea and his damp, herbed rags.

The Steward's breath caught as Daurannon took the cloth, with its stinging astringents, and wiped the blood from his scalp. When he went on, his thin voice stumbled on the words. "I thought that I could heal her—I have healed others before—and that no one would be wiser. That Witchfinder—he would have blamed it all on her, said she was a madwoman . . . At the very least she would have been dropped from the Council. Phormion . . ."

He shook his head desperately, as if knowing they would

315

not understand. "Phormion is proud. I owed her at least concealment from them. Then she accused me of trying to poison her—said Rosamund was spying on her, plotting to destroy her rivals for the Master-Spells, were Minhyrdin to die. I couldn't let them find her. I did not think she'd try to hurt me."

"And exactly when *did* she begin to go mad?" Silvorglim asked softly, his fox yellow eyes glinting in the soft flicker of the witchlight that hovered in clouds around the wizards' heads. "Who can tell, when a madness begins? A month ago, when the abominations began to appear . . . ?"

Sergeant Hathen turned, hand on her sword, and said, "There's six others on the Council who can tell you it wasn't, chum."

The little Witchfinder's nostrils flared with disdain. "Who *will*, I'm sure."

"And in any case," Daurannon said smoothly, rising to lay a hand on Silvorglim's arm and unobtrusively putting his own body between the Witchfinder's and that of the bristling sergeant, "it's a matter for the Council to deal with. Why don't you sit down over here and be comfortable?"

"Joanna . . ."

She turned quickly at the harsh buzz of Ninetentwo's voice. Leaving the outer edge of the dispersing group, she rejoined the bony monster within the circle of generators.

"Whether one wizard went insane and tried to rip another with her claws—or those pitiful little things you people pretend are claws—it is not the worst of our problems." His long tail lashed uneasily, and even as he spoke he moved from screen to screen, the maggotlike tentacles of his hands flicking nervously at keys and dials. "The spells of Daurannon and his cohorts cannot keep the field stable much longer. Unless we complete our setup quickly we'll begin to lose parts of the Citadel. My instruments show me wormholes and spell-fields opening everywhere in the Citadel above us, as well as the

Vaults beneath. If the outer parameter of the spell-field is breached, we may get air leakage.''

"Christ, I'd forgotten about the air." Joanna went back to the next reflector screen, withdrew its small data chip, and knelt again to insert it into the computer's entry port. She punched through the memorized sequence, and superimposed the new data lines with the model. "We've got a misalignment here."

The Dead God moved over to her to check the findings, clicked deep within his huge skull, and made the necessary adjustments, bending over her slim form like some nightmare horror from Special-Effects Hell.

"Even if we don't get a hole in the biosphere of this joint," Joanna continued, taking the chip from the final screen and running the check, "what happens when the air gets exhausted?"

"It is not something with which we need concern ourselves."

She brushed back the feathery mass of her hair from her face and sighed with relief. "Thank God for small . . ."

"Long before that happens," Ninetentwo went on inexorably, "if what Antryg tells me is correct, stabilization field or no, the polarization energies will disintegrate and the enclave bounded by the Citadel's outermost air/stone interfaces—the original parameters of the spell—will dissolve."

He returned to her side, hunkered down into an angular ball of bones, and reinserted the corrected screen's data chip, looking over Joanna's shoulder to confirm that the adjustment was in line. As he did so he balanced himself on her shoulder with two of his hands. Looking at them, she realized that the thick-muscled strength of his upper set of arms came from the fact that they were actually necks—the tentacles, in fact, were tongues, emerging from mouths in the palms of the claw-armored upper hands. *I guess it takes all kinds,* she thought queasily.

"Though presumably once the Citadel itself fell into the Void, the faulting along the energy lines in the various worlds would cease," he continued, as if unaware of her momentary flinch of revulsion. "The reflection that we have saved our universes from abominations will comfort me little when we implode. This should take place in approximately," he checked a gauge, "two hours."

"Two hours?" Joanna stared up at him, completely forgetting the ephemera of his appearance in her horror at his words. The rigid exoskeletal face was expressionless. After a moment he turned away to check another set of gauges.

"Look," Joanna said, when he had finished his final adjustments a few minutes later. "According to Antryg, the whole problem stemmed from one of the Gates in the Void being kept jammed open, right?"

"Correct." The light node on his forehead flickered, casting a gruesome firefly glow over his big upper hands as he changed one of the air bottles on his breathing apparatus. Joanna noted two other bottles among the general pile of tool kit, spare coax cables, and what might have been extra ammo heaped in the dense shadows behind the backup batteries. "It is his theory that once that link is broken, the Citadel will snap back to its correct position in the time-space continuum, and the entire continuum will return to its normal orientation. Since this Gate seemed to be moving around, probably as a result of being kept open, he established the stabilization field and attempted to chart the Vaults where it had been seen, but he was effectively prevented from completing even that task."

Joanna squatted next to the smooth, knobby bulk of the alien, half-hidden in the darkness of his gleaming-eyed machines, and folded her arms around her knees in an unconscious mimicry of his own position. "But if your field of study is xchi-particle flux—the energies that were polarized to stabilize the field—were you taking readings before the period of stabilization?"

"Of course. But they wouldn't tell us which of the loci of flux was the Moving Gate. That was the first thing we thought of."

"No," Joanna agreed. "But it would tell us something. If nothing else, there might be some kind of pattern to it that isn't obvious until it's laid out. And Tom the gardener tells me Antryg did get some of the Vaults charted, so we can overlay your findings with his, and see where we are. Can you get a three-dimensional graphic on your computer?"

"Four dimensional, if you need it—but no printer."

"Damn," Joanna muttered, glancing at the tiny screen. "Looks like it's chalk-on-the-floor time again." *At least,* she thought as she stood up and dug in her purse for chalk, *it'll give me something to do until the Antryg comes back—if he comes back—or the place disintegrates.*

It took her only a few minutes to round up most of Antryg's charts. The two Juniors Mick and Cylin had some of them; Tom remembered Antryg emptying a creased wad of papers out of his coat pocket in the baths, and hurried out, candle in hand, through the eastern doorway into the still and waiting blackness of the kitchen to fetch them. After a little asking, Seldes Katne produced the rest. "They aren't complete," the librarian said, looking worriedly down over Joanna's shoulder as she sketched out in chalk on the planked oak floor the preliminary plans of the several levels of the Vaults. "Brighthand had some, and others were left up in my rooms in the Library."

"Just what we need," Joanna said, turning the scribbled charts this way and that to orient their pattern. The situation was made easier when Tom returned, rather white and shaken but bearing a mass of grubby papers, scribbled over in Antryg's looping, illegible scrawl, which Tom obligingly proceeded to decipher for her. The Dead God produced a long, folded readout of greenish flimsiplast with all the readings taken before the field went into effect—sheet after sheet of what looked like a badly photocopied, black-and-white version of Van Gogh's "Starry Night"—and Joanna took notes on the back with a ballpoint pen from her purse, while the physicist keyed through the later screens of data during stabilization.

"As you can see," he said, "not everything registered on the multiscanner, and some of what did register was undetectable by human senses. We still don't know what this disruption was, or that." The massive claw touched the screen with incongruous delicacy.

Anything, she thought as she worked. Anything to keep from looking at her watch, counting down how little of the two hours was left.

It was definitely growing colder.

*Great,* she thought, warming her stiff fingers in her armpits. *We may not be losing air, but we're sure as hell losing heat. I wonder why gravity still works?*

Behind her, Daurannon had called the wizards together again for a muttered conference, their voices carrying clearly into the tense hush of the shadowy room. "According to our scryers the water's up to the fifth level of the Vaults," he said.

From somewhere in the dark of the kitchen there came a thin, alien piping, the scramble of unseen feet. The mages glanced quickly at one another. Daurannon went a little paler, but continued, "Nandiharrow, take twelve of the sasenna with you."

From the north door came a muttered confusion of voices. Joanna looked up, to see the guards there step back. Two gray-robed Juniors—a rawboned, red-haired girl and a dark-eyed boy—carried in between them a stumbling little man in a yellow nightshirt, whose black, greasy hair cascaded like a woman's down his shoulders. Behind them, haloed by witchlight, flitted the androgynous form of Issay Bel-Caire.

"Brighthand—Otaro." Daurannon strode across to greet them.

Joanna bent back to her work. This patch of moss and that wormhole were related here in this configuration, which meant that probably this map went this-way-around, and thus that Gate there had opened twice . . . or two different Gates had opened there a day and a half apart.

"What's that note say?"

" 'Cold field,' " reported Tom.

"Well, they all seem to be lining up."

"It's where the energy-tracks run through the Vaults." The Dead God's shorter, thinner lower hand snaked past Tom to trace a line on the map fragment. "That chamber is the one with the Glass Pillar, at one point of the field axis. There are Gates—concentrations of flux—here and here, outside the Vaults, indeed outside the Citadel altogether."

"Is the cold field on the next map? How about the one that says 'cat magic'?"

"That's over here . . . not in the Vaults . . ."

Her eyes sneaked to her watch. Forty-five minutes had passed.

"My lord . . . !"

The guards on the east door of the refectory stepped aside. Nandiharrow, tall, gray, and grim, strode through the door in a billow of dark robes, trailed by a very shaken-looking Pothatch and twelve guards. Daurannon put aside the crystal he had been studying for the past ten minutes and walked quickly to meet him, probably, Joanna guessed, to keep whatever ill news Nandiharrow had to impart from being called out across an assembly of folks already teetering on the knife-edge of panic. Silvorglim, at least, had for some time been pacing and fidgeting, staring around him at the wizards and across at the darkly gleaming circle of oscillators and transmission screens in a way she did not like.

Daurannon might as well have saved himself steps. The attention of every person in the place, with the exception of Bentick and the heavily sedated Otaro, was riveted on the dark forms of the two Council mages from the nine-fingered clock-maker's first utterance.

"There's something moving down there," Nandiharrow said softly. "There are . . . things . . . throughout the cellars now, but this seems to be coming up from the Vaults. I've looked and cannot see it properly, but I felt it . . . we all felt it. A drawing, a coldness not of the air, but of the bones within the flesh . . ."

"Oh, Christ," Joanna whispered, knowing instantly what it was that he had seen. Something seemed to sink and tighten behind her sternum, and her heart began to pound.

Daurannon returned quietly to his chair, and the light that had flickered over his head while he'd scried grew brighter as he held his crystal once more to its glow. He gazed for a long time, and the wizards grouped around him in the curious, flickering ring of multiple shadows grew very silent. By the stronger glare, Joanna could see the sweat glisten upon that short upper lip.

"Miss Sheraton . . ."

She came to him, dusting the chalk from her hands. "The *tsaeati*," she said softly, pronouncing the word as Magister Magus had done. "That's what it is, isn't it?"

The mage shut his eyes for a moment, not surprised, but with the gesture of a two-pack-a-day man who'd been hoping the doctor would say, 'Oh, no, that cough's just a summer cold . . .'

"I don't know," he said at length. Joanna looked down over his shoulder at the chunk of gray-yellow quartz the size and thickness of an avocado pit that lay in his well-kept hands. In the flat, reflected brightness she could see nothing in the glass-smooth facets.

"In the Vaults," Joanna said softly, "one of those two-legged Shriekers came running after us, and I thought then there was something moving behind it—something I couldn't exactly see. I thought . . . I thought almost that the floors bulged up, like the stone itself was alive."

Sweat flashed as a muscle jumped in Daurannon's jaw, but he said nothing.

"Antryg had Magister Magus remain behind to put the strongest illusions he could muster across the passageway, so that nothing on that side could perceive anything beyond them. We had to get the machine up here."

"And it has followed," he murmured. "Or perhaps it is only that it sensed the smell of our blood, our souls, from afar."

He turned the crystal over in his fingers, which remained oddly steady; Joanna herself was a bit surprised at how calm she felt. "I can see the walls move," he continued in a voice that was audible only because of the deadly hush that had fallen all around them. "I can see a mound of water and mud, and out of it the torn limbs and necks and bodies of unknown creatures are waving and snapping, surrounded by darkness. And past that darkness, I see the arches and brickwork of the storage cellars."

Across the refectory by the east door, other sasenna had come in, their panting voices clear for all their quiet: "We couldn't stop it. We had to fall back. It's on its way."

Daurannon got to his feet, counting his forces with his eyes. Without being ordered, all the sasenna in the room including those of the Church—save the guards on the north door—had gone to the eastern archway, ranging themselves across it. Their faces were grim, and Joanna reflected that, though the sasenna trained throughout their lives for a death-fight, in these peaceful times very few of them—Church, Council, or the private forces of nobles or Emperor—ever actually saw true combat. Near the north door Otaro stirred in his poppy-induced dreams, mumbled something that sounded like "Father . . . ," and then began to scream, a horrible, harsh, animal noise, and claw at his face with his bound hands. Brighthand and Issay, who had joined the group around Daurannon's chair, raced back to him, catching at his wrists—his cheeks and forehead were already a mass of scabs—and pulling them away; in time the Singer quietened to weeping, and so once again to sleep.

But as if the screaming had raised the temperature of some volatile liquid over boiling point, the stillness of the refectory, with its shifting patterns of yellow torchlight, pale witchfire, and shadows, dissolved into nervous convection currents of movement.

"Nandiharrow, Issay, Brighthand . . ." Daurannon was moving among them, his choirboy face very white but resolute. "Gilda, contact Q'iin, get her and her party back here—tell them to come through the north doors if they can. Whitwell . . ."

Seldes Katne, seated near the quilt on the floor where Bentick lay, got to her feet and made as if to come over, and Daurannon waved her back. Bentick, too, climbed shakily to his feet, catching the corner of the nearest table.

"Lie down," the little librarian ordered. "You'll kill yourself . . ."

"Nonsense. They need everyone with any pretension to strength."

The Senior mages were drawing together, with a few of the Juniors—Brighthand and Kyra—under Daurannon's quiet-voiced orders. "If it is the *tsaeati*," he was saying, "it was said to be drawn by life, to absorb life. Thus we need to form a Blood-Bond among us, to pool our life and our strength against this thing."

As the mages began to turn up their sleeves and form themselves into a ritual circle, Joanna faded back to the ring of transmitter screens and generators—Compu-Henge, she termed it mentally—and knelt beside the Dead God and Tom, who were still laboriously marking and annotating the master maps. "Back up your data chips and take the computer down," she said softly. "We're going to have the worst kind of company in a couple minutes and I wouldn't want the disk to crash."

The Dead God swore. Translated by the Spell of Tongues

directly mind to mind, some of the images were fairly startling. "What comes?" he asked, as the screen colors redshifted themselves away into darkness.

"Something that eats life."

"We *all* do that." He unfolded himself in long-boned increments and fished his weapon from behind the main generator. "We can bring the screens inside the main ring and still maintain the configuration, but if it comes near the oscillator or the batteries . . . see?" He showed her the triggering and targeting mechanisms of the gun, which had clearly been designed for operation by one upper hand and one lower. "It doesn't kick much, but hold it tucked, this way, and by all Those Below keep your arm clear of the vent."

Joanna checked the infrared targeting system and found it unfamiliar but comprehensible. When she'd admitted, to her own embarrassment, a delight in armament, her instructor had demonstrated some fairly esoteric weaponry. Antryg had generally been more curious about how the stuff had worked; Joanna, always practical, had merely striven to be able to hit anything with it before that thing could hit her. Though the gun was awkward to hold, the trigger was no more than a button, designed for the tiny tongue-fingers of Ninetentwo's kind and easily adaptable to her own small hand.

Ten feet away, the fifteen or so top mages stood in a chalked Circle of Power, bared forearms pressed together; here and there, between the joins, slow trickles of blood dripped out. Among the ashy grays and blacks of their robes, Tobin, the Witchfinder's Dog, stood out like flame among cinders. Though Joanna could hear no words, she knew there was magic being raised and shared among them; could sense it in the quiet stillness of those vastly disparate faces. Teenagers like Zake Brighthand or fussy old men like Bentick, whatever their feelings about one another, about the role of wizardry or the operation of the Citadel, when it came down to it, they would back one another to the death or beyond. They were what they were, and even those who loved them—herself; her friend Caris the sasennan, Salteris' grandson; Pothatch, Hathen, and Tom—could never fully understand. Silvorglim the Witchfinder, who had remained seated among the torches and lanterns when his guards had joined the ranks before thc doors, now approached the group with a glint of protesting fire in his eyes: Pothatch caught him by the arm and whispered, "Not now."

"My lord!" Sergeant Hathen called from the eastern door, and around her the black ranks of the sworn warriors stirred.

Daurannon raised his head and opened his eyes. As she had briefly during their argument, Joanna saw the middle-aged man who hid beneath the wizard's smooth disguise—saw, with some surprise, the naked terror in his eyes. He walked forward, bracing himself for what would come.

The circle of mages re-formed itself into a rough line. Daurannon nodded to the sergeant to get her warriors back. She signed them to withdraw but remained herself—Joanna saw the big, heavy-boned woman's glance cross Daurannon's, asking some question; the mage took a deep breath and motioned her away. After a moment's hesitation she went. Crouching behind the stack of batteries with the Dead God, the muzzle of the gun protruding between them, Joanna thought that momentary hesitation—that wondering whether she ought to remain at her master's side in spite of the creeping coldness, the sensation of slow-building evil that had begun to flow into the room—was one of the bravest things she'd seen.

Neatly and very rapidly Daurannon sketched signs upon the door with his left forefinger—or presumably, Joanna thought, they were signs, since she herself could see nothing of them in the soft whiteness slowly strengthening in the room around them. The waiting line of wizards grouped closer, heads bowed, some with eyes shut as if meditating. One or two of them, Joanna saw, held hands, the blood that streaked their forearms staining the clasped fingers.

A stream of bloodstained water began to trickle in under the door.

Daurannon stepped back, panting as if with some strain or

exertion, his hands visibly trembling now. Sweat misted his face and dripped from the strings of his long hair; his lips moved a little in the torch glare from behind. The witchlight, after its final blaze, began to fade, and like the cold dark that waited beyond the doors, night closed in.

The bolt across the door quivered, creaking under some massive weight; then from the wood of the door itself came a scratching, tearing sound, and Joanna saw the heavy oak planks at the bottom shift and start. Daurannon took another step backward and spread out his arms, gathering what was left of the light about him until his form was haloed in shuddering wings of brightness against the gloom. He cried out *"Tsaeati, tsaerat, anambo mishia tathet!"* and steam began to curl from the surface of the water still trailing thinly in.

The scratching stopped.

Otaro moaned with terror in his sleep.

Then something smote the door with a blow like a steam hammer, like a freight train slamming at floor-level, and oak splinters three inches thick went spearing like shattered match-wood in every direction. A cacophony of howls and screams burst out, and claws pawed and thrust under the widened space beneath the door, ripping, grabbing at the wood while all around them water, mud, and blood came pouring in. Daur-annon and several others in the line made a slashing pass with their hands, and blue lightning smote the floor, turning the water to hissing steam and raking at the searching claws. But the steam itself sprang upward into a cyclone, flung itself in the Handsome One's face, and as he threw up his arms to protect his eyes, the oak of the door bulged, swelled, heaved out into an impossible bubble as if the molecules of the wood itself had softened to liquescent gum.

Then, with a report like a cannon-shot, the door burst, and a monstrous thing, shining slimily with mold and niter, stink-ing of rot and curtained in a swirling fog of water from which the heads and arms and feet of unimaginable creatures snapped wildly and eyelessly, rolled in.

The blast had flung Daurannon backward, a splinter of oak tearing through his left arm like a javelin head. At a cry from Brighthand, lightning smote the thing again, the darkness that streamed in with it like noxious fog exploding in a white clap of blinding electricity, and Issay Bel-Caire dove forward under cover of the bolt, to drag the stunned Daurannon out of the *tsaeati*'s path. Joanna shaded her eyes against the searing glare as the mages flung the lightning again, and the thing before them took fire and hurled itself in a swollen, blazing wall of steam and flame and burning meat at its attackers.

They fell back before it, dragging Daurannon with them. A bolt of lightning leaped from the fog to strike the Herbmistress Q'iin; she stumbled, and the column of burning mud fell upon her, sweeping her along with it, screaming like the damned. The stench of blood and charred meat billowed suffocatingly from the heaving mass.

"Cold!" yelled Daurannon, struggling to stand. Blood spouted from a severed artery, splashing Issay and all those near him with gouts of crimson. "Not fire—COLD!"

The mage Whitwell Simm and two of the Council's sasenna had sprung forward, slashing with swords at the gory serpent heads, the clawed hands, fighting to get to where Q'iin had been. Already the mud was whitening, stiffening with frost, smoke mushrooming off it as the air temperature plunged and spreading over the floor of the refectory. For an instant the *tsaeati* slowed, settling into immobility . . .

And then, as the door had done—as Joanna had half sensed the stone floor of the corridor doing—it began to move again. There was a creaking, a thin, hideous *snickle* of shivering ice. From its slow bulging it burst into horrible speed, pouring itself over the feet of the nearest sasennan. The man pulled back, hacking at the slithering thing with his sword, but the hairy arms of a Shrieker reached out to him from it, pulling him to his knees and then forward, screaming, face-first into the frozen muck. Whitwell Simm leaned down to drag the young man free and the sasennan's hand shot out, seizing the frail old wizard by the arm and hauling him down inexorably into the slime that heaved up to meet him. The water was ice, frozen solid and moving, impossibly, like clouded and filthy gelatin—where she stood behind the batteries Joanna could feel the smoke of cold radiating from it—but the hands and heads of the abominations, hung now with spines of frost, still lashed and snapped within it, ripping at Simm's flesh as he twisted frantically to get free. Brunus and the remaining sasennan managed to hack through the tentacles, the claws—the arm of the warrior it had devoured—and carried Simm, with gobbets of the thing still clinging to his flesh, back to the far end of the chamber. Within the thing itself Q'iin's voice screamed on and on as it advanced upon the wizards.

And then, opposite the cluster of generators and screens, it stopped.

And turned.

For a nightmare second Joanna felt as if she were dreaming, separated from self and reality by the mere fact that this thing, creaking with the scrape of ice as it began to advance on her, was the embodiment of her nightmares.

Then she realized what was happening and yelled, "It's going for the batteries!" In the same instant the Dead God loosed a charge into the thing nearly point-blank. Shards of ice and mud spattered everywhere as the round exploded deep in the gelid mass, Q'iin's voice breaking off with a hideous, gobbling choke.

Each separate glob, including the one from which the sasennan's torso and legs still projected, kicking with a horrible life of their own, began to crawl toward them again.

"Dammit, it eats energy!" Joanna screamed. "If it takes the batteries, the whole Citadel will collapse."

*What the hell am I getting so excited about?* she wondered blindly, casting a frantic glance at the group of wizards but too terrified to leave the protective wall behind which she crouched. *The whole Citadel's going to collapse in twenty minutes anyway.*

Daurannon shouted something in the trained, booming voice of Power; she had a glimpse of him from the tail of her eye, clinging to Brighthand and Issay, fighting to stay on his feet, his face chalky from loss of blood. The air in the long chamber seemed to glitter and crackle with static, her hair rippled and swirled.

And behind the creature, directly opposite the pile of batteries, another pile of batteries appeared, twice as large and coruscating with blue flickers of lightning.

A second look showed Joanna it was illusion. Antryg had once told her that there were limitations on what could be done with illusion, and this one, though clearly very, very good, still looked wrong in some fashion she could not determine. But for a last-second effort it was far from bad, and the *tsaeati* did not appear to be a particularly discriminating judge. It hesitated for an instant, its various parts melding stickily into the main mass, then slowly started to crawl toward what it clearly sensed was a still greater concentration of energy.

Daur's voice was a broken gasp. "Open the north door, somebody . . ."

Seldes Katne, torn from the immobility of horror, lunged across the monstrosity's path and threw the huge oak panels wide. The illusory pile of batteries—Joanna noted obliquely that they'd reproduced the brand logos exactly—flickered, wavered, then reappeared in the corridor outside.

The *tsaeati* moved toward it in a thick *crickl*ing of ice, leaving a horrible wake of bloody, frost-rimmed water and slime. Daurannon and Brighthand were clinging to one another like drowning men, kneeling now with heads bowed within the circle of the other mages, focus and laser of their power. Joanna saw the Junior's lips move, heard Nandiharrow repeat to the others, "The Library. The top floor of the Library. It's the farthest place . . ."

"No!" Seldes Katne cried in a voice of despair. None of them heeded. The mages of the blood-circle were all clinging together now, supporting one another, sinking in on each other like the ruins of a burned-out house. Their eyes shut, they poured out the last of their magic into the maintenance of the illusion, the drawing of power.

Daur's head fell back against Brighthand's shoulder; from under the boy's pressing fingers blood still pulsed, thick and stinking and redder than anything Joanna had ever imagined. "Issay . . . barriers . . . illusion. Keep it from finding its way back." The little mage flitted like a white-haired spider to the doorway through which the creature had passed and began, with long, emaciated hands, to form infinitely stronger versions of those same signs that Magister Magus had written across the corridor in the Vaults not three hours previously.

"Not the Library!" Seldes Katne wailed, standing as close behind the Silent One as she dared. "They can't . . ."

In the corner, Whitwell Simm was still groaning and sobbing as the slimy shreds of the *tsaeati* slithered from what was left of his arm and crawled like filthy ribbons toward the door, leaving a pustulant black mildew behind. Issay stepped aside to let them past, as if they had been no more than snakes. Beside Joanna, the Dead God set his weapon down and said, "And how long will that illusion foil the thing's instinct to seek out and absorb whatever it can?"

Joanna, nauseated and trembling with shock, had to lean on the stack of batteries to keep her knees from giving way. Reaction was setting in, and despair, on top of swirling light-headedness that left her short of breath. Her own voice sounded weirdly matter-of-fact in her ears as she said, "In fifteen minutes that question's going to become academic . . ."

"What?" The Dead God lunged to check a gauge. 'Nonsense! Barely an hour has elapsed."

Joanna looked at her watch, then up at the tall figure towering above her. "It's been damn near two by my watch." Then she paused, feeling suddenly foolish. "Oh," she said. "You have different hours than we do, don't you?"

And her knees buckled, and she slipped slowly to the floor.

Clawed hands caught her, lifted her as if she'd been a spray of lilies, and carried her to one of the piles of blankets heaped along the wall. Though she didn't lose consciousness, in her grayed-out dizziness Joanna was aware of all things in small vignettes, still-lifes without meaning: Daurannon's face white as eggshell against the black of his hair while Pothatch ripped open his sleeve and Sergeant Hathen tourniqueted his arm; the other mages of the Blood-Circle huddled numbed and shaken on the floor, like the stunned survivors of battle, too shell-shocked to move; two of the novices holding Otaro back from beating his head to pulp against the wall behind him; Whitwell Simm, deep in shock, staring at the greenish brown slime slowly thickening on the melted flesh and half-stripped bones of his arm; a tiny abomination like a bug-eyed purple rat skittering nervously back and forth along the far wall.

She noted, as if from some great distance off, that all the light had died from the room save the torches and lanterns of Silvorglim's sasenna—noted how the ruddy glare danced across the faces of the Witchfinder as he called his warriors about him.

She wondered a little distantly why Seldes Katne should be slipping away unnoticed through the north door.

Then Brighthand called out, "Hold on, what the hell you playin' at?" He staggered to his feet as Silvorglim and his troops closed in on the bank of batteries. Two of the Church sasenna caught the young man unceremoniously by the arms, a third struck him hard over the back of the head with the long, iron-hard hilt of a sword. At the same instant the Dead God, kneeling beside Joanna, snapped to his feet and sprang like a skeleton dragon toward the Witchfinders. Two crossbows came up and there was a wicked snap of iron and hardwood; the huge, spiderlike shape collapsed with a crash, long arms stretching toward the machinery that was all of their lives.

There was a moment's stunned silence. Then, into it, Silvorglim spoke.

"What am I doing?" he said softly, addressing the unconscious Brighthand, the other Council mages who stood, immobilized—those of them who *could* stand—facing the ranked crossbows of the Church's guards.

"I am saving the world. I am doing what should have been done six hundred years ago, no matter what the cost would have been to the Church and to the free armies of human-kind."

In the shadowy torchlight Silvorglim's eyes had the strange, clear yellowness of nearly colorless amber, cold and hard and without emotion, and in his level voice there was a quality of almost exaltation.

"Instead, they bargained with the mages—believed their promises of the half use of power, the lie of noninterference in human affairs. They let them live—they paid them off, *worked* with them even, did their bidding—not understanding that *no* mage is capable of good, that the use of these powers *to any degree* can bring nothing but evil, and plots, and disas-ter. You say that when those batteries are destroyed, the Cit-adel will disintegrate into the Void. So be it. I am destroying the Citadel of Wizards—destroying wizardry forever and sav-ing the world from its pollution, once and for all."

On the whole, the older a teles is, the more powerful its capacity for magic; yet such implements must be observed straitly, and tested often. For whenever such spells develop strange fields of heat and cold, or the random movement of things within the chamber, it has been my experience that it was when the teles was a very old one.

—GRIMOIRE OF GANTRE SILVAS

# CHAPTER XXII

JOANNA SCREAMED, "NO!" AND STARTED TO HER FEET AS THE Witchfinder strode toward the dark ring of the oscillators, a silent, blinking rampart in the flickering gloom. A sasennan swung toward her, crossbow leveled.

And the next instant the darkness was riven by blinding brightness, ozone cutting the stinks of torch smoke and blood with the searing crackle of lightning. Joanna cried, "NO!" again in the same instant she realized Silvorglim had cried out, too—cried out in shock and thwarted rage.

As the Witchfinder sprang back from the spitting curtain of purple-white fire that had ripped upward from the floor between him and the equipment, a deep, familiar voice from the eastern doorway chided, "Really, Yarak, I had no idea your dedication ran so deep."

Silvorglim rounded like a scorched weasel as Antryg came striding out of the shadows of shattered wood and darkness, his scarecrow tangle of shawl and coat skirts and glittering beads fluttering absurdly and a long killing sword stuck casually through his belt. Three more dark shapes materialized

334

from the dripping hell-mouth on his heels: the Lady Rosamund, leaning heavily on her staff but with a drawn sword in her other hand, and Aunt Min, leaning upon Magister Magus' arm, her pale eyes sharp and bright.

The Witchfinder whispered, "You . . ."

"Well," Antryg said, "there are two schools of thought on that subject. Don't you think it's time you took a little nap?" He'd reached Silvorglim by that time—the Church sasenna being momentarily too nonplussed to know if, or whom, to attack—and extended a mitted hand to touch the smaller man's forehead.

Silvorglim struck his hand away and nearly suffocated on an enormous yawn. "You can't smother me with a—aargh . . ." He yawned again, his sulfurous eyes blazing with fury even as they fought to remain open. ". . . a cantrip like that one." His hand fumbled at the sword at his belt.

"I realize that, of course." Very casually Antryg dropped his other hand over Silvorglim's sword wrist and caught the Witchfinder a terrific crack across the chin with one bony elbow, considerably supporting him as he dropped, stunned, to the floor. The sasenna, taken by surprise, moved in, but the interval had given time for Sergeant Hathen and her troops to collect their senses and spread out. There was a swift clatter of weaponry and then the sudden, fraught silence of a standoff.

"No, no, no," muttered Aunt Min, pulling one fragile arm free of Magister Magus' grip and doddering purposefully to Antryg's side. "You and you," she pointed to two Church sasenna at random, "take poor Mr. Silvorglim over to his blankets. Kyra, see what you can do for his headache, please. Q'iin . . ." She paused, and Joanna knew that she was aware of what had become of the beautiful black lady with the sea blue eyes. "Ah, Q'iin." The old woman sighed and bowed her white head. "My poor little girl." On the other side of the refectory, the novice Gilda huddled in a corner, her cheek pressed to the plaster of the wall, weeping without a sound.

Lady Rosamund limped to Aunt Min's side. With the neutralizing of the Church troops she had sheathed her sword; she put her free arm protectively around the old lady's shoulders as she looked up at Antryg. "And what now?" Her hair was damp and stringy with sweat, her dark robe torn and blotched: evidently the route to the Brown Star's gate had been less than easy. Antryg, despite a makeshift bandage on his left hand and black rings of exhaustion around his eyes, looked better than he had, as if a weight had been lifted from his bony shoulders. Magister Magus simply sank down in a corner and put his head in his hands.

"The battle with the *tsaeati* has exhausted the powers of nearly everyone on the Council without defeating the creature, and we are where we were before."

"Well, hardly that," Brighthand pointed out, looking up from Otaro's semiconscious form. "Once that thing gets to the top of the Library and finds nothin' resemblin' energy up there, it's gonna be back."

"You had to say that," Tom sighed.

But Antryg had already turned away, to kneel, as Issay Bel-Caire was already kneeling, beside the great, bony shape of the Dead God. "Ninetentwo," he whispered, his crooked fingers traveling with feathered lightness over the long bone planes of the alien temples, brushing the heavy clawed hands and corded wrists. Joanna, coming up quietly on the alien's other side, checked the gauges on the air tanks. They seemed less than half-empty, and as she watched, the green lights flickered and varied with the slow draw of breath.

Leaving Antryg and Issay together to bind the wounds the crossbow bolts had made, she returned to the oscillators and, plagued by a deep sense of embarrassment at what she perceived as truly unfeeling behavior, systematically checked what she could of every gauge and dial. As far as she could tell, all the lights that should have been amber were still amber, nothing was blinking or white . . . the equivalent of danger-red. Fortunately, the dials and screen were self-illuminated, for the witchlight that had been drunk away by the *tsaeati*'s power had not returned, and the great refectory was sunk in almost total darkness. Only the torches and lanterns of Silvorglim's sas-enna provided a smoky, eerie light, which played nervously across the faces of the wizards while their shadows loomed and staggered on the walls like shredded battle flags borne by dying men.

Laboriously, she followed Ninetentwo's original instructions, feeding the wafer chips into the computer's port and overlapping the samples with the actual readings to make sure nothing had altered. Behind her she was aware of Antryg rummaging through the spare equipment behind the main oscillator to locate a black plastic case roughly the size of a loaf of bread. Presumably, she thought, it was the first-aid kit, with drugs and stimulants proper to Ninetentwo's alien physiology. *He wouldn't have known what it was or where it was unless Ninetentwo told him,* she thought, as he strode back to the Silent One and their patient, and allowed herself a hesitant sip of relief.

The sound of Gilda's sobbing had quieted; Joanna raised her head to see the dark-haired novice being rocked in red-haired Kyra's arms. Brunus, fat and deft and serious, was applying hot cloths to Whitwell Simm's ruined arm, steam from the basin beside him rising in wreaths around his kindly face. Nearby a rather shaky-looking Brighthand, his gray robe still soaked with Daurannon's blood, was holding on to Otaro's bound wrists and saying something to him in the soft tones of healing-spells, while the mad wizard stirred in his dreams and sobbed incoherently. Lady Rosamund and Aunt Min had gone to kneel beside Daurannon, the Lady binding and stitching the wound in his arm by the light of a tallow dip while the Arch-mage listened to Durannon's stifled account of the events of the past hour and a half.

She heard Aunt Min say softly, "And it was not so much then, to face Death when it came?"

Daurannon's breath whispered in a laugh, as at some old conversation, and he murmured, "Believe me, Auntie, if there'd been any place to run, you'd *still* be trying to coax me out of it." But the old lady only smiled.

Magister Magus, Joanna noted, hadn't moved from his corner near the eastern door, where he was rather numbly consuming a cup of tea under the watchful eye of two of Silvorglim's guards. The Witchfinder himself slept heavily in his corner among the cluster of torches.

Yet a waiting tension filled the dark room like an indrawn breath. Joanna knew—they all knew—that Brighthand was right. It was far from over.

"He'll be all right." Antryg's deep, flamboyant voice breathed like the soft-brushed note of a temple gong in Joanna's ear. Turning, she saw that he and Issay had brought the Dead God back to the shelter of his equipment, covering him with blankets. The iridescent orange eyes were open, but since Joanna had never seen them close, she wasn't sure what this meant. Steam curled from the palms of those huge, toothed hands and drifted in ribbons from along his spine.

"I hope so," she murmured nervously. "Aside from the fact that he's the only one who can really tell if anything goes wrong with all the hardware . . . Dammit, none of this is really any of his fight. I mean . . ." She hesitated, looking worriedly up into Antryg's face. "He could have stayed in his own world, you know."

"Don't talk foolishness." The buzzing from the Dead God's skull was barely louder than a mosquito circling somewhere, invisible, on a summer night. "If you saw a long-odds opportunity to enrich your knowledge by leaping through a Gate into another world, would you not seize an air bottle and leap?"

"Hell, no," Joanna replied promptly, then realized that it was exactly what she had done in returning to this world last fall, to attempt to rescue Antryg from the Council.

Antryg's eyebrows shot up, with a kind of startled, nervous question, and she realized she wasn't the only one who'd considered the implications of their love in the light of the danger it had brought her.

Magister Magus had cautioned her not to make a choice. But her utter joy at having the choice—at having him there to choose—was, she understood, choice in itself.

She added softly, "Not knowledge."

In their bruised pits, the gray eyes warmed, and he sighed a little, reaching out to touch her cheek with the backs of his fingers. "It's good to see you again."

"You don't know how good."

"Joanna, I'm so sorry . . ."

She shifted her grip to his coat sleeves and pulled him to her. Their kiss was slower and stronger, without the first unthinking desperation; she felt, for an odd moment, that had things been a little different they would have retired then and there to some corner, curled up together like a couple of puppies, and gone to sleep.

Instead she said, "Now come over here and have a look at this."

"Filthy French postcards?" he inquired hopefully, and she poked him lightly in the ribs.

"I'll give you a filthy French postcard. How about a filthy French map of the Vaults, with all your information totted up and whatever I could pull out of the Dead God's graphics. And I hope you can see some kind of pattern in it all, because I sure as hell can't. Other than the obvious one, that they all line up along the leys."

"Yes, but we knew that going in." He coiled himself down cross-legged to study the nine maps roughly sketched on the floor. "The problem is . . . where's Kitty, by the way? She was here when I left."

Joanna frowned at the sudden memory through the jumbled events of the last half hour. "She dodged out of here right after the fight with the *tsaeati*—which, as Brighthand so sapiently pointed out, *is* going to be back as soon as it gets to the top of the Library and discovers there's no supersonic lollipop up there. She might have had some idea of protecting the books, but I don't think it would devour them. They aren't an energy source, are they?'

"Well, some of them are, but that's another story. What worries me is that there were supposed to be two or three teles stored in the Library. Which ones, and how strong, I don't know, since Kitty never got a chance to give me the results of her research. What's this?''

"Just my notes.''

"No, on the back.''

"Ninetentwo's raw data from before the stabilization field went into effect. You can see the concentration in what has to be the Vaults . . .''

"Yes,'' he murmured, and began to riffle the pages like a cartoon flip-book, so that the images seemed to skate nervously here and there with the rapidly falling sheets. "How did Kitty act?''

Joanna looked at him blankly for a moment, then said, "Scared, like the rest of us. Why?''

"Well . . .'' He frowned and riffled the pages again, watching the illusory movement of all the Gates through the almost-patterns of the maze. Then he looked across at her, the torchlight sliding opaquely across the lenses of his spectacles for a moment, then showing his eyes grave and worried. "You see, two of the three people who actually saw the Moving Gate went mad.''

"You mean from something in the Gate itself?''

Antryg nodded. "Kitty didn't get as close a look as the others did, and so mightn't have gotten the full dose of whatever it was—probably an atmospheric poison—but she did get some, because she, too, described the Gate as rushing toward her. Now, there may very well have been some kind of noises and lights connected with it, but . . .''

"Wait a minute,'' said Joanna, catching his hands as he began to riffle the sheets again. "Are you saying that the Moving Gate *didn't move at all*?''

His long mouth quirked. "I suspect not. I thought it was impossible at the time, you remember—no, you don't remember, you weren't there. Anyway, from what I know of the physics of the Void, for a Gate to slide around in that fashion is extremely unlikely. What is likelier is that the initial hallucinations involved the sense of the darkness of the Gate rushing toward—or in Kitty's case, away from—the victim; pursuing them, as Otaro described. Then later come pain and increasing paranoia: Phormion's belief that Lady Rosamund was using me in a plot against her, Otaro's visions of the Moving Gate appearing in his rooms."

He glanced across at Bentick, who was helping Brunus with Whitwell Simm. The Steward moved with the jitteriness of the cats that had begun to congregate in every corner of the echoing darkness of the room; his face was haggard under the raked red lines of its wounds.

"I began to wonder about it after I spoke to Otaro, but other matters intervened. It's been a rather busy night. But looking at all the evidence, it's quite plain to me that what appeared to be an anomaly was in fact not an anomaly at all, and therefore probably no more significant than any other Gate. In other words, I—we all—have been pursuing a chimera."

Joanna looked around her at the refectory, the tense, exhausted white faces of the wizards, the stinks of smoke and burnt flesh and blood. Her voice shook. "So we're back to square one?"

"Oh," Antryg murmured, returning to riffling through the pages and making all the various Gates move, "I think we have a long, long way to go before we achieve the comfort and security of square one. But if Kitty's started to go mad from seeing this Gate as well . . ."

Then he paused, staring down at the top sheet of the pile. Lifting them again, he let them fall, holding them higher and wider, so that not only the closer patterns of the Vaults showed, but, here and there, the dark blurs of fields elsewhere appeared and vanished.

Looking down over his shoulder, Joanna was silent until he'd finished.

Then he said slowly, "Yes."

"That one spot isn't moving at all."

"No."

"But it isn't even in the Vaults. I saw it on those charts and thought it was the one out in the Green King's Chapel."

Antryg shook his head. "It isn't anywhere near far enough out for that. By its placement it's definitely in the Citadel."

"But if it's in the Citadel," Joanna argued, puzzled, "I mean, not in the Vaults—wouldn't somebody have seen it?"

"Not necessarily. Kitty and I searched all the places in the Citadel where no one ever goes in quest of you, but it's conceivable that we missed some . . ."

"Ninetentwo . . ." Joanna bent anxiously toward the prone shape of the great dragonoid. The nodule of light flickered, then brightened like a feeble star. "Could you show me how to run up a three-D projection of the Citadel and feed in this data?"

"I could," responded the buzzing voice, the words forming up in her mind. "But it would take me four times as long as it would simply to do it. Bring the computer here."

"Antryg . . ." Another voice spoke from the fitful glare beyond the shadows of the oscillator ring.

Antryg rose; Lady Rosamund stood silhouetted in the fitful light. He stepped closer and saw how the shadows showed up the lines of pain around that perfect mouth, the aching soreness in every move she made. Her hand shook where it clutched the staff.

"Brighthand was right, you know," she said. "The *tsaeati* will be back, and soon. I have some power, and you also, now, and the mere fact that he could read the marks in the Vaults tells me that Magister Magus is more than the charlatan he pretends to be. But the *tsaeati* . . . In all the legends of Berengis' meeting with it, it is said that the thing cannot be defeated. That it will absorb whatever is used against it, whatever it touches, as poor Whitwell found. It has Q'iin's magic now, too.''

"Yes," murmured Antryg, leaning his elbows on the generator that separated them. "And the worst thing about the *tsaeati* is that it *isn't* the worst of our problems. We have to find the Gate—which, as it turns out, is neither moving about nor in the Vaults at all—and we have to find it within the next hour, before the stabilization field starts to disintegrate."

"Not in the Vaults?" Her dark brows plunged down. "But what Phormion and Otaro and Seldes Katne saw . . ."

"Was a hallucination which appeared to be more significant than it was. Bentick . . ."

The Steward, kneeling beside Otaro, twitched as if struck. His eyes met Antryg's across the room with a kind of shamefaced defiance; then he sighed, and crossed to the dark ring of blinking equipment.

"I never thanked you for saving me from Phormion," Antryg said quietly. "It was enormously appreciated, in spite of subsequent events, and once you realized she was going mad, I can't really blame you for doing whatever you could to keep the Inquisition from meddling in the search and finding her. Is she still in her rooms?"

The old man shook his head wretchedly. "She is wandering. I . . . she . . . she said I was trying to kill her. Said we were all plotting to poison her." His hand strayed to the clawrakes on his scalp. "She said the Moving Gate was appearing to her in her rooms, that she heard voices within it plotting her death." He bowed his head, his hands straying nervously again to his watch. "She hasn't eaten or slept . . ."

"Well," Antryg sighed wistfully, "when it comes right down to it, neither have I. But unfortunately she's one of the few wizards in the Citadel capable of using her full powers at the moment—or any power at all. While she was ill, did you enter all the rooms of the Castle?"

"Yes. She thought that Lady Rosamund had put spies there and made me come with her to search them."

"Hmn. Well, that rules out the Castle. I had thought . . ."

"Antryg . . ." Joanna looked up from the screen. "We've got it."

Antryg excused himself, leaving Rosamund and Bentick talking quietly while he went to kneel in the tiny circle of greenish light from the computer screen.

"I'm using as parameters the outer limit of the spell-field you set." The thin, clawed fingers of Ninetentwo's lower left arm—the only arm not immobilized by wounds or bandages—picked swiftly among the computer keys. "The green spot is the area in question. It isn't a Gate at all, if you'll reexamine the raw data, but a field of some kind surrounding a small wormhole. The wormhole would appear from time to time as a floating area of blackness, not large enough for a human to pass through."

"Yes," Antryg murmured, as the Dead God manipulated the knobs to turn the digitalized construct of the Citadel here and there. "I'm familiar with them."

"I still think it's odd that nobody would have noticed it, if it were in the Citadel," Joanna said. "Particularly if you and Seldes Katne searched the place for me."

She looked up at Antryg's face, the amber lines of the graphic reproducing the Citadel in miniature in the lenses of his glasses. In the dark of the electronic ring that surrounded them, the reflection of the single pixel of green burned like telltale fire.

He shut his eyes, and his breath escaped him in a sigh; etched in the pallid flicker of the screens, the lines of pain and weariness in his face seemed to deepen. He brought up his hand under his spectacles and rubbed his eyes, the gesture of a man defeated, comprehending that which he would really rather not comprehend.

"What is it?" Joanna asked worriedly. "Where is the field?"

"In the old Conservatory." His voice was matter-of-fact. "Adjacent to Seldes Katne's rooms."

"But wouldn't Seldes Katne have . . ." Her voice trailed and faded, as she understood. "But Seldes Katne doesn't have any power. At least, she's supposed to be the least powerful mage in the Citadel, according to Magister Magus."

"I know." He rubbed his eyes again and readjusted his spectacles to look at her, bone-deep weariness and bitter understanding in his eyes. "And that's why she used teles to power the magic-circles which keep it open; why she would have done *anything*, from discreetly fanning Bentick's fears to attempting to murder me, on up to destroying the stabilization field, to keep the Citadel from being searched, once she knew I wouldn't—or couldn't—help her."

He stood up, his shoulders bowed tiredly, and looked at the square, blinking wristwatch strapped incongruously to his arm beneath the tarnished beading of his coat cuff. "And I'm very much afraid, judging by how much time has elapsed since the *tsaeati*'s departure, that by this time it will have entered first the Library, then the Conservatory, and devoured the energies of the teles. Technically, it *is* a teles now, which means that we're going to *have* to destroy it in order to close the Gate."

"Unfortunately," Lady Rosamund's clear, cool voice sliced into the quiet like a trickle of ice water, "it has long been established that nothing *can* destroy it."

There was an awkward silence. At length Joanna said, "If nothing can destroy it, Nothing is probably what we need."

She got to her feet, staggering a little from the cramps of crouching in front of the computer so long, and crossed to them, her arms wrapped around herself against the growing cold.

"Considering that *nothing* is precisely what we're doing at the moment," Bentick retorted caustically, "dare I predict a large-scale victory in short order?"

But Antryg and Lady Rosamund were looking at one another, half-worried, half-speculative.

Down by Lady Rosamund's elbow, a piccolo voice said,

"Nothing," and looking across, Joanna saw Aunt Min, hunched like a bright-eyed little witch in the shadows.

"Antryg," Joanna said slowly, "you told me once that the Dead God—the *real* Dead God, not Ninetentwo—was Nothing. The opposite even of Entropy—a kind of antimatter, or antienergy, anti even the movement of randomness . . . pure Nothing. Is it possible to summon that?"

Antryg ran his fingers through his long gray hair, his eyes a little absent behind the thick lenses of his spectacles, delving around in the chaotic darkness of his memory. "Theoretically, it's possible to summon anything which can be imagined," he said. He started to say something else, hesitated a moment, then went on, "I suspect it would kill me."

"Suspect?" Lady Rosamund gave a single, high-bred sniff. "I can assure you, Windrose, that if you summoned a tithe of the . . . the *essence* of the Dead God, the emptiness, the coldness, the nothingness of absolute Nothing, it would finish you before the words were out of your mouth. And while the sight of you committing suicide in such a fashion might momentarily startle the *tsaeati* . . ."

"Not did he hold a spell of protection about him," Aunt Min said, reaching up to grasp her pupil's torn sleeve.

"Don't be silly," Bentick snapped. "To summon Nothing is more than most wizards can do in the first place. To summon a protective spell powerful enough to hold that Nothing at bay—that Nothing which would swallow even the magic of the teles—would kill the spell's wielder. And to summon half of each would end in leaving the *tsaeati* sufficient power to swallow you up, protection-spells and all. And in any case, the Summoning of Nothing is impossible."

"Bentick, Bentick," Antryg chided, "where's your imagination?"

"In the strict charge of my reason, thank you, where it belongs," the Steward retorted, tilting his head haughtily.

Joanna looked from one to the other, her heart slamming hard in her chest; from the table where a few candles had been lit,

Nandiharrow said softly, "Antryg . . . Lady Rosamund . . ."
Looking across at him, Joanna could see a scrying-crystal rest-
ing between his mutilated hands. He looked exhausted, slime
and filth and Daurannon's blood smeared across his face.
"There's something moving in the upper floor of the Harlot.
Coming back this way."

Antryg drew a shaky breath. "I'd have to wait," he said
softly, "until the thing was right on top of me."

Joanna shuddered, not even wanting to picture it. His own
death aside, the thought of standing in the darkness, of waiting
for the thing whose mindless, devouring malice she had felt in
the sightless labyrinth of the Brown Star, froze her to the core
of her being. She whispered, "No . . ." but knew he didn't
hear.

"Two of us could do it," Aunt Min piped.

Lady Rosamund's head snapped around to face her. "No!
You couldn't . . ."

"Don't make difficulties, Rosie." The old woman cut her
off placidly with a gesture of her clawlike hand. "Do you be
telling me now what I can and cannot survive?"

Any other woman, Joanna reflected, would have had tears
in her eyes: her Ladyship's were cold and dry and bitter. "I'll
go."

"Because your magic is greater than mine, or because with
a hole in your leg and pain throughout your body, you are fitter
to withstand this than I? No." As Rosamund opened her mouth
to protest, the old lady reached out and touched her hand.
"No," she said again, softly. "I will do this thing." The
firelight turned the white halo of her hair for a moment to
honey gold and caught the gleam of her eyes, brighter blue
than they had seemed before, and more alive, the eyes of a
wildcat girl who had never feared gods or man.

She turned back to Antryg. "It would need a Blood-Bond."

Antryg's gray eyes were sad and bitterly resigned. "So it
would," he said gently, and disengaged his arm from Lady
Rosamund's sudden, furious clutch. "It is the only way," he

said to that white, rigid face in the fidgeting torchlight. "The *tsaeati* has to be hunted down and destroyed if the Gate is to be closed, and we have very little time."

"Then do as Berengis did and return it to the Brown Star. You don't have to . . ."

He shook his head. "Since the Brown Star's probably up in the Library we'd have to get past the *tsaeati* to reach it, and anyway at the moment it's breached in a dozen places. If we leave now we can intercept the *tsaeati* on the bridge between the Harlot and the Junior Parlor—that's the way it went up and seems to be the way it's coming back."

Dread and panic had risen to a gray roaring in Joanna's ears; she wondered why she wasn't hysterical, and came to the conclusion that she must still be half expecting to wake up. *Come on, alarm clock, RING!* In the dark of the computer screen, she could see the amber schematic of the Citadel on its hill, the squat, heavy bulk of the Library that wore the faceted Conservatory like an unlikely purse at its side; the vertical, flatiron shape of the building called the Harlot (*Why?* she wondered obliquely); the narrow, covered bridge that led across to the upper floors of the Polygon at the lower part of the hill.

If Antryg didn't manage to kill the thing, those lines, those final parameters of life in the airless darkness of the Void, would dislimn as though they had never been.

As if another person were acting within her body, she walked over to where the Dead God lay and picked up the heavy weapon from the floor beside him.

Her knees were shaking so badly she could barely stand as she walked back to where the four wizards grouped.

"Look," she said quietly, "I know I can't put another round into the *tsaeati* without making it stronger—but if that thing's going to be coming at us across a covered bridge, if you two can't stop it with magic, what would be the chances of precipitating it into the Void by blowing the bridge?"

Antryg's eyebrows vanished upward into the tangle of his hair. "My dear . . ."

"I know what would happen to the air in there," Joanna said, looking up into that tired, bespectacled face. "And I know I'd . . . I'd be dragged out into the Void by the vacuum, along with you, and it. But would that destroy it?"

There was long silence, as Antryg debated, she knew, the possibility of lying to her, of keeping her from sacrificing herself as he was proposing to do. Then he sighed, defeated, and said, "Yes. Yes, it would."

"It's moving down the stairs of the Harlot now," Nandiharrow said quietly.

Antryg shivered, his face turned away from her momentarily, the absurd, sensitive mouth taut and colorless with strain.

"Antryg," she said gently, "if that thing kills you, I'm going to die anyway when the Citadel collapses."

"My dear Joanna," he whispered, "have I ever told you how difficult logic makes things for those of us who are trying to be gallant?"

A Howard Hawks heroine, she supposed, could have come back with some nervy wisecrack to that; she only slung the gun strap over one shoulder and threw her arms around his waist, pressing her face to the shabby purple velvet of his preposterous coat, holding him tight. For a moment his long arm was around her, ropy muscle and the smell of woodsmoke, candles, and the niter of the Vaults; then he said, "Rosamund, you and Magister Magus start weaving a spell of air—you'll have to coach him, Rosie—in case worse really does come to worst. If we do blow out the bridge and the *tsaeati* is thrown into the Void, the Citadel will be released and will snap back into its own world, but if the air goes, it may be a fortress of corpses when it gets there. You can probably hold what's in this room. Hathen, my incomparable beauty . . ."

The sergeant came over, her square face grave.

"I'm going to need a halberd—not the single-bladed kind, but the one with a point and a cross guard like a boar spear . . . Thank you, my dear. Aunt Min . . ." Disengaging himself from

Joanna's grasp, he reached down and took the ancient lady by the hand. Brunus and Brighthand rose from their places near the wall and went to open the north door; Otaro had begun to keen again, a high, thin wailing of pain. The Dead God's bazooka weighed like lead on Joanna's shoulder; looking into the utter blackness that lay beyond the stone archway, she was finding it difficult to breathe.

With a sudden movement Lady Rosamund strode to intercept Antryg and laid a white hand upon his threadbare purple sleeve.

Her voice was very low, but such was the silence that Joanna heard her clearly. "If she dies of this, Antryg Windrose, I swear to you that, whoever inherits the Master-Spells—whoever becomes Archmage after her, whether it be myself or Daurannon or whomever—you are a dead man. But not before you discover just why wizards are forbidden to use their powers for vengeance, and hatred, and pain. Do you understand?"

A muscle tugged at one corner of Antryg's mouth, a rueful half smile of memory. Even more softly than she, he replied, "I know why wizards are forbidden to use such powers, Rosamund. There was nothing which Suraklin did not teach me, in one fashion or another. Wish us luck."

But Lady Rosamund turned away, to kiss the old Archmage, and hold her close, before retreating to the darkest corner of the hall and folding herself into bitter silence.

There are those who say that wizards are subject to temptations and addictions beyond the understanding of ordinary men: the addiction to shape-changing, or to meditation under the influence of certain herbs and conditions of the stars; the obsession with knowledge, and the development of power. Yet this is not so. Temptation is temptation, obsession is obsession, and choice is choice.

—ISAR CHELLADIN
*Precepts of Wizardry*

# CHAPTER XXIII

TRACKING THE *TSAEATI* WAS NOT A DIFFICULT TASK. THROUGH the north door and across the little vestibule beyond, up the oak and iron of the staircase and across the Junior Parlor, up the three steps to the bridge and so across, it had left its trail of bloody water, slime, fragments of dimly shining flesh and the overwhelming stench of fishy rottenness. Save for the glow of Joanna's pocket flashlight, masking-taped to the barrel of her gun, the darkness here was absolute. Up its three steps, the bridge plunged away into an echoing, aphotic pit. The cold here was bitter; by the flashlight's yellowish beam, Joanna could see the smoke of her own breath. Dimly, somewhere up above, something was moving.

"Can you get a xchi-particle reading on the Conservatory, my dear?" Antryg asked, walking to the carved archway that led to the bridge. "Is there still activity up there?"

Hesitantly, Joanna examined the Dead God's sensor, which the alien physicist had set for her with masking-taped marks. "Yes," she said after a moment. "There's still a field reading." Beneath her feet the floorboards creaked alarmingly.

351

Where the *tsaeati* had passed, the wood had become desiccated, runneled with dry and crumbling streaks of rot, and only by clinging close to the railings had they been able to climb the twisted, clapped-out remains of the stair. Niter and slime dripped from the eaten-looking ruins of carved chairs, filthy water stood in puddles; Joanna shivered and checked her ammo loads.

"What a pity magic itself makes no reading on the sensors," Antryg murmured. "I wonder why that is? Are you aware, my dear, that insofar as I have been able to decode it, the information in the patterns of tortoiseshells is of a completely different nature in your world than it is in mine? I wish I'd had time to unearth Munden Myndrex's rubbings. I suppose we shall simply have to assume that the *tsaeati* visited the Conservatory and devoured the teles there."

"It did." Aunt Min's high, fragile voice was decisive as she hobbled painfully forward to stand at Antryg's side. "It has swallowed all its energy, all its being. It returns now, hunting, smelling out magic, mindless and greedy as the ghost that was the heart of it, malicious as a demon. It is time." She fumbled in her knitting basket for a piece of chalk.

Antryg had already given his shawl to Joanna in the dead and terrible cold of the upper floors of the Polygon; now he shed his tawdry coat, shivering a little at the bite of the air on his shirtsleeved arms and, taking off his spectacles, tucked them carefully into an inner pocket. In the dim yellow finger of the flashlight beam Joanna could see the old scars that straggled from wrist to elbow as he rolled up his sleeve, tiny punctures and slashes, and here and there long, cockled threads where the veins had been repeatedly slit. Aunt Min drew a circle around the two of them and pushed up her own black homespun sleeves like a housewife preparing to do dishes; Antryg drew the sword that was still thrust through his belt. The dim light winked on the blade, then glinted red-black on the sudden, gleaming lines of the blood. As the old lady marked Antryg's forehead and wrists, she seemed to straighten a little, and Joanna glimpsed again the wild dancer in her pale old eyes and recalled, for no reason, a pair of pink silk slippers carefully preserved on a dusty shelf.

Everyone who had seen her dance was dead now, she thought inconsequentially. And perhaps everyone they had talked to firsthand, as well.

Though Joanna was usually not conscious of magic, it seemed to fill the room like a strange scent, a fiery lightness to the air.

Antryg, who had knelt to receive the marks from the old woman's fingers, stood again, and his voice was very calm.

"Keep the spells of protection around me with whatever you've got. I'm going to have to wait until it's right in front of me before I do the Summoning . . . then it's going to come down on top of me and draw off the field of Nothingness, and if there's any of it left by the time it's absorbed everything I can conjure, God help us all."

"God always has helped us, my son," Aunt Min replied serenely. Taking his hands, she made a final, invisible sign upon the bared tips of his fingers and on the shabby wool and leather of the writing mitts he still wore. "In all God's forms, and in all of ours."

In the darkness beyond the bridge there was a sudden, dry, scritching crash, the sound of falling wood and plaster, then more loudly a huge, foul slither, as of some vast quantity of half-liquescent flesh sliding from great height. A moment later a cloud of stench rolled from the bridge: plaster dust, carrion, the cold wet stinks of mold and underground.

Soft and terrible, a thin, wailing ululation began, not human, not beast, keening and utterly mindless, and a thick, wet dragging.

Antryg's hands were shaking as they closed around his halberd. "Protect me," he whispered, his face ghastly in the dim flashlight beam, and Aunt Min gave a tiny, creaking chuckle.

"If I could protect you all this while from Rosie and Daur, can I not protect you also from a mud pie?"

With the tiniest flicker of answering smile, Antryg walked forward onto the bridge.

Min followed him to the bottommost step. There she sank to her knees, fumbling a piece of chalk from her knitting basket; around herself she drew a swift circle, perfect in its roundness with the perfection of years of practice. Joanna knelt at the far end of the Junior Parlor, Ninetentwo's weapon braced on her shoulder, and flipped forward the sight. It seemed to her that Antryg was now silhouetted against a kind of foul purplish glow emanating from the far end of the bridge; not light, or anything resembling light, it seemed to beat the air with a thousand vibrating wings and flicker hellishly in the crystal of his earrings and the beads still strung around his neck.

And in the darkness, something moved in response. Where the *tsaeati* had been dark, darkness within darkness within darkness, now it glowed. Its every claw, its every eye, its every drunkenly lashing fleshless head was outlined in an obscene radiance, sickly yellow and growing brighter, stronger, diffused by the fog still clinging about it and fed by the glow that throbbed within the swollen embolism of water and filth like a ghastly, sulfurous heart.

Antryg cried out once, a handful of words, a spell of summoning in a voice Joanna had heard him use only once before: the booming bass outcry of a lost and exiled god. His head thrown back and his arms flung wide, he stood for one instant in the narrow entry of the bridge, earrings and halberd blade flashing, and light seemed to glance from the rivets of his jeans and the brass hardware of his boots and from the ends of crooked fingers in their tattered, fingerless gloves. Then the air around him changed, and Joanna felt that, too: terrifying, leaden cold, a leaching stillness; darkness beyond concept of shadow, inertia untouched and untouchable by blood heat or synapse or chemical bond. Nothing. Even in the Void, pressing so close against the frail glass of the windows, there was a wildness and magic and chaos. He had become a Dead God, and around him the molecules of air seemed to collapse inward like the crumpling of a punctured star.

Lightning streamed from the shimmering corpseglow shape of the *tsaeati*, light that elongated itself, rising above him; then it fell upon him in a devouring wave.

Half-hidden in the glowing fog, Antryg gave back and braced himself, twisting with the halberd against the raking claws that slashed from the shadow around him. At the foot of the steps, Joanna heard Aunt Min utter a broken sound of pain. Even when it had had no strength, Joanna had felt the terrible drawing of the *tsaeati*'s greed; what it was like now, drinking at the energy of Antryg's magic, she could barely stand to imagine. Across the room she felt it, heat or cold, she could not tell; wind whipped the fog into a maelstrom of phosphor and darkness, tore and swirled at her hair, half blinding her, and her chest ached from the vacuum of its presence.

On the bridge Antryg slashed at it, playing it for time, keeping the physical elements of it—taloned feet, chisel-toothed serpent heads, and here and there, horribly, a human hand wielding a sword—from tearing at him physically and so breaking his concentration. But the sweat ran down his face in spite of the terrible cold, and there was desperation in the movement of his arms and back.

Around them the fog was swallowed in darkness, and the air began to shudder and burn. There was a noise to it, Joanna thought—or the noise was in her head—a kind of hissing that was almost a metallic scream, razoring her skull apart, rising in volume and intensity, like wind, like air escaping, like the fizzing roar of chemical bonding amplified a hundred thousand times. The wind strengthened and Joanna felt the throb of a pressure headache stab behind her eyes, smelled and tasted blood running down out of her nose; she could see, silhouetted against the chaos on the bridge, Aunt Min's black robes lift and pull with the dragging of that chemical wind and the tight knot of her thin white hair shred into a wild, fragile cloud.

The yellow glow within the *tsaeati*'s dripping bulk flared brighter, then slowly, steadily, began to dim.

There was blood on Antryg's face, from his nose and from a cut where a chance talon had scored him. He seemed to be holding something from him on the end of the halberd, the weapon itself shrouded in blowing clouds of utter dark. A half-rotted serpent head lunged along the shaft, and he twisted, dodging and, when it struck down to tear at the back of his knee, stomping with all his strength to shatter the brittle skull. Above the hissing roar of the energy, Aunt Min's voice rose like the thin, shrill wailing of a storm-whirled gull, crying words of power and protection again and again, her skinny arms upraised in the roaring sizzle of the air. A glow of light seemed to swirl around her, streaming from her hands; Joanna shifted the heavy grip of the weapon on her shoulder, goose-flesh sandpapering her arms and sweat rivering down her cheeks and sides. *Come on, Antryg, keep it off you. I really don't want to have to be dragged out into the dark.*

She saw Antryg stumble, as if, within the shadow, whatever he braced against had jerked back.

And the next instant he lunged at the darkness, dropping the halberd and catching with his bony, crooked hands at whatever he could seize—taloned claws, writhing coils—and dragging at it with all his weight.

*It's realized what's happening,* thought Joanna. *Demon—ghost—simulacrum of a magic soul . . . it knows it can't help absorbing the field around him, the field that will destroy it. It's trying to flee.*

The screaming roar of the darkness increased, shrieking, keening, a hellish cacophony of whatever half-living abominations were still imprisoned in the water and slime. The tightening pressure in Joanna's head made her wonder how long she could last without blacking out from pain or suffocation. Antryg was still on his feet, blood pouring now from bites and claw-rakes on his back, his head bowed and his body twisting to avoid what damage it could. A thing like a barracuda, flesh hanging in long flaps from spine and skull, eyeless sockets filled with orange mold, curved from the shadows engulfing him and buried its fangs in his shoulder, only barely missing his neck; it was Aunt Min who screamed.

The noise had increased to a deafening roar, a wind that filled the bridge and the ruined chamber before it; the burning, sulfurous glow around the struggling shapes had shrunk and intensified, then began rapidly to fade.

*Dammit, hang on! You're winning.*

Antryg screamed as the thing pulled him off his feet. Blue lightning seared from the darkness, stitching lines of black down his arms and sides. Something like glowing smoke seemed to fold around him, but the darkness no longer filled the entire bridge. Beyond him Joanna could see discarded bits of bone and flesh and nameless things strewing the floor, desiccated and lifeless as the ruined chairs and tables around her. Wind tore the breath from her lungs, seemed to scour the very skin from her bones. Beside the steps Aunt Min lay motionless in her circle, save where the winds tore at her robes and hair. Within the heart of the *tsaeati*, the yellow light glowed feverishly bright, and Antryg cried out again as lightning struck him in the chest; she saw him on his knees, struggling to rise, coils of glowing darkness wrapping him like a crushing hand. He shouted, "The bridge!" his voice hoarse with his fight for air. "Joanna, blow the bridge!"

She froze. She had, she knew, come for that purpose—and faced with it, she could not make her finger move on the trigger.

She could not kill Antryg. She could not bring herself to blast away those walls, to feel, even for the few seconds it would take for her to die, the icy drag of vacuum pulling her out . . .

"JOANNA . . . !"

Darkness swallowed him.

In the next second, something moved beyond the darkness. Joanna had only a confused glimpse of a squat black figure at the far end of the bridge, a slick, glassy gleam of some object flashing through the air . . .

And with a shattering report, like the hideously disproportionate explosion of a bursting light bulb, the object flung by the figure broke as it struck the floor in the midst of the collapsing field of darkness. A glare of brittle light blanched the smoky shadows to nothing; Joanna saw in a skeletal flash Antryg's body, the bodies of the semianimate abominations clinging to his flesh in a tearing pile and, around them, the very fibers of the floorboards, the mortar of the stones.

Then it was all changed.

For the first few seconds, Joanna had the weird sensation that none of it had ever been. Her mind groped, numb, as if a photo negative had been abruptly reversed, transposed to something completely different—a different medium, a transposition to another key . . . as if a light had been turned on.

She realized, getting slowly to her feet, her head ringing in the sudden stillness, that a light *had* been turned on.

Bright and soft as molten silver, moonlight poured through the bridge's little windows to stream in a luminous bar over the defiled floor.

She barely heard the footsteps running away, scrabbling up the remains of the stairs, heading back to the safety of the Library. Still holding the gun, she strode the length of the Junior Parlor to where water and blood trickled thickly down the steps, a little stream that touched the fingers of Aunt Min's tiny, outstretched hand.

Antryg lay across the threshold of the bridge, draped in the coils of what appeared to be a many-legged sea snake at least twenty feet long. His gloved hands still gripped the wrists of two half-dissolved Shriekers amid a reeking charnel house of portions of whatever and whomever the *tsaeati* had ingested. The halberd, haft charred and blade melted, lay a little distance from him. Everywhere around them glittered fragments of broken glass.

Joanna took one fast look at the sensor and saw that the

energy which had marked the *tsaeati*'s movements was gone. That didn't necessarily mean the *tsaeati* itself was gone, she thought, with a sickened throb of fear even as she shed the gun to kneel at Antryg's side.

His flesh was cold. His wounds seemed superficial, even the horseshoe-shaped ring of tooth-punctures on his shoulder, but there was no pulse in his scarred and bitten wrist or in the big veins of his throat. The charring of the *tsaeati*'s lightning etched a crooked black line from his temple to the pit of his throat; his shut eyes had a naked look, vulnerable, as in sleep.

Joanna whispered, despairingly, "Dammit," hesitantly located the target spot just below his sternum, and proceeded to administer CPR.

After somewhat less than a minute, Antryg flinched, gasped, and threw up; Joanna sat back, her hands shaking and cold, and for a moment all she could feel was astonishment that the whole process had worked the way she had been taught in class that it would. In time Antryg propped himself up on his elbows, his head hanging so that his dripping gray hair covered his face. In the moonlight his earrings sparkled, bright as the glass shards that scattered the floor.

"Here's your glasses." Her voice sounded blasphemously loud in the stillness. She fished them out of the pocket of his coat.

His hands were trembling so badly he could barely put them on.

Outside, a nightingale called, a warbling note like the hurtful mourning for a lover long gone. More distantly a wind chime spoke in the breeze.

With a crooked forefinger Antryg turned over one of the shards that strewed the filthy swamp of the bridge's floor and murmured, "Good Heavens. I didn't think they *could* be broken."

"Was that the teles?"

He nodded and slowly, achingly, sat up. For a moment he looked ready to vomit again; then he rubbed his hand wearily over his face. "Probably being drained of energy rendered it friable. Trying to break it was an absolute longshot . . . There must have been just enough of a link between the semianimate magic of the thing and its original housing to release the last cohesion of its energies when it burst." Leaning heavily on Joanna's arm, he got to his feet and limped to open the casement. The sweet, heady mixture of rain and wild roses poured in, the endless, silent benediction of the Sykerst night.

Then, moving stiffly and painfully as an old man, he went down the steps to where the Archmage's crumpled form lay.

"Aunt Min?"

Her hand moved a little at his touch upon her shoulders, groped to find his fingers. He lifted her gently. In the vanilla moonlight her face was gray, her lips turning blue under the smears of blood. She whispered, "Rosie . . ."

"Rosamund isn't here, Aunt."

The old woman smiled a little, and her eyes opened, sunken and huge, transparent in the wan light. "My dearest girl," she murmured. Her hand reached up, as if to wipe some of the blood-tracks from Antryg's face, but fell back again.

"It will be hard for her," she breathed. "It always is. Tell her I loved her best."

"I will."

"Tell her . . ." she sighed, "forgive." And her eyes slipped closed.

Antryg stayed kneeling for some minutes, cradling the wasted body to him and rocking her, his head bowed. Standing behind him, though she had barely known the old lady, Joanna felt her throat hurting with tears, with a sense of the passing of something great, some spectacular tale of fire and magic and delight that now she—and others—would only know secondhand, as Magister Magus had told parts of it to her. *A dancer or a vixen, or an angel made for sin . . .*

And now she was gone.

A shudder passed through Antryg's body, his shoulders bowing as if under the weight of some sudden, terrible awareness. "Oh, dear God," he whispered. When he raised his head, Joanna caught the shadow of shock and dread in his eyes. He murmured again, "Dear God . . ."

"What is it?"

He turned, startled, as if he had momentarily forgotten her presence; then he shook his head. "Just . . . never mind. It doesn't need to be dealt with now. I can't stay, my dear." He bent, laying Aunt Min's body down. "She said forgive," he added, looking down at the toothless crone face, like new ivory in the moonlight, with its intricate scrimshaw of years. "But Lady Rosamund will never forgive me . . . this."

He got stiffly to his feet and took Joanna's hands. She saw the glitter of blood through the gashes in his green calico shirt and how gray and weary his face looked in the bleached light. He shivered a little, with cold, or something more. "I fear I cannot even take the time to return you to your own world before I seek out the ending to this tale. Afterward . . ."

"I think Lady Rosamund will get me home," she said softly.

"If she doesn't, Ninetentwo said he had a xchi-flux generator in the Vaults that would open a way through. My dear . . ." He hesitated, and she caught his wrists, suddenly realizing by the pain in his voice that he was bidding her good-bye.

"Will you come back to L.A.?"

He looked down at her, his gray eyes weary and resigned behind the Coke-bottle glasses. "After all that I've led you through," he said softly, "after nearly getting you killed," his long arm took in the stinking ruin of the bridge, "or worse than killed, I don't really think that's such a good idea."

In the dark of the Brown Star, Joanna remembered she hadn't, either. Her hands tightened grimly over his. "Antryg, I put my life on the line every time some stockbroker in Westwood offers me five grand to get on the 405 freeway and come down and reason with his mainframe, and I don't think twice about it."

He smiled. "Five grand pays your rent."

"You . . ." She stopped, unable to say what she had been thinking, desperate with the knowledge that somehow, she had to call him back. To convince him . . . to say the right thing. She couldn't lose him—couldn't let herself lose the years ahead. For a moment her mind was a blank of panic and pain.

But the only thing she could think of to say was "You make me laugh."

He looked aside, saying nothing.

Very softly, she whispered, "Don't go."

He sighed, and there was a wryness, almost a bitterness, in the flex of the corner of that absurd mouth. "I really should be stronger about this."

For the second time relief flooded her, an ache of release as deep as the pain of her fear.

"Ah, hell," she said unsteadily. "Whether or not you come back to L.A., you know that if the Council comes looking for you, they're going to start with me anyway. This way, instead of being apart and miserable, at least we can both get laid while we're waiting for the next disaster."

The sadness in his eyes vanished into a wicked twinkle, like a star in the gray depths. "My dear Joanna," he said, "you do have a point. If I can . . ." He turned and picked up his coat from the floor, the hem discolored with water and blood. "When I'm across, blow out the bridge. They won't believe you if you tell them I was killed in the battle. Just tell the Council that I've deserted you and fled. God help me, it will be the truth."

He leaned down and kissed her, while she put her arms around his shoulders carefully, mindful of the gashes underneath; she could feel already where the blood had soaked into the velvet of the coat. Then he turned and walked away through the Niagara of spring moonlight, and the sparkle of his earrings winked at her as he vanished into the darkness beyond.

Wearily, her heart hurting within her, Joanna took a few steps backward and picked up the Dead God's gun. As Nine-tentwo had promised, it didn't kick much. The nightingale outside broke off its songs, shocked by the roaring explosion of flame and shattering wood, and there was a crashing *whoosh* as the shards of joist and wall and tiled roof cascaded down into the thickets of laurel and honeysweet below.

Night air breathed over Joanna's sweat-streaked face. For a time she stood, gun tucked loosely beneath her arm, inhaling the sweetness and realizing how long it had been since she'd smelled any air at all, let alone this fragile combination of wet ivy and rain and open leagues of freedom.

At last she bent down and drew Aunt Min's shabby, randomly knitted shawl over the little body curled at her feet. Turning, she walked back toward the lower reaches of the Citadel, to find the Council again.

It is a forbidden thing for those born with the powers of wizardry to marry. First, because the children of the mageborn are often mageborn themselves and, in the eyes of the Church and the law, are damned and without souls. Second, because however good his intent, natural feeling would prompt a wizard to use his powers to further the interests of his family at the expense of others.

Third, because wizards in their greed for knowledge frequently desert their families when they travel to seek it. Likewise, it is known that no person—husband, wife, or child—is as precious to a wizard as the search for knowledge and power; thus union with them leads only to grief for all.

—FIRTEK BRENNAN
*Dialogues*

# CHAPTER XXIV

"KITTY?"

Nothing moved in the shadows of the ruined chamber as Antryg slipped quietly through the crumbling wood of the door.

It was breathtakingly obvious that the *tsaeati* had turned aside from its quest for an illusory grailful of backup batteries at the top of the Library and had come here instead. Slime and niter dripped down the stair from the Library's main floor, water puddled the pitted sandstone flags. Here, in what had been Seldes Katne's private study, chairs and tables had been overturned and heaved aside by the slow, lumbering crawl of the thing toward its goal: the wide French doors leading into the disused Conservatory beyond.

The glass had been burst from the twisted frames and glittered crystalline in the ice-cream moonlight beyond. All around the floor, sodden heaps of notes soaked in the general mess, like soiled leaves raked on the threshold of winter, among the broken-backed corpses of books. Notes, he thought, on the natures and histories of the teles in the Citadel . . . not that she'd ever intended to convey the truth to him, even if she'd guessed why he needed to know.

He shook his head. He'd been a fool to trust her.

But it hadn't been until after his walk to the Green King's Chapel that he'd realized the culprit didn't necessarily have to be a member of the Council; even when he'd begun to question the reality of the Moving Gate, he had feared for Kitty's sanity, not questioned the truth of what she said she'd seen.

And then, he reflected, he'd always trusted too easily.

Oddly, he felt no anger. There was only an overwhelming sadness, for he knew perfectly well why she had done what she had done.

Nevertheless, he edged his way cautiously across the room. She was still in possession of the Brown Star—a fist-sized hunk of molasses-colored crystal that Suraklin had kept in an iron box in his study. With the Citadel back to normal, all the Star's Gates would be closed again, and at the moment, he knew he had not the smallest power left in him to resist its imprisoning spells.

Moonlight falling through the dirty panes of the Conservatory showed him a moist line of foot-tracks through the mud and broken glass. He followed to the doors, his shoulders smarting under the sticky abrasion of his clothing. The long-term effects of repeated doses of jelgeth made his bones ache, as if the marrow had been reamed out with a pipe cleaner; if he fell, he thought, leaning for a moment against the jamb of the broken French doors, he felt he would shatter like glass.

Through the burst panes, the air of the old Conservatory breathed upon his face, damp, icy, but still weighted with all the thick green smells of the plants that had been suffered to grow there unheeded in the old forcing pots. Banks of grape vines rioted heavily over what had been an old table; around the tarnished brazen pots of stunted and unpruned lemon and orange trees, leaves had risen in such drifts as to support tiny ecosystems of their own—mushrooms, molds, trailing coleus and pothos, or perhaps those were rooted in smaller pots long since buried in the general mulch. A number of those twisted trees had been heaved over and lay in ruined clouds of leaves, root and branch sticky with foulness and burning slowly from some horrible chemical combustion inside; orange moss thickly coated the trailing vines and shrubs, dissolving all into a foul-smelling black muck.

Somewhere water gurgled, the old pipes still pumping their moss-cysted fountains.

Wind moved his hair, cold and sharp, a silver knife in the rank stenches of greenery, carrion, niter. Someone had opened one of the long windows at the Conservatory's far northern end.

Straightening his aching shoulders, Antryg picked his way through the jungle.

Seldes Katne stood where a little bay had been built out, a curving seat in a shell of intricate glass. Before her, space had been cleared on the floor, further thickening the jungle all around it; in the latticed moonlight he could see the crossing lines of a huge Circle of Power, smeared and fouled now by the slobber of the *tsaeati*. There were three windows in the bay, looking out over the tor's sheer northeastern face, and the little librarian was silhouetted in the central one, her short arms spread out, crucified across the narrow frame in the lucid silver of the moon.

The light showed her face, rinsed of color, and he was shocked at how fallen it seemed. The dark eyes were smudgy with fatigue, as if someone had ground a thumb into the sockets. Her iron black hair, torn from its braid by the colliding energies on the bridge, hung in a raveled swatch over her plump shoulders. He hadn't realized how long it was, or how thick.

Behind her, rags of cloud strewed the sky, the wind a reminiscence of the night's rain, though mostly the storm was heaped up around the horizon like an untidy job of sweeping, iced silvery white. It was a sheer drop from the window to the rocks at the foot of the tor: five hundred feet.

The wind moved the ends of her hair.

She sighed but only said, "She's dead, isn't she? The Archmage . . ."

"Yes," he said.

There was silence.

Then, "I take it that when Daurannon first began to experiment with opening the Void—what was it, nearly two months before the abominations began?—the field that appeared up here was one which transformed those of little magic into . . ."

"Into what we all of us want to be." Seldes Katne finished the sentence, brought her arms down, and folded her plump hands before her girdle knot. The eyes that met his were unapologetic, ravaged. "Yes."

"And you used a teles to generate the power to hold it open?"

She nodded. "I had two up here, little ones—Freath and Nicarynko. Later I took the strongest, the oldest I could learn of, from the storerooms: Vyrayana. I was going to Angelshand to look for more information about the Void, trying to find some way of making the field permanent or of carrying its effects into . . . into the real world. The world outside this room. I had to know its strength would hold the circles intact until I returned."

"I see," Antryg said softly.

"And then when I read in Salteris' notes about the Brown Star—when I heard that he had had it, that it was there, in Angelshand . . . I conceived the idea of bringing you here, of forcing your help. It wasn't difficult, even for me, to locate the man who'd stolen it from Salteris' house, and take it back. I didn't know then how you . . . how you felt. Or that the Lady would conceive the same idea. Or that the Council would take your powers away. Only that you were a dog wizard at heart—not one of them."

"You spoke for me," Antryg said. "When they were getting ready to lay me under the geas, you protested . . . I was grateful."

Seldes Katne looked away. "I meant it," she whispered.

"Having so little power of my own . . ." She raised her head, her eyes meeting his again. "I do like you, Antryg. I truly do. It's just that . . ."

Antryg looked around him, at the smeared and faded lines of the circles on the floor. "I don't suppose, once you got back from Angelshand, that you had any difficulty opening a Gate through the Void from this spot."

"Oh, no," she said. "No, I had no difficulty doing . . . anything. Anything at all." There was a lingering glow of ecstasy on her face, a reflected joy. It faded, and her thin mouth pinched tight. "Only, when I came back from Angelshand, I found that the teles had . . . had changed. It held more power than I had thought. Sometimes I couldn't even see it. When Daurannon told me about the abominations, I—I wanted to bring you here, to make the magic permanent, quickly, before more evil happened. But they were ahead of me. So when Phormion spoke of a Moving Gate, all I could do was say I'd seen it, too, and keep you from looking anywhere but in the Vaults. And then, when they put the geas on you, I . . . I knew I had to get rid of you, too. Because you did know about the Void, and eventually you'd find out and tell them."

She spoke simply, her dark eyes in shadow, her voice filled with the logic of obsession, of desperation—with the knowledge that, in some way, he would understand. "And after what they did to you, I knew that if they found out about what *I* had done . . ." Her voice cracked a little, despair strengthening it. "Antryg, if they took even what powers I had from me, it would have been more than I could bear! I couldn't let them know! I couldn't let anyone know."

Her small hands clenched again on the window's half-rotted frame. "After Otaro saw the Moving Gate—after you said the situation in the Vaults was growing worse—I did try to replace Vyrayana with the two little teles I'd had there before. But it—it wouldn't let me near it. And you kept asking about the teles. Sooner or later you would have found out . . ."

"Just tell me this," Antryg said quietly. "If you had succeeded in killing me—either knifing me in my room that first night in the Pepper-Grinder, or tricking Gru Gwidion into doing it at the Green King's Chapel, where I would be out of any possibility of protection from Aunt Min—what would you have done with Joanna? Would you have released her?"

"Yes," Seldes Katne said, startled at the question. "Yes, of course. Not immediately, because—well, because the Void was becoming so unstable I was afraid to try to cross it again. I followed Salteris' notes the first time, but I was never—never easy with my power, used in that way. But I would have eventually, when I'd gotten myself more . . . more straightened out."

"Except that it was impossible to straighten out," Antryg murmured. "It never would have straightened out—and the power of the Void kept feeding into the teles, distorting and increasing *its* power . . ."

"I studied," Seldes Katne said desperately. "I read all the notes, studied everything anyone had written—about the Void and how to cross it; about the teles, about magic . . ." She slumped down to sit upon the window seat, her head bowed, the rain-touched night wind stirring at the ends of her hair. "What *is* magic, Antryg? Why are some born with it in such abundance, and others born with only enough to realize what it is they lack, and will always lack? All my life I wanted magic, the same way all my life I wanted to be beautiful."

Antryg leaned a shoulder against one of the twisting pilasters that supported the glass-paned roof. "And had you been beautiful, it would have brought you troubles of its own, you know. Magic is only magic: it isn't sanity, or goodness, or the ability to be a friend or live a decent life. Because I was born with talent in magic, I was shunned by my family, and . . . Well, I can't say I was precisely kidnapped by Suraklin, but he would never have used me as he had, had I been . . . " He hesitated, and again she finished for him.

"As untalented as I?"

"I was going to say, had I been of less potential use. For when it came down to it, I was really only a thing to him. I fought for years to go on believing that there was something more to it than that. That he would have cared had I not been what I was, but only *who* I was. But there wasn't. I suppose dazzlingly beautiful girls get a little of that."

"Maybe," Seldes Katne said softly. "But that knowledge doesn't help us dumpy little squabs, with our big noses and our coarse hair and our crooked teeth. I would have willingly been a . . . a thing to be used, a vessel to be emptied, to Suraklin or to anyone else, for the sake of having all I knew that others like me could have. And when it came . . ."

She shook her head, and again the wonderment of it, the memory of that brief and shuddering joy, illuminated the puffy, square-jawed face. "Can you understand that I couldn't give it up?"

*We give up everything for it,* Suraklin had said. *Our lovers, our parents, our homes . . . the children we might otherwise bear, the people we might otherwise be. And we consider ourselves fortunate to be allowed by God to make the trade.*

"I thought," she whispered, "I thought if I studied long enough, if I searched hard enough, I might still be able to find a way to transfer some of the powers I had within the field to . . . to be effective outside of it. But all the while you kept getting nearer to the truth . . ."

"You never could have, you know," Antryg said gently. "That field was an enclave of another universe, another place and time—a might-have-been lying parallel to what is for you and me. It is simply not possible."

She sighed. "I know," she murmured. "Maybe in my heart I knew it then. But Antryg, within the field my powers were so great. I could cast spells at a distance of miles, shape-change, scry the wind and summon the darkness. I was powerful enough to . . . to be one of those who might inherit the powers of the Archmage. I've been librarian here for years, Antryg. I've seen students who were Juniors to me when I was a student, like Nandiharrow, and then students I've *taught*, like Issay, sit on the High Council . . . children like Zake Brighthand and Kyra the Red, scattering power like sunlight from their hands. And I just stayed here, reading about power I could only barely touch, sorting books, making lists, organizing knowledge that to me could be little more than academic, while Daurannon and Rosamund were spoken of as candidates to become Archmage. And my hair got gray. And I got fat and got old, and I knew it would never be mine. It was mine," she said softly. "Just for a little while."

Softly, he reminded her, "Only within the field."

"Oh, yes." She raised her head, to look at him with those sad dark eyes. "Yes. But how different is that from the others, who only permit themselves to work magic within the bounds of the Citadel? Just knowing it was mine was enough. Just knowing that for once I was . . . was one of you."

She turned back to the window, her knees pressing the sill as she looked out over the long drop to the ragged pelt of black spruce that cloaked the stones below. Beyond that window, the sky seemed to stretch forever, the heart-shivering sky of the far north on the threshold of summer, even near midnight pulsing with liquid light. "I couldn't let them take that away," she said softly. "And they would have, if they'd found out. If you'd . . . you'd learned. I just . . . couldn't let it happen."

Moving her head, she looked back at him over her shoulder. "Do they know?"

"Joanna will have told them."

"I'm—I'm sorry about Joanna," she said. "About you, too . . . She wouldn't have come to any harm in the Brown Star."

*No*, he thought. *Nor would she have come to good . . . or to anything at all. Only a life going on and on, without ending, without variation, until, like all those others, she went mad . . .*

"It's on my desk, by the way, in the other room . . . I suppose," she added, "they'll be coming for me." She caught his eye. "For us both."

Antryg sighed. "Yes," he murmured. He was sorely tempted to simply pocket the Brown Star and take it with him when he left—if Lady Rosamund laid hands on it, the odds were good he himself might end up trapped in its dark, endless mazes. But it was Rosamund and the Council who would have to release, and care for, the prisoners Suraklin had left trapped within. The spells of release were there, in Salteris' notes. He wondered if the Council would heed his written note, begging that the Star not be used again, at least not on the innocent.

But no, he thought. Simply trapping him would now not be enough for them.

He raised his head, his magpie beads glittering in the moonlight. "For us both indeed," he said softly. He came forward to Seldes Katne's side and rested his hand on her shoulder, and she looked up, startled, into his face.

When Joanna reached the refectory again, it was to find all the long windows of its northwestern side thrown open to the cool stirrings of the night air. Silvorglim and his entire contingent of hasu and sasenna slept stertorously on the piled blankets in their corner, under the novice Kyra's calm, sarcastic eye; Joanna had the feeling they'd be sleeping quite some time. Near them, Magister Magus, clothed in a Wheatlands farmer's bright-colored shirt and baggy breeches that had quite clearly come from the Citadel's slop chest, engaged in a passionate, whispered argument with Nandiharrow and Pothatch. Tom, arms folded and his usual expression of mournful interest on his face, stood by with a couple of small bedrolls and a sack of food.

". . . can't ride all the way to Angelshand looking like this!"

"Well," the cook said, slightly miffed, "they're the only

things your size, Miss Joanna having taken Tom's spare shirt and all. We could fit you out in a mage's robe.''

"Never!" Magus turned pale. "Good grief, it's bad enough that *they'll*," he jerked a thumb at the sleeping Witchfinders "be after me for being in league with you lot. D'you think I want to be lynched?"

Nandiharrow smiled, and there was an ironic but genuine warmth in his eyes. "What, with Tom there to protect you? I suppose you could ride off in your dressing gown if you chose."

"Very funny. I don't suppose," his voice dropped still further and he leaned closer to the tall, gray-haired man, "I don't suppose you could . . . well . . . I know there's spells of forgetfulness. You couldn't arrange it so that none of them would remember they'd seen me here, could you?"

Nandiharrow shook his head. "It's trespassing the borders of our vows already, to keep them sleeping. You're a wizard, Magus . . ."

"I am *not*!" the little man insisted, rising to his full five-foot-six. "I am a spiritual counselor, and the only reason I'm not working such a spell upon them myself is because your monopoly on the teaching of magic made it impossible for the master who taught me to learn such a spell."

"Well, if we keep on arguing," Tom reasoned, "it'll be dawn, and that lot'll wake up, and the whole question about what you're wearin' for the trip'll get a little academic."

Joanna stepped past them, looking quickly around the long room. Torches still provided most of the illumination, though here and there, feeble threads and feathers of witchlight had begun to burn in the air. Ninetentwo, she noticed, was up and about, a huge, silently moving troll tinkering among the innards of the now-dark oscillators, the bandages on his shoulders and back pale streaks against the smooth-stretched olive sheen of his skin. Closer to Joanna, a little knot of mages were grouped around an old woman, thin and straight like some elderly warrior-priestess, who seemed to be subsiding into an uneasy, nightmare-ridden doze. Bentick was holding her head on his lap, and under the disheveled white mane Joanna could see horrible claw-rakes on the woman's face and dried blood on the fingernails of her twitching hands. The Steward's face was tracked with tears.

In a corner, near the sleeping Gilda, the boy Brighthand sat with his head bowed almost to his knees. He looked up when Joanna touched his shoulder, and in his dark eyes she saw the dry, brittle deadness of one who has shut out every feeling, every touch of life, rather than endure the pain inside. In a corner Otaro the Singer moved and whispered fitfully in his sleep; Brighthand did not even turn his face to look.

"It's the same as your master Otaro, isn't it?" she whispered. The boy nodded, his eyes avoiding hers.

"It must have been somethin' about the Gate they saw." There was an academic detachment to his voice, as if he spoke of a stranger. "I should have told someone earlier," he said softly, his dark eyes sick with guilt. "I should have disobeyed him and got someone to look at him. Then tonight, when the Gates all closed, I hoped . . . when the Citadel went back the way it was . . ."

Personally, looking about her at the long, unnaturally quiet room, Joanna doubted that the Citadel would ever go back to being as it had been.

"It might have done that if magic were the cause of the madness," she said, laying a hand on one bony shoulder. His gray robe was still patched with stiffening swatches of blood, brown and smelly. "But it sounds like the madness was caused by a gas of some kind, some sweet-smelling toxin that came through a wormhole down in the Vaults and caused the hallucination of the Gates moving, and the voices, and all those other things."

"Maybe." For a moment she thought that would be all and almost turned away, embarrassed to have spoken, shaken by the absolute deadness of his eyes. But something told her this boy needed not to be alone, and after a time he raised his head, and there was a faintest flex in the muscles of his face, like a stone statue reluctantly coming to life.

"You mean like the air of another world, like old Nineten-two breathes?" He nodded toward the angular, insectile shadow in the darkness, more monsterlike than ever in his ring of electronic trilithons. Even in his grief, she thought, Brighthand was a wizard. It was his ingrained nature, as it was Antryg's, to listen to anything and to consider what it meant.

She nodded. "Because of the pain involved and the progressive nature of the paranoia and hallucinations, my guess is that the gas caused lesions of some kind—hemorrhaging from one area of the brain into another. That would bring on pressure, and with it, pain and madness and further hallucinations. I don't know whether, once you located the lesions . . ."

His eyes widened—the darkest eyes, she thought, that she had ever seen, suddenly ablaze with a hope that was painful to see. She had been half-afraid of him, knowing him for a wizard, and with the echo of her old reflexive fear of men. Now she saw only how young he was and how scared.

"How?" he demanded, lurching to his feet, towering over her, but the hands that seized her by the arms were trembling. "Heat? Blood-heat?"

"More likely some kind of disruption of the brain's electrical field. The brain has an aura . . ."

"We know that. Issay!"

The little doctor rose from Phormion's side, flitted over with gray eyes inquiring; Brighthand caught the skeletal arm in a grip suddenly alive with the desperation of hoping again, and the two of them plunged into a soft-voiced maelstrom of medical theurgy. Joanna stepped back, the weight of the gun she still carried suddenly leaden on her shoulder. All she wanted to do, like Silvorglim and his troops, was stagger to the nearest blanket and sleep.

Someone came up beside her. She turned and saw Daurannon, his choirboy face lined with fatigue and chalky with pain, the streaks of gray in his hair glinting a little in the flickering of the witchlight around Bentick, Phormion, and the mages of healing. For all the spells of healing that had been worked upon him, he still looked like ten miles of very bad road.

For a moment she stood, looking up into that face—Antryg's friend, she remembered, so many years ago.

"Are you all right, love?"

She nodded, and the gun slipped from her shoulder to the floor. "He left me," she said slowly. "He said . . ." She tried to draw breath, but the tiredness came down on her, grief for Aunt Min, exhaustion at what she had been through, the sudden conviction that she would never see Antryg again. Idiotically, she burst into tears.

"Here . . ." Joanna felt herself drawn into the comfort of a strong arm, surrounded by the familiar smells of candlewax, woodsmoke, medicinal herbs. "Here, love, we can't have you breaking down now it's all over with."

Instinctively, she knew that Daurannon was one of those men who always had words of easy comfort for a crying woman. Still, it was good to lean her forehead on his shoulder and cry, to be led to a bench and held. As Ruth always said, *God gave men those nice pectoral muscles for a reason.*

"And I suppose," said a chill, sweet, silver voice above them, "that a few tears are sufficient to wipe away Minhyrdin's death? Or to make you forget how close the entire Citadel came to destruction because of that . . . that *dog wizard* and his meddling?"

Joanna raised her head, shook back the tear-matted tangles of her hair from her cheeks. Lady Rosamund's face looked ravaged, its steely beauty shredded away by the night she had endured. Her cold green eyes were ringed with the purple of sleeplessness and the red of tears, the first tears Joanna had ever imagined that the Lady could shed. Her black hair, tangled like a harridan's—or like an Amazon's after battle—was for the first time visibly threaded with gray. In a strange way the terrible ruin of that icy beauty made her far more human, and for the first time Joanna pitied her.

The Lady's voice was bitterly sarcastic as she went on. "Now that I know a few tears are all that can get around you, Daur," she used the pronoun of social inferiority, as she would have addressed a dog or a servant, "I'll have to try them the next time I want to put something across you in Council."

"I'll give you a nice spell to bring them on, then," Daurannon retorted, his arm tightening around Joanna's shoulders. "You'll need one."

Joanna shook her head, scrubbed at her eyes with the back of her wrist. "I'm sorry," she said. "It's just that . . ."

Coldly, her ladyship turned away.

"Don't mind her." Daurannon produced a clean handkerchief out of nowhere—*I suppose pulling handkerchiefs out of nowhere is the first thing they learn in wizard school,* thought Joanna illogically, and had to suppress the urge to giggle. "She's . . ."

"No." Joanna got quickly to her feet and followed the Lady down the length of the darkened room, to where she stood, her back to them all, staring out the window.

The moon was setting above the frivolous marble roofs of the Birdcage and the Pavilion; it had the matte pearliness that came from the lightening of the whole expanse of sky around it as dawn breathed grayness into the dark. Below the windows Joanna could see a wide, flagstoned courtyard, from which two or three small stairways arose, and one flight of imposing sandstone steps; last night's rain puddles gleamed with the gray of pussy willows under the growing reflection of the sky. A stately cloister of yellow sandstone curved along the knee of the hill, and under its eaves, pigeons and doves began to flutter from their nests.

From under the gateway opposite, a small band of warriors appeared, walking cautiously and gazing about them—Implek and his missing sasenna. A cat picked its way along a wall. In the tower across the court, a clock struck five.

"Lady . . ."

Rosamund's head was erect, her profile unflawed as she stared out over the Citadel that was her home, her domain, the place of her being and her soul. The corner of her strong mouth flinched a little, but her eyes were dry as she turned.

"When Minhyrdin died," Joanna said quietly, "she told us—told Antryg and me—to tell you that she loved you best."

Rosamund's mouth tightened with some bitter retort, the delicate nostrils flaring. But she did not speak, and in the moment of quiet, the hatred relaxed from her and her hands began to tremble where they rested on the sill; tears filled the pale green eyes and ran down over the perfect cheekbones when she closed them against the cut of remembrance.

Her lips moved, but it was a moment before she was able to command her voice to utter a sound. "Thank you."

"She said that she knew it would be hard for you," Joanna went on, gaining a little courage. "She said that it always is. But she said she loved you best . . . and she said, Forgive."

The Lady sighed, releasing something, it seemed, from the deepest heart of her body. There was no rage in her voice, no hatred, only a kind of tiredness, and regret. "No," she said softly. "No. I will never forgive."

Joanna heard Daurannon's step behind her; turning, she saw the look that passed between the two wizards: question, answer, debate and decision, all in the traded glance of green eyes and hazel. It crossed her mind that these two were of an age, young for Council wizards, no more than forty. Had the enmity between them, she wondered suddenly, grown from the fact that once they had both been twenty, and the most beautiful girl in the Citadel would have nothing to do with the facile charm of a common wool-stapler's son?

"Come," Daurannon said quietly. "You're tired—you need to rest. You've been brave as a half-sized tiger. Old Pothatch'll get up a room for you."

"No." Joanna shook her head wearily and shivered a little in her borrowed shirt and breeches, though the air that whispered through the windows was barely cooler than the spring afternoons in California. "No, all I want to do is go home."

She felt Daurannon and the Lady speak again with their eyes and felt their silence.

Daurannon drew his breath and let it out; then he said, "It's something we have to talk about. All this came about through tampering with the Void, you see, and I for one am not willing to do that again."

*And you need a hostage*, thought Joanna, *to trap Antryg again*. Her voice was low and quite reasonable. "But what about Ninetentwo? He can't stay in this world, and his air supply must be just about exhausted."

"Well, of course, we'll do for Ninetentwo what we can."

But his eyes avoided hers.

She looked down at the floor and made her shoulders slump a little, and ran a small, square hand over her face. "Look," she whispered, "can we talk about this tomorrow? I'm just . . ." She stepped back away from his comforting touch. "I just need to rest, all right?"

"Of course," Daurannon said understandingly. "You rest now, love, we're going to be working for days, sorting out the mess and trying to get the water out of the Vaults, but there's no reason for you to deal with that. Pothatch'll find you a place to sleep."

But when she left Lady Rosamund and Daurannon, absorbed in intent and quiet-voiced converse by the windows, she stumbled, not to where Pothatch and Tom were still arguing with Magister Magus, but to the dark and silent monoliths of the Dead God's ring.

"They're not going to let us go back," she breathed, kneeling beside him where he squatted, adjusting the wiring in the main generator. "They say it's dangerous to open the Void again, and they probably have a point. Daurannon claims they can do something about your air."

"I wouldn't let that pack of hocus-mongers guess my weight," came the deep, buzzing voice from within the Dead

God's skull. "They are indeed right. Though the time-space continuum has, as far as I can ascertain on what equipment I have here, returned to normal, were I in their position I would hesitate to tamper further with it." He picked up his computer, which he had folded back into its black box, and straightened up to his seven-foot-plus height, stiffly, like a chilled insect, a slow unraveling of sinew and bone and breathing tubes. His iridescent ocher eyes gleamed eerily in the shadows of the coming dawn.

"However, I am *not* in their position—and I have no intention of remaining in this world and having my body suffocate and my mind deteriorate into a nameless whirlwind of psychokinetic madness, as it did before." The segmented tail moved in a restless sidewinder crawl, and he nodded toward the shattered ruin of the eastern door, crusted with the drying strings of the *tsaeati*'s slime and completely unguarded now that Hathen and her sasenna had divided themselves to patrol the resurrected Citadel and to keep guard over Silvorglim and his sleeping beauties.

"It shouldn't take us long to backtrail the *tsaeati*'s wake to find the way into the Vaults; I was careful to mark the walls there so that I could locate the experimental xchi-flux generator. It should—I hope—open a Gate into my own world and, at the place to which I originally returned Antryg four months ago, to yours."

*Great,* thought Joanna. *I get to show up at five in the morning in the parking lot of the San Serano Missile Plant.* She comforted herself with the reflection that at five in the morning, Ruth would still be up, painting.

They could stop for breakfast at Feeding Frenzy in Reseda.

The thought was so bizarre as to be almost completely disorienting.

The Dead God reached down to pick up his rifle and sling it over his shoulder, and to collect a last battery. "I've set a timer to fuse the circuitry of all this," he went on, the glowing nodule on his forehead twitching. "I'll set one likewise on the slave relay which opens the Gate. Thirty thousand eldacta worth of the Corporation's equipment,'' he added bitterly, tucking computer, battery, and gun under his various arms. ''But like Daurannon, I feel it will be a good long while ere I have sufficient nerve to tamper again with the Void. Are you ready?''

Joanna looked around. Dawn light was slowly growing in the long room, making the yellow flicker of the few torches, the dim blue glow of the witchlight, seem dirty and sleazy. In her chest was the queer anxiety attendant upon leaving a party far too early, walking away from people she really wanted to get to know better: Brighthand and Issay, bent anxiously over the thin, skeletal Phormion, their fingers tracing arcane patterns over her skull while Bentick looked on with growing hope and the pain of the only love of his life naked in his narrow face; Nandiharrow and the fat, good-natured Brunus rewrapping Whitwell Simm's arm; Kyra the Red tripping over the stacked weapons of the sleeping Witchfinder's troops and exchanging a good-natured grin with the friend—Mick or Cylin, Joanna didn't remember which was which—who steadied her.

By the window, Daurannon and Lady Rosamund were still too intent on their frigidly polite confab to even look up.

Antryg's world, she thought. The people he'd grown up with, the life, the place, that he knew. They'd bring Aunt Min's body back here soon and lay her in state in some assembly hall— that delicate, withered scrap that had once been beauty and power and life.

''Just a minute,'' she murmured and walked to the door where Pothatch, Tom, and Magister Magus still stood.

Putting her arm around the little dog wizard's shoulder, she tiptoed to kiss his cheek. Though they'd spent God knew how long together in the Brown Star, it was only now that she felt the beard stubble beginning to emerge on that stretch of jaw between Van Dyke and ear.

She whispered, ''Good-bye.''

Magus looked surprised; Pothatch caught her glance with one bright little porcine eye and winked; Tom gave her a discreet thumbs-up.

If she was lucky, she thought, she would never see any of these people again.

But she had a feeling she wasn't going to be that fortunate.

She walked quietly back to join the Dead God in the shadows of the ruined east door. "All right," she said softly, shivering inside at the thought of the terror of the jump. "Let's blow this Popsicle stand. I want to go home."

God does have a sense of humor—but I've encountered more sophisticated ones in some taverns I've visited.

—MINHYRDIN THE FAIR

# CHAPTER XXV

FRIDAY NIGHTS WERE ALWAYS BUSY AT ENYART'S. THE LIGHTS were low and artistically placed to shed slats of white across the bubble-gum pastels of the walls, an illumination kind to strain-puffed features and fatigue-reddened eyelids. The floor was slick fake marble, the chairs—in the small area along the wall for those who really wanted the more popular combinations of carbohydrates to soak up the booze—slick black Italianate paper clips; the clientele, for the most part, slick refugees from the law offices, real-estate agencies, and production companies along Ventura Boulevard. There wasn't a soft surface in the place, and conversation ping-ponged off the angular walls. In the background, jacked to carry over the general noise level, a ragged-edged Liverpudlian voice wailed Ben E. King's "Stand By Me" over the modern, upscale equivalent of a jukebox.

Standing uncertainly in the doorway Joanna craned her neck to see over the heads of the crowd. After a moment she spotted the flash of round-lensed glasses up behind the bar, the tangle of graying curls half a head over the tallest of his customers, and the silhouette of a long, beaky nose.

Beside her, Ruth said, "You want me to get a table?"

"Not unless you're really crazy about waiting an hour and a half for *coq au merde*."

Her voice shook a little. Though she'd found his absurd purple coat and bloodied calico shirt on the bed when she'd come home from Galaxsongs this afternoon, and a note in his careful and nearly unreadable block printing, not until this moment, actually seeing him, did the anxiety truly leave her, the anxiety that had followed her through the dark terror of the Void and all through the twenty-four hours which had followed: the fear that, after all, he would change his mind. That she never would see him again. That all the years to come would be lost.

"I dunno," Ruth said thoughtfully. "That blond waiter's gorgeous."

"*All* waiters in Los Angeles are gorgeous," pointed out Joanna. "They're all actors between jobs."

"That one's not," Ruth objected, pointing to another.

"He's working on a screenplay. Come on."

As she edged her way toward the bar, Joanna, though clad in the leather minidress she believed she'd paid far too much for, felt curiously protected; every male eye in the place zeroed automatically and instantly on Ruth's spectacular cloud of moussed raven curls and the exotic perfection of her face. Not much to Joanna's surprise, Ruth did not make it to the bar with her.

"So you got back okay," she said quietly, as Antryg turned to catch her eye.

He came out around the end of the bar and bent his tall height to kiss her, and there was a desperate relief in his touch. It was as if he, too, almost couldn't believe he was there. Without a word exchanged, his partner behind the bar, known to all as the Beautiful Kevin, had moved to take over dispensing tequila and Chardonnay. "I'm delighted to make the same observation about you, my dear."

"I didn't . . ." She hesitated, shy of speaking her true thoughts though she knew that he, of all people, wouldn't laugh. "I was afraid you'd suffered a fit of gallantry and changed your mind."

"I did." Antryg looked down at her with a small, wry smile. He was wearing his usual faded Levi's, a shabby T-shirt inscribed BROKEN GLASS WORLD TOUR, and earrings that had to have come from some East Valley K mart in the early seventies. "And then I found I couldn't go through with it."

Her smile was one of genuine amusement, not at him, but at herself, realizing how like her in some ways he was. "Antryg," she said softly, "tell me this. You'd have believed me if I said, 'I really want you to go.' Why can't you believe me when I say, 'I really want you to stay, in spite of what may come'?"

The rueful answer flickered deep within his eyes. "I suppose because I want it so much." Then he drew himself up with great dignity and added, "And because it's more gallant to sacrifice all for love instead of sticking around and enjoying it like the thoroughgoing moral coward I am."

She nudged him in the ribs, gently, for she felt the bandages under the thin cotton of his shirt. "For a man who'd abandon his sweetheart in another universe surrounded by people who are talking about killing him, you should talk about gallantry."

He sighed and hugged her again; there were bandages on his arms, too, where the worst of the claw-rakes cut, and one still on his hand. Among them his tattoo stood out like the label on a beer bottle. She wondered what he'd told his colleagues . . . The truth, undoubtedly.

"Were they?" He shook his head. "I was afraid of that."

She looked up at him, her arm still around his waist. Over the chatter of the crowd—"Steven was saying on the set today . . ." ". . . corporate buy-out's going to result in a bloodbath like the St. Valentine's Day massacre in Accounting . . ." "You know, baby, I can tell you things about yourself that probably you don't even know . . ."—she caught a flying wisp of Linda Ronstadt's voice: "Desperado," a song that always brought a burning to her throat.

"You let Seldes Katne go," she said, "didn't you?"

And felt again how well she knew him, how well she read him, in the defeated bow of his head.

"Joanna, I couldn't judge her," he said. "Maybe if I hadn't spent seven years imprisoned in the Silent Tower, unable to use the magic that I knew was mine . . . Maybe if the Council hadn't put me under the geas . . . Maybe if I hadn't lived here for four months, existing on sippings and dreams." He shook his head. "And she'd had over fifty years of wanting it, of knowing what it is and seeing everyone around her using it, and not having it, not *ever*. I don't know what I'd have done in her place."

Joanna was silent, leaning her head against his chest, standing in the shelter of his arm. The shuddering darkness she'd seen in the corner of her room returned to her, the absolute depth of terror, knowing what was to happen to her . . . Seldes Katne had done that. Seldes Katne had given her those hideous hours—days—in the Brown Star's sightless mazes, wondering if she were mad, wondering if she'd be there forever.

And yet, all she remembered of the stocky little librarian from those hours in the darkened refectory was the sad desperation of her eyes. An echo returned to her from her own days in school, watching the pretty girls, watching the girls who were sure of themselves, of their beauty, of their skill with words and wit and social situations, while she retreated into the safety of her books and her cats and the computer games that let her forget about the world outside.

"I take it you opened a way for her into the world where her magic was strong? Where she'd be a powerful mage?"

Silently, Antryg nodded.

Almost as an afterthought, Joanna remembered that Seldes Katne had tried repeatedly to murder Antryg, too.

"Do you think she'll be happy there?"

"No." His sparse eyebrows quirked a little with regret. "No, I don't think Kitty has much capacity for happiness. She may find that out there—or she may meet someone, or encounter some new situation, which allows her to develop it . . . But it would be presumptuous of me to say. The future is the future, Joanna—maybe we all need to spend a little time in the City of Dreams."

He shook his head, and leaned a shoulder against the wall. Over on the bar's minuscule dance floor, a blond studmuffin with shoulders like a door and, Joanna guessed, an IQ that rivaled his shoe size bobbed and weaved with Ruth to a semi-slow reggae version of "Do You Wanna Dance?"; both smiling, like animals purring under strokes, happy simply to be what they were. In high school, Joanna reflected, she would have hated Ruth without ever speaking a word to her.

In those days she had had very little capacity for happiness herself.

Antryg's voice was very low. "They'll be after me now, you know."

"Daurannon said no one was going to open Gates in the Void again—that it was too dangerous to tamper with. Of course, he may have been lying."

"I don't think so," Antryg said. "Daurannon usually believes what he's saying, while he's saying it. But when it comes to a thing which stands in the way of what someone really wants, people tend to have shockingly bad memories. He truly loved Salteris, as Rosamund truly loved Aunt Min . . . and neither of them will ever forgive me."

*If she dies,* Rosamund had said, *you are a dead man . . .*

But Antryg had known that from the start.

"With all the confusion I forgot to ask them," she said after a time of watching the dancers. "And I meant to . . . who inherited the Master-Spells after Aunt Min died? Who *did* become the Archmage? From the way Daurannon and Lady Rosamund were being polite to each other I have the feeling it wasn't either of them. I take it you know."

"Oh, yes," Antryg said softly, and a shiver went through him, although the bar, with its close-packed bodies, its smells of cigarettes and beer and synthetic aldehyde, was warm as a Jacuzzi. In the upside-down flicker of the slanting light his eyes were wide and daft behind his spectacles, and filled with a haunted grief.

"It's a curious thing, the Master-Spells," he said at length. "No one can tell to whom they will pass until it actually happens, but when it does, most of the Academics know immediately, some of them even without having met that person . . . though of course wizards of that strength are usually on the Council, these days. I was rather hoping they would pass to Zake Brighthand, as I'm certain they eventually will. He's a good boy and will grow to be a good man, with a core in him like a note of white music—and he doesn't hold a grudge against me, which is getting rather rare among wizards these days."

"I take it they didn't," Joanna said dryly.

"No." There was a look of pained regret in his face, and he propped his glasses onto the bridge of his nose with a long forefinger. "No, in fact, they didn't. I'm sure Rosie and Daur are going to blame the disruption caused by the surrounding presence of the Void for the fact that neither of them became Archmage, or the fields of alien magic which were everywhere . . . all of which, they will say, I engineered. And perhaps they did affect it. In a way I wish they had fallen to either of those two. It would be better for me if they had."

"Someone who hates you more than they do?" asked Joanna doubtfully. "Who . . . not Bentick?" Another thought crossed her mind at the thought of the fields of power, appearing and disappearing in the Citadel during those last hours, giving powers undreamed of to people no one had suspected . . .

"Not Seldes Katne herself? Or . . . *Silvorglim*?!"

Down at the far end of the bar someone called his name; Kevin was making change for a platinum blond waitress who was also clearly between acting jobs. Antryg raised a finger in a be-there-in-a-minute gesture and turned back to Joanna.

"No," he said, his voice small with regret. "Even at that, I might have some chance of being let alone—some chance of escape. But no. I'm afraid they fell to me."

Joanna was still looking up at him in silence as he reached down to put a knuckle under her chin and shut her open mouth for her. Then he leaned over and kissed her lips and, with a rueful grin, hooked a bottle of Sauza Especial from beneath the counter and strode off to pour drinks.

# ABOUT THE AUTHOR

At various times in her life, Barbara Hambly has been a high-school teacher, a model, a waitress, a technical editor, a professional graduate student, an all-night clerk at a liquor store, and a karate instructor. Born in San Diego, she grew up in Southern California, with the exception of one high-school semester spent in New South Wales, Australia. Her interest in fantasy began with reading *The Wizard of Oz* at an early age and it has continued ever since.

She attended the University of California, Riverside, specializing in medieval history. In connection with this, she spent a year at the University of Bordeaux in the south of France and worked as a teaching and research assistant at UC Riverside, eventually earning a master's degree in the subject. At the university, she also became involved in karate, making Black Belt in 1978 and competing in several national-level tournaments. She now lives in Los Angeles.